BY MILA KANE

The Original Sin Series

Unholy Vows

Brutal Legacy

Sacred Ruin

SACRED RUIN

MILA KANE

DELL • NEW YORK

SACRED RUIN

A NOVEL

Dell
An imprint of Random House
A division of Penguin Random House LLC
1745 Broadway, New York, NY 10019
randomhousebooks.com
penguinrandomhouse.com

Dell Trade Paperback Edition

ISBN 979-8-217-29969-0

Printed in the United States of America

1st Printing

BOOK TEAM: Production editor: Dennis Ambrose • Managing editor: Saige Francis • Production manager: Linnea Knollmueller • Copy editor: Lossie Channing • Proofreaders: Caryl Schwartz, Michael Burke

Book design by Caroline Cunningham, after the design of Unholy Vows *by Fritz Metsch*
Angel frontispiece: zwiebackesser/Adobe Stock

The authorized representative in the EU for product safety and compliance is Penguin Random House Ireland, Morrison Chambers, 32 Nassau Street, Dublin D02 YH68, Ireland.
https://eu-contact.penguin.ie

Welcome to Mila Kane's world. It's not the one you know, and here the Kings and Queens of the Underworld reign supreme.

Along with life-or-death stakes, love, darkness, and mayhem rule this corner of the book world. If that's your thing, read on.

This book contains themes of criminal enterprises, including trafficking, abuse of religious authority, medication manipulation, forced marriage, kidnapping, abuse by authority figures in a medical setting, and a possessive, dangerous anti-hero love interest.

If these topics aren't your thing, I'll see you in the next one!

SACRED RUIN

PROLOGUE

"Hell is empty, and all the devils are here."

—William Shakespeare, *The Tempest*

PART I

KATARINA

THEN

"Katarina, there's a young man here to see you," my mother called from the sitting room as I let myself into the small apartment we called home.

I locked the door and took my shoes off, nerves gathering in my belly.

A young man? Who?

Who do you think? Your stalker. The one who will curse you to hell, the voice inside my head said in her ethereal tone. The damn voice that had appeared a few months ago.

I hadn't told a soul about it except my local doctor, and my mother, though I was regretting that already. I didn't want people to think I was going mad, and my mother was eyeing me lately like I was possessed. She was probably planning on booking me an exorcism or something. Dr. Blackwood had given me several reasons why the voice might be happening: stress, anxiety, bad sleep . . . there were plenty of possible causes.

I was certainly under stress, with my final teaching exams coming up at the end of the semester, after which I'd be qualified to get a job at a real school. I couldn't wait. I had to eat something and get studying tonight. I wasn't going to let anything get in the way of finishing my degree, especially not some local smooth talker who had for some reason decided that I was "the one."

I drew my shoulders back and walked into the sitting room, freezing at the sight before me.

I was used to the religious artifacts on the walls. My mother was a devout woman, and one glance at her house would prove it. She'd never met a picture of a saint she didn't think wall-worthy.

What I hadn't expected to see was Father Vargas, the head of our local church, sitting next to the skinny guy who had been the bane of my existence for nearly a year.

Ivan Markovic.

My mother sprang to her feet as soon as I walked in.

"You're late," she said, a hint of worry in her tone.

Whether it was concern for me or worry over keeping esteemed guests waiting, I wasn't sure.

"I had to pick some books up from the library," I explained, unwinding my scarf and giving Father Vargas a tentative smile. "Father. What brings you here?"

He sighed and tilted his head to the side. "This is a delicate topic, but I want you to know, Katarina, that I'm here for you and your mother. This is what I'm here for. Ivan has brought your situation to my attention, and I couldn't live with myself if I didn't help."

"I'm sorry, I'm not sure what you're talking about," I managed to get out, my gaze flying to Ivan's. "Can we talk?"

He followed me out to the hall while my mother pressed tea and cookies on Father Vargas.

"What's going on? Why is Father Vargas here?" I asked Ivan, bewildered.

Ivan slouched against the hallway wall and eyed my skirt-and-tights combo with ill-disguised disgust.

Nearly a year ago, we'd been on one date, at which he'd told me, as soon as I'd showed up, that my dress was more suited to a whore than a woman who wanted to teach kids. For me, that had been the end of it. Unfortunately, the same couldn't be said for Ivan.

"He's my uncle, didn't I mention that before?" Ivan said.

I shook my head. "No, you didn't, and regardless, it doesn't explain why he's here."

Ivan sighed. "You remember how I told you that you'd regret turning me down?"

Now it was my turn to sigh. "Ivan, who asks someone to marry them after one date? And we didn't exactly hit it off."

"Maybe you didn't, but I thought we did. The problem with you is that you've been influenced by the media to think you're supposed to be this career woman, sleeping around with different men, whoring yourself out—"

My hand moved before I could call it back. The slap was quiet but mighty.

Ivan glared at me and then leaned forward, getting in my face. "Look how panicked you are that your nights of living wild and free, whoring around, are about to be over. When you're my wife—"

"I'd rather die than marry you," I said between my teeth.

Almost a year he had been pestering me with this ridiculousness, and I'd had enough. I was twenty-two years old. I wasn't a kid he could order around.

"But you will . . . I told you that and you didn't believe me, so now you'll see what happens when you defy your future husband."

"You're insane. You've gone mad," I muttered.

Ivan chuckled. "From what I heard from a nurse in Dr. Blackwood's office, you're the one who's gone mad. Hearing voices and refusing perfectly good marriage proposals."

I stepped back, my cheeks heating. He knew about the voices? Shame and fear coated me. I felt exposed.

"I want you to leave," I said stiffly.

My mother appeared at the sitting room door.

"The tea is poured," she said, wringing her hands. She was nervous.

What was going on?

We dutifully followed her into the sitting room and sat.

Father Vargas shifted forward, his face morphing into the sympathetic expression I had seen countless Sundays for years.

"Now, Katarina, Ivan has told me what is going on with you, and I want you to know, first of all, you are not so lost that you can't be found."

"What?" I asked.

Father Vargas went on. "Modern medicine would have you believe that delusions and voices and loose behavior"—he paused—"can all be traced to hormones and diseases of the mind, but it isn't so."

"I don't know what you're talking about, and Ivan doesn't know anything about me."

Vargas nodded as if he'd been expecting me to say just that. "And your own mother? She's been worried sick by these voices you're hearing in your head."

I spun to catch sight of my mother, betrayal stinging deep. She'd told Vargas? Probably in confession. Her blind trust in the

Church had always bothered me, and now it was being used against me.

A tingling fear had started at the base of my spine and was working its way up. My mother wouldn't meet my eyes. The nerves in my stomach intensified.

"My colleagues and I have been developing ways for faith to heal these ailments, but it must be done in a supervised environment. Being free to act out your licentious fantasies can be dangerous for you. You need supervision and care . . . and since you're so important to Ivan, I'm here to offer it to you. Hallow Hall is waiting to help you, Katarina."

I stared at him for a long time, unsure what the hell to say. My mother got up and left the room, weeping.

I looked at Ivan. *That motherfucker.* He'd gone and told his uncle lies about me being promiscuous to punish me for not saying yes to his marriage proposal.

I shook my head.

"There's been some kind of mix-up here," I stated firmly.

Then I heard them. The soft rustle of people in the hallway. Several people. I turned, and they were there. In pale-green scrubs, strong arms outstretched.

Orderlies. At least four of them.

They were here for me.

I stumbled backward and bolted for the door on the other side of the sitting room while screaming for my mom. She stood in the hallway, crying softly, her face showing her resignation. Ivan caught me as I crossed the room.

"You should have accepted me when you had the chance, Kat. Now you'll beg me to still marry you," he whispered to me.

He held me still and the men in scrubs advanced. One had a long needle in his hand.

"No! Don't touch me. I'm not crazy, this is all wrong," I shouted, frantic.

Then the needle pierced my skin, and the strength went out of my limbs. Suddenly, I was so tired, and all I could think about was closing my eyes.

Yes, close your eyes, child. You are going to need your rest—to survive.

The voice was the last one I heard, clear as day, speaking in my ear.

PART II

Three weeks.

Three weeks I'd been trapped in Hallow Hall, and I was worried that the place might be starting to rub off on me. Was insanity contagious?

Every morning, an annoying hymn played over the loudspeakers in the patients' cells. Sorry, rooms. That meant you had to get up or be doused in freezing water by a nurse to get your ass moving.

They called the place an institute and said they helped troubled souls, but it was better fortified than a prison. It was crazy. I still couldn't believe I was in here. I was missing studying for my end-of-term exams. I was missing my life, and all because Ivan Markovic couldn't take no for an answer.

My mother didn't visit; she wrote me letters. She claimed it upset her too much to see me here. I wrote back, urging her to come, telling her it was all lies, but she never answered. I suspected my letters weren't getting through.

A knock sounded at my door mere seconds before it opened.

There was only the illusion of privacy here. The staff had keys to all the rooms, and they could and would come in whenever they wanted to. Even the bathroom stalls didn't lock properly.

"Dmitrova? Medication." A nurse wheeled her cart in and used a checklist to tick off the pills in a little paper cup. Then she held it out to me.

"I respectfully pass. I don't need it, thanks." I attempted a smile.

She stared hard at me. "You have to take it or go and see Father Vargas."

"Okay, take me to see him," I answered her quickly.

She frowned at me and put the cup down. "Let's go."

I followed her along the hallway. I just needed to explain to Father Vargas what Ivan had done. None of this was right. It was all messed up.

His office was on an upper floor. The nurse knocked before letting me in.

Father Vargas's office wasn't like I'd imagined it would be. It was . . . opulent. He sat behind a huge desk and waved for me to sit. There was another man in the room in the same dark robes of Father Vargas. Another priest.

He nodded to me as I took a seat.

"This is Father Pavol. He is going to be in charge of your rehabilitation."

"Rehabilitation?" I repeated, wary. "Look, there's been some kind of mistake. I don't need rehab. I haven't done anything wrong."

"And so believe all sinners."

I stared at Pavol.

He nodded again. "I'm going to help you, though. Don't worry."

I turned back to Vargas. "Please, Father. This is all a misunderstanding. You've drugged me, and abducted me, really, but I'm not going to make a fuss about it. I just want to go home."

"You won't be going home for some time, Katarina, unless you've changed your mind about Ivan."

I shook my head vehemently. "Never."

Father Vargas's jaw ticked with annoyance for a second, a crack in his serene mask.

"Very well, you leave us with no choice. You see, Katarina, you are *special.* Having our families be joined is important to me. You'll be here until you see that."

"Special how?" I echoed, completely confused. "I'm as run-of-the-mill as they come."

Vargas just shrugged. "As far as you are aware, child, yes you are . . . and we will treat you like we would any other young lost soul who needs help curbing the desires of the flesh. Pavol, I think now would be a good time to start."

I tensed. Pavol got up and crossed to the door behind me. Fear rushed through me at the thought of being locked in alone with these men. Terrible, crushing panic . . . but there was nowhere to go and no one to help.

The lock engaged with a loud snap.

PART III

It was Sunday. I knew it was Sunday because my mother had started visiting on Sundays. I was slumped in my seat and could barely keep my eyes open. Whatever they gave me on Sundays was strong. They didn't want someone acting out during visiting hours.

When all the people came to see the freak show.

The voice in my head had become my closest friend, my confidante, my only companion through the dark times.

My mother clutched at my hand, never thinking to pull my damn sleeve up and see the track marks on my skin. They'd started to shoot the Sunday sedatives intravenously since I'd gained a reputation as a biter.

"Ivan visits me once a week. He can't wait for you to get better," my mother cried, real tears tracing down her cheeks.

I looked away. I couldn't stand the sight.

How long had I been here? I'd lost track. Between the weekly sedative and whatever else they gave me on a daily basis, I was growing more and more confused. Only my therapy sessions stayed etched in my mind forever.

Those I'd never forget. And one day, when I escaped here, they'd all answer for this.

"He says that if you get better soon, you could have a summer wedding. Isn't that lovely?"

Summer? At least six months, then, that I'd been rotting in here. I felt sick.

"Aren't you going to speak to me?" my mother asked.

I opened my mouth, but only drool came out. The sedative made my salivary glands work overtime. It was disgusting, but I was past feeling embarrassed about it.

None of this was my fault. I had to hold on to that fact above all else.

"Take me . . . home, please," I murmured past my rubbery lips.

My mother stared at me.

"Thisss-is a b-b-bad place."

Exhausted by the effort of speaking through a regimen of drugs that could probably fell an elephant, I slumped back.

My mother shook her head, more tears running down her cheeks. "I can't. You're not better yet. If you leave before you're better, then all of this will have been for nothing."

She was so close to getting it, but she could never seem to cross that final barrier to full understanding.

It *had* all been for nothing. She'd accepted the advice of strangers. The only person I'd trusted in the world willingly kept me here and ignored my pleas.

My only family.

I'd never been more alone.

"Hi, Mrs. Dmitrova," a warm voice said.

My mother turned.

Mira stood beside us, belly huge, a big smile on her young face. She was my friend, the only one I'd made at Hallow Hall. Pregnant at sixteen, she'd been taken in by the institute to help her through her difficult situation, whatever that meant. She had no family and had been on the streets before coming here.

"Ah, Mira, you must be due soon." My mother was clearly grateful for the change of subject.

Mira nodded. "This week."

"This week! Goodness."

They chattered away while I tried not to fall asleep.

Another visitors' day passed, and my mother did nothing to help me.

Another day, left alone here to rot.

PART IV

Wake up. She needs you.

I woke with a start. The sedative had finally worn off, and I was in control of my body again. Usually I was out all night after a Sunday dosing, but maybe I was building some kind of tolerance.

I lay in bed and wondered what had roused me besides the voice in my head. Then I heard it.

There it was, a far-off sound.

A scream.

I got up and fumbled toward the door in the dark. It opened, and I rushed out into the hallway. They didn't usually lock our doors at night, considering that patients like me were under heavy sedation and usually slept like the dead.

Mira. I ran toward the infirmary. It had to be Mira and the baby. I had no idea why I was so sure about that, I just was. I needed to see if it was her. I didn't want her to be alone for such a scary thing.

The infirmary wasn't teeming with doctors like I'd thought it would be. In fact, it was quiet now. I slowed and walked more cautiously through the darkened rooms. Ahead, a light glowed under the operating room door. The institute had a bare-bones medical team headed by my own physician from before I'd arrived here, Dr. Blackwood. Silence pulsed through the air of the infirmary, and tension notched along my spine. Why wasn't Mira screaming anymore? Had she fainted? Was she unconscious?

I crept closer just as a cry split the air. A baby's cry. It was jarring and out of place in such darkness. I crept closer, trying to see.

The baby cried and cried, and a sister in a nun's habit appeared, bustling out the door and pushing the baby, surrounded by blankets, on a small cart. She didn't see me.

Mira.

I swiveled back to the room just in time to glimpse blood on the floor, dark red against the white, aging tiles.

I went to step forward, but Vargas's voice stopped me.

"Call the extraction team in. She's young, it's a good yield. Fresh."

"She's still breathing." Pavol's voice.

"Not for long, without lifesaving measures. You could have shown a little more finesse with the C-section, Pavol. I can see why they took your license away. Regardless, she's worth more to us in parts than alive. Take the blood, though. Don't let it spoil. The rest the extraction team can take when they get here. The kidneys and eyes will fetch a pretty penny."

What are they talking about?

As if in a trance, I walked through the swinging doors of the operating room, forgetting to hide, forgetting everything but the words they'd just said. There were three men in the room, all dressed in scrubs. Vargas, Pavol, and a third, Benedict. He was the father in charge of the medications at Hallow Hall. It was jarring to see them without their robes.

"Katarina!" Benedict snapped, and looked hurriedly at Vargas.

"What are you doing?" I asked, my gaze going to Mira.

She was so small and delicate on the table, and her middle . . . I nearly fainted, swaying dangerously into the wall.

"Call an ambulance," I said. "Quickly!"

"No." Vargas's voice was like a whip. "No ambulance. The girl has passed, sadly, and so has her baby."

I shook my head, my thoughts rushing and confused through my head.

"The baby w-was alive. I saw it," I stammered. "I heard it crying."

"You're confused, Katarina." Pavol appeared at my back. He'd snuck up behind me while I was frozen in horror.

The needle sank into the back of my neck, and my gaze held Mira's half-open eyes until the world went black.

PART V

I woke to the sound of the morning bell ringing out through the loudspeaker in my room. I bolted upright and immediately felt sick. My head thumped, and I was sweating. I glanced around wildly before last night hit me with a devastating smack.

Mira.

I got up and tried the door. This time it was locked. I waited impatiently for someone to come. After what seemed like hours but was probably only ten minutes, the nurse from the day before arrived. I flew past her, running as fast as I could up the hallway toward the infirmary.

Orderlies scattered before me, people shouted, patients screamed, but I didn't stop. I burst into the operating room and stilled.

It was empty. Everything was gone. The blood on the floor, Mira's body on the table.

There wasn't a single sign that anything had happened there last night. Had I imagined it all? Had it been just another horrific nightmare? I got them often. I dropped to my knees, suddenly unable to stand for one more second.

I stared in a daze at the bottom of the instrument tray and saw it. Startlingly red against the chipped and yellowing ceramic underside of the table.

A spray of blood. A spot someone had missed.

I pushed myself to my feet. I had to do something, tell someone. I had to get justice for her, the teen runaway no one else would miss. I felt dizzy and sick.

I staggered back, crashing into the wall. My head hit something hard, and I turned to look at it.

A phone?

I grabbed it off the wall before I could second-guess it and called the police. It rang and rang, and then, finally, someone picked up.

"You have to come to Hallow Hall, the institute on the hill.

They—they killed someone. They stole her baby. They're crazy," I fired down the line, trying to get everything out before someone could stop me.

"Calm down, miss, and tell me again, who?"

"Father Vargas, Father Benedict, and Father Pavol. They killed someone, I think they—I think they harvested her organs." A wave of nausea passed over me at the words.

They'll never believe you. You're just another crazy girl.

This time, I was pretty sure the voice in my head was correct, but I had to try.

"Ah, Katarina, there you are."

Varga appeared beside me and tugged the receiver out of my hand, then put it to his ear.

"This is Father Vargas. Yes, Officer."

He listened, and I stood there and waited for the officer to tell him that the police were on their way. There had been a report, and they had to investigate, right?

Vargas nodded. "You tell Giuseppe that next time, dinner is on me. I'm sorry about this trouble. Of course, you know we are only here to serve the community. I'll see that she gets calmed down. And do me a favor, Officer, if you see Mrs. Dmitrova around at the market, tell her I'm coming over later for a visit."

My mother. He was talking about my mother.

He hung up as my heart broke into pieces.

Vargas faced me and sighed.

"Well, Katarina. You just don't seem able to stop making things harder on yourself. Now, you've put me in quite the predicament. Ivan wanted to marry you, but now—how can I let you leave? I can't kill you, because, like I said before . . . you're special . . . but I can't have you remembering any of last night. Luckily I've planned ahead."

"You can't keep me here! I'll expose all of you and the sick things you're doing—"

His slap sent me spinning around. He followed me to the floor and took something from his pocket. It was a picture, grainy and a little unfocused, but I could make out the person in the image. My mother, in church. She went every day. She trusted Father Vargas more than anyone.

"You keep your mouth shut, be a good girl, and take your medicine. You'll jump when we say jump, and you'll do your therapy . . . or else your mother is next. Her organs won't be worth much, so they might just end up at the local butcher. The whole town will be eating sausages made from your mother if you don't fucking cooperate. Got it?"

I tried to lean away, but he gripped me hard by the hair and yanked my head back.

I bit down a whimper. I wouldn't whimper for this man.

I tasted blood in my mouth. The threat to my mother was real. I believed everything this monster said. He and his fellow devils had carved up a sixteen-year-old girl last night. He'd really feed my mother's flesh to the town to punish me if I stepped out of line.

It was a chance I couldn't take.

"So, tell me you understand." He shook my head so hard my teeth rattled.

I nodded slowly, and Vargas released my hair. I fell forward.

"Time to up your doses, dear girl. You can't tell what you can't remember. It's a mercy. Be grateful. Welcome to the real Hallow Hall, Katarina."

PART I

INFERNO

"Before me nothing but eternal things were made,

And I endure eternally.

Abandon all hope, ye who enter here."

—Dante, *The Divine Comedy*

1

MASSIMO

NOW

Fear has a smell. It took me years to figure out what the particular odor was. It's not to be confused with desperation or regret; maybe they have their own scents. Fear is something different.

From the little kid falling and scraping their knees, to the person about to go into surgery, fear has a particular smell . . . and it's one my life has made me intimately acquainted with. The tap of my boots echoed through the old building. It had been abandoned halfway through construction, leaving a hollow shell. Exposed studs and rebar jutted out in places. Handwritten measurements and notes in chalk and marker littered the walls and floors like drawings on cave walls in a forgotten place. The vast open-plan rooms were exposed to the elements on all sides, and there were plenty of corners to hide in. A breeding ground for dark deeds.

I passed by a group of men standing around a fire in the bottom of a trash can. They talked quietly, the Neapolitan dialect a lullaby to my ears after years far from home. They went quiet as I passed them by. They might have noticed my clothes and weapons and fancied trying to take them from me, but I didn't think they would.

They didn't want to die tonight. There was only one person who was dying tonight, and he'd just scrambled up the stairs before me.

I followed slowly, letting him hear me coming.

Scraping sounds and a muttered curse came from ahead.

What my target didn't know was that I'd herded him this way on purpose. After these stairs, he'd end up on the fourth floor—where there was no other way down but to jump.

I arrived at the top of the stairs just as that fact sank in for him.

Fabio spun around as I clapped in a loud, slow way that sent his shoulders inching up.

"Well done, Fabi, you found a quiet place for us to talk," I said.

"What is it you want?" Fabio called urgently, backing up as far as he could before he got too close to the roughly hewn building edge, hovering over the drop to the gravel below.

"Well, *you*, silly . . . Why do you think I've been searching for you for so long?"

"I-I didn't hurt her," he said, his voice wavering.

I nodded, pulled black leather gloves from my back pocket, and slid them on. I usually only used sterile gloves, given they were more flexible and I could forget they were there, but tonight was cold. A harsh wind blew across the open sides of the building, and frost lay on the ground. It was only a few days after the holidays, and winter crouched over us. Even in the South, we couldn't escape the cold.

"Didn't you?" I asked him, and drew closer.

He shook his head. His face was a mess. I might have gone overboard. It had been a while since I'd killed for anything other than a contract. My nine-to-five might be careful and meticulous assassination, but it was a job like any other. I didn't torture or maim, or get carried away. No, letting the beast inside play with its food was always a mistake. I couldn't let the lines blur.

Tonight, however, was personal. Tonight I'd let it eat its fill.

"I-I loved her."

He'd barely gotten the lie out before I grabbed him, hauling him to me and smashing my fist into his face, once, twice, three times, before I let him sag to the floor.

I exhaled my fury into the cold air and flexed my fists.

"You knocked her up and then had her sent away in case it looked bad for you to be screwing your employees. I already know all of that, Fabi, you can't change our past."

"*Our* past?" Fabi rolled over on the floor. His white hair was dark red now. It suited him. The man had lived far too long on borrowed time.

"Why do you even care about some random employee I fucked around with and knocked up anyway? I can pay you to stop this. I'm well-off. You need money? I can get it for you," he babbled away.

I sighed heavily and crouched before him. "Fabi, Fabi, I'm richer than you can imagine. Your money is no good here. I just want your confession before I send you to the next life. Think of me as the reaper come to collect your soul, and repent before it's too late."

Grim humor filled me as Fabi shuddered and crossed his chest. There was nothing quite like dirty sinners who had lived a lawless life fearing divine retribution, as if their blood-soaked old souls still had a shot at heaven. I was a sinner too, but I didn't expect anything other than the inferno at the end of my days. I'd always been a realist.

The sight of Fabio crossing himself called to mind my next target. A priest, no less. My job as a contract killer had taken me to all kinds of places, from palaces to gambling dens; diplomatic summits to boardrooms to holding cells; but never church. How exciting to have something new to look forward to.

"You sent her to a hospital to have your bastard, and she never left. Your sentence is already written—that's not up for discussion," I told him, taking a knife from my belt. It was thin and delicate. The kind that chefs used to separate flesh from bone.

I twirled it expertly between my fingers, and Fabio stared at it, petrified.

"The only thing you're dictating now with your silence is how long your end will take and how much it'll hurt."

Fabio wet his shiny, bloodstained lips. "She went crazy, you know. In the end, she was a danger to that baby. She thought she was talking to angels."

"And who are you to say she wasn't?" My anger kindled, and I lowered my knife to his hand. A few cuts later, I raised a flap of skin in the air on the tip of the knife and waved it. "Call her crazy again, and I'll do your ball sack next."

Fabio went white. He clutched his hand to his chest. "I don't remember, I swear. It was so long ago."

The anger growing in my chest went quiet for a moment.

"I need the name," I insisted.

He nodded. "Fuck! You think if I knew I wouldn't tell you?" He glanced around. "Santa something . . ."

"Where is it?" I demanded next.

"How should I know? I never went there," he spluttered.

"Oh really? I suppose you really loved her, didn't you?"

"Why do you want to find it anyway?" Fabi gasped out as I flipped my knife between my fingers.

I shrugged. "Maybe I want to pay my respects. Put flowers on her grave," I said, and then gave him a bloodthirsty grin. "Talk to the doctors in charge."

He shook his head. "There are no graves. It's gone, all of it. It burned down, and I'm sure they salted the earth after it. I can't remember anything else about it except that."

His words cut through my calm and sent black fury racing back along my veins. I hauled him to me just as his hand rose toward my face.

Dust hit my eyes, gritty and blinding. I dropped him to swipe at them, and he stumbled back.

I didn't have time to throw out a hand or take a step forward before Fabio stumbled too far backward and disappeared from view.

I walked to the edge of the drop and stared down. He was already sprawled lifelessly on the cement below, his head cracked on the ground, dark-red juices peppered with bits spread all around. Just like watermelon seeds . . . but brains.

With a sigh, I straightened up and tucked my knife away. I took a cigarette from my coat pocket and lit up.

Finding Fabio had taken years, and now I was once again at a dead end. The hospital where she'd died had burned down? Why were there no records of it? No graveyard to visit, no explanations for the families?

None of it made sense.

I smoked, enjoying the quiet of the night, then stubbed out the cigarette and tucked it into my pocket. I hadn't gotten to where I was by leaving my DNA at crime scenes.

"I care, Fabi, because men like you shouldn't get to do whatever they want to the women they employed, and then stuff them away somewhere when they were inconvenient," I murmured, finishing my conversation with the man who had destroyed my life. "They had lives and families of their own before you ruined it all."

I crouched and studied Fabi's lifeless body. It had been too quick in the end.

"My mother deserved more from you, and from the world. And in her name, I'll burn it all." I spit down at his body. "See you in hell; keep it warm for me. I'll see you soon."

A shuffling sound pulled my attention to the stairs. A teen stood there. He couldn't have been more than fifteen. Dirty and wrapped in rags. He stared at me with hungry eyes.

"You got a cigarette?" he asked in a rasp.

He'd seen me. I was sure of it, but he didn't flinch when I walked toward him. I never flinched in the face of death either; usually, quite the opposite. I welcomed the final darkness with open arms. It was some cruel twist of fate that I'd never been caught for my crimes or killed in the line of duty—or the countless other times I'd put a target on my back. Living was my punishment, and I had no idea when it would end.

I took my wallet and the cigarette pack out of my back pocket and slipped a fat roll of bills into the slim box.

"Here," I called, and tossed it to him as I approached.

He caught it and held on to it like it was a life preserver in a stormy sea. He wouldn't tell a soul the things he'd seen in the dark. Maybe by now he'd stopped even noticing them. We, the damned, were all so similar, really. A family you never wanted to belong to.

I passed him by and he didn't say a word.

• • •

There was no time to stick around and read in the papers about the tragic death of local millionaire Fabio Carrozza. I had a job waiting for me, and I was behind schedule.

I flew first-class to Torino. The hands that only hours ago beat the shit out of someone were now being pampered with hot, lemon-scented towels and flutes of champagne. I glanced around the cabin at the other people sitting in their little pods, their towers of wealth and power. I'd bet good money my hands were no dirtier than the majority of them.

I landed and made my way into town to see an old friend. Father Vittorio had joined the Church not long after we'd both left the Italian Special Forces a lifetime ago. The Col Moschin changes a man. It had led Vittorio to God and me in the other direction. It wasn't the Col Moschin's fault. I'd been hell-bound from birth.

I knocked on the door of the apartment situated in the back of the little chapel in downtown Torino.

After a moment, the door opened, and Vittorio was there. He looked up at me with his warm, round face. He'd always been small but strong. The kind of guy who could sneak in anywhere. He'd been a hell of a soldier, but even I could admit, he was also a hell of a priest. The only one I'd ever trust.

"You made it," he said, and smiled at me.

I nodded and stepped into the apartment. "Duty calls. I need to get over to that sanatorium or whatever it is tomorrow."

Vittorio followed me down the hall. He had an electric fireplace on and a teapot with a cozy on it. His apartment was humble and heartfelt, and I relaxed for the first time in months when I sank into his overstuffed sofa.

"It's a hospital, apparently, one that used to be very loosely affiliated with the Church, or so I've heard. You have to go there to reach him?" Vittorio asked.

"Mm-hmm, it looks that way. He has some kind of private security most of the time, which seems strange as hell for a man of the cloth, but perhaps it's just delusions of grandeur. Anyway, my brief is very specific. This mark needs to die in a particular place, and it pays extra." I grinned at Vittorio.

He tugged at his dog collar and glanced away.

"Come on, don't be judgmental; you know who I am and what I do for work. If not me, then someone else would take that contract and the mark would still die."

It was our well-worn argument. Vittorio worried for my immortal soul, while I argued that I needed to be practical about my talents and skills and find a job accordingly. I'd never been good at anything else.

"How did you get on in Napoli?" he asked, changing the subject.

I told him briefly of Fabio.

"So you killed him? That was no contract," Vittorio reminded me.

I stared at him. "So? I wish he'd died slower for what he did to my mother, and me, and who knows how many other women before her."

Vittorio nodded slowly. "I know, and believe me, I expect that he will be judged and his soul will be sorted accordingly, but the act damages your soul. You will be punished for taking justice into your own hands."

"And by removing evil from the world, don't I save someone?" I said with a sigh, sinking back into the couch and staring at the blue light of the electric fire. "If I save even one person from my mother's fate, isn't that worth my soul?" I eyed my friend. "Their soul isn't worth less than mine."

Vittorio sighed and shook his head. "My brother, you break my heart sometimes."

"You'll get over it. Now, what about these holy robes you promised me? I have an important part to play starting tomorrow . . . I need the right costume."

2

KATARINA

"And what do you get if you mix red and blue?" I asked.

Tatiana wrinkled her little button nose. "Green?" she guessed.

"Let's see, shall we?" I murmered, and watched as her chubby six-year-old fingers closed around the paintbrush eagerly. She dipped the end into the two colors before carefully swirling them onto the last blank corner of my notebook page.

She gasped. "Purple!" She sounded enraptured, making me smile.

"Yes, purple. Green is yellow and blue. You want to try it?"

She bit her lip and nodded. "But there isn't any paper left."

With a shrug, I reached for my journal and tore out another page. Yes, it was my most prized possession, and journals were hard to come by at Hallow Hall, but Tatiana deserved to paint as much as she wanted.

"Here, let's use this one next. Let's finish the picture of Hallow Hall."

Hallow Hall. Home. Hell.

Tatiana smiled and nodded, happily going on to try different colors. I sat back and glanced around the rec room. It was morning, and the common space was filled with the usual suspects. Nurses walking briskly to and fro, orderlies making sure no one caused any kind of trouble. The odd nun, their stark black robes somber compared to the riots of color of the medical staff's scrubs.

Dr. Blackwood, the resident physician, was talking with Sister Vera, head nun, in the doorway to the dining hall. Their gazes moved toward me, and I turned away.

"Who is Myra?"

Tatiana's voice jerked me from my reverie.

"Who?" I asked.

She stared down at the journal lying open on the table in front of me.

"My-rah," she sounded out slowly. "Myra."

I peered down.

Mira

It was written in scrolling cursive text in my book, over and over again.

"I don't know." I sighed. "Maybe it's just a nice name."

I should have known the answer. It was on the tip of my tongue, but I couldn't quite grab on to it. Most things were like that nowadays.

Tatiana giggled. "Did you forget things again?"

"I think so!" I smiled back, but it felt strained.

"You're always forgetting things."

"You know what I told you. My brain likes to act like a block of Swiss cheese . . . full of holes!"

Tatiana laughed merrily and then glanced shyly down at her paper.

"Can I see?" I asked her.

She put her brush down. Teaching Tatiana here in Hallow Hall was the highlight of my days. It was the only thing I had to look forward to.

Tatiana pushed her drawing toward me. She had drawn Hallow Hall as a long rectangular building with a spiky roof. Turrets on top of the childlike Gothic structure. Green grounds surrounded the building, and then a black line. The perimeter fence.

"What about outside the fence?" I prompted her. "The world doesn't end beyond the gates of Hallow Hall." I smiled at her gently.

She slow-blinked at me. "What is it like?"

I turned to gaze out the window at the grounds outside. Snow had fallen during the night, and everything was white. The black fence was still visible, though, holding up the edges of our world. I tried to picture outside. I tried to imagine walking out of the gates. What would I see there?

I'm starting to forget.

I turned back to Tatiana and her sweet, innocent curiosity and shrugged.

"It's more beautiful than you can even imagine. One day, you'll see it." I wrapped my hand over hers. "One day, it will all be yours."

The schedule at Hallow Hall wasn't hard to follow. Breakfast and exercise in the gymnasium, followed by group therapy. After lunch it was individual therapy for some and rec time for others. Since coming here, I'd done more shitty crafts than anyone should be subjected to.

Oh, so you actually remember yesterday?

Not really, I mentally snapped back at the voice in my head.

So, I couldn't remember doing crafts yesterday, but as I sat at the rec room trestle table and tried to feign enthusiasm for winding pipe cleaners around popsicle sticks, I just had a feeling I was sick of it. Still, today, I felt reasonably aware and less tired than usual. That meant that I'd somehow managed to avoid taking my medication yesterday. It took about three days for the effects to really wear off. I couldn't remember the last time I'd managed to make it that long. It could have been last week or last year.

"Katarina Dmitrova." Sister Vera, perching like a crow in the doorway, all black robes and pointed beak. "Father Benedict is ready for you."

I tightened my hands hard around the popsicle stick in my hand, and before I realized it, I'd snapped it in two. *Oops, there goes an hour's work.*

"Katarina, don't keep the father waiting," the nun barked, her pretense of empathy disappearing like smoke.

I stood, dropping the two ends of the popsicle stick on the table. As I followed Sister Vera in the direction of the private offices where the heads of the institution spent their time, I found my hands were shaking.

I squinted down at them, perplexed.

I couldn't make them stop.

Scaredy-cat. The voice in my head was mocking and sad at the same time.

"Scaredy-cat," I repeated. Was it fear making my hands shake?

"What do you have to be scared of?" the nun in front of me asked. "You should be thanking God that you found your way into this place and are able to be helped by men like Father Benedict. His heart is so true and pure, he doesn't mind treating even the lowest of filthy sinners." She shot me a glare that made it clear she was referring to me.

I just followed her without comment. After all, my mind was still foggy and would be for a good bit longer . . . unless I took my medication, in which case, I'd start all over again.

The nun ushered me into Father Benedict's office, shaking hands and all, and shut the door behind me.

"Katarina. Sit down." Father Benedict stared at me from across the room.

I slowly approached his desk and sat in the chair opposite him. The leather squeaked faintly, and I knew I'd been there before. I couldn't always remember specific things, but sometimes the details were crystal clear. I also knew I'd sat in this chair before, many times, I was willing to bet, by how familiar the creak of the leather sounded.

"How are you doing?" Father Benedict asked.

I shrugged. "I don't know. I'm okay, I guess. The same, anyway."

The priest sighed. "Are you any closer to working out whose name it is that you write on your wall?"

"Ivan Markovic," I dutifully repeated, and shook my head. "I just can't figure it out."

Father Benedict sighed again like I was the most disappointing case of crazy he'd ever encountered. The name on my wall was one I'd never forget, no matter what they gave me. I'd never forget. Ever. But this was Benedict's little test to see if I was taking my medication. There was only one acceptable answer.

"Tell me what you do remember," he prompted.

I hesitated and then told him about my mother. Her, I would always remember. Her and the little apartment we'd lived in after leaving Bulgaria and arriving in Italy. In my memory it was clear as day. The smell of the small wood burner spitting, the taste of black tea, the feeling of the scratchy, stiff blanket on the tiny sofa in the living room.

Father Benedict nodded as I spoke, but I had the feeling he wasn't really listening.

"I'm sorry, have I told you this before?" I wondered, suddenly self-conscious.

"Only every day." He gave me a tight smile. "But don't worry. The therapy that we do isn't a fast process. It takes time, and I'm committed to helping you get better so you can go home to your mother and fiancé."

The suggestion that Ivan was my fiancé boiled my blood, but I knew better than to fight back. I had to wait, bide my time, find the right moment. If I didn't, my mother would pay the price, or I'd end up drugged up to my eyeballs and lost for three months.

So I nodded. I nodded like marrying Ivan was what I wanted. Like it was the only thing that mattered.

"Have you had any other . . . licentious thoughts?" Benedict tried to sound disinterested, but a catch in his voice gave him away.

I shook my head quickly. My fingers shook again, so I tucked my hands under my legs to hide them.

"No? I find that hard to believe, given the kind of behavior that brought you to us."

I shook my head again. "I don't think those kinds of thoughts anymore."

Father Benedict watched me for a long moment before getting up.

"I will be the judge of that," he said, and came to stand behind me.

I stared out the window behind his desk and focused on the spiny branches of a frozen cherry blossom tree.

Benedict leaned against my back, pressing his midsection into my head, and his hands touched my hair. I dug the small, delicate chain I wore around my neck out of my clothes and gripped the tiny crucifix on it, pressing the shape into the pad of my thumb.

"To cleanse the sinner, a good man must take the sin out himself, with his hands," he murmured.

I stared at the branch. It was dead. Gone.

No, the voice in my head disagreed. *It's only sleeping. Soon, it will wake and be more beautiful than before.*

I lost track of how long he stood behind me. I didn't listen to the noises he made. He only touched my hair. My mind was outside on that sleeping branch. From there, I would be able to see beyond the fence. I was sure of it. I imagined what I'd find there. One day, I'd walk through those gates and find the road. I'd walk into town and find my mother. I'd hold her close, and this nightmare would be over.

Until then, I knew better than to protest. It would only make it last longer.

Benedict moved away with a sigh and heaved his bulky frame over to the window, where he fiddled around with a little paper cup before coming back to stand over me.

"Here. Take these. It's a new dose; let's see if it helps."

I reached out automatically for the medication, but a screech cut the air. It sounded like the building was screaming. I covered my ears, a headache immediately spiking through my temples.

"It's the fire alarm, some fool's set it off again," Father Benedict said, swearing. "Take your medication, don't forget."

I nodded just as the door opened, and Sister Vera gestured me out.

I followed the crowd in the hall down the emergency stairs. Cold wind billowed up from the open door at the bottom. Snow covered the grounds. The institute sat on the outer border of

Turin at the foot of the Italian Alps, and the snow often fell until Easter.

I shuffled through the snow, watching as the slush soaked through my socks. I only had sandals on, not really any protection against the harsh weather. The rest of the patients milled about outside, their breaths freezing into puffs of hot air above their heads. I shivered violently in the wind and ducked into a recess to escape it. There was a small area where the old, rambling institute butted up against the chapel that sat on the grounds of Hallow Hall. I couldn't remember finding out about it. It was lost to a past that I couldn't quite put my finger on. I hurried toward it now, reaching the wall and slipping around it before any of the nuns could call me back and make me stand with the group in the howling wind.

In my hurry to escape the gust, the cup of medication brushed the wall and fell from my fingers. The tablets landed in the slush, quickly dissolving into an icy puddle below. Gone.

Oops, that's a shame.

I stomped the pills into the melting snow and leaned against the wall in the sheltered area. I'd done it; I'd managed to avoid two days of medication. By tomorrow, my mind would be clearer. I needed to make sure I missed medication doses whenever I could, or I feared I'd lose myself completely.

Tucked away in the corner was a metal bowl I'd smuggled outside for the cat that lived on the premises. The tabby, affectionately nicknamed Gravy, heard me banging his bowl on the stones and, meowing at me, ran down a tree where he'd been perched, spooked by the sound of the fire alarm.

"Here we go, boy, my little stray. I got you bacon this time." I pulled the greasy, dried-up meat out of my pocket and eyed it critically. It wasn't in the best shape, but judging by the way Gravy wrapped around my legs, he was into it anyway. He dove for the bowl just as a low, scraping sound made me jump out of my skin. No one came around here but me. Until now, apparently.

Across the recess, facing away from me, was a man.

He was dressed in black robes, just like all the rest of the clergy who gave their time to the patients of Hallow Hall. He was standing strangely, leaning an arm against the wall before him, the other in front of him somewhere. The arm on the wall moved lazily toward his face, and a plume of smoke rose over his head. He was smoking, but there was something odd about the way his legs were planted. It took me a long moment to realize what he was doing.

Pissing. The priest was pissing . . . against the wall of the chapel. Smoking and pissing on sacred ground.

I stared. I'd never seen anything like it. It was brutish somehow, shocking for sure. It was unsettling. A priest desecrating holy ground. Smoke rose around his head and the piss, adding to the disquieting sight. He let out a deep, masculine grunt as he peed on the brick of the chapel. Unease spread through me. I watched his back jerk as he finished up and pulled his robes closed. Then he spun around, stepped a few paces away from the steaming snow, and leaned back with a satisfied sigh.

He lounged against the wall, uncaring of the snow dampening his black cassock. His profile was striking. He was tall and so very broad. He smoked calmly, ignoring the shrieking fire alarm sounding overhead. He pushed his black sleeve up and scratched his arm, revealing dark tattoos that crowded his skin. I thought there might be one on his neck as well.

The one on his arm was terrifying. A face without eyes, just deep, dark holes. They seemed to stare right at me.

He didn't look like any priest I'd ever met. There was an aura of violence about him that clung like a second skin. He didn't just wear it, he *was* it. He was brooding, with long winged eyebrows the same black as his hair. Thick stubble molded over the lower half of his face, highlighting the strong jaw and firm planes of his chiseled cheeks. His dark eyes were expressive. Pools of warm sepia that felt like they would suck you in if you stared too long.

While the rest of the institution's staff rushed to and fro in the courtyard behind us, trying to keep patients calm, this man leaned on the wall smoking a cigarette, very much like someone who wouldn't care in the least if the whole building burned to the ground.

Snow swirled down, turning the sky white. The fire alarm screamed, and the man with the tattoos wearing the priest's robes turned my way, tapping the ash of his cigarette to the snowy ground.

For a second, when my eyes met his, his appeared black as night.

Demon. Devil. He's finally come for you.

"Shh, don't be rude," I muttered.

The man stilled and took me in.

His head tilted to the side, his gaze straying from the top of my head to my feet in a slow, leisurely perusal.

Over our heads, the fire alarm finally went silent, and the lack of noise felt like a scream.

"Okay, everyone back inside!"

The nuns were trying to round up the wandering patients.

The stranger watched me closely.

"They're calling you, little lost lamb," he said quietly. His voice was deep, carved from stone . . . no, not just stone. Brimstone.

Devil.

As if he could hear my thoughts, his full, wicked lips turned up in a smirk.

Then, just when I thought he couldn't be more disturbing, he brought the lit cherry of his cigarette to his mouth and extinguished it on his tongue, grinning the entire time.

I spun and ran.

3
KATARINA

That night, the dream returned. Maybe it was because of the devil I'd seen on the grounds of Hallow Hall, or because I'd missed two days of medication, but whatever caused it, it was nearly unbearable.

In the nightmare, there was always a baby crying. The crying sound seemed to be coming from the next room, but when I went there, it was gone, moving farther and farther away.

In the dream, I was locked in Hallow Hall, but none of the doors would open, and the windows were all nailed shut. The smell of smoke came from somewhere, but I didn't know where. People rushed around, but no one stopped to tell me what was happening. I tried to find the fire or the baby, but I just went from empty room to empty room.

I'd been having the same dream for so long, I wasn't expecting a deviation.

This time, I saw her.

My mother.

She kept leaving every room just as I entered it. I had to catch up to her. I needed to ask her something. It was always on the tip of my tongue, just out of reach.

I almost caught up with her. My fingers brushed her sleeve, but when she swiveled around, it wasn't my mother.

"Mira?" I cried out, pain and grief crushing my heart in half.

My best friend stared at me with wide, bleeding eyes. I stumbled back from the sight of the long lines of blood falling down her face. Fire licked the walls behind her.

"Mira! Be careful of the fire," I managed to pant out, reaching toward her. My fingers only just managed to touch the hard shape of her swollen belly. In her clinging, paper-thin white hospital gown, her nine-month-pregnant belly strained against the material. Her long hair streamed around her shoulders, and her eyes wept red.

"*Prosti mi, zashtoto sŭgreshikh,*" she whispered right in my ear, despite the distance between us.

Forgive me, for I have sinned.

Then she wheeled to the fiery doorway behind her, stepping toward it.

"No!" I pushed myself forward and reached for her, but a hard hand tugged me back. I stumbled into a bony chest and looked up to see who had grabbed me.

Ivan Markovic.

I woke with a start and tumbled out of bed, hitting the hard tile floor below. It was freezing and dusty, and I soon started to cough. Through my bleary eyes, I stared underneath the bed. I was just about to get up when I saw it. A slip of journal paper tucked under a loose spring on the underside of the mattress. I pulled at it.

I opened it slowly, a sense of déjà vu filling me.

Do not take the medication. <u>Find a way.</u>

The last line was underlined so hard, the paper had been pierced through. A pencil rolled out of the mattress, too, and I picked it up.

This was my fail-safe note, just in case I ended up being on the medication for a long period without a chance to skip. A strategy to help me find my way out of the confusion again. It had saved me a few times.

I tucked the paper back under the mattress, hoping that somehow this would be the last time. That I'd never need it again, because I'd figure out how to leave this place, and Vargas would let me and my mother go. With every single day that passed, that dream felt more and more impossible.

I got back into bed. Usually I fell back asleep easily, but tonight I was restless, tossing and turning. I watched the moonlight move across the ceiling for hours.

Mira, I'm sorry. I still haven't made them pay for what they did. I'm still failing at every turn.

But I'd try again tomorrow.

What else could I do?

"Katarina, time for your physical therapy." The same nun as yesterday stood beside me.

It was after lunch, and I'd been staring out the window at the fat snowflakes falling for an hour, my mind going over the dream from last night again and again, looking for clues. They made all the patients do physical therapy because they said it helped heal the mind. But everyone knew they did it to feed their own twisted desires.

"Who with?" I asked woodenly.

"Father Pavol."

I barely turned my head in time before my lunch rushed up my throat.

"What is happening!" the nun exclaimed, jumping back so as not to get splashed. "You dirty girl," she snapped at me, shouting orders for cleaning supplies over her shoulder.

I heaved and heaved until nothing but bile came up.

The janitor arrived and dropped a bucket with soapy water, a sponge, and a bottle of vinegar beside me.

"Clean this up quickly; you're keeping Father Pavol waiting. Don't make him come down here for you."

I rose, knowing that if Pavol had to come down, it would be much worse.

You know he's just waiting for an excuse to play his perverted games with you. Stop giving him one, the voice in my head, evidence of my growing insanity, said.

"I know, but I'm not a robot," I retorted. "I feel things, too, sometimes."

"What?" the nun demanded.

I just shook my head and continued to clean.

Everything was all neat and tidy far too quickly, and I was being marched toward Pavol's offices before I knew it. My heartbeat felt irregular. My palms were sweating violently. I couldn't even really remember my last session with Pavol, so what was with this reaction? But my body remembered even if my mind didn't.

We arrived at his door. His office was on a lower floor, far away from the residential and rec floors. Underneath Hallow Hall was a network of basement rooms and tunnels. It was creepy down here. The air smelled fetid and old.

The nun knocked on the door and waited until she was bidden to enter before pushing me inside.

"Katarina Dmitrova. I apologize for her lateness; the fool girl was ill." She grabbed me by the forearm, her nails digging into my skin. "Apologize to the father and his guest."

His guest?

"I apologize," I managed. I had to fight the urge to go for her eyes with the way she was bruising my arm. The woman didn't have an ounce of gentleness in her.

"It's fine, Sister Vera. She's here now. Come in, Katarina."

No. No. No. Don't go. Don't leave me alone here.

I watched Sister Vera leave, the door shutting heavily behind her.

"You were ill, Katarina? That's not like you. You haven't been skipping your medication, have you?"

Don't tell.

I shook my head, my tongue feeling numb.

Pavol sat behind his desk, his pale eyes eerie, his attention fixed on me.

"Good. Must have been something you ate in that case. You'd never want to come off your medication too quickly, or you would feel quite terrible."

"What's she on?" a deep voice asked.

I flinched.

The voice had come from the other side of the room. I whirled in that direction, my heart all but jumping into my mouth.

A man sat on the velvet couch on the far side of Pavol's office.

Not just any man.

Him. The man from yesterday.

The devil himself.

He's here for us.

"That's enough," I snapped at myself.

His dark, wicked-looking eyes . . . His gaze latched on to mine, and the result was electrifying. I couldn't look away. I was transfixed somehow.

"A mix of carbidopa and levodopa, as well as some sedatives to calm her other ailments."

The names of the medicines went over my head. I couldn't stop staring at the demon wearing a cassock.

The man raised an eyebrow, seeming surprised by the medicinal cocktail they gave me every day.

"Does she have Parkinson's? She's young."

Pavol shrugged. "It's a complicated diagnosis; I won't bore you with it at present. Let me introduce you," he said as he stood from his chair.

I know who he is. The voice in my head was confident.

"Father Lucciano," Pavol said.

Lucciano. The light one. He's not even hiding it. Light bringer.

"Lucifer," I whispered.

The man on the couch stood, unfolding to a towering height.

"Not quite. That's a little rude even for you, Katarina." Pavol chuckled awkwardly. "Katarina suffers from delusions, occasional hallucinations, voices. It's all quite mixed up in her head."

The newcomer approached me, and I shrank back against the wall, jerking away from Pavol's hand when he reached out for my shoulder.

"Call me Father Massimo. And your name, little lamb?" he asked.

"He already gave you my name," I found myself saying pedantically.

Massimo smirked. "But I'd rather have it from you."

I shook my head. I wasn't giving my name to the devil himself. I might be crazy, but I wasn't dumb.

"Katarina, but she goes by Kat around here, don't you? She's a long-term resident of Hallow Hall," Pavol said, and took my arm in his, clearly growing weary of our long introduction.

"Now, sit down, and let's get your session started. Father Lucciano is here to observe my groundbreaking methods of exposure therapy. He will watch your session today."

"What? No. I don't want anyone to watch," I said quickly.

Massimo had moved back to the couch, and I watched him like he was a snake about to strike.

"Why not?" Pavol suddenly seemed interested in my response. "Do you remember last week's session?" He watched me intently.

"I—no, I don't," I confessed. When I tried to think of the reason I didn't want anyone to watch, there was nothing there. Admitting that just the thought of his therapy made me ill didn't seem smart. If he thought I was remembering, he'd shoot me up with something himself.

"Well then, don't be churlish. And don't be self-conscious. It's all part of getting better. Sit down."

I sank into the seat opposite him, all too aware of the gaze of the black-eyed devil behind me.

"Now, some background for Massimo about why you are here."

Massimo. Father Massimo Lucciano. His name was powerful somehow, just like him.

"Katarina was checked in by her mother for dangerous behavior . . . attention-seeking and the like. Her mother felt that she was sliding down a dark path and needed an intervention to prevent her sinful nature from taking over."

My face burned hot. I looked at the surface of the desk, fighting helpless tears stinging behind my eyes.

I would not cry for these men.

I would not. I had nothing to be ashamed of. I'd done nothing wrong. It was all lies. Lies they'd used to steal my life. That was one thing I'd never forget.

Massimo was silent.

Pavol continued. "Now, we are trying a technique where we simply use a stimulus to provoke an instinctive reaction, and then use a punishment to train the brain to associate those two things. Katarina, dear, go and change behind the partition."

My fingers shook again as I rose and made my way behind the partition at the side of the room. As soon as I stepped behind it, the memory flooded back. The TV and the sound of grunting. The lash of pain at the same time. Oh, God. He was going to perform his degrading, painful therapy on me, and this time, I had no cushion of pain pills to fall back on.

Well, if you ever want to get out of here, you need to get your head clear, the voice in my head said reasonably.

It made sense, but it was much easier said than done. Father Vargas was in a predicament with me. He couldn't get rid of me because, as he constantly reminded me, I was special, though he'd never deigned to explain why. He couldn't let me go, because I'd talk and bring the police up to Hallow Hall as soon as I could. So, he was stuck with me here . . . In order to torture me, or maybe just to please his partners in crime, he'd made me their plaything. All the weird experiments and therapies they longed to try on their patients they tested on me first. The only saving grace was that my being "special" held them back from full-on assaulting me.

I changed from my thin white T-shirt and long, loose pants into a hospital gown, tying it as securely as I could in the back, painfully conscious of how easily it came open.

"Katarina, hurry up behind there, I have other patients to see today."

I stepped out from behind the partition and met Father Lucciano's eyes first. His dark stare was curious, and something else . . . angry, perhaps.

I turned from him and walked to the leather therapy chair in the middle of the room. Pavol had wheeled over a TV on a stand, and now he gestured for me to sit and tied me into the leather straps.

"It's best to restrain the patients, as they can be resistant to treatment for their addictions. Lust is one of the hardest to curb. Poor Katarina is one of the worst cases I've ever seen."

He fiddled with the TV, and a movie played. A porno. In it, the couple was undressing on a bed. A city skyline filled the window behind them. I focused on it. My face burned. Pavol had tied my ankles and wrists to the chair, and now he fitted a gag and glasses that blacked out everything except the TV sitting right in front of me.

"Now we wait until the arousal starts—her sinner's instinct coming to the surface—and then we apply the therapy."

"What's the therapy?" Father Lucciano's voice was dispassionate.

"The whip is effective; electroshock we have only tried once. She had a bad reaction to it."

He forced me to stare at the TV for a good ten minutes, pausing it when the couple was fucking enthusiastically on the bed, and took a strap to my thighs, lashing my skin twenty times before he unpaused the TV.

I didn't cry. I was too numb. I was the branch of the cherry blossom, swaying in the wind.

"How do you know she's . . . feeling aroused?" Father Lucciano asked in a tight voice halfway through the session.

Pavol sighed. "I admit there is room for error in that aspect. Of course, checking for bodily fluids would be the most surefire way to tell; however, in application, we found that it was impossible to perform such a physical check without sullying our own consciences. As men of God, we must always be aware not to put ourselves into the path of temptation or dirty ourselves with a sinner's touch."

"You. Checked." Father Lucciano's voice sent goosebumps across my skin.

Pavol sounded surprised by his deadly tone. "Well, yes, in the interest of science, but alas, the benefit didn't justify the cost."

He eyed me. Even without touching me, Pavol always sweat during the session. His flaccid face went pink, and his eyes glassy, and he ambled around in a bumbling way.

"Now, I will just step out to attend to another matter quickly. You may end the session and let Katarina gather herself, Father Lucciano."

He disappeared into the bathroom beside his office, just visible beyond the TV, leaving us with only the grunting sounds coming from the screen in front of me.

After a long moment, Lucciano walked behind the TV and surprised me by taking a small, sharp blade from his pocket. Instead of switching the TV off by unplugging it, he cut cleanly through the wires.

Silence fell. I guessed the rest of this week's exposure therapy was canceled.

He crouched before me, still holding the knife in his long-fingered hand. My cheeks burned as he looked me over and then raised the knife toward my mouth. I didn't flinch when he slid the blade beneath the gag and sawed it back and forth. The gag fell away, my face uncut beneath.

He folded his little knife and tucked it away somewhere in his cassock.

Then his hands moved to my feet. He untied the restraints. I sighed with relief at the sudden absence of pain. Pavol had tied them so damn tight. Strong, callused fingers touched my ankles, and I jerked my feet forward. They bounced off Father Lucciano's steel-like chest. He gripped them tighter, and fear laced through me for a moment, until I followed his gaze down to the ugly red marks on my skin.

He tutted deeply. He muttered something that sounded awfully like, "Such an amateur," but I couldn't be sure.

The blood rushed back into my feet as he rubbed, waking up my circulation.

Next, he focused on my hands, still kneeling before me, his black robes pooling on the floor. This close, fiery specks of amber were visible in his dark eyes. Embers of hellfire. He was beautiful, like fallen-angel beautiful. The very tips of a black tattoo licked up the underside of his jaw, mostly hidden by his starched white collar.

My hands had already stopped shaking by the time he untied them, so when he went to massage my red wrists, I pulled back from him. I couldn't take his suffocating presence this close. I kept forgetting to breathe. He smelled . . . too good. He smelled like the trees outside, and the snow. Wild, unbound things, the real world. A place I'd nearly forgotten. I wanted to lean into him and breathe deeply. Give him my soul to free me from this place. But another part of me wanted to hide away from him and keep my soul for myself; I wasn't for sale to any devil.

"What's your name, *micetta?*"

Micetta. Little cat. Little stray.

"You already know," I murmured.

"I want you to tell me." His mouth curved around his words.

I couldn't look away. That was a mouth made to sin. It was

carnal. Tempting in a way I had no experience with. How could this man be a priest?

"Father Lucciano? Any questions?" Pavol's voice jerked us both from the reverie that we'd fallen into.

"Hmm, none at present." Father Lucciano stood before me and stepped aside.

Pavol jerked his head toward the partition. "Change into your clothes and return to your room to recover from your therapy."

I stood, and my thighs burned. Had he broken the skin? It sure felt like it.

I walked stiffly to the partition and hid behind it.

But instead of getting changed, I peered through a small hole in the carved wood and watched Father Lucciano as he spoke to Pavol.

So, the devil really was the most beautiful angel of them all. Who'd have thought?

As if Lucciano could see me, he looked up at the partition, right at me, and I ducked down, my heart beating hard.

4

MASSIMO

"The work we do here is groundbreaking, truly. Society doesn't care about those who are suffering from sin. But their families do. These patients, with the right therapy, could be released to live a normal life again someday. The director believes in the power of holiness and science working together. We are blessed to have him as our patron."

"And is this an official scientific research arm of the Church?" I asked Father Benedict, one of the most senior officials at Hallow Hall. I knew it wasn't, of course. It was unsanctioned, a pet project of the powerful. A remnant of a murky past.

He paused, and I sensed his brain frantically working through what to say.

"What did Cristoph say?" he finally asked.

Ah yes, Cristoph, my "in" to Hallow Hall and the one who had made me my fake credentials and letter of recommendation, and vouched for me. Father Benedict had no idea that his colleague was lying dead in a river about ten miles away. All he and the rest of the higher-ups at Hallow Hall knew was that the company that funded Hallow Hall was sending in a new senior manager for training. Me. It was supposed to be the man called Christoph, now a John Doe in some Torinese morgue.

"I didn't ask Cristoph that question, as I wasn't sure how familiar he was with the project. But I assume this work is sanctioned by the Church, yes?"

"Not as such. Because of the delicate nature of the work, we can't really afford to make it public; you understand."

"Yes, of course, I understand completely." Fucked-up old perverts preying on defenseless innocents was a tale as old as time. Yes, I understood exactly what was going on. Luckily for me, I had a job to do here, and once it was done, I was gone. The place made my skin crawl, which took a lot for a man like me.

Father Benedict said good night and invited me to sit in on another session tomorrow, then left me alone finally.

With a bone-rattling sigh, I pulled the fucking dog collar that had been strangling me all day free and dropped it on the bed. The cassock was next. The fabric was suffocating. It joined the rest of my disguise on the covers. Of all the disguises I'd donned to reach important, well-hidden men, this was the worst.

The room they were putting me up in was in the basement and didn't have a single window. It had stone walls with candles instead of real lights. The space was as spartan as you would expect, with a twin mattress resting on a simple, wooden bed frame and a desk and chair where you could do Bible study.

It was pretty bleak, honestly, but I'd slept in far worse places.

I sat and fished a cigarette out of my pocket, lighting up and inhaling deeply. I'd never needed a cigarette more than today after the shit I'd seen at Hallow Hall.

All these perverts parading under God's name, carrying out their foul therapies and believing themselves to be holy.

I wished there was a shower in the simple quarters because I needed to wash myself clean of the filth of the day. Not of the patients. No, those poor souls were to be pitied. It was the filth of those in power.

Well, soon enough, there would be one less head of the monster for the patients to deal with.

I took my brief out of my bag and flipped it open.

Michal Vargas. Now Father Michal Vargas, second in charge at Hallow Hall. Apparently he'd had quite the misspent youth. Why someone from his past had taken out a hit on the man I had no idea. I didn't ask why. I did the job, and I got paid.

I was seventeen when I discovered my calling.

"Alora, bravo, Edoardo!" My high school math teacher, Mrs. Vasco, was the kind of woman who thought a cheerful expression and a few enthusiastic claps could lighten the atmosphere in a room full of juvenile delinquents. She frequently attempted to engage the kids in my class in something approaching learning but never quite managed. Luckily, she hadn't bothered to bring in her spirit stick again after someone had gotten stabbed with it.

"Edoardo wants to be a doctor—that's amazing!" she enthused. She looked around the class and smiled warmly. "So, between all of us in here, we have just about everything covered. From detectives to doctors to chefs! You kids are the future, and don't let anyone tell you different."

It was really quite admirable how she managed to say such blatantly false statements with a straight face.

"Now, have we covered everyone?" she mused, counting

the names on her list, and then seemed to falter. “Oh, there’s one left.”

Her gaze dragged across the room toward me. I sat in the back corner, a no-man’s-land of empty chairs where not a soul dared venture. Even in a school for troubled kids, no one wanted to sit with me.

“That leaves just you, Massimo. What do you want to do when you grow up?”

My desk was a pitted mess of knife points pressed into the shiny wood. What could I say? I was a fidgeter. I twirled the small knife I always carried between my scarred fingers and used the flat of it to scratch my neck. She’d confiscated it once, but after I took out my restless energy by beating one of my male classmates, she never made that mistake again.

“I don’t know, Signora Vasco, maybe you have a suggestion for me?”

I gave her a lazy grin that only sent her shoulders higher.

“Something especially suited to my talents . . . something I could excel at,” I added.

“Mafioso.”

“Murderer.”

The murmured whispers made me laugh. I glanced around, but no one dared to meet my gaze.

“Enough!” Mrs. Vasco snapped, her positive, sunny attitude fading for a moment.

A mask-slip moment where I could see how much it cost her to stand in front of this class of lost souls every day and pretend so hard that they were going to be anything but losers when they were older. More than half were headed to prison; the rest would be in gangs, on welfare, or sponging off family for the rest of their days.

Me? I had no intention of doing any of that.

"Now, you see, I might not have learned much this year in this shithole, but even I know that you need to get paid from a job . . . so murderer is out."

Mrs. Vasco let out a long sigh, not even trying to hide her relief.

I twirled my knife between my fingers.

"But you did get me thinking," I continued. "Sicario. That sounds much like me."

Sicario. Hitman.

"That sounds about perfect."

Maybe Mrs. Vasco would be proud to know that her career day had helped at least one of her students find his profession. I doubted it, however. She was too good of a person to be able to stomach that a kid she'd once taught had really grown up to be a killer for hire. A mercenary, an assassin. A dark mark on the world.

She was good and kind and godly, like none of the men in robes at Hallow Hall. Real goodness. No, God had no place here at Hallow Hall. There were only men and the evil they did. The place reeked of it. God had forsaken Hallow Hall and all the souls within. Maybe I'd finally found a place to belong. I'd been forsaken by the world for longer than I could remember.

I placed the brief back in my bag.

It had taken a while to track Vargas down. Hallow Hall wasn't exactly well-known. In fact, far too many people went out of their way to keep it secret, which only made me more curious about the company that was funding this place. It wasn't the Church, that was for sure. There was no way they would. But someone was. That was clear.

Still, I didn't need to get involved with any of that. I was only here to carry out a contract. Kill Vargas and get out of here, throw salt behind me and try to forget that such a place existed.

I couldn't help. I'd given up trying. No matter what I did, someone innocent got hurt. I'd learned that the hard way, and not getting involved was the only answer.

Still, if I were going to get involved . . . I'd start with her.

The girl who spoke to the voices in her head.

The one who'd stared at me like she knew every single bad thing I'd ever done, like it was written across my face.

The one who'd called me Lucifer.

I chuckled as I remembered her wide eyes, gaze fastened on me, and her look of pure certainty. Tipping my head back, I exhaled a plume of smoke up to the ceiling. It had been too long since someone had *seen* me. The real me. I'd gotten good at hiding in plain sight. A wolf in sheep's clothing, and these robes should have made me invisible. Beyond reproach. But not to her. One glance and she'd known. Maybe she really did have an angel on her shoulder. But if she did, it was a shitty one if she'd ended up here.

That fucker, Father Pavol, was a new level of low when it came to humanity. Subjecting a poor young woman to his bullshit therapy just to get turned on, so he could go to his bathroom and jerk off over the john, was depraved, and not in a fun way.

Maybe the good father could have an accident while I was here. Why not? Accidents happened all the time.

Katarina Dmitrova.

Her name was beautiful, just like her. She was distant, elusive, living in a world in her head, speaking with spirits, or voices. She didn't seem of this world. With her white clothes, long, tumbling blond locks, and serene expression . . . she was the fallen angel, not me. Otherworldly beauty.

She wasn't the first woman I'd met who believed she was talking to angels.

My bag was gaping open, and I spied the top of a notebook calling to me from the depths. It was in my hand before I could question it.

It was the only thing that the hospital where my mother had died had bothered to send me, along with a letter informing me that she'd passed. I carried it with me everywhere. My last remaining artifact of the life I'd lost. Once upon a time, when there had been a person in this world who'd loved me.

I opened the book to a random spot, my mother's spidery script scrawling over the page.

> And the devil would lay his hand upon his shoulder and take him to Hell, for the fires that awaited his return . . . and then, my son, my only, would be at home. For his eyes had always burned, and his skin had smelled of ashes, and in his reflection, the end of all days was shown. This is the prophecy the angels showed to me, my boy, my only, and it opened my eyes. For I lay with the beast, and his son I did birth. You will be all and nothing, the beginning and the end of this world. I'm sorry to the world for producing such a sin. I am damned for all time, as the mother of the Devil.

The writing was jumbled and nonsensical. It ran on and was hard to make out in places, and yet the gist remained the same.

My mother, my poor, hardworking, beaten-down, angelic mother, had lost her mind before her death and been sent away.

I traced my fingers over the words scribbled on the page, my mind drifting over my conversation with Katarina Dmitrova. I was clearly the subject written about on these pages. My mother's devilish son. The boy with the soulless eyes and the hellfire smell.

If my mother thought it, wasn't it true? She'd called me a devil first, and now that little stray, Katarina Dmitrova, with her angelic sweetness and all-seeing gaze, saw it too.

I was a devil.

My reputation had only gotten worse once my mother died and I'd abandoned all hope. If I couldn't beat back the darkness of the world, I'd join it.

No. I'd rule it . . . and Katarina saw me.

Mother, there's someone else like you.

Fuck, what was I thinking? This fucked-up place was getting inside my head. I didn't have time to get distracted. I had a job to do, and another lined up right after, and another after that. L'Ombra didn't take vacations, and if I did, it certainly wouldn't be here. I'd built a fearsome reputation with my skills and was paid well for my work. I killed. I hunted. I earned my money, and I paved my path to hell. One day I'd get there. Probably in the not-too-distant future.

Fine by me. I wasn't entirely convinced I wasn't there already.

I had one thing to do before I went, and I was getting closer and closer to that goal every day. Then, I'd take my long-awaited vengeance: for me, and for my mother and the life that had been stolen from us . . . and bathe in the blood of those who had crossed us. The people who'd taken her from me. They would wish for the sweet release of hell by the time I was done with them. Slowly, I inched closer to them, my anticipation growing day by day.

How nice to have something to look forward to.

That night, I lay in bed and stared at the ceiling, smoking silently, dragging the poison into my veins as deeply as I could. My mind kept returning to Katarina, and then my mother after her. They had Katarina on a powerful mix of drugs that, as far as I knew, should only be used for the treatment of Parkinson's disease. My mother had briefly been on the same ones before she'd been sent away.

Don't get involved.

A quick search revealed that that exact combination administered incorrectly could produce all sorts of psychosis symptoms, including auditory hallucinations. How long had Katarina Dmitrova been taking those drugs? As long as she'd been hearing her voices? Who'd been slipping them to her before she'd even arrived here?

Don't get involved.

I couldn't save Katarina if she even wanted me to. I couldn't save anyone, not even myself. I destroyed everything I touched.

I stubbed out my cigarette and turned on my side. A roughly hewn cross was nailed to the wall. It looked just like the one that my first boss had hung over the old TV in his café, the one the whole neighborhood would gather around to watch football on. His altar of choice.

Old Ricardo had been the last well-meaning adult to give my teenage self a lifeline . . . one that I'd promptly dropped. A man like him hadn't deserved to be associated with someone like me.

Midnight, and I finally finished at the bar where I worked after school every day, or sometimes during if they needed cover.

"Here, take this home with you." Old Ricardo, the owner, pressed a box full of leftover pastries and paninis into my hands.

"No need," I muttered, and pushed it away.

Ricardo sighed. "Well, then, it goes to the cats," he grumbled, opening the box and laying it on the wall outside the bar.

"They need it more."

I watched as the usual little gaggle of strays made their way eagerly toward the box. Ricardo was softhearted with the animals around this part of town. The weekend would see him setting down bowls of leftover pasta for whichever animals were brave enough to try his wife's cooking.

"No they don't, and we both know it." Ricardo salvaged a panino and wrapped it in a napkin, then tucked it into my pocket—and I let him, because he was right. It just stung to have to take food out of needy animals' mouths. In the end, I was a stray, just like them.

I shook a cigarette out and lit up, taking a long inhale.

Ricardo locked up the bar and leaned against the wall next to me.

"Basta, boys your age shouldn't smoke," he chided, and hit me on the back of the head, even though he had to reach up high to do it. He stole the cigarette from me and put it to his own lips, inhaling deeply.

"And how about bad-tempered old men?" I teased.

He smoked the rest of the cigarette, then ground it out and flicked it away. Cigarettes were foul, but they helped with hunger, and a pack lasted longer than a sandwich would.

"We're old and on the way out anyway. We've got nothing to lose," Ricardo said.

"That's not something exclusive to age, you know. Some of us were born that way."

Ricardo gave me a sideways glance. "And your mother?"

That little reminder felt like a shard of ice piercing my heart. Anger threatened to erupt at his poking such a raw nerve, but it drained away at the kind look on my old boss's face.

"Exactly. Even if you had something—someone—worth saving, it doesn't mean that you can. Then you're lonelier than ever, worse, maybe, than if you'd never known what it was like not to be alone."

We stood in silence for a beat or two before Ricardo spoke.

"I think that's the most you've ever spoken to me at one time."

That pulled a chuckle from me. "You sound like my teacher."

"Ah, Signora Vasco was cursed with you as a student, wasn't she? Poor soul. She's aging rapidly, teaching that class."

"The school year's almost over. She'll recover. She's well-meaning and irritatingly optimistic," I muttered, and pushed myself off the wall. "We had career day today."

"Yeah? What did you tell her you wanted to be?"

I grinned at him. "What else? *Sicario*."

Ricardo coughed, and I patted him on the back when he didn't stop.

"Take it easy, I'm not getting paid yet to take you out."

"Very funny," he said, wheezing. "You told your teacher during career day that you want to be an assassin?"

"Well, she said to think about your talents . . . so . . ." I sighed and shrugged.

Ricardo shook his head. "If you need help coming up with a list of your talents, I'll tell you them. You work the coffee machine like you designed it yourself, you cook well, you clean diligently, you're always on time. You respect the customers, you help with the books. You have a lot of talents, Massimo. A bounty. You're just not counting those ones."

"So, I can be a barista the rest of my life with those gifts?"

I wondered curtly, flattered by his compliments while knowing they were undeserved, and feeling pissy because of it.

Ricardo shrugged. "I've no children. You can take over the bar, and I'll retire. Problem solved."

My breath hitched in my chest. I couldn't turn to look at the old man who had treated me with kindness from the very start, even when I'd fucked up. Especially when I'd fucked up. In my most selfish heart, I wanted to take him up on that offer. Become part of his family. Keep the café going and make sure this town would remember him, even when he went . . . but I couldn't. I was a person who ruined things. Everything I touched crumbled to ashes. I didn't want to be Ricardo's burden. He didn't deserve that.

He could tell my answer by my expression. He sighed. "Come to church with me this Sunday, Massimo. It's not too late—"

I tutted and shook my head at Ricardo. Hope was a dangerous thing. Hope that a soul could change, be redeemed or saved . . . that a life could turn around, could be deadly. I wouldn't risk Ricardo for an ill-fated shot at changing my life. I knew my worth, and it was lacking.

"You think some man in a costume can save my soul? Cleanse me from my sins? My confession would burn a mere mortal to ash on the spot," I murmured.

Ricardo held my gaze. He couldn't understand a life without faith . . . in a greater power, in humanity, not only in others, but in yourself.

"There is no forgiveness for me. I know what I am. I know I'm destined to burn—I do not fear death, or the hell that awaits me. But I will see my vengeance served before I go . . . and then I'll happily burn."

Ricardo stared at me for a long moment, like I was the Antichrist, and then crossed himself.

Ouch. If I had a functioning heart, that might have hurt.

"Your mother, God rest her soul, wouldn't have liked hearing you talk about yourself like that," he said quietly.

I nodded. "I know, but she's not here, is she? She's not here, and I'm just the leftovers."

Silence fell between us. I wanted to call back my harsh declaration and make Ricardo smile again, but I couldn't find the words.

Ricardo cleared his throat. "Well, I better get home. The wife worries."

I reached out and clapped him gently on the shoulder, and to his credit, he didn't flinch. He was a good man. Better than I'd ever be.

"Go on home to your wife. Cross your chest to ward off evil and throw that salt over your shoulder. Very few people don't deserve the pit, but you are one of them."

He hesitated there a second. Usually, he tried to make me come home with him for a hot meal, but not tonight. Probably never again. I didn't blame him for it.

"You live your good life, keep being kind and generous with strays like me. One day, you'll keep the heavens godly, and I'll keep the hell fires burning. Everyone has their place."

I watched Ricardo leave, calling cats as he went, picking up little pieces of litter from the street and chatting with everyone he came across.

I lit up another cigarette and stared at the Napoli skyline. There was a concert going on at Arena Flegrea, and the orange cast shining over the building made it look like the entire city was burning.

Sicario.

Assassin.

It really did have a nice ring to it.

What would Old Ricardo think of me now, lying here in a cassock? But Old Ricardo had passed years ago, leaving the café to a nephew. Sometimes I thought about how different my life might have been if I'd taken him up on that offer.

I lit another cigarette and stared at the cross.

I guess I'd never know.

5

KATARINA

On Tuesdays, part of my rehab program was working in the institute's office. Of course, they didn't let me handle much of anything important, but still, it felt good to look at something more intellectually stimulating than craft paper and popsicle sticks.

As I worked on filing, two cleaning ladies were wiping the floor beyond the reception desk.

"But have you seen the man?" One of them crossed herself feverishly. "No man of God should be so tempting. It is a sin."

"Yeah, I saw him, too. *Molto bello, e vero*. But I heard that he's a little strange . . . Father Benedict doesn't like him."

"Really? Why not?"

"I don't know, but I think he's deciding whether or not he'll allow Father Vargas to come on his monthly visit next week."

"Why wouldn't he? Father Vargas is the guiding light of this place. Hallow Hall is lucky to have such a high-profile person taking an interest in it."

"But you know how there have been threats; he has a bodyguard now. It's all political. They don't talk about Vargas at the local church anymore . . . There was some scandal."

They moved out of earshot, and I took a deep, steadying breath.

Father Vargas. I might despise Pavol, and I might hate Father Benedict—but Father Vargas? I didn't have the words to describe how much I detested that man.

Mira, I promise. I'm going to get him. I'm going to get him for you. I won't escape here until I do.

I wiped away an errant tear. Any thought of Mira made them fall. I focused on the paperwork I'd been given. Invoices for bulk amounts of food. Flour and porridge oats featured heavily. The board, or whoever ran Hallow Hall, was a big fan of gluten, that was for sure. There was always the same company name at the top of the invoices.

Centrium Group.

Whoever they were, they were the ones paying for the food, heating, and lights at the institution. I'd gotten a shift in this office just to find that out. That conversation between the unholy trinity the night Mira died would never leave my heart. I might forget it when I was being a good little patient and taking my pills, but I always remembered eventually. Someone was profiting off this place, and someone was paying the bills for it. Were they one and the same? Until I figured that out, I'd show up for my shift and dig into Hallow Hall's secrets. Not that it had gotten me anywhere at all. I was stuck here. I couldn't escape, and no one was coming to check me out. I had gaps in my memories, and sometimes, when I wasn't able to skip the medication, I could go whole weeks without a single lucid thought. I would surface and find that a month had passed.

Lately, it had felt like I was doomed to spend my entire life here, forgetting things, trying to recover those memories, trying to leave and finding out I couldn't.

I had no idea how to break that cycle. Centrium Group . . . Were they the ones selling the organs? Were they trafficking the babies?

"Hey there, *bella*." Alonso, an orderly, appeared at the edge of the reception desk.

I gave him a quick smile. Alonso was one of the only people I could trust in this place. He wasn't a nun or priest; he was just a local guy who was strong enough to force meds onto people and discreet enough not to run his mouth. Still, he wasn't a sociopath, so he had an advantage over the rest of the men in Hallow Hall. He had no idea about the true business of the place.

"Hi."

"Did you enjoy your day yesterday?" he asked, raising an eyebrow at me. Reminding me that he'd done me a favor.

I nodded. "Thank you."

"Why did you want the fire alarm tripped anyway? Just itching to get outside into the snow?"

"I love the fresh air, what can I say?" I gave him a winning smile. When I was clearheaded enough, I got Alonso to set off the alarm for me during my sessions with Benedict. He was the only person I saw every day and got my medication from. Others simply lined up for a little paper cup of pills in the morning, but not me. I couldn't be trusted.

He pulled his phone out and tapped the screen. My fingers itched to get a hold of it, but there was no point. In the beginning, I'd stolen phones a million times and called the only number I could remember since that morning with Vargas in the operating room, but I never let it ring. I was putting her in danger every time I reached out. I also refused her visit requests. I couldn't see her sitting across from me and not go completely insane.

"What's wrong? Lael giving you trouble?"

Alonso sighed. "She wants jewelry for her birthday, but I've got no ideas. Care to take a look?"

"Sure, but don't tell her another woman picked it out. It ruins it," I added quickly.

We scrolled through the store's website together, and I pointed out some pretty items for his girlfriend. I could almost imagine it for a second. Going on a date, to a real restaurant, in a town. Getting a present and wearing it. Walking home down the café-lined street, tables out on the sidewalk, people laughing and talking with friends.

The simple nothingness of being an ordinary person.

Something I'd taken for granted until I'd come here.

Something I vowed that, one day, I'd never take for granted again.

If I ever got that chance . . .

That afternoon, I had therapy with Father Benedict, and of course, my medication. I didn't plan on taking it. I was already gearing up to hide it. I'd gotten pretty good at keeping it under my tongue, and Benedict didn't always check. If I could manage not to take it today, then that would be the third day without any. It had been a while since I'd gotten to the third day.

I followed Sister Vera to Benedict's office just as the door opened and the man himself appeared.

His face was pale, and he seemed to be sweating.

"Come in, come in," he cajoled.

I entered the office and immediately spied Lucifer sitting in one of the seats in front of Benedict's crowded desk.

My hand rose before I could help it, and I crossed my chest fearfully. Massimo's mouth tilted up in a bemused smirk.

Benedict jerked upright and issued a small yelp. We all turned and stared at him.

"Excuse me, Sister, Father," he said, panting. "I seem to be a little off. I will leave the patient in Father Lucciano's capable hands, since I must take care of some private business."

The way he waddled off clenching his butt cheeks together made it clear his personal business was with the toilet.

Sister Vera seemed a little flustered as she ushered me farther into the office.

"Ah, yes, well, Father Lucciano, how nice to meet you again," she said, beaming at the devil in black sitting across the room.

Damn, Sister Vera's got the hots for the new priest, the voice in my head sniggered. She'd been pretty quiet since yesterday.

"Shh," I said before I could help myself.

Sister Vera glared at me.

"Well, I'll leave you with this one, but be warned, she's known to be . . . tempted by sin." Sister Vera flashed me a look up and down.

It was obvious she wanted to call me a whore but had only just restrained herself.

"Also, she needs her meds," Sister Vera continued.

Father Lucciano stood, looming over both of us, and strolled to my side.

"I've got it handled, Sister. Thank you for your careful attention to each patient. They are lucky to have you here."

Father Lucciano took both of Sister Vera's hands between his and squeezed them. I thought the good sister was going to pass out for a moment, or come, or something equally embarrassing, but she just squeaked a thanks and headed out the door.

"Come in, Miss Dmitrova. Make yourself at home." He crossed the room back to the desk.

I let out a snort at that phrase.

Father Lucciano arched an elegant black brow at me. "Something amusing?"

I glanced around. "Yeah, the thought that this place could be anything like a home. It's a prison, Father, if you've not worked that out yet."

"Please, call me Massimo. No need for formalities." He reached for a chart on the desk and flipped it open. Sat down in Benedict's chair.

I fought a flinch. That file held all my history. Every painful moment that had led me here, to this place.

"Why don't you tell me what brought you here?" Lucciano said.

I nodded to the file. "You can just read it for yourself."

"I'd prefer you told me."

I scoffed. "I need to give you my name, I need to tell you my story . . . do you get off on making people do things?"

His face didn't move. "You have no idea. Why are you here?"

"Didn't you catch Sister Vera's drift? I'm a whore, remember? That's what the unholy trinity think, anyway."

Lucciano considered my words and shook his head. "Try again. I see your mother petitioned the board for your admittance."

"She was worried about my eternal soul. She thought that getting me in here would save me from the corruption of the world," I said, parroting her words from so long ago.

"And has it?"

I eyed him up and down. "What do you think? Anyway, no one listened to my mother until Ivan Markovic got involved."

"Ah, yes, your boyfriend—sorry, fiancé."

"No, not my boyfriend or my fiancé. He'd never be either. Never. I hated the guy, but he didn't like hearing that, or the word *no*." I wrapped my arms around myself, trying to keep it together.

Lucciano simply watched. "And so?"

"And so, he went telling on me to his uncle—Father Vargas. Told him I was a fallen woman, that I went after married men, that I practiced witchcraft and spoke to spirits. My mother handed me over, and the fuckers locked me up in here."

"Three years ago," Lucciano supplied.

The number stole my breath. My lungs seemed to close. I'd worked out as much, in my bouts of lucidity, but hearing it so plainly was hard to take.

"Three years ago," I echoed, and a tear dashed down my cheek.

"So, that makes you twenty-five years old, correct?"

I just shrugged. What did I know? My life was slipping through my fingers like sand.

"It says in your file that you're a flight risk, violent with the orderlies, and known to self-harm."

I forced a jagged laugh. "Quite the catch, aren't I? I'll have a hell of a dating profile when I get out of here."

Lucciano's mouth twitched, and I felt sure for a second that he was going to laugh, but the moment passed. Unlike the man I'd seen smoking and peeing against the side of the chapel, the Father Lucciano who haunted the halls of the institution was sober and unreachable. An emotionless well so deep, it pulled you in if you stared too long.

"Do you plan for life after this place?"

"No—here, all my wishes have come true. Of course I do," I snapped.

"What kind of things do you wish for?"

"To be normal. Next question."

"So, you think about leaving?" Lucciano continued.

"Every day. I should never have been here in the first place. Sleeping around with married men?" A bitter chuckle left me. "I've never so much as kissed a man."

Lucciano's eyes narrowed at me. "But you did stab an orderly and slash a nun across the face, did you not? And you do hear voices in your head."

I sighed. He'd definitely read my file. I lowered my lashes and batted them. "Like angels whispering . . . or devils. Either one would work."

"You hear angels speaking to you?" Lucciano pressed. "What do they say?"

"Nice try, Lucifer," I murmured, and sank into a chair opposite him. "You're not getting any divine secrets from me."

He looked bemused at my refusal to share. But what could I really share? Sometimes I heard a voice in my head saying the stupidest shit. Other times it was screaming absolutely terrifying shit. Most of the time it was quiet. It had all started when I'd met Ivan.

He peered at the clock on the wall.

"We'd better end there." He glanced down at the file. "Oh, one last question. Who was Mira?"

I froze.

Mira. An angel.

"It says here that you were close. She comes up often in your psychotic episodes."

"I don't have psychotic episodes. I have moments of lucidity where I realize how much the people who run this place need to suffer for what they've done. What they continue to do to the patients here," I burst out; probably not a great idea, but the mention of Mira had stirred my emotions up too far to wrestle them under control.

"If you don't have these episodes, then why do you have a list of medications a mile long?"

"That's a good question. Maybe Father Benedict can answer it one day in court," I snapped.

Lucciano narrowed his eyes at me again.

"Let me guess, you're going to report back on everything that I just said, right? Like a good little demon. I expect nothing less. This is a cursed place, forsaken . . . Only evil can walk through these doors. You are no different from them. Your hands are stained just like theirs . . . I can smell the copper . . . and ash. You smell like the pyre of the people you've killed." The words left me thoughtlessly on a wild rush. I had no idea where they'd come from, but that was all just part of losing your mind. From the brain fog, sometimes crazy shit emerged.

Lucciano stared at me, his hand tightening on the desk. I wondered what the other fathers thought of the tattoos on the back of his hand.

Then he stood, and my heart stopped. He was so imposing, so threatening without even trying. It was in his effortless strength, his onyx eyes, his callused hands.

He crossed to me in three long, measured strides and placed a hand on either arm of my chair, caging me, then leaned in, staring into my soul with that brimstone gaze.

"How do you know that?" His voice was low, a husk. A rasp. A call to sin.

"Know what?"

"What I am?" He leaned down so his face was only inches from mine, leaving me nowhere to hide.

My spine felt like it was liquefying. Jesus, save me. Sure, controlling my mouth wasn't my strong suit, but now I'd gone and pissed off an actual devil.

"How do you *see* me?"

His eyes searched mine. He really wanted an answer. Some way to explain how I could know just by looking at him that he had bloodstained hands. I had no explanation except that the voice in my head told me so. No reason except for the fact that surviving in Hallow Hall had honed my ability to tell when monsters walked among ordinary people.

"Do you really hear angels inside your head?" He sank a hand into my hair and gripped the back of my head. He gripped it hard, as if he'd like to crack it open and peek inside.

Fear laced down my spine.

He straightened slightly, forcing my head back so I was staring right up at him, supplicant.

"What do they sound like?"

"Insanity. I think they're what insanity sounds like," I whispered, honest and disarmed.

"But I thought you weren't crazy, remember?" he reminded me.

A lump formed in my throat so large I couldn't dislodge it. A tear welled in my eye. It trailed down my cheek.

"I don't know," I admitted. "I don't know anymore."

Fear was making my heartbeat spike, and I wet my suddenly dry lips. His gaze fell to the movement. He tilted his head to the side.

"What are you?" He matched my quiet tone.

"Just another crazy girl. Or another victim of Hallow Hall. Take your pick," I whispered back.

Lucciano shook his head. He seemed disturbed by me. "No, neither of those is all you are. You are something else," he said.

"Hey, at least I'm unique," I wisecracked, feeling like if I didn't ease the intensity of his inspection, I might cry. I hated to cry in front of anyone. I hated to let them see they'd gotten to me.

"Unique, but not alone . . . I've known another—" He cut himself off when the door to the office suddenly opened.

I jumped.

Father Lucciano didn't release me right away. He took his time letting go. Father Benedict moved around his desk, ignoring us for the most part.

"My apologies. That coffee you gave me didn't sit right for some reason, Massimo. Old age, never let it catch you."

He sat and studied me. "How was your session?" He glanced at the file on the table. "Oh, you got to Mira already? You've made progress."

"We had only just started on the topic," Father Lucciano said.

"It's one of the most difficult ones for Katarina. Isn't it? Shame what happened to that girl."

I shot up in my chair. "Can I go?" I couldn't hear Mira's name come out of Father Benedict's mouth. I just couldn't stand it. My mind was clearing every day, and the memories were nearly too painful to recall.

"Not without your medication." Father Benedict peered at me. "You seem upset today. I hope you remembered to take yesterday's dose with all the fire alarm kerfuffle."

"I did," I lied brazenly, looking him in the eye.

"I've got it ready, Father, if you'll allow me." Father Lucciano was right there.

God, I hated him. How beautiful he was. How strange and unsettling. A striking demon come to play in this little playground that the men in power had made, hidden away from the world. Somewhere they could let the beast out.

"Go ahead, Father, as you see best." Father Benedict sank back into his chair and watched us with interest.

He was a man who had observed me kick and scream in pain, injecting different stimulants and sedatives into various veins and taking notes on the effects. Vargas was in it for the money, or the power, it seemed. Pavol was in it to satisfy his twisted sexual desires. But Benedict? He has his own sick kinks, but what really got him going was the need to experiment on human subjects. To see what happened when you combined different variables.

"Miss Dmitrova, open wide," Father Lucciano said. He'd moved in front of me when I was glaring at Benedict's balding head.

I glanced up at him, fighting the urge to scream. He held my medication in his hand.

Open wide?

I stuck my hand out, palm up, waiting for the pills, but he didn't drop them.

Instead, he held a pill to my lips and waited for me to open my mouth.

"What? Why?" I demanded lowly, disappointment crashing into me. I wasn't going to be able to avoid taking today's medication, which meant resetting the clock all over again. Staff at Hallow Hall were pros at checking that you'd really taken the pills. There was no escaping their inspection. It had happened to me countless times, but this time, I felt like my heart might snap in two.

"To ensure there are no mistakes," Lucciano said dispassionately. He was a different demon from who he had been before, questioning me about my voices. Now, it was like a mask of cruel indifference had slid over his handsome features, cloaking them in ice.

There would be no mercy from a man like this.

My face felt hot as I slowly opened my mouth and let him slip his fingers inside. They were long and thick, the kind you might find on a man who sculpted marble. I had to widen my mouth to fit him. There was something twisted and shameful about the feeling. He was staring down at me like he was committing every scorching second to memory. It was violating. It was titillating. It was wrong and yet it made me burn.

Crazy is as crazy does.

His fingers caressed my tongue for a second before he moved them deeper, filling my mouth, choking me as his dark eyes sucked up all the air in the room. He watched the place where his fingers disappeared in the cavern of my mouth, and I watched him back.

Then he was pulling away, leaving my mouth strangely empty.

Empty?

Before I could process that fact, he brought the paper cup of water to my lips and tilted it up. Water ran down my chin and dripped onto my chest, wetting my T-shirt.

"Now, swallow," he commanded in a voice that had probably never once been defied.

I swallowed, my throat bobbing, pushing the water down my gullet. Only water, and nothing else. I was so relieved I could have cried.

He nodded. "Good girl."

My face burned hotter, but I didn't turn away from him. I couldn't seem to make my eyes leave his, or the words they seemed to be speaking to me in secret.

"Interesting technique for giving medication," Benedict said from across the room, the spell breaking.

"It's the only way to know for sure that the right dose has been administered," Father Lucciano replied, and stepped back from me. "If it suits you, I can oversee Miss Dmitrova's medication schedule from now on. It might be a nice way to continue my training on her case."

My pulse jumped as Benedict considered his words and slowly nodded.

"Very well, go ahead."

Sister Vera appeared in the doorway. She reached for my arm with the meat pincers she called hands and grabbed at me.

"Thank you for today, Miss Dmitrova. I look forward to working with you," Lucciano murmured, his gaze not leaving me for a moment.

I nodded, confused and flustered.

We left the office, and I hurried down the hallway, eager to escape before either Benedict or Lucciano could change their mind. I glanced back before turning a bend in the hall and saw him standing in the doorway, a spot of darkness watching me go.

Strange as he was, demonic as his aura may have been, there was no denying one simple truth . . .

He hadn't given me the medication, but he'd made it seem like he had.

Maybe I'd been wasting my time asking God to save me this whole time here, locked in Hallow Hall, forgotten by the world.

I should have asked the devil instead.

6

MASSIMO

"And when can we expect Father Vargas?" I asked Pavol.

We were eating dinner in the private dining room exclusively reserved for the three men who ruled over the institute in their holy robes, the ones Katarina called the unholy trinity. An opulent, dark-paneled room with velvet chairs and polished silver.

The Church wasn't paying for this place; I'd stake my reputation on it. In fact, I was a little unclear on how much the real Church knew about Hallow Hall. It was an interesting discovery.

"He has to show the director around. Benedict likes to make sure that the grounds are up to scratch and that our more colorful patients are safe and sound and in solitary." Pavol belched discreetly. I'd been topping his glass up continually, and it seemed like it was finally having an effect.

"Despite its appearance, Hallow Hall turns quite the tidy profit. It benefits all parties—the shareholders make money, and Vargas, Benedict, and I get to continue our work, as you know..."

"And the patients?" I mocked gently, but he was too far gone to notice.

"They are saved, or at least become useful for something, instead of being out there in the world sinning." He hiccupped and stood, off to search for water.

Father Benedict hadn't made it for dinner. The laxative I'd slipped into his coffee this afternoon had continued to take its toll on his colon. Such a pity.

I sipped my red wine, noting it was an exquisite vintage. Yes, the unholy trinity of Hallow Hall wasn't exactly on a strict budget.

I let my mind wander over the day. Killing time here until Vargas showed up was irritating, but I'd already ascertained that getting to him anywhere else would be near impossible.

I was impatient to be gone, though, given the information I'd uncovered only a few weeks ago. When I'd gotten out of the Col Moschin, the Italian Special Forces, I'd started to poke into my mother's past. I had found out where she'd worked, but figuring out who had been in management at the time had been a challenge. I'd hit a dead end with the search until an old friend found a lead. Fabi Carrozza . . . the now-dead millionaire who had knocked up my mother and sent her away. But he'd fucking died without giving me the name of the place he'd sent her. I needed to start working my way through his list of coworkers and acquaintances to see if anyone remembered more than him. Maybe he'd had an assistant who had handled the admission paperwork or something. I'd taken one step forward and two steps back and burned with the need to continue my search, but I was here, working. Haunting the halls of this cursed place, waiting for my fucking target to appear.

Haunting the halls and watching her.

Katarina Dmitrova.

Just the thought of her sent a flurry of heat and curiosity charging through me. Earlier, I'd nearly gotten carried away in Benedict's office. She was afraid of me but fearless at the same time. Perfectly sane and sweetly crazy all at once. Blessed by angels and talking to devils. I couldn't understand her, but it was clear that she was being mistreated here at Hallow Hall. Yet, if you read her file, she was the one who had drawn blood, the one who was violent and unpredictable.

Interesting. I hadn't met anyone interesting in a long, long time.

More than anything, she reminded me of my mother. A woman the world had turned their backs on. Was there anyone looking for Katarina? Would anyone miss her when she was gone?

I mused over those questions as Pavol made his way back to the table and sat heavily. I raised an eyebrow at him, taking in how much time had passed.

He was flushed.

"Apologies for keeping you. A patient was having some problems sleeping. She needed . . . tucking in." He chuckled, his beady eyes darting about. His whole face was as pink as the ham we'd just eaten.

A dark feeling spread through me.

"Which patient?" I curled my fingers around the knife beside my plate. I could already imagine driving it through his fleshy neck. The white tablecloth would be so pretty sprayed with his arterial blood.

"No one you know," he assured me. "You've only met Katarina so far, haven't you? She's a special case. Not to be touched. The director's pet."

I narrowed my eyes at him, wondering what the hell that meant.

Pavol sighed and leaned back, a smile playing around his lips. What the fuck had he done in the twenty minutes he'd been gone?

Kill the fucker. Make him bleed. I could cut his balls off and feed them to him before he passed . . . some alternative therapy for him to choke on.

But then Father Vargas would never schedule his visit, and I'd never leave this place. I had a job to do, and that had to come first. Always.

"She's a special case," he said again. "Honestly, she might have been released a long time ago if not for the incident with her friend."

I thought for a moment and took a leap. "Mira?"

Pavol blinked at me. "She told you about Mira? She needs her medication adjusted, then. She's not meant to remember anything about all that."

"What happened?"

"Oh, nothing new. Mira was a street kid, some other poor Bulgarian rat who Katarina became friends with here. She was pregnant, at sixteen, no less. Just street trash. She ended up here instead of on the streets, a lucky break for a girl like that."

I watched him speak, letting my anger curl around me like smoke, savoring it. I couldn't act now. I would act later. This man wasn't leaving here alive, I decided.

"And?"

"And she didn't appreciate what she'd been given," Pavol said, touching his cheek in a way I was certain was subconscious. He had a thin scar there. So Mira had gotten him somehow. Good.

"She was in solitary when the baby came. She had a rough birth; she and the baby both passed."

I was watching Pavol's eyes at the moment he lied. He was a

piss-poor liar. His eyes glided to the side, gaze fixing somewhere in the distance.

"Katarina took it hard, I guess. She blamed the staff and the doctors here. She didn't understand that accidents sometimes happen."

"Of course, you seem to have a disproportionally high number of pregnant patients." You could hardly ignore the number of young women, some little more than girls, who were clearly expecting.

Pavol shrugged. "A lot of fallen women come to the Church for aid when they have nowhere else to go."

I nodded. "But this isn't the Church. It's a private enterprise, isn't it?"

Pavol's jovial expression dropped as my words sank in, but I plastered a smile on my face, trying to seem as nonthreatening as possible.

It worked somewhat, but I'd still made him nervous.

"Still, it must be such a comfort to the community to have a place people can go if they find themselves in trying times," I added to smooth his ruffled feathers.

He nodded vigorously. "Exactly! It's not like we're encouraging them to have relations outside of wedlock. We just help clean up the consequences."

Clean up the consequences. There was something utterly distasteful about that phrasing.

I nodded. "Bless you, Father, and everyone at Hallow Hall. May you reap all the *consequences* of your hard efforts."

I stood on the crumbling balcony outside the dining room and smoked. Pavol had disappeared again, and Benedict was still on the john, probably. The night was sharp. Snow blanketed the trees and grounds. Spring should be coming soon, but this close to the mountains, you never really knew when it would arrive. Torino was a majestic city. The weather here was nothing like the weather where I'd grown up in Naples.

Thinking about the pregnant patients brought thoughts of my mother to the surface. A subject I rarely let myself dwell on. But here, in Hallow Hall, it struck too close to the bone.

My mother's descent into madness started when she'd gotten a job at a steel plant in a town outside of Naples. For a while, things had been good. My mother had always been religious, pious, and God-fearing. She'd prayed every day, never missed church, and whenever she looked at me, for a bright and shining moment, I thought that maybe I could be good, too.

Then she'd gotten pregnant. My father was long gone, having died abroad in the military. My mother hadn't dated; it just wasn't even a possibility. She'd gone to church, worked, and cared for me. That had been her life, and she'd never once complained about it. Then the pregnancy. After that, people started to see her differently, and me by extension. I was no longer a war hero's son but the son of a whore. They turned away from her at church and ignored her conversation in the street. Silently, as a whole, the entire community had turned their back on her. She soon had only me.

No matter how many times I'd asked her, she wouldn't tell me who the father was. She'd only told me it was her shame and she'd bear it alone. Regardless, the pressure got to me. I'd started to get into fights and learned how to inflict damage quickly to even the score. I'd started to skip school to avoid those fights, and then got arrested.

Slowly, my life slid off-kilter.

The owner of the steel mill, that rotten prick Fabio, had her institutionalized when she'd tried to take her own life at work one day . . . Well, that was his story, anyway. I didn't believe it. I hadn't believed it at thirteen when it had happened and overnight I was shipped off to live with my aunt and uncle, and I didn't believe it now, decades after her death.

The hospital she'd been at had sent me her journal and a letter informing me that she and my sibling had died during the birth. One day, I vowed, I'd find everyone responsible for her death and send them to hell. It was the only thing that got me through those early years after her death.

It was like someone had switched the power off on the world, and after that, I only lived in darkness. For decades I'd lived without a single light in the world and no one who would care if I lived or died. Before then, I hadn't known how loneliness could feel like a tattoo across your forehead, setting you apart from the world. Those were the times when living started to feel like an unnecessary burden. A cruel punishment.

Seeing the pregnant girls walking around the institute here, getting treatment for mental illness, I wondered how many of them would be missed if they disappeared.

They were just like me.

Unwanted.

Unmissed.

Strays. The lot of us.

After the late dinner, I walked the darkened halls back toward my room. The upper floors were quiet except for the occasional shout. Some of the doors I passed had people murmuring in a constant stream behind them. Others were still as the grave.

I strode the halls, casting a long shadow in the moonlight. Dressed in a priest's robes, I resembled my own worst nightmare.

I was halfway along the high-security corridor when a terrible scream rent the air.

I stopped, surprised by the sudden sound.

It came from a door up ahead on the right. I approached. All the doors had observation panels cut into them with thick shatterproof glass. Slowly, I slid aside the metal flap that hid the glass and peered into the room.

At first glance, I couldn't quite make out what I was seeing. White sheets and a white nightgown.

Is she floating?

Then she moved, and I saw how it was only a trick of the light. Long hair spread across the pillows, the sheets tangled up around bare legs.

Katarina Dmitrova. Of course it was her. Since our very first encounter, it was like a tether had formed between us. When she'd looked at me outside in the snow and had immediately seen me. The real me. The monster inside. That link was pulling us together, again and again.

"I'll open the door, Father," a burly orderly said. "Kat can get a little worked up sometimes and needs to see a familiar face. She just needs to be woken up at night now and again. She'll be fine once it passes."

Kat? The orderly's overfamiliarity annoyed me.

"Leave treating Miss Dmitrova to the professionals," I ordered, and brushed past him as soon as the door opened. I stepped inside and tossed a glare over my shoulder.

"You can close it up. Lock it."

"Lock it? But . . . she's been dangerous in the past to the staff . . ."

"She's not a danger to me; now hurry up and stop questioning my authority," I commanded him.

He snapped his lips shut and pulled the heavy metal door shut behind me. It clanged loudly but didn't seem to snap Katarina out of her nightmare.

Was it a nightmare or a fit? I wasn't sure as I went to stand over her. She thrashed, the sheets coiling around her straining limbs.

She whispered something in another language over and over again. Was it Russian?

"*Toï idva.*"

Not Russian. Wait, hadn't Pavol said her friend, Mira, had been Bulgarian?

"*Toï idva,*" Katarina repeated, tearing now at the neck of her nightgown.

I was going to have to wake her up before she hurt herself.

"Katarina, you're dreaming," I murmured with a gentleness I hadn't known I still possessed.

I reached out and touched her feverish-looking skin. She was burning. Her skin was sinfully smooth. She was like a perfect marble angel, not meant to be touched or sullied with blood-stained hands. She twisted from side to side, dragging the neckline of her nightgown down, exposing the slight swell of her breast.

Blood snapped through my veins, surging hot. *Jesus.* Maybe I really was a devil. I wanted to touch this woman. I hadn't wanted to touch a woman in a long, long time. It had all grown wearying. Hookups and awkward conversations afterward. Clinging hands and missed phone calls. Pretending to be normal . . . I didn't want anything to do with that. I was done with it.

But Katarina saw me exactly as I was. Somehow, she knew.

Her smooth, pale skin called to me, and in that moment, I wanted to mark it with my fingerprints. Make it red with my lips. I wanted to hear her scream my name.

"Sleeping around with married men? I've never so much as kissed a man."

I'd never met such an untouched person. Her soul was squeaky-clean, her body inexperienced, her heart—lonely, just like mine. She couldn't stay in this place. It would destroy her. She was special. She needed to be protected. Sheltered. Isolated from the real, harsh world.

I can take her with me when I go, a small, devilish voice whispered in my mind. *She could be ours. We've never had someone to call our own.* The devil inside me salivated at the thought.

Ha. And Katarina thought *she* was crazy.

She had no idea.

No one would miss her. No one would come for her. She'd be all yours.

Putting aside those thoughts, I tugged up her nightgown and covered her chest. Christ, she was rail thin. The girl needed food and sunlight, fresh air. She needed the real world. She was dying without it. She needed someone to take care of her . . . someone to belong to.

"Katarina, wake up, *micetta*. It's only a dream."

I touched her cheek when she failed to rise from the clutches of her nightmare. Her skin was downy and plush, like the most expensive of fabrics. She still failed to rise. Was she drugged? I lowered my hand to her neck and circled it, pressing in just enough to inhibit her breath. Her pulse surged beneath my fingertips. Life and warmth, right there within reach for once. *What is it like to be so vividly alive?* I wondered idly, enjoying the feeling of her slender neck between my fingers.

I sank down on the bed beside her. A moth to her luminous flame.

Then the long dark fans of her eyelashes suddenly lifted, and she was staring right at me.

"*Toï idva.* He's coming. He's coming . . ." she whispered feverishly, her eyes wide.

"Who's coming?" I asked. Was she talking about me? Her Lucifer?

"He's coming, Mira—he's here. He's already here, hide. Hide." She turned to look at the corner of the room, and her face crumpled.

Ah, so she was still lost in her nightmares. But then, weren't we all?

Then the tears came, spilling down her cheeks like someone had turned a tap on.

I froze. I didn't know what the fuck to do. Anger was easy to cope with. Rage, mockery, fear, all of it was simple . . . but this grief?

I was lost.

I began to pull back just as her fingers sank into my cassock and she held me close to her.

"Don't. Don't leave me alone." Her heartbroken whisper was enough to move even the dead lump of stone that lived in my chest, where a heart used to beat.

Her plea stilled me. People routinely begged me for mercy when their fate was already bought and paid for. I was used to those desperate pleas. But comfort? No one asked me for comfort. No one felt safer in my presence. The idea was laughable, and yet, there was a tenacity in Katarina's fingers in my cassock, holding me near her in a moment I knew I'd never forget.

She sank into my side, sliding down until her head was cushioned on my lap, and then her tears were sinking through me. I froze; my breath stuck in my chest as she shook with her grief. Slowly, like she was made of spun sugar, and one wrong touch would dissolve her completely, I rested a hand on top of her head. Her hair was like satin.

She cried, and I bore witness.

She wasn't alone . . . and for once, neither was I.

7

KATARINA

Coming to with my own personal Lucifer leaning over me was unsettling, but the dream had left me too rattled to do anything other than dissolve in his arms. When he'd tried to leave, terror had struck me at the thought of being alone with the memories in my head.

Mira. Oh, Mira.

When the tears ran out, Father Lucciano's robes were soaked through, my face was swollen, and I could barely crack my eyelids open. My nose was running, and I wiped it inelegantly on my nightgown. It was also soaked by tears, sweat, and snot.

Lovely.

It didn't matter, though. Nothing mattered now that I'd remembered everything. Three days. Three days without medication was the sweet spot. The day when I remembered the exact events that had led up to my incarceration here in excruciating detail. Details I was always grateful to drown out.

What had happened to Mira.

"You were dreaming about your friend," Father Lucciano said quietly.

I nodded. "Because you didn't give me my medication."

"Does the medication keep the nightmares away?" he asked.

We were sitting side by side on the floor, leaning against my bed. My legs were crossed, bare and scratched up in places. I had a hundred old scars, slices I used to make in my skin when I felt like I was truly losing my mind, before they took everything sharp away from me.

Now I felt Father Lucciano studying them. They were silvery in the moonlight. He had his long legs stretched before him, crossed at the ankle. His legs were strong, the muscles clearly defined even through his dark trousers. If I were strong like that, could I have escaped here with Mira?

"It keeps the memories away. They aren't nightmares," I told him tiredly.

"What happened to your friend?" he asked after a long moment.

"Didn't you read it in my file? She died."

"I'm asking you what really happened, not what's written in that folder."

I thought about telling him, only for a moment, before letting the urge fade away. I couldn't trust him. I couldn't trust anyone. He worked here at Hallow Hall. He was on the same side as Pavol, Benedict, and Vargas. He wouldn't believe me, even if he wasn't really a demon. Why would anyone believe me over those upstanding pillars of the community? Even I wouldn't believe me.

"Why didn't you give me my medication?" I asked instead. "What do you want from me?"

He turned toward me, and I felt the weight of his eyes on my skin.

"What do you think I want from you?" His deep voice sent heat billowing through me.

I risked a glance at his face and found it right there. So close I could smell every note of his unique scent: ashes, incense, pine, and sweet, fresh air.

His gaze traced over my face, taking me in. I didn't know how to handle it. No one had looked at me like that in a very long time. Years. Like I wasn't crazy. Like I was . . . beautiful?

I blinked and quickly glanced away, my salt-burned cheeks tight. Then his hand descended onto my leg, and I jumped.

"What are you . . . ?"

"This can't start again," he said firmly. His long fingers traced the scars on my thighs. "If it does . . . we will have a problem."

He traced the cobwebs of silvery scars on my legs, sending my knees weak. It had been so long since someone had touched me with anything other than firm professionalism or sadistic disinterest.

But my own personal devil's touch was warm and insistent. Not just a touch. A caress. All the hair on my arms rose, and I shivered. Electricity seemed to hum under my skin at that touch. It was him. He was magnetic. The ultimate temptation.

He wants you. He's going to devour your soul.

The voice in my head had been quiet all day, and now she piped up. My angel.

"Too bad. My soul is mine to keep," I murmured, answering the voice without worrying how odd it sounded.

Father Lucciano's hand flattened on my thigh, high up, where the skin got softer, and his fingers dug in for a moment, squeezing.

"I have no use for your soul. I've collected enough to see me through."

My eyes shot to his. Was that a confession? Was he confirming my wild theory that he had blood on his hands?

He smirked faintly at me. "Father Benedict is overprescribing. I'm here to check up on him. If you need the medication, just say."

"No. I don't need to take it."

"We'll see. No lashing out. No acts of violence toward others or yourself . . . Got it? Or I'll have you back where you started faster than you could cross your chest to ward me off."

He rose smoothly, elegant in his long black robes.

He headed toward the door and rapped on it, indicating that he was ready to leave.

"Thank you," I called quietly, but I knew he'd heard me from the soft jerk of his powerful shoulders.

He paused and looked back at me.

"Don't thank me, *micetta*. Don't be confused. I'm not here to save you."

Then he walked out the door and left me alone.

Another scintillating day at Hallow Hall, and another chance to poke around the office. There was a safe in the back that I'd love to get into. I knew they had money and other valuables in there. I'd seen it once when Vargas had opened it. There had been a lot of money. Some of the people who checked their family members in here for treatment could afford to pay out of pocket and did so in cash. Others, like me, didn't pay. We were the charity cases.

"Did you know Vargas is coming tomorrow? Along with the director of the board, apparently." Alonso leaned against the reception desk watching me rifle through papers without a word.

"Really?" I paused.

Vargas. That motherfucker. Today, I was myself again. I remembered the night Mira had died like it was yesterday. Vargas had been the one leading the show in the operating room, watching over Pavol cutting Mira's baby out of her without a single regard for her life.

"Director of the board," I considered for a moment. "Is that for Centrium Group? Their name is all over the invoices here. They bankroll this place."

"Do they? Isn't it like a charity or a church thing?" Alonso wondered, and then pulled his phone out and searched for something.

"What are you doing?"

"Seeing what company name's on my paycheck."

"You haven't noticed that in two years?"

He sighed. "A paycheck is a paycheck; most of the time it doesn't pay to look too deeply into who signs it as long as it's in my account on payday." He stopped typing and frowned at his phone. "You're right, Centrium Group."

"That doesn't set off alarm bells? Why is a private business paying for this place? What do they get out of it?" I mused.

"Katarina! What are you wasting Alonso's time with?" Sister Vera had appeared out of thin air behind me.

"Nothing," I muttered, and wandered a little ways off as Sister Vera chastised Alonso for fraternizing with a patient.

As soon as she turned to me, Alonso pulled a face that made me smile, then made his escape.

"Katarina, you seem cheerful this morning. Are you on the verge of an episode?"

Ah, yes, an episode. That was Hallow Hall psychobabble for when I was lucid enough to start protesting my involuntary confinement and pointing fingers at all the fucked-up shit that went on here.

"No, Sister. Not at all. In fact, I'm so tired," I said, and feigned a stretch. "My medication must be making me so exhausted."

"Hmm." She eyed me distrustfully. "We'll see. Now, you better be on your best behavior today when the director comes. He's not a man to be trifled with."

"Oh, I wouldn't dream of it, Sister." I sighed.

She scowled at me, clearly searching for a reason to reprimand me but coming up short. "Well, make sure that you don't, or there'll be hell to pay."

"Literally," I murmured as I busied myself with filing again.

8

KATARINA

"Here, have some tea, it's got lots of milk in it," I told Mira, and set down the mug I'd had to spend half an hour begging for in the kitchen.

She wrapped her bony fingers around it and shivered. The back of her hand was bruised. I knew that bruise.

I picked up her hand, anger welling up inside me that couldn't be contained.

"Was it Benedict? What's he been giving you?"

She swallowed, her slender throat bobbing around the movement. She was so thin. It was a miracle the baby continued to grow when her mother was wasting away.

"I don't know . . . He says it'll make the birth easier. I'm scared," she admitted.

I wrapped my hand around hers. "Of course you are, because you're smart. But women have been having babies forever. You'll be okay. They'll take care of you here." I was lying and we both knew it, but what else could I say?

She took a sip of tea and put it back down quickly.

"You feel sick?"

She nodded slowly.

"Did you sleep okay?"

She sighed. "I had therapy before . . . I couldn't sleep well after."

"What therapy?"

"With Father Pavol," she confessed in a whisper.

The anger inside me turned red-hot. What was the bastard doing to a nine-months-pregnant sixteen-year-old?

I gripped her hand tightly.

"One day, he and Benedict, and Vargas, too, they will all get what they deserve. You believe in God, don't you?" I looked down at the small gold crucifix around her neck.

She shrugged noncommittally.

"Yes, you do. I know you do."

"If so, he doesn't believe in me. I'm a fallen woman."

"Don't repeat those monsters' words to me. I know you, the real you. You're forgiven. You haven't done anything wrong. Everything is going to be okay." I said the words and believed all but the last.

"When we get out of here, we'll raise the baby together in a house by the sea," I told her. It was our ongoing story, one we had made up to make us feel better about the sorry state of our lives. I waited for Mira to continue.

With a sigh, she nodded. "And we'll put our feet in the water every day, and make *mekitsi* and drink tea, and all of this will just be a bad memory. One day," she finished like she always did.

I nodded. "One day."

I woke to the sound of someone banging on my door. The metallic sound clanged around my head. It was early, before the usual wake-up time, which could only mean one thing. It was visiting day.

Twice a year, Father Vargas visited and brought along the head of the board of directors to tour the facility. Everyone was washed and dressed nicely. The more problematic people were drugged up and hidden away.

I could barely remember the last visit day, I'd been so drugged up.

Today, I was painfully aware.

Today, all three of the worst people I'd ever met would be in the same room. The unholy trinity of evil.

My dream of Mira was fresh in my mind as I walked to the showers with the other women from my ward. That memory had been near the end. Only a week later, she'd been screaming in the operating room, and I'd snuck in to see her after they'd carried a screaming baby out. I'd seen the light leave her eyes and—

I forced my thoughts away from that particularly dark memory. I couldn't go over it again or I'd lose my mind. That had triggered the start of the heavy medications. Before then, I'd been on something light . . . but what I'd seen had changed everything. Three years ago. Three long and terrible years.

My breath grew short, and I struggled to stay calm. I couldn't let them know I was off my medication. If I did, I'd be drugged up again in minutes, or worse.

You might still end up like Mira. I wonder how much your organs are worth these days?

I didn't bother shushing the voice in my head. The terrible question haunted me while I washed and dried my butt-length hair. I tied it into a braid then helped the girl in the room next to mine with hers. If we were good, then we'd get extra dinner tonight and maybe a communal movie. If we were bad, well, that really didn't bear thinking about.

My nerves were jumping by the time we were told to line up in the hallway, waiting for Father Vargas and the director to arrive. I was watching through the windows when an expensive car pulled up. It was flanked by men on motorcycles and another two black utility-sized vehicles. It was a large security presence for the director of some random, backward institute like ours. I'd long suspected that Centrium Group had a lot of fingers in different pies and Hallow Hall was just one of them. How exactly they made enough money here to justify the expenses I had no idea.

I told you—an organ harvest can bring in a pretty penny.

I felt sick. Surely the company that owned this place had no idea what Vargas was doing. He was just taking advantage of a situation where he had access to vulnerable people no one would miss. If not, why would he go to such trouble to put a professional, respectable face on the place whenever the director came to see his investment?

A flurry of whispers erupted along the corridor; our VIPs appeared in the entrance.

Father Vargas was just as I remembered him, tall and severe in ceremonial robes, but everything holy about that man seemed performative. He swept inside and waited for the director to follow. The man entered with an entourage of black-clad bodyguards. He didn't look like any CEO I'd ever seen on TV or in movies. He had a squat build and thick shoulders. His bald head gleamed under the lights overhead. His hands resembled ones that had suffered busted knuckles more than once and were adorned with rings. He appeared bullishly strong. The man was more like a brawler than a businessman.

They walked along the hallway, glancing this way and that at the patients they passed by. Benedict and Pavol led the way, and I felt dizzy at the sight of them all together in the same place. Father Lucciano was conspicuously absent. Maybe because he was new? Would I feel reassured or more afraid with him present? I had no idea.

I wanted to kill them all. I wished I had even half the power Father Lucciano commanded. Just the way he moved told me he had lethal skills. His body was a weapon, and he knew how to use it like one. I was jealous. If I were like him, I could take them all out and make it as bloody as I wanted. My savage thoughts were shocking, honestly. For a girl who had grown up spending every Sunday in church, learning goodness from my mother's side, Hallow Hall had changed me, damaged me.

Ruined me.

The director was silent for the most part while Vargas rattled on, gesturing around with expansive movements. They stopped here and there, never for more than a few seconds, until they reached me. To my horror, Father Vargas stepped forward and put his hand on my shoulder.

"And you remember Katarina Dmitrova."

The director stared me up and down, a suffocating inspection. He nodded slowly.

"*Buongiorno,* Katarina. You look well," he said slowly in stilted Italian. He had a mildly Eastern European accent.

I held my tongue, unsure what to say. Pavol, Vargas, and Benedict all watched me expectantly.

"You won't speak to me, child?" The director pushed. "I said you look well."

I shrugged. "I guess appearances can be deceiving."

"Katarina!" Vargas snapped, anger transforming his serene expression into one of ugly rage before he quickly smoothed his features.

The director chuckled and held out a hand to me. "Don't worry,

Michal, I like a woman who speaks her mind. I'm Sergei. Nice to meet you."

I just stared at his pale tattooed hand. Why was I being singled out like this?

I shook his hand limply and willed this to be over.

"How old are you, Katarina?"

I shrugged. "Twenty-five, I think." Well, that was what Father Lucciano had said yesterday, so I was going with it.

"Twenty-five, wow. I have a daughter your age," Sergei said, staring at me with an intensity that made me feel like something was on my face.

"We are going to tour around the institution and then have something to eat," Sergei continued. "Would you like to join us?"

"No," I blurted immediately.

Pavol stiffened, and Benedict jerked like I'd slapped him.

Vargas, though, just laughed and clapped a hand on the director's shoulder.

"You know the youth, so temperamental."

Sergei nodded and peered back at me. "Well, I'd love to know the opinion of a young person into how we are performing here for our patients. How are the care and standards in your view? Things can't improve without input."

Improve? Was it really possible that the company that ran Hallow Hall didn't know what kinds of things were going on under its crumbling roof? Maybe I should try to speak to Sergei after all.

"Katarina isn't well enough to give any kind of feedback," Vargas interjected before I could speak. "Now, I have someone to introduce you to, just down this way."

He turned Sergei, and they started to walk away.

Vargas shot me a glare over his shoulder that chilled me to the bone.

One thing was for sure: I'd pissed Father Vargas off. More importantly, I needed to speak to Director Sergei alone and tell him what was going on here, tonight, before I missed the chance for another six months.

The rest of the day was unusual because the higher-ups were entertaining Sergei, so there was no therapy. Our medications were delivered to our rooms, and it wasn't hard to avoid taking mine.

I lay on my bed and waited until all the lights had gone out in the hallway and everything was quiet. When the director visited, it was one of the rare nights that they bothered to lock us in. However, earlier today, I'd managed to sneak Alonso's key off his key ring. I'd use that to get out of my room and find the director.

When it felt like the whole place was sleeping, I got up, threw on a hoodie over my nightshirt, and pulled socks on. The tile floors were wickedly cold at night.

Then I headed to the door. I slid the key into the lock, turning it slowly so as not to be heard.

Adrenaline surged through me as the door was suddenly yanked out of my gentle grip.

It wrenched open, banging against the wall, and then Vargas was there, pushing into the room. He had two orderlies with him. I stared at them in shock.

"Going somewhere, Katarina? Looking for new ways to embarrass me?"

He sneered at me, staring me up and down and seeming to find me pathetic, standing there in my socks, my arms up defensively, like I could protect myself against these men.

"Bring her," Vargas snapped, and spun on his heel.

I opened my mouth to scream for help, whom from, I had no

idea. Strangely, the image of my own personal Lucifer filled my head for a moment before the orderlies grabbed me. One brought his wrist too close to my mouth, and I sank my teeth into his skin, hanging on doggedly. He growled and tried to shake me off. Hot copper filled my mouth, but I hung on, right until the other guy sank a syringe into my neck.

Then, it was lights out.

I came to slowly, the pain in my neck dragging me from my chemical slumber. I blinked a few times, trying to clear my head. I was in a room . . . more like an apartment. There was a TV in the corner, and a sofa, as well as a dining room table, and doorways leading off toward a bathroom and bedroom. I could see it all from my vantage point on the floor.

"Finally decided to join us?" The smell of cigar smoke drifted to me.

I moved my head to see Father Vargas sitting in a wingback leather chair, a phone in one hand, the cigar in the other.

"Take your time, clear your head. I'd rather you were of sound mind for the lesson I'm about to teach you."

Dread filled me. I'd never been alone with this man. I was one of the lucky ones, unlike the stories I heard sometimes from other patients. Unlike Mira's stories.

I didn't want to get up. I wanted to close my eyes and pretend this was all a dream.

When I tried that, though, I opened my eyes again straight away, too afraid not to watch and see what Vargas was doing.

"Why am I here?"

Vargas clamped his cigar between his teeth and listed reasons off on his fingers. "Let's see, because you embarrassed me? Or maybe because you're the only crazy bitch in this whole place I can't touch? Or you're the thorn in my side that I'm stuck with because of that whore, Mira?"

"Don't say her name," I said, panting, and sat up. "Don't you ever say her name."

He raised an eyebrow at me. "Mira. Mira, the whore . . . just like you, except you weren't really a whore, were you?" He smirked. "When my nephew, Ivan, first told me about you, I thought you were just another faceless baby machine who would disappear inside these walls and do something productive for the institute . . . I had no idea who you really were. Then I realized who you were, and I knew . . . Ivan had good taste."

"What are you talking about?" I muttered, swaying on the floor. Fuck, I was dizzy.

"Nothing." Vargas sighed. "Nothing for you to worry your pretty little head about."

He stood and strolled over to me. I fought a flinch. I wouldn't flinch from this man. His rosary clinked softly when he crouched before me.

"You know, you are so much more lovely than anyone else in here. You tempt a man to sin, Katarina, and I'm tired of being a saint around you."

The snort left me before I could stop it. "Saint? I've never met such a foul-hearted, filthy sinner in my life," I said venomously.

"Are you referring to your friend Mira? Everyone should be useful to the institute. Her heart paid for the new carpet in my office, and her eyes paid for that TV."

I lunged at him, but he was ready. He stepped back, and I fell flat. It had been a pathetic attempt, but I had to do something. He laughed and pulled his foot back, then let it fly at my abdomen, kicking me hard once, then twice. My ribs groaned, the muscles around them taking the hit, bruising and tearing. I felt like I could hear the sound, but Vargas's laughter had drowned everything out. It had to be my imagination.

He kicked me until I was quiet. I spat a mouthful of blood onto the carpet and fought for breath.

Vargas crouched over me again.

"I'm sick and tired of not being able to touch you, Katarina, not for discipline or anything else. But, you see, Benedict believes we've finally found the cocktail that'll keep you and whatever other whores come through here quiet. No voice, no memories . . . and soon enough, no mind. The only downside is that it triggers psychosis in some people . . . but it's a small price to pay. So now, no one has to know what happens to you, off-limits or not, because soon there won't be any of you left. You should thank Benedict. I was favoring lobotomy before he hit upon the ideal cocktail of drugs."

"The baby—" I said.

"What?"

"I just want to know what happened to Mira's baby," I pleaded.

Vargas sank back, perplexed. "You don't know? I thought you saw everything . . . sneaking around and spying."

"What happened to the baby? Please, I just want to know."

Why I was begging this man I had no idea. He had no mercy, no humanity at all. But Mira had cared about her child, and the least I could do was find out what they'd done with the baby.

Vargas considered my words and then sighed. "It died. Stillborn. That's what the death certificate says."

I shook my head. "No, that's not right. I heard it crying."

Vargas sighed. "Did the psychosis really start already?"

"It wasn't dead," I repeated on a wheeze, growing hysterical at the thought.

"Prove it," Vargas goaded, and smirked at me with a look that told me he was lying.

God, I wanted to kill this man more than I'd ever wanted anything in my life. More than I wanted to escape Hallow Hall, I wanted to kill this man. I wanted to bathe in his blood, and Pavol's, and Benedict's, too. I wanted to stick their heads on spikes around the gates of this place as a warning.

Vargas laughed at my expression. Why wouldn't he? I was weak and powerless. I couldn't do anything except imagine their gruesome deaths. I was never going to get my justice. A tear fell from my eye and plopped onto the carpet.

He moved his foot closer to me, aiming for my hand, and stomped his heel down, grinding it hard.

"Come on and scream for me, Katarina."

I bit my lip, holding the sound inside, determined not to give him the satisfaction. I felt the scream building, though, higher and higher, undeniable.

Then, shattering my concentration, a loud knock sounded at the door.

"Christ," Vargas muttered, and stood.

I dragged my hurt hand across the floor toward me and cradled it.

"Who's there at this hour?" Vargas called.

A muffled response that I couldn't make out.

He swore again and turned to me.

"What am I going to do with you?" he muttered, and then pulled his satin fascia off, tying it around my head like a gag. He picked me up and dragged me toward a large wardrobe in the corner.

He stuffed me inside, banging my head off the side for good measure. Once I was sagging down in the bottom, he reached into a pocket and drew out a rope, quickly tying my hands together. He was good at it. He'd clearly had practice.

"Not a sound, or when that fucker leaves, you're dead, and your mother is, too. Don't test me."

He shut the doors, and his thudding footfalls drifted away toward the door to his apartment. We had to still be in Hallow Hall. I knew that Benedict, Pavol, and Vargas all kept rooms on the top floor; that had to be where we were. Was it the director?

I strained to see, leaning forward despite my aching ribs to peek through the empty keyhole. I could just about make out a patch of the room.

Deep voices spoke, muffled and far away. Dark figures slipped past where I could see. My head ached where Vargas had banged it off the side of the wardrobe, and the drowsiness of the sedative from before hung over me, slowly lowering back over my head like a cloud. I couldn't keep my eyes open.

The soft murmur of male voices floated to me, but it was too late.

I lost the battle and fell into darkness.

9

MASSIMO

Waiting for a target to move into position was always tedious. Today, waiting for the high-and-mighty Michal Vargas to finally visit the institute had been especially mind-numbing.

I spent the day following up on my other jobs, and the most important thing: researching the steel mill in Castel Amaro, and Fabio Carrozzo, who, the story went, had ties to organized crime. I was no stranger to the Cosa Nostra, though I'd never swear allegiance to any one family. I worked for the highest bidder, and that was that.

Unraveling Fabio's past seemed paramount to moving my search for my mother's final resting place forward. If only the fucker hadn't died so fast. I'm sure I could have tortured something useful out of him. The next questions I had were which family he'd been affiliated with and who else might have helped him organize my mother's hospital stay. I had a dim memory of a logo but nothing else. Maybe they would remember more about it than he had.

I returned to Hallow Hall when all the festivities had died

down. I couldn't afford to be hanging around when the director was here. After all, I wasn't who I was supposed to be, and the unholy trinity thought I was here at Centrium Group's request. My cover story was flimsy but would hold long enough for me to get my job done. My business was with Vargas. After tonight, I'd have no reason to stay here in this cursed place.

Except for her.

Last night, holding Katarina Dmitrova as she'd cried her heart out on my lap was stuck in my memory. She was like the stray cats I fed whenever I found them. An unwanted creature. Just like me. Did she feel it, too? Was that why she'd sought comfort from me? Who turned to a devil for comfort? She was distracting.

I put all personal thoughts aside and prepared for work. I checked my bag for gloves, rope, a gag, sedative. All the tools to cover a few different scenarios, should things go sideways. Next, I tucked my loaded gun into a holster at my hip hidden beneath my cassock, and a silencer into my pocket.

Vargas had an apartment on the top floor of the building, and sure enough, when I made my way up there late at night, he was home.

I knocked and waited an unreasonably long time for him to open the door.

Finally, it swung open. He looked flustered, his face flushed and clothes askew.

"I'm not interrupting anything, am I?" I asked when he invited me inside.

"No, no. It's fine. It's good to meet you, Father Lucciano. Benedict told me that you'd finally arrived. It's been a while since Centrium sent us anyone to train."

"Likewise. I've heard so much about you," I said with a smile, and took his outstretched hand. Where the fuck they thought I was going to go and use their sick and twisted therapy training, I had no idea. This whole place was fucked.

We shook hands, and Vargas looked around.

"Let me fix us a drink and we can talk about what brought you here to Hallow. Sergei mentioned that he has someone here on a day-to-day basis keeping us honest." Vargas smirked at me like the very idea was an inside joke.

I nodded, playing along. "That sounds ideal." Luckily for me, my cover was holding. Christoph had been the ideal person to bump off and steal a position from.

But now, none of that mattered. After this, I would go back to the shadows and try to forget this place ever existed.

I waited until Vargas turned to his bar, then came up behind him and locked an arm around his throat.

He thrashed a little, nothing that could dislodge my arm, however, and then went limp.

It was almost too easy. Disappointing, really. Since coming here, I'd had to restrain myself from killing far too much, and it was wearing on my nerves. Pavol and Benedict were begging for it, but I'd ignored the urge so I could carry out my job.

I lowered Vargas to the floor and reached for the rope I'd coiled into my pocket. The client wanted him hanged; they were very insistent. There was probably some allusion to Judas in there somewhere, but I didn't care. Or maybe they wanted him scorned in the eyes of the Church by having his death ruled a suicide? Regardless, dead was dead, and I was good at any which way that was achieved. Since suicide was specifically requested, I held off leaving my usual calling card . . . a broken hourglass.

Rigging the rope up didn't take me too long, and soon I balanced Vargas's inert body on a stool to take his weight. I wanted him awake when I killed him. I wanted him to know what was happening.

Yes, Mrs. Vasco, the most unfortunate public school teacher in the borgo, *I did find my calling in your class. Thank you.*

I sat at the opulent table and lit a cigarette, filling my lungs with nicotine. I looked at Vargas. He was a man with secrets, and I wondered how many of them were born right here in Hallow Hall. The place was still a mystery and not one I was particularly eager to unravel except for where it concerned her.

Katarina Dmitrova was complicating things.

She wasn't going to be easy to leave here, or forget.

I pondered it as though I hadn't already decided to take her with me.

Then I heard it. A whimper. The sound of pain muffled by a gag. I'd heard it a hundred times, but never from someone who wasn't my victim.

Fuck.

Someone was here.

I rose slowly, senses on high alert. Since leaving the Col Moschin, I'd built a reputation for myself. That of a fearsome assassin, the man who could get to anyone, L'Ombra. The Shadow. They'd even given me a nickname.

But my ability to enter anywhere and get close to anyone was rooted in the fact that very few knew my face. As soon as my anonymity was lost, it was all over.

I couldn't afford to leave loose ends, and witnesses were exactly that.

I coasted around the room, approaching the wardrobe from the side, making it harder to see me coming. If the person inside had any kind of survival instinct, they would attack me first.

I reached under my cassock for my gun. It fit my hand like an old friend. I rolled the silencer on, took the safety off, aimed it toward the doors, and opened them.

The person inside launched at me, a blur of white and red. I leveled the gun at them. They had too much momentum. They weren't lunging. They were falling.

I backed up, gun pointed at the person as I finally made out who they were. Who else needed to die tonight.

She landed on her side, her hands over her face. Despite that, I recognized her.

A little stray cat getting into places she shouldn't.

Her clothes were bloodied, her hair wild. Her focus landed on me, and her lips moved around a thick satin gag. I stared at her, surprise rooting me to the spot.

What had Vargas been doing when I'd interrupted him? Had she seen me attack him? She only had to glance to the left and she'd see my suicide setup in progress.

Katarina had just made herself a witness, and I didn't leave witnesses. Ever.

I crouched before her and reached out for her gag. She flinched away from me, afraid. Her gaze fixed on the gun in my other hand.

I tugged the gag down. Her mouth was ringed with blood, her eyes red. She looked like she'd been to hell, and now she was staring at me as though I'd come on cue to collect her soul.

"Don't, please don't kill me," she whispered, staring at the gun. "Don't shoot me. Please. Please, I beg you."

I sank back on my heels and considered how to handle this unexpected development.

"You're somewhere you shouldn't be, Katarina."

"I didn't see anything, I didn't." The way she kept her eyes from the left side of the room, where Vargas was bound and ready to be hanged, told me otherwise.

"You're a terrible liar. Try again," I suggested.

She swallowed. "Fine, I saw. I don't care. I won't tell anyone."

"You won't tell anyone? What about when the police question you? What about when Benedict and Pavol question you during therapy, maybe when you're floating on whatever they give you?" I shook my head. "It's not a risk I can take."

"I hate him, too, though. I hate him so much—"

"I don't hate him," I interrupted her curtly. "I don't give a fuck about him. To me, he's just a paycheck."

I waited for her reaction to that confession. I was a contract killer. It was a bit of a conversation stopper, in my experience.

She wet her lips, and I watched her, unabashedly curious about everything that concerned her. Her and her unkissed lips. A virgin mouth at twenty-five years old in this day and age? Unheard of.

"I've killed a lot of people, and I haven't stopped to ask why . . . so many, I'm a millionaire many times over. My hands are as blood-soaked as your angel's voices told you they are."

She swallowed hard, and I could see those words sink in. She was afraid of me. Of course she was. How could someone so sweet and pure not be afraid of a man like me?

"The only rules I live by are get the money first and leave no witnesses. You, my little stray, are putting me in a difficult position."

A low moan sounded across the room. Vargas waking up. I pressed my gun into Katarina's temple for a moment.

"Stay here," I commanded, and rose.

Vargas slowly lifted his head, looking around in a daze. He hadn't registered the rope around his neck yet.

I sauntered over to him.

"Good evening, Father. Thank you for not keeping me waiting too long."

"What's going on? Where—" Vargas glanced down and saw the rope. "Wait! What's happening?"

"We're playing a game." I pointed the gun at him. "Now, stand on the chair, nice and slow. Be careful, you wouldn't want to fall."

Vargas blinked at me, my words taking a long time to penetrate. I jerked the gun.

"Hurry it up."

He moved, carefully balancing on the precarious stool. It had three spindly legs. He had turned white as a sheet.

"What game is this?"

"Truth or dare. Which do you choose?"

"Truth, I choose truth," Vargas cried.

"Why is Katarina in this room? Tell me the truth."

"I had her brought here to discipline her. She embarrassed me in front of the director, and I'm sick of her. She's clearly off her meds and running wild."

"Did you hurt her? Where did you touch her?" I asked, my tone conversational, which was quite a feat, considering how much my blood boiled.

"I didn't. She just woke up. I stuffed her in the cupboard so you wouldn't see her, I swear."

I glanced to Katarina for confirmation and stilled.

She was gone.

I turned to find her, and it was like the world slowed for a second. A second that lasted for an eternity.

She'd gotten herself up and moved around behind me, coming at me from the opposite side and taking me by surprise. I brought an arm up to defend myself, but it wasn't necessary.

I wasn't her target.

With a cry built of pain and blood and hate so deep—I

recognized it as the twin to the feeling inside my own heart—she lunged forward.

I thought for a second she was going for Vargas. She was going to pull my rope system down and I'd have to start all over again.

I was wrong.

She lunged for the stool, throwing her entire body weight at it. It skittered across the floor, and Vargas fell. The drop wasn't long enough to snap the neck, and that had been by design. Few suicides got the distance right. Also, it was too quick. Only friends deserved a merciful death, and Vargas was no friend.

He swung, his face blooming red, a gargle coming from spit-flecked lips. He tried to push his fingers beneath the rope. But it was no good. I was a master of my trade, and I dealt in death. There was no escape once the contract was out.

Katarina stared in fascination, never taking her attention off the man who technically she had given the final push. I couldn't look away from her. She watched him, and I watched her. In the dark, decadently decorated room, she seemed to shine. Her pale blonde hair and fair skin and white, stained clothes.

A light in the dark. A light who had just killed someone. An avenging angel.

I'd thought I was attracted to her before. It couldn't even compare to now.

She observed him losing the little air he had left in his lungs, hyperventilating with panic and running out even more quickly. She bit her lip.

She stepped closer when he jerked, and his eyes fluttered to her.

"For Mira," she murmured, and held the dying man's gaze until the final throes of death had passed over him and he was gone.

Then, she pressed her arms around her rib cage as if merely

standing were killing her, but the sight of Vargas dying had been worth it. She turned to me and raised her chin like a queen. No, an empress, peering upon her loyal subjects.

"Now," she said heavily, pushing her hair off her bloodied forehead, "you're *my* witness."

Fuck.

I think I just fell in love.

10

KATARINA

"We need to leave in case someone comes. It won't look like a suicide if we're hanging out with the body." Massimo's deep voice reached me through the haze in my head.

I simply nodded. My gaze kept returning to Vargas's bloated, purplish face. It was fascinating. In the end, it hadn't been hard at all . . . with the right accomplice.

"*Micetta*. Time to go." Father Lucciano's hand closed around my upper arm, an unbreakable grip. His expression was unreadable. His forceful hold on me was a reminder of how easily he could kill me, too, if he wanted. And he had seemed ready to do that not five minutes before. At least he seemed to have changed his mind about getting rid of me immediately. That was something.

I nodded and let him guide me across the room. My ribs screamed. *Fuck,* they hurt.

He sighed as if reading my thoughts. Stopping by the door, he tucked his gun into the holster on his hip and pulled the cassock over it, then reached for me.

He swung me up into his arms before I realized his intention. I let out a short scream. My nerves were shot; I couldn't help it.

"*Now* you're scared?" he muttered incredulously. "You just stared down a gun to the temple and murdered someone, but sure, now you're scared."

He carried me out into the dark hallway, checking this way and that. His focus was as precise as a laser. He scanned the empty doorways and listened carefully for any telltale sounds that someone was coming. This was a man in his element. I'd be impressed by his professionalism if it weren't so terrifying.

"In my defense, you're pretty scary," I said.

One corner of his beautiful mouth lifted in acknowledgment of my words, but he stayed focused on getting us away from the off-limits area of the building. He was heading toward my room.

"I could say the same to you, my little stray."

Was he going to deliver me back to my bed and stage his second suicide of the night? He didn't leave witnesses. He was an assassin. A professional. Cold and calculating. I doubted he'd built a business by sloppily leaving witnesses behind.

He might try to kill me as soon as we got into my room. No, not try. In reality, if he'd decided to kill me, he wouldn't have to try hard at all. He wouldn't even break a sweat.

So, do something about it, the voice in my head whispered.

I'd missed her.

His knife. He always carries that knife, she reminded me.

Before doubt could steal my courage, I shifted in his arms, sliding a hand down my side. One of his pockets was under my hip. I was almost sure that was where I'd seen him take the knife from the other day when he'd used it to cut the cord on Father Pavol's TV.

I felt around as discreetly as I could, making sure to wriggle my body to hide my hand movements.

I was sweating by the time I touched the smooth handle of the folding knife and the door to my room loomed in front of us.

We were back. Judgment time.

My heart pounded so hard it hurt as we got to the room and went inside. The goons who had dragged me off earlier hadn't bothered locking it behind them.

It was dark inside, with just a square of moonlight shining on the bed through the window.

He carried me across the floor and lowered me to the bed, pausing when my weight was on the mattress, but his arms were still under me. He was so close.

This is it. End of the line.

I eased the knife open. He didn't notice. He was staring at my face as though he'd like to climb inside my head. God, he was beautiful. Death and destruction and temptation all in one.

"What am I going to do with you, *micetta?*" he murmured, his voice stroking over the words.

"Maybe I should be the one asking that," I said, my voice a mere breath, and moved my hand.

He raised an eyebrow and then seemed to register what I'd done.

His knife was pressed to the underside of his strong jaw, right against his jugular.

A moment of tension held between us, and then his mouth split into a grin.

"If this is your idea of foreplay . . . I like it. Keep going."

His grin was disarming, but I couldn't afford to be charmed by him. I couldn't forget what he was and what he did for a living.

"You're going to kill me, and I'm not going to let you."

His smirk turned wicked. "Is that right? How are you going to stop me?" His magnetic gaze drank me down. "What are you going to bargain with?"

"I-I have a proposition for you," I stated as confidently as I could.

"Hmm, I'm all ears." He seemed to be getting closer, closing in, making it harder and harder to breathe.

"I want to hire you."

There. I'd said it.

The statement stilled the man above me.

His dark brows drew together. "That isn't where I thought this was going."

"You kill for hire, right?" I forged on, growing more confident in my plan with every passing second. This made sense. "I want to hire you. I need your services."

"Katarina—" he started.

"It's just business. A business proposition. I'll hire you, and you won't kill me because I'm just as complicit as you are."

He sighed. "Being hired means being paid. I don't work for free. How are you going to pay me?"

Damn it. I'd kind of forgotten that detail. I chewed my lip, his gaze riveted by the sight.

"I don't know, but I'll work something out. Just tell me your price. I'll find a way, no matter what," I rushed out.

"No. Matter. What. At any cost? Those are dangerous words, Katarina. You have to understand something about owing a debt to a man like me."

He leaned forward, uncaring about the knife at his throat. It pressed in, and a dark line of blood ran down his neck.

"I always collect. Always." His words were a dark promise. His body was heavy on mine, his leg nestled between my thighs, and I had the wildest, most inappropriate urge to rub against it.

"The safe!" I exclaimed as the solution suddenly popped into my head. "There's money in the safe here. Money and all kinds of valuables. I can find out the combination somehow; I work in the office. I'll find it out and give it to you."

He studied me for a moment then sighed. "Who do you want killed?"

"Pavol and Benedict. They're monsters. They deserve to die."

He cocked his head. "Are you sure you want me to do it? You did a pretty efficient job yourself earlier."

"Only because of you. I can't do it without you, I'm not strong enough," I admitted, breathless from the steady ache in my ribs. "I need your help."

A muscle ticked in his jaw. "As unorthodox as my work is, I do have a schedule, commitments . . ."

"Please, Massimo," I begged with as much quiet dignity as I could muster. It was the first time I'd ever called him by his name. "I need you."

His hand moved to my jaw and gripped my chin in a firm hold.

"I like the way my name sounds on your lips. Say it again. Tell me you need me," he ordered.

His voice had dropped, and tension dripped through me. His leg between mine pushed into me, and I felt him. A long, hard line pressing into my hip. I might have been a virgin, but I wasn't clueless. He was hard, and that was his dick lying against me.

"I need you, Massimo," I whispered. "No one can help me but you."

His eyes closed for a split second, like he was savoring my words, and then snapped open with renewed focus.

"Killing two men will cost you. It's not cheap," he told me.

"I'll give you everything in the safe. There's a fortune in there. It's all yours," I vowed.

"It'll cost you all of that . . . and more. There's something else I want from you, Katarina."

"What?" I asked, my skin suddenly feeling too small for my body. I was so aware of his closeness.

He still had my chin gripped between his thumb and forefinger. He used it to tilt my head down so all I could see was his face.

"You. I want you. That's my price."

His words took a second to register. He took advantage of that moment of confusion, and before I could move, the knife was plucked from my hand. He twirled it between his fingers and then put it to my throat when I tried to sit forward.

I froze, terrified again.

He really does want your soul after all.

"He said he didn't want it, though," I argued softly with the voice.

Massimo looked fascinated.

"Is your angel speaking to you? What does she say?"

My jaw clenched. "She says you want my soul after all."

He tutted. "I don't want your soul. I don't need one where I'm going, but you intrigue me. Keep your soul, I'll take your mind and body . . . given freely."

"Why?" I burst out.

He cocked his head at me. "Do you really not know, are you really that naive?"

I shook my head. "I'm not that naive. I know what you mean, but I mean, why me? I'm—crazy. I'm . . . I haven't had a haircut in three years," I blurted out.

Long hair was just the tip of the iceberg. I hadn't voluntarily looked in a mirror in years, but I was sure I fell short of the kind of women who must be interested in a man like Massimo. He was beautiful, strong, rich, charismatic. It didn't make sense.

"You . . . You're unique, Katarina, and I like exclusive things. You interest me."

Like a freak show. He wants to sleep with the freak. For once I didn't respond to the voice.

"Besides, there is no why when it comes to desire, *micetta.* It just is. And I want you, end of story. I want to be all your firsts."

Those words sent a twisted kind of heat rushing through me. All my firsts.

"If we make this deal, you'll kill Pavol and Benedict, and you won't kill me after we're done."

"Why would I if you're my client?" Massimo said with a smirk.

He looked like he was enjoying himself now, plotting the death of two men and *being all my firsts.* I couldn't even think the words without my skin getting hot.

"I'm your witness," I reminded him. I needed to know that I was safe from this man.

He nodded. "And now I'm yours. We guarantee our mutual destruction."

I thought furiously about any downsides to his proposal.

"Do you need to see the full t's and c's, or are we making an agreement?" Massimo asked, dryly amused.

"When you make a deal with the devil, you have to check the details," I pointed out.

He chuckled. "Check away . . . make sure you do, because I plan to enforce them and take every single thing I'm owed."

Then he dipped his head and shocked me by licking my cheek from my jaw up to my temple. I shivered at the wet stripe on my overheated skin. There was something primitive about that movement. Primal. Ancient.

His lips moved over the sensitive flesh.

"Every. Single. Inch."

His hand found my chin and he turned my face to his, holding me captive with effortless strength.

His mouth lowered to mine and brushed across my lips. It was electrifying, and somehow not quite enough. I panted, and his tongue slipped inside my mouth and stroked along mine. Not exactly a kiss.

A taste.

A faint growl sounded from deep within his throat, like it was hard for him to pull back. Like the beast inside didn't want to.

"Agree, Katarina. Give me your word and sign this deal with your devil."

I nodded slowly, the weight of what I was agreeing to hitting me. I was killing two men. I was ordering their deaths. No one deserved it more, but it was still sobering.

"I need your words; I need you to agree." Massimo waited for me to clear my throat.

Then I spoke.

"I agree to your terms. I need your help; I can't do it alone. I need you, so I agree."

"Good girl," he whispered, and then stole my breath one more time by bringing the hand that held the knife to his neck. The line of blood that I'd spilled was still there. He smeared it on his thumb and brought it to my lips.

"Bargains with the devil are signed in blood," he said, his gaze fixed on the sight of his blood painted across my lips.

I was frozen there, transfixed by his actions. When my lips were wet with his blood, he sank his sullied fingers into my hair and tugged my head back, baring my mouth to his ruthlessly.

He closed the space between us and kissed me. No, not just kissed me. He savaged me. He bit into my lip, drawing blood, and I gasped. His kiss gentled then, and he slid his tongue in my mouth, caressing it against mine. It was suggestive and wicked. It felt like being invaded by darkness . . . and I liked it.

It was unholy. It was perfect. Our blood mixed between us, sealing our agreement.

For better or for worse.

It was done.

11

KATARINA

The next day, the morning hymn sent me out of bed at the usual time. The halls were quiet, and there wasn't a nun to be seen. Usually they watched over the cafeteria while patients ate, but this morning, it was bedlam without them.

I sat with Tatiana. She ate cereal and played with a small corn-husk doll we'd made together. Moving was challenging. My ribs were a colorful array of purples and dark blues.

Dr. Blackwood walked through the room looking harassed. I spied Alonso, but he barely had a second to wave to me before he was striding away.

I shot out of my seat before remembering the state of my mid-section. *Ouch.* I collapsed back into my chair, and Tatiana eyed me curiously.

"Where are you going?"

"I just wanted to speak to my friend," I muttered.

She turned to look at Alonso's departing back. She seemed un-settled. All the patients were. The staff might not have announced that something was wrong, but the tension was palpable.

"Knock, knock," Tatiana said after a moment.

I summoned a smile for her. "Who's there?"

"Howl," she said seriously.

"Howl who?"

She bit her lip, her gaze moving to Dr. Blackwood, who was now walking toward us.

"Howl we ever get out of the haunted house?" she whispered just as he arrived at our table.

"Katarina, a word," he snapped at me.

I jerked at his tone. Blackwood was usually civil—well, civil enough. He didn't seem to share the perverted interests of the unholy trinity.

Tatiana tensed, and I patted her hand.

"Be right back, don't worry."

I felt her watching me as I walked across the room.

"How can I help you, Doctor?" I asked Blackwood.

He stopped just outside the doorway. "Did you see Father Vargas last night?"

I fought to keep my expression neutral. "No, why?"

He peered at me. "He asked me about you . . . It seemed he was about to speak to you about something. Are you sure you didn't see him?"

I swallowed, my throat too dry to answer. I wasn't like Massimo. I was no seasoned killer who could lie with a straight face, and it felt like Blackwood was trying to crack open my skull and inspect my memories.

I shook my head, not trusting myself to speak.

"Why don't you just ask him?" I wondered suddenly, remembering that I shouldn't know there was anything wrong with Vargas.

Blackwood narrowed his eyes at me, then gripped my upper arm.

"Liars have tells; I'm sure you know that, Katarina. They have tells for when they don't want to appear like they're lying. Too much eye contact is one, and not blinking is another. Come with me."

He tugged me along the hall. *Crap.* I'd been so busy trying to avoid seeming like a typical liar, I'd acted weird enough to make him suspicious. Or maybe he was just suspicious because he'd known what Vargas's plans were going to be last night. Either way, he was pissed off. There was an urgent, frantic sort of energy hiding behind his usual stern and dispassionate demeanor that was unsettling.

We reached his office, and he pushed me inside. My ribs twinged hard, and I hid a flinch.

"Doctor, I don't know what you're talking about, I didn't see Father Vargas last night," I attempted, and stumbled across the floor.

His office was roomy, with a desk and seating area and another area behind a medical curtain. He pulled the curtain back and pointed at the exam table there.

"You're overdue for your checkup. Sit."

I took a deep breath and slowly walked over. Resisting now would only get me thrown into solitary. Blackwood had never hurt me, as far as I remembered, and I *was* overdue for my checkup.

It was the usual routine. Blood pressure, weight, pulse. He checked my eyes with a little light and then my throat.

"I suspect you're anemic again," he said, and sighed, as if the nutritional choices I made at Hallow Hall were my own.

He fiddled around with an IV bag before wheeling it over to me.

I drew back. "I feel fine."

"But you're not. Aren't you tired? You haven't been skipping medication doses, have you?"

I shook my head. "No. I'm always tired, so it doesn't feel any different." *Crap.* I was getting myself into all kinds of trouble today.

He took my arm and cleaned it with a sterile wipe, then slipped the fresh IV needle in. It didn't hurt. My arms were a patchwork of small, silvery lines of scar tissue. I'd been stuck and poked and prodded so much in the three years I'd been here, an IV going in hardly registered.

"Lie back and relax. Take half an hour to enjoy the quiet," he said, picking up my medical chart and making copious notes on it.

I lay back, my arm feeling slightly cold where the iron infusion was passing into me.

"So, when was the last time you saw Father Vargas?" Blackwood suddenly asked me. His focus was still trained on his notes, but I had the feeling he was watching me more closely than ever.

"I don't know, when he walked around with the director, or maybe in the dining room . . . I think he passed through while the patients were eating."

"And you're sure it wasn't at any other time?"

A wave of tiredness washed over me. It was soft, and gentle, like the breeze of a peaceful sea. Well, what I imagined a breeze off a peaceful sea might feel like. I'd only ever read about them and dreamed.

My skin prickled, and heat washed through me from my arm. It felt different than any other IVs I'd ever gotten.

"I feel strange," I said, my voice surprisingly deep.

Blackwood nodded. "I popped a sedative into the solution to

keep you calm. Today isn't the day for hysteria or acting out, and besides, I thought you might remember something more about last night if you relaxed."

He pulled a chair up closer to me and shined the light in my eyes again.

"This solution is just one of Bendict's passion projects. I confess, it hasn't been tested yet, but I'm going to observe how it affects you and make a note of it."

"You're testing a new drug on me? Is that ethical?" A ridiculous question considering how often they did so, but I was panicking. Strangely, my body didn't feel that way at all. His words should outrage me, but instead, I felt nothing. No, not nothing . . . I felt hot. My clothes were harsh and uncomfortable on my skin, and suddenly all I could think about was taking them off.

"It's not unethical . . . People care more about animal testing than humans these days, anyway. This isn't a new drug; it's just a new combination. It's no big deal . . . unless you want me to get that stray cat from the chapel and test it on him?"

"Gravy? How'd you know about Gravy?" I asked.

Blackwood pushed the hair back from my sticky forehead. I was sweating. I felt like I was burning alive.

"Because I know everything about you, Katarina. You were the first patient I referred here to Hallow Hall. You might say I'm invested in your recovery. About last night—"

"I'm too hot, I can't breathe," I muttered, and tugged at my sweater, but the IV was still in my arm, and it hurt. I flopped back on the bed.

Blackwood frowned and glanced down at his notes. "The sedative should just relax you, make you feel good and willing to answer anything I ask you." He kept reading his notes for a moment before raising his brows. "Ah, is that what it is?" He wrote something down in small black scribbles. "Too many dopamine agonists? Maybe an interaction with the antipsychotic."

I reached out and grabbed his hand, and he jolted, shocked into looking at me.

"I feel strange," I confessed in a rush.

His pale cheeks reddened, and he gave me the once-over. I became aware of how my body was moving. Fidgeting, and rubbing my thighs together.

"Tell me exactly how you feel," he murmured.

"My skin hurts, like the clothes are too rough, and it's so hot." I squeezed my eyes shut. The awful truth filtered through my overheated brain. I felt turned on. Completely against my will and at odds with anything I'd naturally feel around this weed of a man, this monster who worked in Hallow Hall and did the bidding of the unholy trinity.

Blackwood flushed even more and wiped his mouth with the back of his hand.

"Doctor?" *Knock, knock.* A hard, urgent sound.

Blackwood tore his attention from me and stood. He put the clipboard over his crotch, though it was plain to see he was hard. A sharp feeling of disgust cut through my arousal.

Blackwood pulled the door open.

"Yes, what?" he all but barked at Sister Vera.

"There's been an incident. One of the seniors has cut himself badly, and he needs to see you. He's lost a lot of blood."

Blackwood cursed and peered back at me. "I'll return shortly, Katarina. Do not move from this spot."

Then he strode out of the room. Sister Vera looked into the room and saw me. She took in my posture, the way I was writhing on the bed, and her eyes gleamed with judgment. Her face full of disgust, she closed the door.

Alone in the silence finally, I shoved my hand down the front of my sweatpants and found my pussy. I was wet. Pressing my fingers on my folds gave me a vague sort of relief, but it wasn't enough.

I rubbed at myself inexpertly before giving up out of frustration. It just wasn't enough.

"Don't stop on my account, little stray. I was enjoying the show."

Massimo's deep voice sent me scrambling upward. He lounged against the closed door. He must have entered while I'd been attempting to get myself off.

He raised an eyebrow at me. "I'd ask what the hell you're doing, but that seems pretty self-explanatory. I do question your setting, though. I wouldn't have thought this room capable of turning anyone on."

"It's not me," I said, and tugged at the IV. "Please, take this out."

Massimo crossed to my side and slowly drew the curtain shut, hiding us from anyone who might enter the room.

"What's in it?" he wondered.

"Some kind of sedative. Blackwood suspects me. He was trying to question me about last night . . ." I panted.

"Interesting way of questioning someone," Massimo said, and carefully withdrew the IV from my arm, letting the end drop.

A little blood ran down my arm, but the hot sensation at the injection site immediately faded. Thank God. Massimo pressed a cotton ball from the nearby instrument tray over the trail of blood, blotting it away, and then tossed it to the side.

"He gave you MDMA," Massimo mused, sounding far more entertained than he had any right to be. He was checking my notes.

"What's that?"

"Some people's party drug of choice. Increased happiness, less filter . . . increased libido." He set the clipboard down and ran his gaze over me. "Unfortunately, you seem to be experiencing at least one of those effects."

"How did you know I was here?" I murmured. I toyed with the top of my sweatpants. I felt like if I didn't touch myself again, I'd die, but Massimo was watching me. Only shame kept my hand from sliding between my legs.

"You weren't anywhere else," he said shortly. "We have a deal. I need you in one piece to satisfy it."

"You were looking for me?" I asked. My fingers had crept below the waistband, and I couldn't even bring myself to care.

"Hmm, yes. It's becoming a habit. Whatever room I walk into around here, I'm looking for you."

He stared down at my hand, which was now fully snaked beneath my sweats. "Are you touching yourself while speaking to me?"

I nodded and wet my lips. "Does that mean I have your protection until the end of our contract?"

"No one touches what's meant for me," he said slowly, and then his shadowed eyes flickered to mine. "That includes you."

He reached out and grabbed my wrist, taking my hand away from its inept groping.

I groaned, the disappointment too much for a second.

"Wait it out. It'll pass," he told me, still gripping my wrist.

I shook my head. "I can't. It hurts. I just want, *need* something, please."

"I won't take any of your firsts like this, drugged up and confused. I want to look in your beautiful clear eyes, little stray, when I take what you promised me." Then he brought my hand to his nose and inhaled. My fingers felt wet still, coated with my juices.

He closed his eyes as he inhaled, as though he were breathing in the finest perfume.

Heat scalded me, made so much worse by this man, a man I actually wanted.

"Please, make it stop hurting, Massimo, please," I asked.

His mouth quirked up at the corner. "You sound so pretty when you beg. Do it again."

I had no shame in this hot, desperate place, and so I did.

"Please, take this feeling away," I pleaded.

He was quiet for a moment and then sighed. "I won't take any of your firsts this way, but I don't like to see you suffer, either. Get up," he instructed.

I immediately complied. He unbuttoned his cassock and pushed it open. He had a black button-up shirt on with the clerical collar, and black pants.

He sank into the wide, leather armchair Blackwood had been sitting on and patted his lap.

"I won't touch you, *micetta*, but you can touch me. Take what you want. What you need."

I wasted no time slinging my leg across him and sinking onto his lap. Reason whispered to me that I had no idea how to take anything I needed. I'd never felt like this before. I had no idea what to do. Then, I felt it. Long and hard and lying right against my center. Massimo, my own personal devil, was hard. He was big as well, or seemed to be by the way he was filling out his pants. The bulge was an impressive size, rigid and demanding even through the rough material of his slacks.

I pressed my core on him, my pussy perfectly lining up with his cock. Then I moved on him. Back and forth, right and left, shamelessly grinding as much of my center on his as I could. It felt like cool water after wandering in a desert.

"Does that feel better, Katarina?" he murmured, catching a handful of my hair and tilting my head back just enough so my ear and throat were exposed to him.

"Hmm . . ."

"Use your words."

"Yes, it feels good. So good. I wish it was inside me, but this feels good, too," I moaned, moving faster and faster, spurred on by something only my body knew how to do, chasing the pleasure that spiraled up my spine.

"Soon I'll be inside you and all around you. There won't be a hole on this beautiful body that I haven't marked as mine." His filthy words only turned me on more.

I humped my hips against him, rising and rising, knowing that there was relief coming, so close I could taste it.

"From now on, you want relief, you come to me. You need to come, you come to me. You feel like touching yourself . . . you come to me. You gave me all your firsts. Don't forget it."

His final growl sent me over the edge. I bucked into him, grinding along his length. He jerked beneath me, stiffening suddenly, his hips nudging up toward me as if he wished as much as I did that the material between us was gone.

He let out a soft sigh of curses as I continued to grind into him, squirming against his pulsing bulge, drawing out every last second of pleasure. The roaring need inside me dulled to a gentle ache when I finally sank down on him, spent and relieved. He opened his arms, and somehow, I was sinking into his chest. Still astride him, I felt his arms close around me, and I was . . . warm from the inside out. Warm in a way I'd never felt before.

Safe, even.

It was new. It was terrifying. It was addictive.

I breathed out in a long, grateful exhale.

"Better?" Massimo said, his chest rumbling under my ear.

"Better." I tilted my face up to look at him. "Thank you."

He stared down at me, a curious expression on his face.

"No one thanks me, little stray. No one, until you."

I found a smile touching my lips. I felt light and happy. Maybe I liked the MDMA cocktail after all.

"Well . . . no one's ever helped me, until you."

Then I closed my eyes and fell asleep.

12

MASSIMO

The coroner arrived in the afternoon. I had no idea who had discovered Vargas's body, but the director and his goons had left immediately in heavy-duty armed cars.

Pavol and Benedict suspended the usual therapy schedule, so patients were free to wander around in the rec room for the rest of the day.

I grabbed a coffee and sat at a table in the staff kitchen, staring out at the frozen ground. Yesterday had been unexpected, and now my schedule was fucked.

Of course, I could have just refused and tied up the loose end that was Katarina Dmitrova, but honestly, there was nothing I'd like to do less. Our time together earlier in Blackwood's office returned to me with force, the sight of Katarina's cheeks flushing as she came, the feel of her dragging her pussy against my hard-on . . . I'd been erect all fucking day even though she'd made me come in my pants. She was completely unexpected, and I was hooked. Getting her out of my head was a challenge, and saying no to her proposal hadn't been a real option.

I always built flexibility into my schedule. You couldn't really promise that someone would be dead by a certain date, so I could adjust. Killing Benedict and Pavol would be a pleasure, honestly, I just couldn't do it too soon. It would raise suspicion. Clearly they had smoothed Vargas's death over and had it ruled a suicide, so as not to bring the authorities into Hallow Hall. It wouldn't end well for them if detectives started to question the therapy that was done here, the pregnant patients. A lot of things didn't add up in this hellhole, and Pavol and Benedict were hiding things. A lot of things. The only worry on the horizon was my cover story. If Centrium Group got too involved, it was only a matter of time until someone worked out that I wasn't the man they'd sent here for training. Or worse, Christoph's body would be identified. I'd cross that bridge when I came to it.

I took my phone out of my robes, fighting a shudder. The fucking material of the cassock was hot and scratchy.

I checked my emails, waiting to see if my hacker friend had made any progress investigating the people who might have worked with Fabio Carrozzo in the past. He'd said that the hospital burned down. Surely that was the kind of thing that made local news. I was sure the hospital had been in the South. However, the whole thing was so clinically scrubbed, even from legal record, I had no doubt that officials had been involved in the cover-up. The question was why. My old Army commander's father-in-law, Prosecutor Bellisario, had been the kind of official who'd been up for sale for the right price. He could have helped to remove every trace of a catastrophic fire at a hospital from local record. I wished I could ask him directly, but unfortunately, it wasn't the kind of thing that he'd remember since it was so long ago, and Bellisario had bigger problems these days. He was imprisoned and likely never to see the light of day.

No new emails. I tucked my phone away, questioning the odd sense of relief in my chest at finding out I was no further ahead. Making progress on my mother's past would mean leaving here to go and deal with the people involved.

It would mean leaving Katarina . . . But I wouldn't leave her here while she owed me. Where I went, she went. She hadn't quite realized that when she was negotiating her terms yesterday.

She had given herself to me . . . and not once mentioned a time limit. And that worked well with my plan to keep her.

I caught myself smiling in my faint reflection in the window.

That oversight was going to cost her dearly. She had given me license to take whatever I wanted from her, for however long I wanted to.

Finishing my coffee, I stood and tapped my pocket to check for the roll of tape and painkillers I'd taken from the infirmary.

"Oh, you're here, Father Lucciano." Dr. Blackwood stood in the doorway watching me.

He was another unsettling fucker, but Katarina didn't seem to lump him into the same category as Pavol and Benedict.

"Just leaving, actually." I stepped away from the table. "I take it everything is wrapped up with Father Vargas, may he rest in peace."

Dr. Blackwood nodded absently. "Yes, it's a shock, honestly. Suicide by a man of the cloth is a sobering thing. How did he seem to you last night?"

Blackwood poured himself a coffee and collapsed into a chair by the window.

"I didn't see him, I'm afraid. I was busy all day."

Blackwood scrubbed a hand over his face. "I wonder what deep, dark secrets a man like Vargas had that could drive him to take his own life."

"Perhaps something went wrong with the inspection. The director of the board was here, I heard. Maybe Vargas wasn't performing well as the head of this business."

Blackwood looked surprised by my words. "Business? We help people here."

I studied him for a long moment, holding his gaze silently until he fidgeted.

"Right, so you do. Still, it's not funded by the Church and is run by a board of directors for profit. That describes a business to me."

Blackwood shrugged. "I suppose. I don't know your background, but in case you don't know, in medicine, trying to make a difference, trying to help people without worrying about bureaucracy and funding and insurance, is next to impossible. Hallow Hall is the only place I've worked where the objective is just about helping people."

The man was either very calculating or painfully naive. I didn't have time for either.

"Hmm, yes, indeed. If you'll excuse me, I think I'll go and make sure the patients don't need anything. They must be unsettled by all of this."

Blackwood nodded. "Good idea. In times like this, people need guidance. Help them." He trailed off, his eyes fixed on mine.

Did he know something? There was a look in his eyes that held something I couldn't quite read. Dr. Blackwood was a man to keep an eye on, clearly.

"Yes, of course. That's why I'm here, to help people . . . just like you."

I found Katarina in the office. She volunteered her time there, and it seemed to be encouraged, seeing as she was one of the more lucid patients. There were plenty of younger patients who weren't interested in volunteering, and then those who wouldn't be capable.

I watched as she sat at a desk and stared down at some files in front of her. She traced her finger along lines of text on a spreadsheet and then jotted down something on a notepad. A bruise had bloomed on the back of her hand from last night. I didn't like the way the sign of injury appeared against her skin. An orderly hung over the desk watching her. The same orderly I'd seen with her before. His expression showed he was fond, overly fond.

I didn't like that one bit.

"Miss Dmitrova," I said from the other end of the desk.

Katarina glanced up and jolted so hard her teeth clicked shut, and she winced. The orderly looked between us.

"Father Lucciano," Katarina said, her eyes dancing away from mine. She bit her lip, right over the small cut my teeth had ripped last night.

"Ah, Father. You are the new holy spirit around here. Nice to meet you. I'm Alonso." The orderly approached, sticking his hand out to shake mine.

It wavered in the air until he realized I wasn't going to shake it. He dropped it to his side.

"Alonso, aren't we keeping you from something?"

Alonso faltered and then shrugged. "I'm observing patient Dmitrova. It's all part of the job." He grinned and wiggled his eyebrows at Katarina.

She smiled at him, a small, trusting smile. No one had ever smiled at me that way.

"Well, I'm here now, so you can move along," I found myself saying.

Alonso shrugged. "I'm on a break, and there's no one else I'd rather hang out with here at Hallow. Me and Katarina, we're tight. Maybe she'll tell you in therapy." He chuckled at his own words and peeked back at Katarina.

"You should go," Katarina said, still maintaining eye contact with me but speaking to Alonso. She was growing more and more nervous as my expression darkened.

"What? Really? But I didn't even have a chance to tell you how my date with Lael went the other night," Alonso said, his tone playful.

Katarina's eyebrows rose, and she seemed wistful for a second. "Was the dinner place good? I'm so jealous."

"I'll take you when you get out," Alonso promised, stretching his goodbye to the point where I started to imagine stapling his hand to the desk to make him understand that he wasn't wanted.

Alonso ambled off, pissing me off with his slow, deliberate steps. The fucker was going to pay for that.

Katarina sighed loudly. "Must be nice."

"To date Alonso?"

"To date anyone . . . to have a girlfriend, or a boyfriend—"

"He doesn't have a girlfriend," I interrupted.

She frowned at me. "What? Of course he does. He's always coming and talking to me about her."

I rolled my shoulders to ease my tight neck. The fucking wooden pallet I was sleeping on was doing a number on my neck, and now it was wound tight from interacting with a territorial male.

Alonso didn't understand yet—Katarina was no longer available to flirt with. She was spoken for.

"There is no girlfriend. She's an excuse to come and talk to you. And there I remember you telling me that you weren't naive, and yet here we are."

She shook her head. "You're crazy."

"That's my line," I muttered, and shook off my annoyance at finding that fucker flirting with my little stray, someone so far out of his league it was laughable.

Katarina rolled her eyes and returned her attention to the paper she was writing on.

"You're industrious this morning," I murmured, leaning over the desk.

Putting a hand to her side, she made a soft noise of discomfort.

"Ribs giving you trouble?"

"Nothing I can't handle," she said quickly, and then looked around surreptitiously.

I found myself fighting a grin. She was, for lack of a better word . . . adorable. From an avenging angel last night to this sweet and bright-eyed girl this morning. How could such duality live inside one shell?

"Can you look something up for me?" she asked, and passed me the slip of paper she'd been writing on.

"What's this?" I stared down at her, perplexed.

"The name of the company that pays all the bills for Hallow Hall," she supplied. She waited for me to respond, and when I failed, she huffed. "They have to be the ones involved in all of it. They aren't making money off the patient fees here. Some of the patients aren't even paying to be here, like me. They're making money another way."

"And what do you want me to do about it?" I asked, reading the name on the paper.

Centrium Group.

She nearly said something, then paused.

"I—I don't know," she admitted, her eyebrows drawing together. "I thought you could find something out about them. I've never managed to get on the internet here, so I can't really research anything . . ."

"And if you find out something about them, what are you going to do about it? Go out there and try to bring them down? Tell the police? Expose them to a reporter?" I asked, pushing the paper back across the desk to Katarina.

She stared at me defiantly. "Why not? They can't be allowed to continue. They are the ones who profit off all of it. What happened to Mira is on them, too."

I nodded simply. "Sure, it is, but you don't know who these people are. They could be Mafia. You can't take them on."

"You could," she challenged.

A chuckle left me at her confident words. "Maybe, but I won't."

"Why not?" she demanded.

Something stuck in my throat at her look. It was fearless. It was strong. Katarina had a moral outrage that I rarely witnessed in my world. She was a good person, through and through. She'd seen awful things happen, and she wanted to do something about it, despite what it might cost her. If I wasn't careful, that look on her face would enchant me into promising to be her white knight, and that wasn't a role I was qualified to play. I could be her grim reaper, but never her guardian angel. After all, I'd never managed to keep my mother safe, so what chance did I have to save anyone else?

"Because I don't care. I'm not being paid to care," I said.

She flinched at my caustic tone. It was better she understood who I was now than hide it.

I loomed over the desk and got in her face. She was so lovely with her chin high and eyes blazing, spoiling for a fight.

"I'm not your hero, Katarina, you should understand that now. Centrium, Pavol, and Benedict . . . I don't care about any of them, except for doing the job I've been employed to do. I don't care about the bad guys. I am one of them."

A vein pulsed in her throat, the only sign that she was scared. Scared of me. It was something I was used to, of course. It was better that way. It kept things clean.

"Come into the office," I instructed firmly, deciding to end this pointless conversation. I strode around the back of the desk and into the small private office behind it. Inside, I took the tape and painkillers out of my pocket and set them on the table, then leaned a hip on the desk.

Katarina shuffled in slowly, slightly bent over in a way that clearly pained her less.

"Do a better job of hiding your injury," I muttered.

She glowered at me. "Well, I heard the police already ruled it a suicide, so I guess I'm off the hook."

"Not with Pavol and Benedict. They know something went down, they just don't know what, and they can't afford to have detectives in here poking around."

She nodded and then winced again.

"Close the door and lose the T-shirt," I demanded.

She blinked at me, pink immediately tinting her cheeks. "Here? Anyone could walk by."

"That's why we're inside the office. Take your shirt off now."

She sighed heavily. "You sure get off on ordering people around." She held herself away from me, probably upset that I hadn't offered to help her with her little investigative task.

"And you're sure argumentative with someone you just found out is a stone-cold killer mere hours ago."

She thought that one over for a moment, her hands on the hem of her T-shirt.

"Technically, I was the stone-cold killer last night, so"—she eyed me up and down—"watch yourself, Lucifer."

That pulled a chuckle from me. How the fuck she managed to keep her wit and dark humor in this place was a miracle in itself. I'd been right that morning when I'd first glimpsed her outside in the snow. She was special.

And now, she was mine.

Then her shirt was coming off, and I was staring at the work of art that was her torso. Yes, I'd been right, she was too thin, frail even, but that would be easily remedied when we got out of here. The curve of her waist and line of her spine were beautiful. Elegant in a way that no one should be, standing there in white cotton track pants, frayed as hell, and a graying bralette that had definitely seen better days. None of it distracted from her, however. Well, that wasn't true. One thing did. Mottled purple and blue bruises along her rib cage.

Vargas. That fucker. If he wasn't already burning in hell, I'd bring him back just to kill him more slowly. He'd gotten off too lightly.

"Come here." I nodded to the spot just before me.

She wrapped her arms across her chest, even though it had to hurt, and came to stand before me. A pink blush made its way down her neck. She looked every inch her age just then. Young and inexperienced and painfully unworldly.

I took her chin between my fingers and raised it so her gaze hit mine.

"You're hurt, and I'm going to tape up your ribs to support them a little. Okay?"

She nodded and slowly lowered her arms.

I turned her slightly and checked the damage on her rib cage clinically. Then I started to tape.

"You've done this before? Do you have medical training?"

I shook my head. "Nope, I just had to do it to myself and my guys in all kinds of situations when there was no doctor for a hundred miles."

She pondered that for a moment. "Military?"

I gave her a swift nod.

"Army?" she pushed.

I shrugged. "For a while, then the Col Moschin."

"Is that where you learned it?"

I raised an eyebrow at her while tearing another piece of tape from the roll.

"To . . . kill," she dropped to a whisper.

"No. I was born with that skill. A God-given talent," I murmured, and smoothed the tape over her ribs.

"Well, at least you have one." She was staring off at the wall, her eyes hazy and distant.

"Everyone has one."

She shook her head slowly. "I think my only one so far is my ability to take a punch." She sighed.

"Says the girl with angels in her head." I straightened up and put my hands on her waist once I was done wrapping her ribs. Her skin was pebbled with gooseflesh, and my hands were warm.

She started at first, but I held her firmly until she relaxed again.

"Is that a nice way of saying crazy?" She glanced up at me, dark-blue eyes steady and unflinching.

She might think I'm a devil, but she wasn't afraid of staring me down.

I liked that. I liked that a lot. I didn't meet many people with gumption anymore. Usually they cried and begged for their lives, abandoning all dignity in the end.

I had a feeling that Katarina Dmitrova didn't beg easily. Last night and pleading for her life had been an exception, perhaps the only one she was willing to make, and even then, she'd quickly switched to proposing a deal.

Strength filled that slender spine, and determination angled her chin at me.

No, she didn't beg for just anyone . . .

But she'd beg for me.

"I thought that was unique," I reminded her of her words the other day.

She nodded and then seemed to remember something. "You said you'd met someone like me. Who was it?"

She had grown used to my hands on her bare waist, so now I circled my thumbs. She swayed closer to me. The girl was touch-starved. I knew how she felt. I'd spent long touchless years in the Special Forces. It was a particular kind of loneliness.

I hesitated. Sharing wasn't something I was inclined to do with anyone, and yet, I could tell she needed something from me. A concession.

"My mother," I admitted. I didn't want to lie to her. There was something refreshingly honest about every interaction I'd had with this woman. I'd seen her dark parts, and she'd seen mine. I wasn't changing that now.

"She heard angels speaking?" Katarina asked.

I nodded. "In the end, before they sent her away, and after, too, I guess, going by the journal they sent me of her last days."

Katarina's breath hitched. "She died?"

I nodded and slid my hands slowly up her torso. "She died, her head full of angels, alone, far away from the boy who loved her, without a single person to put her favorite snowdrops in her hair when she was laid to rest. But that's not what's going to happen to you, little stray."

Her breath caught. "It's not?"

I passed my hands slowly over the cups of her worn cotton bralette, and her nipples poked against my fingers, hard and hungry.

I shook my head. "No. It's not. I won't let it. I take care of my belongings, and now that includes you."

"I—" She took a deep breath as I rubbed the backs of my fingers insistently over her nipples. "I'm not a possession. I don't belong to anyone, including myself. I'm . . . I don't know what I am anymore." Her eyes glistened with unshed tears. "The truth is . . . I'm nothing." Her words were so desolate.

I slid my hands up her chest, leaving her pert breasts and passing her pounding heart. I wrapped them around her neck, as fragile as a stalk, and cupped the underside of her jaw. Her face fit in my palms like I'd been designed to hold her, just like this.

"You're not nothing. Not to me," I told her. My tone offered no room for disagreement. "To me . . . you're mine . . . just like you agreed to be."

The phone rang on the desk beside us, the sound jarring after the quiet intimacy we'd just experienced.

Katarina pulled her gaze from mine and picked it up.

"Hallow Hall Institute," she said quickly into the receiver. She turned away from me to write something down.

"I'll make sure Dr. Blackwood gets the message."

She hung up and gazed at the phone longingly.

"Why don't you call the cops?" The question had been nagging at me. She claimed not to be crazy, but her presence here didn't quite make sense. Why hadn't she escaped already?

She looked at me.

"If those men deserve to die, if they're hurting the patients here . . . why don't you call the cops? They leave you alone, unattended in this office, like they trust that you won't."

"I tried once, in the beginning, but they know that I won't try that again. I can't."

She said it so certainly, I knew they had to have some kind of leverage over her.

I thought for a moment.

"Who are they threatening?"

She blew out a long breath, and her shoulders sagged.

"My mother. They're threatening my mother."

Of course. Was there anyone else that a person would never dare risk?

"What's her name?" I heard myself ask.

"Elena Dmitrova." She glanced over my shoulder. "Shit. Sister Vera's coming. You need to get out of here. She won't like me speaking to you." She yanked her T-shirt over her head, presenting her back to the door.

With a nod, I stepped out of the office and met the nun in the hallway.

"Father Lucciano!" Sister Vera said, and smiled coyly at me.

But my mind was a million miles away. So, Katarina's mother was still alive? And yet, she remained here . . . in hell? Why didn't her mother help?

"I've been searching all over for you. Father Benedict needs to see you."

Benedict? It would be interesting to see how he was feeling the day after his boss had killed himself. Entertaining, at least.

"Very well, Sister. I'll go to him right now."

13

MASSIMO

After speaking with Benedict, who'd wanted to reassure me that everything would still run smoothly at the institute, I headed outside.

Benedict was rattled and seemed particularly concerned that I would run off and tell my bosses. Of course the man I'd used to get me in here was linked to the shadier side of Hallow Hall. I could guess that there was nothing the good father wanted less than for their director to get cold feet and pull their funding. Benedict was convinced that I was a representative of Centrium Group, here for training, and therefore would be reporting back on the happenings in Hallow Hall.

Outside, snow swirled in the air. The institute was outside the city, toward the mountains. The nearest city was Torino. I was grateful for the warm cassock when the crisp air of the graveyard hit me.

I walked over the gathered snow, my feet crunching on ice beneath. Ahead, I spied the familiar back of Katarina's pet orderly rounding the corner of the building, holding something.

A rose?

By the time I found Alonso, he was deeply occupied. The young woman he had against the wall was small, even smaller than Katarina. She wore a nurse's uniform, and the rose he'd been carrying was now gripped in her hand.

So, Alonso was even more pathetic than I'd thought he was.

How predictable.

I left the two lovebirds to it and retraced my steps past the front entrance.

I made for the gap that led to a clearing just beside the chapel. The place where I'd first set sight on Katarina. Shivering in the cold, ethereal, her long blond hair streaming over her shoulders, her eyes full of secrets . . . I didn't think I'd ever forget the first time I saw her.

My little stray, feeding the strays. I went to the bowl that Katarina used for the resident feral cat and banged it on the wall. Then I grabbed the leftover ham roll I'd taken from the kitchen and tore it into pieces and dropped them in the bowl.

The cat came running at the sound. As he got closer, he purred loudly, encouraging me to feed him.

He went to eat enthusiastically while I stroked his knobby back. He was thin, poor thing, but surviving. As soon as he finished, he rubbed himself over my legs. Thanking me.

I scratched him behind the ears. Animals were more honest than humans. I could trust animals, but trusting humans had never come easy.

Snowdrops poked through the white layer of snow on the ground, which was melting in patches. A harbinger of the changing seasons. My mother had loved them so much. There was an area beaten down by someone's indifferent tread. I reached out and pulled the flowers from the ground. The tiny bunch was ridiculously inadequate in my hand. Green and white, fresh and new . . . delicate, but strong enough to push through frozen ground.

"Oh! Shit," a voice said.

I stood and turned. I was no longer alone. Resident charmer Alonso stood by the wall lighting up a smoke. I placed the snowdrops in my pocket and eyed him critically.

"That was quick," I muttered.

Poor nurse. It had hardly been worth putting on her winter coat for.

"Sorry, Father, I didn't know that anyone knew about this place, well . . . anyone else."

I shrugged. "Katarina told me about it. I hope you don't mind."

His face betrayed his annoyance before he reined it in. "No, of course not. Katarina's a nice girl. Kind to people."

"Hmm, kind. Too kind for this place."

"Yeah, she's . . . great," Alonso said wistfully.

"Isn't she?" I said, slowly moving toward Alonso.

I could tell he was dumb as shit and had lived a cushy life, because he didn't once seem to realize I had bad intentions.

"Yeah. She's the only good thing about working in this place."

"I'm sure your girlfriend wouldn't be too happy to hear how much you admire her," I added, lashing out and grabbing Alonso's hand. I gave it a quick twist, locked the joint, and forced him to his knees.

He cried out, but the wind stole his voice away. I took his lit cigarette from his captured hand and drew a long drag, then flicked it away.

"Let's get one thing straight, Alonso. I've got nothing against you. You seem great—but Katarina Dmitrova doesn't exist to you anymore. You're not going to talk to her, or look at her, or tell her your fake stories about your girlfriend. Or the nurse you're fucking. Hey, maybe there's even more than one."

Alonso was quiet, so I twisted his wrist harder, and he cried out again.

"Now, if I find out you've been talking to Katarina or messing around with any other patient—you know, those young ones in there, pregnant and alone, only sixteen . . . I find out that you've touched one of them, and it won't end well for you, Alonso. I can find out where you live, I can get to you no matter where you are. Next time, I won't just break the hand, I'll take it with me when I go."

I let go and shoved him away. He fell onto the snow, sniveling with pain.

"Get the fuck out of my sight," I tossed toward him, and leaned back against the wall of the chapel, taking my phone from my robes.

After Alonso finally fucked off, I dialed a number and waited for my IT guy to answer. She was a recent find, sister of my old commander, and there was no one with her skills out there, that I'd found, anyway.

Luckily for me, she'd offered to help me with tech support when I needed it.

"Don't tell me! Let me guess . . . You're undercover in a kindergarten class and need to know the words to 'Baby Shark'?"

Giada O'Connor was always tickled pink by the situations I found myself in to reach marks.

"Guess again."

"Okay . . . You're posing as a top confectioner in a chocolate factory?"

"No."

"Austrian goat herder?"

"Nope."

"Come on, Massimo, give me a clue, then!"

"That's Father Lucciano to you."

"Wait, what? A priest? Send me a selfie. I have to see this. Can you cross the threshold of a church? Does the holy water evaporate before it hits you?"

"It sure does."

"Nice. Okay, lay it on me. What do you need?"

"I want you to check a name for me. Two, actually. First one, Elena Dmitrova. Second is a company."

"Wait." Clacking came over the line as she typed the names. "And?"

"A business. Centrium Group. They do business in Torino."

"Hmm, okay, let me poke into it. It'll take me a second, because the internet at this hotel sucks."

"You're on vacation?"

"If you call a luxury shack in the woods a vacation, sure."

"Where's your husband?"

"He wants to roast something over the massive firepit he's got going outside, so I don't know . . . hunting? While I'm stuck here, wasting away without Wi-Fi."

"Well, don't die before you find out that info for me, okay?"

"Aw, shucks, how sweet. Your concern is touching. Speak to you later, L'Ombra."

I hung up, my assassin moniker echoing around my head. The Shadow. It was a name that I'd been given pretty quickly after I left the Special Forces and went back to the real world.

I'd worked hard in those first few years, building that reputation, figuring out how to use the skills I'd honed.

Looking back, it was all a blur. The only thing that had felt real was the slow uncovering of my mother's past. My abusive POS aunt and uncle had both passed, unfortunately, so torturing them for information would have been impossible.

Trying to find the hospital had also been a fucking dead end, despite having the logo of it. The entire thing had burned down, apparently, only a few months after my mother had died there. So the hospital was a dead end—and the asshole rapist former boss was dead.

Now Giada was nosing into the steel mill staff registry and taking her sweet time. Once she came back with something, my life would carry me away from here and back on the path to vengeance. The only thing I cared about.

Except that wasn't quite true anymore. Now I had something new to care about.

Katarina Dmitrova and our contract.

A change, after so long.

14

KATARINA

The cafeteria was chaotic at lunchtime. There were fewer orderlies and nurses today. Clearly they'd put some kind of lockdown on the whole place. So patients who usually had a lot more support were wandering, confused and upset, with the skeleton crew of staff they'd brought in hardly keeping up with the demand for care.

I grabbed my stale cheese roll, my go-to lunch, as I couldn't stomach the mystery meat in the hot dishes. I went to sit at my usual table by a window, so at least I could stare out at the spindly trees that stretched far into the horizon.

I sat here every day, without fail. So I noticed right away.

One of the branches close to the window was different. I pressed my forehead to the glass to get a closer look.

A tiny, nearly unnoticeable bud.

A loud crash pulled me from my wonder.

"See what you've done? Stupid girl!" Sister Vera's voice was scathing, ugly with her unspent rage; she was looking for an outlet.

I shoved to my feet at the sound. Rough, shouted words set me off like nothing else and always gave me a jolt. Fight or flight, and I always chose fight.

Tatiana stood in the middle of the lunchroom, a tray at her feet, food spilled across the tile floor and on the hem of Sister Vera's black robes.

"You dirty little sinner, look what you've done—wasting food? You might as well spit on a cross!" The nun was raving mad. "Now you're crying? I'll give you something for those crocodile tears!" She drew her hand back.

Sister Vera wasn't holding back today, and there was no one around to stop her. Except me.

I darted between them just as her hand reached me. There wasn't any time to deflect or dodge it without Tatiana getting hurt, so I didn't bother.

Her hand crashed into my cheek, and heat and pain shot through me.

I grabbed her hand when it finished its arc.

"Enough. Get a hold of yourself," I growled into her face.

Her mouth dropped open with shock while she processed that I'd stepped between them.

"Move out of the way, Katarina. You will not let that child escape her punishment."

"She's being punished for accidentally dropping her tray? Where's your mercy, Sister? Or is that just reserved for the priests you suck up to?"

Outrage filled the woman's eyes, and she drew her other hand back to hit me again, but this time I caught it before it could inflict damage.

"Hit me again, and I'll hit you back," I promised.

Silence fell. Every single eye in the lunchroom was fixed on us.

"Shouldn't you be more careful than this, Katarina, considering your situation?" Sister Vera said.

I'd always wondered how much the head nun knew about my presence at Hallow Hall. Was she like the orderlies and nurses who just thought I was mentally unwell and here for my own good? Or did she know that the holy trinity in charge was keeping me here forcefully by threatening my mother?

The question finally answered, I dropped her hand and laughed.

"So, for all your pristine habits and rosaries, you're one of them, too? How disappointing. How hypocritical." Then I leaned in; I couldn't help myself. "I hope your conscience never gets the better of you, Sister Vera, like Father Vargas. Such a shame to be denied entry to heaven after a life of service . . . but then, that ship has already sailed for you and your brethren, hasn't it?"

She jerked back, her gaze moving furiously over me.

"How do you know what happened to Father Vargas?" she asked, staring at me with a note of real fear in her eyes.

Suddenly, I got it. The heady taste of power.

It was beautiful.

"Everyone's talking about it. You didn't think you could really have secrets in a place like this, did you? There are eyes everywhere in Hallow Hall," I whispered menacingly.

She jerked away from me, clearly trying to compose herself.

"Sister Vera, is there a problem here?" Dr. Blackwood had appeared in the doorway, clearly stressed out and harried. His dark hair was tousled, and he had a five o'clock shadow on his normally clean-shaven face.

Massimo stood at his shoulder. He gazed attentively across the scene.

"Yes, there's a problem," Sister Vera announced loudly.

Great. She was going to try and make a fuss to Dr. Blackwood.

I couldn't listen to her lie, so I turned around and went down on my haunches in front of Tatiana. The girl cried silently, big fat tears rolling down her cheeks. She raised her eyes to mine, and I stroked her hair.

"Hey, it's okay. You can have my lunch," I told her.

She shook her head. "I'm not hungry. You got hit because of me."

"No, I got hit because of her, and it's not right," I said back.

I sensed a presence at my side. Blackwood and Sister Vera were still talking behind me, but their annoying voices fell away. Massimo crouched beside me.

Tatiana looked at Massimo, her eyes widening and her lip trembling even more.

"I'm in trouble," she whispered.

I shook my head. "You're not. We'll get this cleaned up and you won't be in trouble."

"I'll go to hell," she continued.

I scoffed, attempting a smile to lighten Tatiana's panic.

"No you won't."

She clearly didn't believe me.

"But how about this. If you do, I'll go with you." I held up my pinkie to her.

She nodded, solemnly wrapping her smallest finger around mine. "You promise?"

"Cross my heart and hope to die," I said.

Her eyes widened; she took those words extremely seriously.

I glanced at Massimo, who watched us with an impassive, unreadable expression, his hands swiftly collecting the utensils and placing them on the tray.

"Katarina, I'm afraid we need to talk," Dr. Blackwood said from above me.

Just wonderful.

He waited as I straightened up reluctantly.

"What?"

"Sister Vera has indicated to me that she's worried you've been skipping medication."

"I haven't," I argued.

"I can vouch for that. I've been administering her medication myself." Massimo rose smoothly to his intimidating height.

Dr. Blackwood wasn't a particularly small guy, but standing next to Massimo, he resembled a gangly teenager.

Dr. Blackwood studied Massimo and considered his words. "Well, in that case, this is a behavioral issue, and you know we have protocols for that. I'm afraid I will have to send you to solitary to reflect on your actions."

I swallowed a protest. I hated solitary. It was a mindfuck like nowhere else. Still, it was worth it to stop Tatiana from being abused by Sister Vera.

"Alonso," Dr. Blackwood called over his shoulder.

Alonso approached, his hand in his pocket, walking stiffly. His eyes darted to Massimo and then down. Had he hurt himself? His hand seemed awkward jammed in his scrubs.

"Take Katarina down to solitary."

"I'll take her," Massimo cut in. "I haven't seen that area of the institute, if you'd be so kind to show me, Doctor."

Blackwood nodded.

"Alonso, you clean up this mess for the little lady and replace her lunch," Massimo ordered, nodding to Tatiana, who had stopped crying but was still crouched over her dropped tray.

Alonso bobbed his head jerkily and turned to Tatiana, lowering to his knees beside her.

She looked at me. I gave her a cheerful wave.

"Thank God I get to go back to bed. I'm so tired today," I confided to Tatiana and winked.

She giggled, her sadness passing.

Then I turned to Massimo. I was ready.

We left the lunchroom. I walked behind Blackwood and Massimo.

"I'll pray for you, child!" Sister Vera called behind me, sounding smug.

I flipped her the middle finger, drawing titters of laughter from the other patients in the dining hall.

Massimo and Blackwood were talking. I listened with half attention to what they were saying.

"No, we don't give the patients anything stimulating in solitary, it's too exciting. No books, no pencils; they could hurt themselves. No chalk after someone ate it. It's a place to find peace within, and it's easier for them to find that peace without distractions."

The lack of something to read or draw on was the worst part of solitary. That and the way the ghosts seemed to come when you had nothing to distract yourself with.

We took the rusty cage elevator down to the lowest floor. Pavol's office was down here too, but in a different wing.

Dr. Blackwood opened the various security doors, and I followed him through. Massimo brought up the rear.

We walked down the long hallway of solitary confinement rooms. I could hear that some were occupied. This was where Mira had stayed near the end so that they could take her for surgery and carve her up with fewer people seeing. Her ghost was everywhere I looked.

Blackwood unlocked a heavy door and switched the lights on inside.

"You know the drill, Katarina. In you go," he said, and stepped back.

Massimo was closer to me. I had to brush past him to enter the room. As I did, his hand touched mine.

He pressed something into my palm and closed my hand around it quickly.

Then I was inside the dingy white room, turning around. The door closed. The observation slot slammed shut, and I was alone. I opened my hand to see what Massimo had given me.

A tiny bunch of snowdrops.

15

MASSIMO

The next day, I left Hallow Hall and drove into the city proper. The institute sat about a thirty-minute drive outside the city. It had only been a week, and yet I was claustrophobic as fuck. I needed to get out.

I couldn't imagine how Katarina was surviving in solitary. I couldn't be locked inside such a small space with my demons. I'd go mad, and I wasn't sure how much sanity I had left anyway.

The neighborhood was quiet early in the morning. Woodsmoke rose from stone chimneys, and the storefronts were just coming to life. Pigeons scattered as I walked across the slick, icy cobblestone. This was the area where Vargas had served as the local priest. I was willing to bet Katarina's mother also lived around here.

I made for a small café and ordered a double espresso. I'd changed into my usual clothes before I'd gotten to town. The key to being a faceless assassin was not to draw attention to yourself. Walking around a hushed city suburb would be cause for gossip. This wasn't the kind of place that had a high turnover of clergy, I was guessing.

I read the papers while I drank my coffee. The first real coffee since before I'd arrived at Hallow Hall. It was like nectar.

I checked my emails. Hallow Hall was in a Wi-Fi dead spot, but fortunately I had satellite internet on my cell.

An email from Giada popped up.

Good morning,

IT guy here with an update.

So, here is Elena Dmitrova's address, attached.

Second of all, Centrium Group is an interesting company, and by that I mean suspicious as fuck. They only own one asset (lol). Clearly they're a shell corp, and it'll take me a while to track down what companies they're associated with. One interesting fact is that they're registered in Bulgaria even though they've always done business in Italy.

I'll keep digging. Also, did you know the so-called spiritual leader of Hallow Hall was excommunicated from the Church a few months ago? Give me the names of the rest of the guys who work up there, and I'll look into them for you.

Talk soon, shithead.

G

I hadn't known about Vargas. It wasn't in the brief, and I had a rule of not researching my targets beyond where they lived and how I could get to them. I had other rules too. No women. No children. Any more information, and I risked feeling something about ending their lives. I wasn't there to pass judgment on who should live or die, or evaluate a person's worthiness.

I was just a deadly bullet, shot from a gun my clients fired.

But Hallow Hall was changing my habits and breaking all my rules. No, not Hallow Hall, really. It was her. Katarina. My little stray. If I hadn't met her, I'd have killed Vargas and already been in Rome on my next job.

She was an unpredictable variable in my orderly life, throwing off my balance.

I wasn't sure how to feel about that yet.

I could ignore it. I could just leave town right now and never go back. When Katarina got out of solitary, I'd be long gone and we'd never see each other again.

But I wouldn't do that. I knew it as well as I knew I'd kill both Pavol and Benedict so I could take everything she had agreed to give me.

All her firsts.

The dark possession that filled my veins when I watched her was a new thing. I'd never felt anything like it, and I was sure I never would again.

It was something specific to her. I wasn't the type to question my instincts; they had always served me well. Now my instincts were telling me to stay and see my deal with my *micetta* through.

I wouldn't let someone else have her.

I used my phone to pull up the address Giada had sent me for Katarina's mother and headed in that direction.

The day was brightening up. The houses of the neighborhood were pretty dusted with snow, overlooked by a backdrop of dramatic white mountains. The area was at the edge of the city, closer to the mountains than anywhere else. Such beauty, and yet just up the road a little was a place where people who needed help were locked away from the world and experimented on.

If I hadn't lost faith in the world long ago, the existence of a place like Hallow Hall would have gotten the job done. Humanity was over, finished. We were circling the drain. Good people were few and far between. They had been wrong . . . the meek wouldn't inherit the earth. The powerful and corrupt—the soulless—had already destroyed the world. And wasn't I just another of them? I certainly wasn't one of the good ones.

I turned the corner and noticed a small market being set up. One of the stalls had fresh flowers wrapped in newspaper. An old *nonna* sat behind the table wrapped up to the nose in a woolen scarf. Only a few bunches of flowers rested on her little table. It was slim pickings in winter.

"*Bucaneve?*" she murmured when I paused in front of her. *Bucaneve*. Snowdrops.

I picked up a newspaper cone and looked inside. These snowdrops were beautiful, not small and trampled like the ones I'd slipped Katarina before she went into solitary.

She asked a meager amount for the flowers, and I pressed a hundred-euro note into her gloved palm before walking away.

The address should have been just up ahead. I strode down the frozen street and came upon tall gates at the end.

What the fuck? Giada had a seriously dark sense of humor.

The graveyard was silent at this time in the morning. I walked through the gates and glanced around the small space. A chapel sat a little way off, the windows already glowing. I walked the rows of graves slowly.

I found her at the end. She had a simple headstone.

Elena Dmitrova. A Mother.

She had passed a couple of years ago. That was why she'd never visited her daughter . . . and Katarina was being blackmailed into staying at Hallow Hall to save the life of a dead woman. I wondered where my mother's gravestone sat. I still didn't know. Did she have one? If she did, would anyone stop by and leave her flowers?

I crouched next to the headstone and brushed the frost off its surface.

"Hello, Mrs. Dmitrova," I said quietly, just for the ears of the ghosts. "I've come to see you."

I placed the bouquet of snowdrops against the headstone.

"The snowdrops are pushing up through the ground, and soon it'll be spring. The snow will melt, and the birds will sing again. The world will wake up, and your daughter will visit you."

What was I doing?

I sighed, and my breath puffed out in a cloud of white. Damn, it was cold here. Cold and dead. All of it.

I straightened up and took a step back, about to leave.

"She thinks about you all the time. Just so you know. And she loved you to the end . . . and beyond."

Okay. Enough. I didn't know if I was talking about Katarina and her mother now, or me and mine. Maybe all the women who had been beaten down and forgotten by the world.

My emotions volatile and restless, I turned away from the neglected grave in the tiny cemetery.

Yes, I was breaking all my rules here at Hallow Hall, but I didn't care.

Those fuckers all deserved to pay . . . and I was here to make them.

And I'd enjoy every second.

16

KATARINA

The next day passed in excruciating slow motion. I slept as late as I could, knowing it was one of the only ways to pass the time more quickly. However, the harsh overhead fluorescents blinked on at seven-thirty a.m. and didn't go off until seven-thirty p.m.

Food was delivered three times. No avoiding the mystery meat this time, so I didn't bother eating. I was used to an empty stomach.

Instead, I focused on the snowdrops.

I'd never had something to look at except my own hands in solitary before.

It was an unexpected gift. The best one I'd ever had.

I found a million things to observe about the perfect flowers. The different layers of the blossoms, the way the colors varied and blended into each other between the stalk and into the head of the bloom. The tiny striations inside the velvet, nearly transparent petals. A network of veins running just below the surface. It was fascinating.

I was still enamored with them when the second full day of solitary came to an end. My stomach was a hollow cavern. When a knock at the door sounded, I was resigned to the fact that I'd have to finally eat the disgusting lump of meat and powdered potatoes that would be dinner. But then Dr. Blackwood walked in.

Hope jumped in my chest. Was I done? I rushed to my feet, swaying a little as a wave of dizziness hit me. *Whoa.* I needed to eat.

"Sit down, Katarina, I'm just here to talk."

Disappointment filled me. I had already hidden my bunch of wilting snowdrops in my pocket, luckily, so I curled my empty hands into fists and sat gingerly on the edge of the metal cot in the corner.

"How are you feeling?" he asked.

I shrugged. "Okay. Bored. What else would I feel here?"

"And your medication? You've been taking it on schedule?"

I nodded, holding my tongue. I had no idea what Massimo had done, but no one had given me medication in solitary, something Dr. Blackwood seemed to have no idea about.

"Tell me, are you expecting visitors this weekend?"

I stared at him, wondering what answer he was looking for. Was he testing my memory to see if I had really been taking my medicine?

"I-I don't really know," I murmured, recalling exactly how it had felt to really not know. The confusion I'd lived in constantly when my medication schedule had been consistent felt like a bad dream.

"No? How about when you think of Hallow Hall and how you came to be here?"

I fought to keep my expression smooth and steady.

"I don't remember. I think I was in trouble. My mom wanted me to come here and get better."

Blackwood nodded. "And does she think the treatment is working?"

I started to answer but realized that I had no words.

I just shrugged. "I don't know. I can't remember the last time we spoke," I admitted. That wasn't a lie. I had been all drugged up when she'd last come, and I didn't even remember saying goodbye to her, though I did remember sending word to her not to visit anymore.

"I see on the visitor records that she doesn't come often to visit. Do you know why that is?"

Because I asked her not to, because it hurt too much. I fidgeted, suddenly nervous. I hated to talk about my mother with any of the psychos at Hallow Hall. I wouldn't give this man the satisfaction of getting anything real from me.

"Busy, I guess. It's not like I have anything interesting to tell her about my day," I snapped before remembering I was supposed to be acting like my usual semi-out-of-it state.

"Hmm, that's true, I suppose. Do you think about getting out of here? Do you genuinely want to get better?" Blackwood asked.

I stared at him. "Yes. I want to get better and put my world right."

He nodded slowly.

A hard knock sounded on the locked door, followed by the sound of the bolt being drawn back.

"I'm not interrupting, am I?" Massimo's deep voice drawled.

I turned to him, relief hitting me hard. I didn't think I'd ever been so relieved to see someone. I was scared to be alone with Blackwood. I was scared of being in solitary any longer. Somehow, his powerful body clothed in the austere robes of the men I hated had become a welcome sight. My wolf in sheep's clothing.

He didn't wait for an answer from Blackwood before gesturing toward me.

"Father Benedict wants Katarina out of solitary; he says she'll have reached her limit being isolated. She's to go back to her room now."

Blackwood frowned and checked his watch. How long had the fucker been planning to leave me in here?

Reluctantly he nodded, but I was already moving.

I reached Massimo's side, and he stepped back, letting me out into the hallway.

I paused at the doorway and glanced back at Blackwood, who watched us with an unreadable expression. The door was right there. My hand itched to slam it shut and bolt it. To give that motherfucker a taste of his own medicine for once . . .

"Let's go, Miss Dmitrova. I will see you to your room." Massimo's voice held a hint of amusement, like he could see exactly what I was thinking.

I moved myself away from the door with effort and followed Massimo down the hall. We passed through the secure doors at the end and into a quiet, dark hallway.

"Did Benedict really tell you that?" I asked. My voice felt weird. Too loud after days of silence.

"What do you think?" Massimo said, a rumble low in his chest.

I tensed. "What if he suspects something?"

"He won't do anything. He doesn't have the balls to pick on someone his own size. And like I give a fuck what Blackwood thinks about me, or us."

We reached the stairs that would take us up to the rest of the building. I shivered in the cool chill that seemed to permeate the air on the basement level.

"Us?" I echoed.

I was so weak I swayed on the stairs, and Massimo's hand came under my elbow to guide me.

"Us. We're partners, aren't we? Partners in sin." Massimo's voice was warm, curling around his words and making them feel wicked. I could listen to him speak all day, though to be fair, being starved of human interaction could do that to a person.

"Partners in sin. It has a nice ring to it," I admitted, and earned myself a small smirk.

I couldn't seem to stop gazing at his face. This man should be everything I was afraid of. A killer, a devil in a human suit. Lawless, remorseless, and comfortable with the idea of going to hell, he should be terrifying, and yet . . . his face drew me in like a magnet.

We reached the door to my room. The thought of going in after I'd just gotten out of solitary felt like a killing blow. So I hesitated at the door. I couldn't exactly ask him in for a coffee.

Hey, you want to hang out in my room and see my crazy drawings on the wall?

Yeah, no.

"Vargas's death has officially been ruled a suicide. So things should be back to normal tomorrow, therapy and group session."

My face immediately heated at the thought of my last session with Massimo, when he'd pretended to put my medication into my mouth. My fingers shook when I pushed them through my hair. Ugh. I needed a shower. I felt disgusting, and yet the memory of Benedict's office, of Massimo fingering my mouth, was making my blood simmer.

He stepped closer. Was he remembering it, too? Or had he really just pretended to put my pills in my mouth, and I'd imagined the way his fingers had caressed my tongue? God, I was really going crazy in here.

"I suppose I'll see you there?" I was aiming for a casual tone but instead made it sound like a question.

"Yes, you will." His deep voice was doing something to me.

"Oh! Here." I suddenly remembered the contents of my pocket. I pulled the battered flowers out and held them to him. Sure, they'd seen better days, but they were still so beautiful.

"Keep them," he said.

"You said you would have put snowdrops in your mother's hair before she was laid to rest?" I ventured. It had felt like such a personal admission, but also one that had helped me feel less scared of him. He'd had a mother whom he'd loved and had mourned. He had a heart that beat . . . once, anyway.

He nodded.

"I can see why she loved them. They are so beautiful . . . so symbolic of spring, the world waking from winter, starting to live again. I think my mother would like them a lot, too. I'm going to take them to her when I get out of here."

He stared at me, those dark eyes seeming to see right inside me, to my damaged soul.

I curled my fingers around the stems of the flowers and pressed them against my chest. "Anyway, thank you for that. You don't know how much you just saved me in there." Words couldn't convey how much the flowers had meant to me in solitary. His simple action of slipping them to me before I'd gone inside had fundamentally changed my view of him, I realized.

"Don't thank me. I don't do anything that doesn't benefit me." Massimo's voice was guarded. He seemed as uncomfortable with gratitude as I was with admitting when I needed someone.

His words were so resigned and knowing. He was so certain of his own badness, he automatically rejected any idea that he might not be as terrible as he'd decided he was.

I shook my head at him with a sigh and said as much. "I don't think you're as bad as you believe you are, deep down inside."

"You're wrong. I'm worse."

His answer sounded absolute. It made me sad somehow. My heart was feeling all kinds of confusing things. There was no doubt an unhealthy attachment forming to the only person who'd treated me like a real human being in years. The only person who seemed to be on my side . . . even if he was only here on business. I had been so lonely for so long. So weak. And now, there was someone strong, someone powerful, someone helping me. No wonder my heart didn't know what the fuck to do.

"Maybe, but I don't think so," I murmured, and then, following an impulse I couldn't quite stop, I stepped toward him, stretched up on my tiptoes, and pressed my lips on his cheek.

It was chaste. Innocent. A nothing gesture, and yet, he jerked under my lips like I'd tasered him.

I'd taken him by surprise, clearly. Even though only a few days ago, he'd kissed me like he was going to eat me alive, for some reason that quick cheek kiss felt more intimate.

It shocked us both.

I stepped back, suddenly embarrassed and terrified of his rejection.

I wouldn't survive it.

"So, thanks," I said. I stumbled out and fled into my room, shutting the heavy door behind me before laying my cold hands on my burning cheeks.

17

KATARINA

By the next day, therapy sessions had resumed and business seemed pretty much back to usual in Hallow Hall. I supposed that the death of the institute's patron saint hadn't really mattered that much, considering he was seldom in residence anyway.

When I thought about him going around town, soaking up praise and adoration from his parishioners and leading his church, with innocent, trusting women like my mother attending every single day, my blood boiled.

Now he'd never stand in the house of God and lie again.

Sister Vera marched through the building, heading for the floor where Pavol's office was. I hurried to keep up with my sore ribs.

We reached Pavol's office in record time. Sister Vera looked tense. Her utter dislike of me was beginning to show more and more every day.

"What's wrong, Sister? What's going on today?" I asked her, unable to stop myself from prodding at her obvious panic.

They hadn't told the residents what had happened yet. They had left everyone wondering and afraid. Excellent mental health support. Maybe they'd tell everyone at some point that Vargas had passed, or maybe they wouldn't even bother.

"It's good that everything is getting back to normal after whatever happened earlier this week."

Sister Vera shook her head. "The schedule of the institute is nothing for you to concern yourself with. Just get inside and don't cause any trouble for once."

"Yes, Sister." I fought a smile as I walked into Pavol's office. Riling up Sister Vera was always fun. Of course, she always got her revenge by delivering me to my dreaded sessions on time, but I had to take my fun where I could get it, or I'd go completely crazy for real.

I stepped into the room and stopped. The door shut softly behind me.

Pavol was a mess, despite a few days having passed since the dark night when Vargas had swung.

He sat behind a messy desk. His eyes were bloodshot, and there was a distinct smell . . . vodka.

Massimo stood in the corner like a demon at the crossroads waiting for a stray soul to wander past.

"Father?" I forced out when Pavol failed to even notice me. He was sorting through the papers on his desk with increasing erraticism. He snapped his head up.

"Katarina, you're here." He stared at me as if he'd seen a ghost.

"You . . . It's time for our meeting."

Pavol nodded and reached for his tea flask. He opened it and looked inside, and then cursed. "Yes, I see. Well, we could have just canceled today's session, but then I remembered that Father

Lucciano is here." He pushed up from the table and nodded toward Massimo.

"He'll lead your therapy today. I've briefed him on the next stage of your exposure therapy."

Then Pavol was heading out, gripping his flask as though his life depended on it.

The door shut behind him, and silence surged in.

I met his inky eyes, and a ripple of awareness moved through me. That kiss on the cheek last night felt like a flashing neon sign over my head, impossible to ignore. Shockingly intimate somehow.

He straightened up and prowled across the room. I could see him in the military. He moved like a man who knew how to use his body as a weapon. A deadly one. He had perfect confidence, and that was intimidating and . . . hot. Undoubtedly hot.

Hot, dangerous, and he was determined to have me.

Massimo walked past me to the door and turned the lock.

He's a killer. How do you know he won't change his mind and decide not to bother with your little deal?

"I don't know. I have faith," I murmured, only a whisper.

My heart beat harder, my pulse jumping in my veins. I wasn't sure if it was fear or excitement. What did I know about excitement? Like I'd told him, I'd never even been kissed properly. Growing up with a religious single mother, I hadn't wanted to make her ashamed by getting a reputation in our neighborhood. The small community had loved to gossip, and since we were immigrants and without a man in the family, we already got more than our fair share.

I want to be all your firsts. That phrase had played in my head on repeat since he'd uttered the words that night. And I'd agreed . . . agreed like a fool without a single thought of how I would handle a man like Massimo Lucciano being my first anything.

I twisted to look at him.

"What are you doing?" I asked. Why was my voice so breathy?

He's going to eat you whole.

"Making sure we won't be disturbed during your session. It's Pavol's protocol."

"But we aren't having a session," I pointed out.

Massimo stood in front of me and leaned against Pavol's huge desk. "Aren't we?"

I stared at him.

"Are you serious?"

"As a short rope and a long drop. Go and get changed."

He jerked his head toward the screen in the corner.

I just stared at him, confused, shocked, and honestly, turned on. My mother would be ashamed of me for the rest of my life if she knew I was getting turned on by a devil wearing holy robes, about to perform some kind of twisted therapy on me as a treatment for lustful thoughts.

Just the thought sent blood rushing to my cheeks. My face had to be the color of a tomato.

"I don't work for free, *micetta*. Clients pay a deposit, at least, before the deed is done."

He let his gaze drop to my feet, pressed primly together in my grubby off-white sneakers. He then dragged his eyes up my legs, somehow making my baggy sweatpants feel scandalous, up my body, slow and steady, until he reached my face. There was nothing disappointed in that inspection. It was . . . satisfied. I forgot about my glowing cheeks and ugly, ill-fitting clothes. I forgot about my scraggly hair that hadn't been cut in years, my ragged nails, and even the silvery scars that worked their way across my upper thighs.

I forgot all of that.

His eyes fixed on mine, warm and wicked. "Time to pay up, little stray."

I found myself standing before I could overthink it. I walked to the screen and slipped behind it. Back there, I laid a hand on the medical gown I put on three times a week. Usually I felt disgusted at the idea of what was about to happen.

Pavol knew why I was here just as well as Vargas had. I wasn't a real patient, I was a hostage, and yet, he'd insisted on conducting his perverted therapies on me three times a week for years. Because he got off on it. Because he knew I couldn't complain. Because Vargas wanted me to suffer.

Now, though, slipping my clothes off, knowing Massimo was waiting outside, I felt something strange and new. A new association forcing itself over the trauma.

Something delicious simmered low in my belly as I stepped out to face him.

Massimo had his arms crossed over his chest, staring at the screen, waiting for me to emerge.

"I can't say I've ever cared much for medical fashion, but you—you make it look good."

I had no idea what to do with that compliment, so instead, I stepped forward.

"Where do you want me?" I asked, then cringed when his grin widened.

"What a good question," he said, and then nodded to the chair I usually sat in while Pavol did my fucked-up therapy. The TV was nowhere in sight.

I lowered myself onto the chair and watched as Massimo approached.

He stalked over and walked around me in a circle.

"Since last night, I've given your firsts a lot of thought," he said in a low tone, sending a thrill through me.

Had that moment in the hallway last night felt as important to him as it had to me?

"Hands," he instructed after a moment.

I swallowed a hard lump of nerves in my throat. I lifted a hand and let him place it into the restraint that was attached to the chair.

"You're shaking," he observed. "Are you afraid?"

"Yes. All the time," I admitted.

He paused when he had one hand tied up and brought one of his to the top of my head. Then, he stroked my hair with a gentler touch than I'd have expected from a man capable of such violence.

"You don't need to be anymore. You've given yourself to me. You owe me a debt, and to pay it, you need to be intact. Our deal makes you mine, and no one touches my things . . . except me."

He tied my other hand to the chair but left the rest of me untouched. No feet straps, no head strap.

Then he knelt before me. He'd never looked more like a demonic priest than in that moment, flicking open his little bone-handled knife with practiced ease and cleaning the sharp blade against his cassock.

"Do you trust me, Katarina?" he murmured.

"No." My answer was immediate.

He chuckled. "Clever girl. But soon you'll realize I always keep my word. If I say you're safe, you're safe. If I say you're dead, you're dead, no matter what. I always keep my word."

Then he put the edge of the knife to the neckline of my medical gown and cut a precise line downward, dividing the material into two flaps.

"I think we'll burn this after today. You won't ever wear it again."

My nipples contracted, and my skin prickled. I was hyper-aware of him as he set the knife down and switched his attention to the fabric. With deliberate slowness, he drew the two sides apart, baring my breasts to his greedy gaze.

My face burned hot, the feeling spreading down my neck to my chest.

He let his gaze wander across my breasts. The edges of the medical tape were only just visible, peeking around the corners of my ribs. My breasts swayed with my rapid breaths; I was so nervous I couldn't stop gulping down air.

Massimo tilted his head to the side, a languid inspection, and then, in an almost involuntary movement, wetted his lips.

He looked hungry.

His huge hands came to my chest.

"Today, I'll make you come, and take this *first*. The first man to show you what you're capable of. The first of many *firsts*."

Then his fingers closed over my breasts, and my brain whited out. His palms were so warm and calloused, in the best way. They enveloped my breasts completely, sending warmth shooting through me. Slowly, he swept his fingers in a caress, growing more powerful as I got used to the sensation. Eventually, he was weighing my small breasts in his palms, his thumbs rubbing across my hard nipples and making me squirm. He was right to tie my hands. I wouldn't have been able to sit still under such an erotic onslaught.

It felt better than I'd ever imagined it would.

"You like that, little stray?" he murmured softly.

I nodded, ashamed, addicted, and everything in between.

"How about this?" he continued and shocked me by leaning in

and pressing my legs wide to fit his body, then lowering his mouth to my chest.

At the first touch of his hot, wet tongue against my heated skin, I cried out. I couldn't help it. I felt like I was melting. I was dripping inside. My thighs felt sticky, and I couldn't stop rubbing them together. This was it. The lustful thoughts that Pavol had been attempting to stimulate for years, and yet, this was the very first time I'd ever felt anything close.

I arched backward, wanting to give Massimo as much of my breasts as I could, and he obliged by ruthlessly sucking on my nipples, tugging and rolling the hard buds between his lips until I was thrusting my aching pussy against the chair, desperately seeking friction.

"Let me help you, *micetta*," Massimo whispered, seconds before the rest of my gown was torn away and his blunt-tipped fingers found my panties.

My wet panties. I'd wet them right through with desire for this man and his devilish touch.

He inhaled roughly, moving away from my swollen, well-sucked nipples to press his face to my panties and inhale. His chest expanded deeply as he breathed in the smell of my lust.

"Now, that is the kind of heaven I can believe in," he murmured, and slid his hand under the elastic of my panties and tugged.

To be honest, the panties had seen better days. They were old and threadbare, but still, a person shouldn't be able to rip material right off someone's body, right?

He took the graying, ugly underwear and scrunched them into his fist, then shocked me by putting them to his face. He stuck his nose into the fabric and breathed in deeply again.

I couldn't look away. It felt wicked. It felt sublime.

"I'm keeping these. The toll for walking the road to hell with me," he said, then shoved the ball of panties into his pocket.

"What now?" I wondered, dazed and barely catching my breath.

"Now I help you see God," he said cryptically, then took both my legs, his hands snaking behind my knees, and pulled.

My ass shot forward until it hovered on the edge of the chair. He hooked each knee over an armrest and spread me wide.

I cringed, and embarrassment filled me. I felt exposed. I felt everything all at once.

Then Massimo trailed his fingers up my inner thigh, and I forgot how to think. He sank his fingers through the curls of my pussy and found my slick, wet folds. He explored, coating his fingers in me, while I squirmed, desperate for more and afraid of it at the same time.

One finger pressed inside me, and I jolted against him.

He swore softly. "We're going to need to stretch this little cunt out before you can take me. It feels like you're going to snap my finger right off," he gritted out.

"You have big fingers," I protested.

He chuckled. "Oh, baby, you haven't seen big yet, but you will."

I rolled my eyes at him as he shallowly thrust that finger inside. Of course he was huge. The guy got his confidence from somewhere.

Then his thumb found my clit, and he slid a second finger inside me. I tensed up, crying out.

"How sweet you sound when you're wet and desperate, humping my hand." Massimo's smirk was infuriating.

I wanted to slap him. I wanted to kiss him.

He circled my clit, thrusting into me with his fingers, while his other hand went to my sensitive breasts. He tweaked one nipple between nimble fingers and lowered his mouth to the other breast.

It was all too much. The onslaught felt merciless. I was rising on a relentless wave of pleasure. There was no escape from the feelings. My pussy throbbed, my breasts were aching, and I knew that I was going to come.

The rising sensation was scary but exhilarating, like reaching the top of a roller coaster and feeling afraid and giddy all at once. I writhed like a wild thing, only held in place by my restrained hands. I was humping his hand at this point, a loud squelching sound filling the air.

"That's you, my little stray. That's you and how much you enjoy my touch," he murmured against my collarbone, and then put his face right in front of mine.

"I-I'm going to—" I trailed off, mortified but too far gone to pull back from the brink.

"Hmm, yes you are, you're going to come, flood this godforsaken chair with your sweet juices, and think of me when you do. Got it?"

I nodded, too lost in sensation to really understand his words. If he'd told me to jump off the roof after this, I'd probably agree at this point.

"Okay, baby, come. Come for me, with my name on your lips and my fingers in your cunt . . . knowing while you do exactly who you now belong to."

Then he kissed me, his hand moving lightning-fast and pushing me right over the top of that wave. I was poised at the top, body contracting, blood rushing, and then I was falling. I exploded around his hand, wetness coating my thighs, the chair, the floor. Massimo kissed me through it and then rested his forehead on mine, drinking down my expression as I came and came.

"Massimo—Mass!" I sobbed out, overcome with the feeling. My body felt like a stranger's. Until I'd met this man, I'd never known it was capable of such pleasure. Just the idea of sex had been tainted for so long. It had been twisted and perverted by evil men . . . which had made something so beautiful feel shameful.

"How can a sin feel so, so good?" I said into his neck when the pulsing in my body had ebbed a little.

"It's no sin, Katarina. It's a blessing. And you are no sinner."

He drew back and hooked a hand around the back of my neck, holding my head captive. He looked me right in the eye.

"You're an angel. My angel."

18

MASSIMO

I tore my loathsome robes off in front of the austere shower near my room and threw them in the corner before stepping under the tepid water.

It hit my chest and slid down to the fucking mess of my cock. Smeared in cum, still half hard at the taste of Katarina's skin. The memory of the sound of her coming undone sent blood rushing back down.

I lowered my hand, giving in to the temptation to ease the ache in my balls one more time. Coming in my fucking pants at the dignified age of thirty-four was not something I'd ever expected to happen.

But then, I'd never expected *her.*

I slid my hand along my cock and spread the cum I'd spilled for her along the shaft and over the head. I instantly fully hardened again as I let that therapy session fill my head. The smell of her, the feel of her slick cunt strangling my fingers, her moans, her glazed eyes fixed on me.

Fuck. I moved my hand faster, pleasure rushing up my spine and down my legs. I slapped a hand to the cold, dingy tiles on the wall and pumped my cock mercilessly.

As I neared coming again, my mind strayed from the therapy session to the night before. Katarina standing in the dark hallway, looking up at me with those wide, clear eyes.

"I don't think you're as bad as you believe you are, deep down inside." Her sweet whisper sent precum leaking from me frantically.

Then the memory of her leaning up toward me and pressing her lips to my cheek. She had kissed my cheek, knowing who and what I was. Her sweet, golden goodness invading my darkness. Fearless.

"Thank you."

I came hard, cum jerking from my balls violently. It splashed the tiles at my feet, striping the drain and mixing with the swirling water that had already turned cold.

I eased my thrusts into my hand, slowly drawing every last drop of cum from my balls, my head swimming with intoxicating thoughts of my little stray.

She'd appeared out of the deepest, darkest place I'd ever been, a blazing light pushing away the black on all sides.

And she had bewitched me. Infected me.

She was dangerous. She was a problem . . .

And I'd never let her go.

There was a tense atmosphere around Hallow Hall the next day, and the reason for that was immediately clear.

A row of black top-of-the-line armored vehicles was parked at the door of the institute. A procession of men in black suits filed through the building, heading for Vargas's personal office.

Centrium Group coming in to wipe all traces of their pet

ex-priest employee. I had briefly considered breaking into Vargas's office yesterday, just to see what I could find out about the inner workings of Hallow Hall, but I'd put Giada on it, and there was no point risking my position.

I kept to the shadows while the men from Centrium worked. I didn't need to raise any eyebrows until I was ready to leave here. Once Pavol and Benedict were dead, Blackwood, too, potentially, and with Katarina at my side.

I'd broken into an attic room with a well-positioned window to observe the front of the building. I lifted the scope of my sniper rifle to my eye to better see the men coming and going with boxes from Vargas's office.

Bulgarian Mafia?

It couldn't have been more obvious; the men may as well have been wearing lanyards around their necks announcing their family membership. They were clearly dangerous men. They didn't move like office drones for some company. So Vargas had been the front man for a trafficking operation. It wasn't a stretch by any means. Vargas had given Hallow Hall a veneer of respectability and Church connections, which were usually unquestionable. As soon as something charitable was linked with the Church, it escaped scrutiny. That was what allowed Hallow Hall to operate in plain sight. And a Mafia family might have connections in the local police to prevent anything from falling through the cracks. Someone like Katarina, who knew too much.

The real question was: Why didn't they kill her? She was obviously a thorn in their sides. There was more to her story, and I had a feeling that not even she knew the full extent of it.

I didn't tell Katarina about her mother. Honestly, it seemed cruel. She was already living in such pain. Finding out that the person she'd endured so much for had died, well, that might very well break her. She'd learn the truth one day, when she was free and safe and all her demons were slain.

I'd see to it.

Another car drew up, this one flanked by motorbikes. The director himself? It was best I stayed out of the way, considering that I was depending on Pavol and Benedict not introducing me to the director. They thought I was here to keep an eye on them for the Bulgarians. That was what the man I'd killed, Cristoph, had been on his way to do. It wouldn't take much for my cover to unravel. I wasn't bulletproof. After all, I'd overstayed my welcome. I was meant to be in and out, kill Vargas, and never set foot here again. No one would have had time to question my purpose here.

Instead, because of Katarina, I was still here, vulnerable to being exposed.

I stared at the director through my scope. It would be so easy to shoot him right now. I could take him out, and maybe the entire Mafia behind him would crumble and Hallow Hall would be shut down. I could go after the ringleaders later, visiting Pavol and Benedict in their homes, after they thought they were safe . . .

But I had no idea what the power hierarchy was in the Centrium Group or the family behind it. Maybe there was an ambitious son waiting to take over the reins. One thing was for sure, shooting the director right now would plunge the institute and all its patients into chaos. I could be separated from Katarina in the fallout. That was a risk I couldn't afford.

I'd taken the liberty of crushing up the medication I was supposed to be giving Katarina every day and adding it to the wine supply that Benedict and Pavol kept in their private dining room. They had certainly been hitting the blood of Christ hard since Vargas's death, and I might have dosed with a heavy hand. I looked forward to seeing the effect it would have, considering that they'd been giving it to Katarina for years.

A fun little experiment of my own. Maybe science was interesting after all. Other than that, I could only wait. Wait for Pavol and Benedict to be in the right position to end them. Wait for Katarina's vengeance to be served so I could take her from this place. Wait for information about Centrium Group. Wait for information about my mother.

Always waiting.

19

KATARINA

They cleared out Vargas's office. What kinds of incriminating evidence did they have in those boxes? I wished I could comb through it. Details about their victims? A record of the patients who had "died" in childbirth and whose children had been "stillborn"?

I itched to get my hands on it but was powerless. Instead, I watched them carry those precious boxes outside.

"What do you think?" Tatiana asked me. She was drawing again. Another day and another landscape.

Tatiana had been born here, in Hallow Hall. Alonso had once mused that she had to be the daughter of one of the higher-ups around here . . . because there were no other children.

Just the idea had been terrifying. That would mean that the powers that be at Hallow Hall actually thought the environment worthy for bringing up their own secret love child. I absently wondered whose daughter she might be as she frowned down at her picture, her features locked in fierce concentration.

Benedict's daughter? Maybe Pavol's? She might have been

Vargas's, but I didn't like to consider that, as it would mean she was currently sitting next to her father's killer.

But once Massimo does his job, won't it be the case regardless?

That was true. If I had my way, all three of the powerful men at Hallow Hall would be dead soon. I couldn't bring myself to be sad about it. Tatiana and all young women would be safer once those men were gone from the world.

I checked the clock and noted it was time for my session with Benedict. I hadn't seen him in days. Pavol was flitting around here and there, his appearance increasingly awful. Benedict was a mystery. I decided to head there before Sister Vera came and reminded me.

I wandered toward Benedict's office and abruptly stopped when I saw the horde of men in black suits in the hallway outside.

Before I could back away, the door to Benedict's office opened.

"I swear, nothing is out of control. The testing is coming along perfectly."

"You seem erratic, Benedict. You need to get a grip. If you're going to take over Michal's responsibilities, you need to step up and get your head on straight."

Benedict's face was ruddy in some spots and pale in others. He looked a mess. Worse than Pavol, honestly, which was really saying something.

"How's the new serum coming along?" The director was there—what had he said his name was? Sergei, that was it.

"Very well, I'm in the last stage of testing."

Sergei sighed. "And yet . . . you're behind on all your other performance indicators; don't think I haven't noticed. Now that you're shorthanded, isn't it only going to get worse?"

"We have Father Lucciano to pick up some slack—" Benedict was saying to Sergei, before the latter turned to see me approaching.

Shit. Was Benedict about to talk to Sergei about Massimo?

Stop him, now!

The voice in my head had been quiet for a good while. Her sudden cry sent me hurrying toward the two men. I wasn't exactly sure why it felt vitally important to help Massimo cover up his presence here, but suddenly nothing mattered more. He hadn't explicitly explained his cover here to me, but I could guess that he didn't want word spread about his presence.

"Director," I unearthed my voice to call out.

All heads in the hallway, Benedict's and the five or so security guys', snapped to me.

Suddenly, I faltered. *Shit, what am I going to say?*

But Director Sergei watched me, his conversation with Benedict forgotten, which was all that mattered.

I slowed as I reached them.

"I—hi. I don't know if you remember me," I rushed out.

Sergei nodded slowly. "Miss Dmitrova. Katarina, yes?"

"Yes," I confirmed.

"How can I help you, child?"

"I-I just wanted to say hi," I managed to get out. *What the hell?*

Benedict glared at me, and an assessing look crossed Sergei's face as he considered me.

"You offered to let me have dinner with you last time. I'd love to do that if the offer still stands," I rambled. Great, now I was basically inviting myself to dinner with the director of Centrium Group for no reason. Oh well, let him think I was crazy. That was why I was here anyway.

Sergei watched me for a long while and then turned to Benedict.

"This young woman seems confused and worried. Is that the state you usually keep your patients in? Is that the state you usually keep *this* patient in?" he asked carefully.

Before I could wonder what the hell he was talking about, he turned back to me.

"Alas, today I am moving on quickly. I appreciate you might be unsettled by the recent events here, but don't worry, Katarina, you are safe."

I wasn't sure what to say to that, so I just nodded.

"Father Benedict will make you feel better. Trust in him and his therapies and medicines. I am a man who believes in the power of medications and prayer."

"Okay," I murmured, nodding to make it seem like I was interested in what he was saying.

"I will see you again the next time I visit, child, and we will have that dinner," Sergei said, and patted me on the hand.

I fought the urge to recoil. There was something unsettling about the man. I instinctively disliked him.

"Sure, sounds fun," I said.

He gave me a tight smile and addressed Benedict. "I leave her in your hands, Father. Do not disappoint me."

Then he was striding off, and Benedict clamped his hand on my arm.

"What are you doing here?" he asked. Up close, he looked even worse than he had only a week ago. His eyes were bloodshot, his comb-over unkempt. His robes were stained with food in places, and he smelled bad. Sour, like old wine.

"Come into my office," he hissed at me and pulled me roughly through the door, letting it slam behind us.

He threw me down into the chair in front of his desk, then walked to his own. Nerves prickled up my arms as I gripped the chair and watched him warily.

"'Don't disappoint me,' he says. What a fucking joke," Benedict muttered.

I'd never heard him speak in anger or swear. He seemed to be unraveling.

He started to mess with some white tablets, and my stomach dropped. Was he going to give me my medication himself? *Shit.*

"Isn't Father Lucciano coming to the session?"

"What?" Benedict's head snapped up. "Why do you ask?"

"Just because he said he was coming . . . and he's been overseeing my medication," I reminded him faintly.

Benedict's eyes stared deep into mine, and a rush of unease went through me. *Crap.* The good father really wasn't feeling like himself. He was volatile and dangerous.

I wished Massimo was here. Suddenly, I was afraid.

"And? I'm the head of Hallow Hall, as of a few days ago, when some people decided they couldn't handle the responsibility. I don't need anyone interfering with my patients." Benedict's eyebrows drew together. "Come to think of it, all the problems started when Father Lucciano came here. Everything was fine before. Then that man arrived, and now everything is falling apart."

He glanced around, a wild look in his eyes. He jerked open a drawer and pulled out a bottle and syringe.

Fuck.

"What did Pavol say you called Lucciano when you first met him?" Benedict rambled. "Lucifer?" He chuckled. "Maybe you were right on the money, Katarina. Let's test that hypothesis."

"Father, I think you should call Pavol or Massimo. You don't seem well," I said, trying to calm him.

His eyes widened as he processed my words.

"Massimo?" he repeated.

Oh no. I'd slipped up and called him Massimo.

Benedict stood abruptly, his chair screeching hard against the tiles. He dropped the bottle into his pocket, as well as the capped syringe, and went back to rooting around his drawer.

My heart hardly had time to calm before he took something else from the drawer.

A gun.

I stared at it in disbelief. Sure—was a gun really that surprising considering Benedict was a man who trafficked babies and sold organs on the black market? Not really. And yet, and yet . . . I was still shocked to see the weapon clutched in his hand.

"I think it's time to test Father Lucciano's allegiance."

My heart seemed to jump to my mouth when he pointed the gun at me. "Get up. Now. You're coming with me."

Benedict marched me through the infirmary wing of the institute, and we didn't see a single soul. Not that anyone could have helped me except for Massimo, and he was nowhere to be seen.

We neared one of the operating rooms, and I came to a stop.

"Go on, go in."

I shook my head. I had a terrible foreboding that if I went into that room, I'd never come out.

The gun pressed into my back, and Benedict spoke in my ear. "Now. Or die right here."

Vargas had told me that I was off-limits and that was why they hadn't just gotten rid of me. And I'd believed him, because why else would they have kept me here alive for so long? But Benedict wasn't acting like himself. I had no idea what to expect.

"Father!" a surprised voice said behind us.

Sister Vera. If there was anyone who wouldn't help me here, it was her.

"Bring Father Lucciano, now," Benedict snapped at the nun.

Whether or not she could see the gun pressed into my back, considering Benedict's robes, I had no idea, but she scurried off anyway, presumably to follow his orders.

"Let's see who Father Lucciano really is," Benedict said, and pushed me toward the doors.

This time, I let him.

Massimo was coming.

20

MASSIMO

The director had barely left, taking his heavily armed escorts and incriminating evidence with him, when Sister Vera hurried over to me. I'd been looking for Katarina, wandering from the cafeteria to the art room to the office.

She hadn't appeared.

"Father Lucciano!" Sister Vera rushed toward me, her pinched face revealing her panic. "Father Benedict requires you, immediately. He's in the infirmary wing. Operating room two."

What the fuck?

I nodded to Sister Vera and took off toward the infirmary wing. What would Benedict possibly be in an operating room for? If he was going to ask me to step in for Father Vargas to help him steal some poor girl's baby, or her fucking organs, he was about to be sorely disappointed. If I delivered a cool box of organs to anyone, they would be his.

I reached the operating room and pushed inside, coming to a stop immediately.

It took a moment for my brain to process what I was seeing.

Katarina, lying on the operating table, strapped down. Her head turned toward me as soon as I walked in, her eyes wide. She was terrified.

Father Benedict stood by the window on the other side of the room, a fucking mask and gown on like he was a surgeon prepped and ready to perform an operation.

He swung toward me when I came in, and I knew there was something wrong. His skin was mottled, and his eyes portrayed madness. Hmm, it seemed a combination of the recent stress and high doses of what they'd been giving Katarina had fucked him up.

What a shame.

Silence fell as all three of us looked at one another. It was absurd, really. I almost felt like laughing.

"You asked for me?" I raised an eyebrow in Benedict's direction.

"Yes, I did. Aren't you supposed to be helping around here? Are you reporting back all the goings-on to Sergei? Or are you here for someone else? Tell me the truth!"

I narrowed my eyes at Benedict. The man had lost the plot.

"Exactly what are you implying, Father?"

Benedict licked his bottom lip, then quickly killed the macabre humor coiling in my chest at the surreal tableau he'd made of the operating room.

He put his hand into his pocket and brought out a gun.

"I'm saying that if you are who you pretend to be, you should be helping with the other business of Hallow Hall, starting now." He gestured me forward with the gun. "Take that syringe off the tray and fill it to fifty ccs from the bottle."

"What is it?" I asked, delaying complying.

"It's a little something I've been working on for years. Sergei's tired of waiting for it." Benedict glared at Katarina. "She can test it. She might as well be good for something around here. Do it now." Benedict cocked the gun at me. It was an older-model revolver with a hammer to draw back. The sound was sobering. He was serious, apparently.

I stepped up to the tray that was set up close to Katarina's side. Her eyes were wild, and now they fixed on mine. A gag filled her mouth so she couldn't speak. Her eyes were wet with tears.

Benedict just moved up his order on my killing schedule.

"And . . . what are we looking for in terms of effects? I know the director is eager to see progress," I bluffed.

Benedict nodded. "Increased memory loss, confusion, painkilling function, and addiction forming. Better control over patients, the ability to perform surgery when and if required with less medical intervention needed afterward. Aftercare is expensive," he said, his gaze falling to the tray.

On it was a perfectly arranged mix of surgical implements. I cataloged the instruments while slowly filling the syringe.

"Of course, the biggest benefit is the curbing of the lustful, sinful behavior of the patients here and all girls who reach maturity. It will be powerful. A means to control the temptation of Eve, finally, so Adam may continue down a more righteous path."

Benedict was rambling now, spit flecking his lips, and he seemed to have developed a tic of some kind. His eye twitched madly.

"Inject her, and we will see if it works. She might be special, but if this works like I think it will, the director will never know we tested it on her. He'll simply be impressed."

I nodded and played along, flicking the air out of the syringe and then stepping closer to Katarina's side.

I brought the syringe as close to her arm as I could and slowly injected a long stream of the liquid onto the floor. From Benedict's angle, he couldn't really tell. He seemed to be having trouble concentrating on anything. Taking advantage of his distraction, I finished pretending to administer the drug and put the syringe on the tray.

"And now?"

He grunted, eyes darting about. He eyed me distrustfully.

"You—you say all the right things, and you seem to do them, but is it all an act? Everything bad started happening when you came here."

He raised the gun toward me again. *Damn it.* Benedict was going to have to go sooner than I'd planned.

A chuckle left me before I could help it. "I'm sure your patients would disagree. I think bad things have been happening here for a long time. Too long."

He frowned at me, the gun shaking in his hand.

"See, you speak with a forked tongue," he said. "If you want to prove you're an ally, take the scalpel there and remove an organ from Katarina, a nonessential one. Nothing too noticeable. A kidney will do."

A scoff left me, and I braced my hands on the metal bed where Katarina thrashed around.

"Jesus Christ, Father. That is dark, and coming from me, that's really saying something. I'd be impressed if your idea were more creative, but as it is, it fucking stinks. I have a proposition for you and this hellhole you live in. Go and round up all the rapists, and human traffickers, and fucking terrible parents who abuse their children, and take those organs. I'll harvest with you all day. But Katarina is off-limits, as are all the other poor, innocent girls you've imprisoned up here."

"Innocent! A fifteen-year-old pregnant girl isn't innocent. She has sinned! And she will pay for it! Cut into that bitch on the table now, or I'll shoot you dead," Benedict warned.

I dropped my hand to the scalpels and ran my fingers over them, selecting the most wicked-looking one.

"Okay, Father, okay. I understand." I glanced down to stare into Katarina's anguished eyes. "I know what I have to do."

I placed the scalpel at Katarina's middle, her body tensing and trying to twist away, her moans escaping around her gag and filling the room.

Benedict followed my movements, chewing his inner cheek in anticipation.

Before the blade could touch her skin, I flipped it in my hand, tossing it and catching it with ease, and then sent it flying.

It hit Benedict in the neck before he could realize what had happened. He turned this way and that, confused, the gun drooping in his grip. Blood dripped from his neck. The carotid artery, severed. He dropped the gun completely to pull at the blade and collapsed to his knees. A snaking trail of blood leaked out onto the floor. I made my way over to him. I grabbed a few paper towels as I passed the dispenser and let them fall to the floor. Cleaning up blood was much easier if you acted quickly.

He squirmed, still trying to get a grip on the scalpel.

"Here, let me," I murmured, and drew it free. More blood poured out, landing on the paper towels. I tutted at the blood spots soaking into the material on my arm. "What a mess. What a disgusting bag of blood and bones you were, you dirty old sinner. But you've managed to make it quick, which you don't deserve."

His eyes grew unfocused.

I leaned in and whispered in his ear, "Enjoy the fires, Father. They burn for men like you and me."

Benedict slumped down, eyes glassy, the last air he'd ever breathe leaving his lungs.

Fuck. I glanced around the room. What a mess. This was the opposite of how I did things in my work. I was methodical and precise, and I never left a mess.

This was going to take a while to clean up, not to mention that I hadn't planned on killing Benedict already. I wiped my red-speckled hands on my cassock, getting them as clean as possible.

With a sigh, I stood and crossed to Katarina. She had her head turned as much as she could, but not far enough to see Benedict's lifeless body on the floor below. I untied her gag, careful to wipe my hands on my cassock first, and then unbound her wrists.

I slowly helped her into a sitting position.

She shook. Her skin was too pale, her breath too rapid.

"Breathe, Katarina. Breathe. You're safe. I have you now," I told her quickly, gripping her shoulders to keep her upright.

She stared at the bloody floor, eyes full of horror.

"Look at me, *micetta*. Look at me," I commanded when it seemed like she was never going to blink again.

She raised her eyes to mine, blinked once, then again, and promptly fainted.

I caught her before she could fall more than a few inches and cradled her against my chest. It had been an eventful few days for my little stray. Not only Vargas's death, solitary, and then our session, but now seeing a man killed brutally in front of her. When had she last eaten?

I scooped her into my arms and walked toward the door, maneuvering around the blood as much as I could. Luckily, the black cassock hid blood effectively. My hands were cleaned, and

Katarina had escaped the splash zone. I needed to get her out of here, and then I needed to start cleaning up.

It was time to get to work.

Hours later, I stripped off the bloodstained robes I'd only made worse when cleaning up the scene and dropped them on the floor of the shower as I stepped in. I had the water turned up as hot as it would go, but it still didn't feel hot enough.

Benedict's blood felt soaked into my skin, permeating every pore. I scrubbed hard with the rough soap bar until my skin was red.

I didn't kill like this. I killed with gloves and tools, and I never got some motherfucker's blood on me. Sure, people could take you by surprise sometimes, but it didn't happen often, and if it did, that's when the backup plan came into play.

Today, though, I hadn't killed for work. It hadn't been professional.

It had been personal.

He'd tried to touch Katarina. Hurt her. Drug her and cut her.

Katarina was mine. *Mine.*

The dark possession that raced through my veins at the very thought of her being hurt, or pushed around, or upset, made me certain I'd kill a hundred Benedicts to protect her.

It had been a very long time since I'd had someone whom I'd cared about so deeply.

It had been a very long time since I'd had anything to lose, and I didn't fucking like it. I felt vulnerable and exposed. I felt threatened by Katarina's simple presence in the world. It was like she was becoming a part of me, but a part that was independent from my body and thus harder to protect.

I showered until the water was freezing and then scrubbed my cassock until black dye leaked down the drain. Stepping out, I squeezed the water out of the fabric as hard as I could, then took it back to my room to hang dry. Luckily, I had a spare. I was also lucky that only Blackwood remained in the medical wing of Hallow Hall since Vargas's so-called suicide, and no one had interrupted my cleanup. I'd never been lucky before, but since coming here, I was beginning to think I might be the luckiest bastard alive. I'd met Katarina, after all.

The operating room and my robes would never hold up to a black light. Though if the priests were slicing and dicing and stealing organs in these operating rooms, I imagined that a black light would find a lot more than just Benedict's blood.

Inside my room, my gaze immediately found her. She hadn't moved much, except to snuggle deeper into the scratchy blanket on my bed. Fortunately for me, Alonso was still shit scared enough of me to lie about someone missing from their room if I told him to.

My own personal angel, sound asleep.

My heart finally unclenched as I locked us in, hung up my wet robes, and crossed to the bed. She was still pale, painfully so, but her breath was deep and even.

Her hair spread over the pillow like satin ribbons. Softer and more luxurious than any manmade texture would ever achieve.

I stroked her cheek, enjoying the smooth, plush feel of her skin.

She looked perfect here, innocent and trusting, sleeping in my bed.

Exactly where she belonged.

I pulled the blankets back and slid in beside her. My chilled skin burned against hers. She shivered for a moment, her warmth meeting my ice. She attempted to turn away from me, even in her sleep rejecting the sudden cool in her cozy bed, but I brought her close, caging her against my chest.

She couldn't escape me. Not now, not ever. I buried my face in the back of her hair, pressed my hard body to her softness, and slept.

21

KATARINA

For the first time in a long time, I slept without dreams.

My mind simply shut off, and I rested in absolute deep, velvet dark.

When I woke, I panicked. *Where was I?* The room around me was strange, and the bed was hard. I was hot, too hot, and there was something around my neck that felt like a restraint.

Then, he shifted slightly in his sleep, and I registered his scent all around me, and my positioning made sense.

Massimo.

He held me against his chest, his arms wrapped around me, barely allowing me any space to shuffle away. Even in his sleep, he held on tight.

Yesterday flooded back. Benedict and the gun, the madness in his eyes. I shivered violently, the memory of the blood splashing against the tile walls taking me back to three years ago, and Mira.

I'm getting them, Mira. One by one.

I took a deep, shuddering breath, and found tears forming. I couldn't stop them. A sob left my throat. I cringed, not wanting

Massimo to wake up and see me crying. It was too pathetic. Why had I always been so weak?

But the avalanche of tears and the dump of trauma blindsiding me when I didn't have my defenses up was too much to hold back.

So, I gave in. I cried. I sobbed. My tears soaked through my pillow. The fabric scratched my cheek. My body shook. I knew I should get up and move away from Massimo before I woke him. I was suddenly desperate to do that. To huddle in a corner and break down alone.

But when I tried to escape, his arms closed tighter around me, holding me to him.

I tapped his arm.

"Let me go," I pleaded through my tears.

"No." His low growl was immediate. His arms only grew tighter, forcing me against his chest, surrounding me with his warmth.

I twisted as much as I could to push at his hip glued to my back.

"Let go!"

He caught my hand and suddenly shifted away, making me fall flat to the mattress. His body slid across mine, his hands circling my wrists, and pinned me underneath him.

His dark-eyed gaze tracked across my hot, tearstained face. "If you're going to fall apart, you'll do it in my arms."

"Why?" I burst out, irritation pressing through my sadness. I squirmed against him, shoving with all my might, but it was no use. There was no getting away from him and his pitch-black gaze. I was laid bare, and there was nowhere to hide.

"So I can catch all the pieces," he murmured softly.

I stilled at those words, my protests clogged in my aching throat. My heart fluttered.

"What?" I whispered.

But he didn't answer. Instead, he leaned in and kissed me.

This time, his kiss was gentle, coaxing me from the dark place I'd woken up in and pulling me from my painful memories.

"Angels shouldn't cry, not over men like Benedict. It's unholy," he said, and traced his lips over my cheeks, pressing kisses to the trails of my tears.

I became aware of how heavy he was, and how his body touched mine in all the right places.

He was hard, long and thick, lying right between my legs against my core. I writhed, sliding my pussy over that delicious hardness, instinctively reaching for something I'd only ever imagined but never experienced. I wanted the clothes between us gone. I wanted his hot skin on mine. I didn't want to think anymore. I just wanted to feel.

His hand cupped my cheek, then slid back and gripped the hair at my nape. He tilted my head back and kissed me deeper. Hungrier. As he did, he thrust his hips into me, rubbing me just right.

I arched my back, thrusting my breasts to his hard chest. I felt suffocated by my clothes. In this small room, away from the rest of the world, it felt like we were the only people left in the universe.

"No more tears, *micetta*," he said firmly, his voice deep and ragged.

Was he as affected by me as I was by him? It seemed impossible. I was the sheltered recluse. The girl who'd forgotten what the world outside the fence looked like.

While Massimo was worldly, older, stronger . . . everything. He'd lived a real life, not just existed as an afterthought, a loose end to shut away.

"I can't fucking stand to see you cry," he murmured on my lips, and leaned up on one hand to trail his other down my chest and slide my T-shirt up. "You're the kind of person who should only ever smile."

He yanked the bralette down and exposed my breast. Then he was swooping down to pull it into his mouth and rub his tongue across the hard point. It felt so good. I jerked against him feverishly, wanting more, wanting everything.

His hands were at the waistband of my sweatpants. Then he was urging them down. My panties went with them. His hands trailed over my thighs, leaving fire in their wake.

I was wet just at the memory of what had happened the last time he touched me there. He sucked on my nipples as he eased his fingers down my slit. He inserted one finger just inside and then circled my clit with his thumb. I thrashed shamelessly, more turned on than I'd ever been. Last night's horrors slipped away, bit by bit, overwritten by these new feelings. New memories to replace the bad.

Then Massimo was heading downward. He left my T-shirt rucked up, my breasts puffy and pink from his tongue. Then his hot breath hit my lower belly, and I tensed, realizing his destination.

"What are you doing?" I said, panicked.

"Tasting you. Taking my next first." He grinned against my belly and dipped his head toward my pussy and inhaled, his chest expanding. "There's that sweet perfume. The one I lost my fucking head over."

"Wait—I haven't showered. I—you don't have to—" I babbled.

He chuckled wickedly. "You think I care that you haven't showered? I want you to smell like you, not shitty soap. I want you to taste like you . . . not chemicals. Your smell drives me wild." He tilted his face up to look at me, his eyes boring into mine. "Take responsibility for this madness you've caused and ease my suffering."

Then he leaned down and licked me. His tongue was hot and wet and really fucking strong. He licked up my slit, surging through my slick folds, searching for my clit, just to drop and press inside me as well. I cried out, and one of his hands snaked upward and slid over my mouth.

"Shh, angel. No one gets to hear you come but me. That sound is mine and mine alone. Got it?"

Then he went back to my clit, rubbing it with the tip of his tongue as I rose and rose. His other hand went to my entrance. He wet his fingers in my juices and then slipped one gently inside. I nearly doubled over. It felt too good.

"We have to stretch you out, remember? We have to be diligent and work on that every day . . . no skipping the homework."

His finger forged deeper inside me, and he slid in a second one. I arched, melting into him. He laved my clit relentlessly, finger-fucking me at the same time. I was so wet I could feel my arousal on my inner thighs and the bed beneath. I wrapped my legs around his shoulders, holding his face in place, and he chuckled as he ate me.

I was shameless. The lust I'd been accused of for so long had taken me over. But mine was for one person and one alone. Only for Massimo. I'd never felt attraction like I felt for him. This chemistry between us wasn't something ordinary. Even in my inexperience, I could tell as much. We were electric.

When I came, I saw stars. Beautiful, crystalline lights exploding behind my eyes. I still pulsed with heat and pleasure when he carefully pulled his fingers from me and stood. Bending sharply, he grabbed my panties off the floor and straightened up, his hand going to his cock. It was an intriguing sight. I'd seen plenty of them during my BS therapy session with Pavol, but never one like this. It was impressive, and scarily big and thick. He pumped his hand along the shaft, positioned over my body. Was he going to come on me? I watched with rapt attention and curiosity. He thrust his cock faster in his hand and held my panties to his face, inhaling deeply.

"Fuck, nothing smells like you, and nothing ever will," he growled.

His hips pistoned faster, and he lowered my panties away from his face and draped the crotch over the end of his cock just as he started to come. He grunted, deep and rough, as his hips jerked. He emptied himself into my panties, catching every single drop of cum perfectly in the material.

I lost track of how long I watched him while he came undone. For a moment, he was stripped of his usual mask of charming indifference. He was just him. He let out a long sigh and dropped his hands, my panties still clutched in one of them.

"Fuck, I feel like I'm sixteen years old again around you," he admitted, and looked me up and down. "My cock certainly feels reborn at the sight of you, little stray. I've never been so ready to fuck as I am around you, any time or place, I'm ready."

"Well, why don't we?" I wondered, eyeing his spent cock. The size had barely gone down. Despite making the most scandalous agreement of my life, I was still a freaking virgin.

I wet my lips, and Massimo groaned.

"Because I'm not taking all your firsts at once. I want them one by fucking one . . . slowly. You won't rush me," he warned. "No matter how much you want to be fucked properly."

His grin told me he was just teasing me, so I rolled my eyes and glanced away.

"Anyway, what happens now?" I asked him. A silver chain glinted around his neck. Something that was usually hidden. A long chain with hanging flat metal discs. Dog tags? There was so much I didn't know about this man, but now wasn't the time. I forced myself to focus on his answer.

"I kill Pavol. Sooner rather than later. Things will unravel quickly here once they discover Benedict is missing. It'll be chaotic." A hint of a grin touched Massimo's lips.

"Why do I feel like you're looking forward to that?"

"In chaos, I thrive. Two down. One to go." Then he lifted his hand, still holding my cum-soaked panties.

"Now, put these on like a good girl, and I'll see you back to your room."

"Put those on?" I exclaimed, shocked by the idea and more than a little curious. Why was the idea hot?

He nodded.

"Why?"

"So you smell like me, angel. So you don't forget who your partner is."

"Like I could forget you," I muttered with another eye roll.

"Hmm, I am rather unforgettable, aren't I?" Massimo teased, and helped me to my feet.

I blushed furiously when he handed me the panties, my cheeks hot and scratchy.

"But," he added, "not as unforgettable as you."

22
KATARINA

Massimo took me back to my room early, before anyone noticed I hadn't slept there. The institute ran on a skeleton crew. Clearly the unholy trinity had been wary of having too many people coming and going. They'd felt the threat even if they weren't sure where it was coming from.

I fell into a heavy sleep and woke up when the midday sun was already streaming in the window. My stomach growled painfully. Shit. Why hadn't the alarm gone off?

I pushed myself out of bed and stretched. My body twinged in new places. I still felt tingly in certain parts after this morning. I could still imagine his mouth on my skin. I could still feel what it was like to orgasm on his fingers and tongue.

I flopped back on the bed, my thoughts hazy and unfocused, lost in that pleasurable memory.

So, it turned out that sex was worth making a fuss about. No wonder everyone was obsessed with it. I coasted my hand down my body, over my breasts, and then lower, and parked it between my legs.

Heat flooded through me knowing that my panties still held

Massimo's cum. It was wrong. A sin. My poor mother would faint dead away if she knew I was writhing around on my bed, touching myself, thinking about the man who'd come in my panties and made me wear them so I'd smell like him all day.

What was I doing? Shame collided with the heat in my blood, and I dropped my hand to the bed and stared at the ceiling. The wooden crucifix on the wall watched me. I crossed myself quickly.

I was going to hell, but at least I'd have good company. *Massimo*. Despite knowing how much of a devil he was, how bloodstained his hands were, how marked his soul was . . . I was falling. He was on my mind all the time. He'd infected me with his poison, and now I burned for him. What would I do when we were done with our agreement? When he moved on? A chill went over me at the very thought. To the girl who had always been alone, finding someone and then losing them felt like the final blow. Would the world afterward feel emptier, with my knowing he was out there somewhere and done with me? Or would it have been better never to have known him at all?

My brain wasn't in the state to ponder big thoughts, and besides, I was pretty sure there was no good answer to those bittersweet musings.

I got up and stretched, thinking I should try to shower while knowing that I wouldn't. The awful truth was that I didn't want to. I wanted to prolong the memory of what had happened between us. An experience that had painted over the horror of yesterday. A shiny new memory that blotted out the others.

When my stomach rumbled too loudly to ignore, I went to the door and pulled at the handle.

It didn't budge. That was odd. Usually the rooms were unlocked for patients to come and go—well, the ones who were unmedicated enough to go anywhere. I pulled again, but it still didn't move. It was definitely locked.

I peered out at the hallway through the observation window. It was empty.

What was happening? Did they already know about Benedict? Did they suspect me, or was everyone locked in?

I watched the hallway for a while, searching for any signs of life. The thought that I'd wake up one day and everyone else would be gone was a persistent nightmare I'd suffered through for months when I first came here. I'd wake up and discover that everyone else had left Hallow Hall, but I was stuck locked inside my room. I'd cry and rage, but no one would ever come. That nightmare had been particularly haunting.

I banged on my door, fear overtaking my patience. *Where is everyone?*

I banged again, as loudly as I could. The sound echoed through the metal and along the hallway. A glimpse of scrubs at the top of the hall sent relief crashing into me.

"Alonso!" I cried out as a familiar face appeared.

He hurried toward my door and slid the food slot open to speak to me.

"What's going on? Where is everyone?" I asked quickly, bending to put my mouth near the slot.

"Did you leave your room last night?" Alonso asked quickly.

"What? No, of course not," I lied.

Alonso was quiet for a long moment.

"What's going on?" I pressed.

He sighed. "I don't really know. They aren't telling us shit. Something went down with the higher-ups. Pavol's freaking out. I think Benedict quit or left or something. I'm not sure. Anyway, Pavol doesn't want anyone out of their rooms today."

"But what about food and the bathroom?" I asked.

"You'll have to use the one in your room today, I'm afraid."

All the rooms had a toilet and a small sink in them, just like prison cells, but I hated using them. I always felt exposed.

Dark figures appeared at the end of the corridor. Massimo, dressed in his black robes, walking quickly with Dr. Blackwood.

He didn't glance in my direction, but Blackwood stopped to talk to Alonso for a second, instructing him to have the cook prepare trays for all the rooms.

I stared at the side of Massimo's face, wishing that he'd look at me, but he didn't. Of course being suspicious right now wasn't a good idea, but still, I sought reassurance from the only ally I'd ever had.

"Katarina, everything okay?" Dr. Blackwood asked me suddenly.

My eyes snapped to him. I nodded and leaned down to speak through the food flap. "I'm okay, just curious what's going on."

Dr. Blackwood nodded. "Well, once you have your meds, you'll feel better. Maybe you can have a little sleep. I know they make you tired. In fact, everyone should eat well today and then rest. The day will pass faster that way."

I nodded and stepped back to watch as Blackwood and Massimo walked away.

"You heard the man, I better get on." Alonso's voice was heavy.

"Okay, come tell me if you find anything out," I said.

He just shrugged and walked away.

It didn't look like I was going to get any answers right now. All I could do was wait.

Luckily for me, I had a lot of experience with that.

I sank down on the floor, my back to my bed, and stared at my wall and the mess of black chalk that lived there: scribbled notes to myself, and words and names of things I'd tried not to forget.

And I waited.

• • •

Come nighttime, my stomach screamed for food. The only thing that had been delivered all day was a single mystery-meat meal. I'd been desperate enough to eat it, but after a few bites, a strange chemical taste had lingered in my mouth. I stared at it, then leaned in and inhaled. There it was—a bitter chemical smell.

Drugged.

Blackwood had had the food drugged with a sedative, probably so everyone would stay in their rooms docilely.

I pushed the rest of the plate away, my stomach still painfully empty, but knowing that I couldn't eat any more.

After a while, I went to bed and lay down. There was just enough of the drug in my system to make me sleepy. I closed my eyes and let myself drift off.

My dreams returned me to Massimo's bed this morning and the feeling of melting into the rough sheets, under the control of his strong, confident hands. My skin felt hot, feverish with want. I writhed on my bed, knowing it was a dream but not wanting to wake up and lose the sweet pleasure.

In my mind, Massimo's tongue worked up my inner thigh, and the cool air of the room against my wet skin had me shivering.

Wait . . . It really *did* feel wet.

I opened my eyes to my darkened room. I looked down and saw him.

My demon. He was just a shadow against the white sheets in the semidarkness, but I knew it was him from the way his scent wound around me, filling my head. I knew it was him from the way he touched me, those callused fingers that were becoming so familiar.

He lay between my legs, having worked my pants off while I

was sleeping. Now he kissed between my legs, his long, hot tongue working up and down my slit. Lapping me up.

The fact that I was extremely close to orgasming dawned on me as I came fully awake.

I sank my fingers into his hair and tugged his face up.

His eyes were pits of shining darkness.

"You're awake?" he murmured, his voice throaty.

"Now, yes . . . What are you doing?" I asked softly.

"Taking care of my things. You were having a nightmare, *micetta*—you needed distracting, and I needed to taste you."

He leaned up, and I clutched at his shoulders.

"What are you doing?" I repeated, panicked. I was so close to coming, the thought of him stopping now was horrifying.

He chuckled, low and dark. "Why?"

"You know why . . ." I trailed off, my cheeks hot.

He shook his head. I could only just make out the movement in the dark.

"No I don't. I need you to tell me." He stood beside the bed, looming over me in his black robes.

"I-I don't want you to stop." The confession felt damning.

"Because?" he encouraged.

I sighed, my cheeks burning at this point.

"Because it feels so good and I want more. Because I didn't know it was possible to feel the way you make me feel. Because even if it's a sin, it feels like heaven." I tore off the stream of shameful truths as he pressed his fingers to my lips.

"Stand up," he instructed me.

Slowly, I followed his instructions, standing beside the bed. He settled himself on the end of the mattress, thick, muscular thighs digging into the edge, and reached for me. He stroked his fingers over my cheeks and then cupped my face. Those hands slid downward and ringed my neck. His forehead rested on mine, and his chest expanded like he was breathing me in. Right then, in that loaded, wavering moment, my stomach let out a loud growl.

I cringed, and Massimo chuckled.

"Have you eaten today?"

I shook my head. I didn't want to talk about food. I was still lingering in that place where he'd coaxed my body while I was sleeping. So close to coming I could cry.

"I brought you something to eat. You don't like the hot food, right?"

"It's drugged."

He sighed. "Of course it is. Motherfuckers. Let's get you something to eat."

"No," I protested.

He stilled and looked down at me.

"I want to eat—after."

He waited. Embarrassment burned through me, but I'd come too far to back out now. Instead, I took his hand and placed it shyly between my legs.

"After," I repeated. "Please."

He was quiet for a moment and then shifted closer, sliding the hand I'd placed on my pussy lower between my legs, and his middle finger curved in, slipping just inside my entrance, pinning me in place.

"You want to come first, angel?"

I nodded wildly as his finger teased me, dipping in and out shallowly.

"Your wish is my command," he murmured, and lowered a hand to his robes. He parted them and pushed down the pants beneath. "I guess I'll eat first, then," he murmured as his cock slapped up his belly, long and hard. He backed up, sat on the bed, and then lay down. He barely fit.

His robes covered everything except for a slice of his lower belly and his cock, pale against the black underneath.

"Come here," he demanded, holding his hand out to me.

I hesitantly approached.

"Sit," he prompted.

I lingered, unsure what to do. I went to sit on the edge of the bed, despite there only being a few inches of space left.

"Not there. Sit up here. On my face."

"What?" I gasped, startled by his words. They were filthy and hot.

"Sit. On. My. Face. I won't tell you again," he warned, and tugged me toward the head of the bed.

Before I knew it, he was lifting me over him, leaving my knees to rest on the mattress on either side of his head. I knelt up as high as I could, horrified by his lewd imagination but curious at the same time.

"And you were the girl telling me you weren't naive only a week ago," he reminded me.

I peered down at his face nestled between my thighs.

"I'm not!" I protested meekly, but really, he wasn't wrong. There was a whole world of sex that I had no idea about.

"Sure you aren't."

I jerked at a soft pinch on my ass and lowered just enough to feel his hot breath on my bare pussy. I lifted back up as much as I could, but his hand quickly clamped on to my hips and held me in place.

"I'm not making fun of you, Katarina. I'm appreciating you. I told you before I want to be all your firsts . . . I want to teach you everything. Now, let me teach you how to ride my fucking face until you drown me. Suffocate me so I can see heaven before I die."

He yanked me down at that, and I squeaked, falling forward

and bracing my hands on the bed. His tongue licked up my slit then slipped inside me, fucking my entrance before heading up to my clit. I shook as he rolled it between his lips.

It was too good. I couldn't stand it.

"Massimo!" I cried, clamping a hand over my mouth a moment too late. I had to get a grip. Anyone could walk past and hear.

"Yes, angel? I fucking love the way you beg, it's so sweet," he murmured, and then bit the inside of my thigh. "But it won't get you any mercy."

He returned to driving me insane, his mouth working overtime to lick and suck and torture me.

He slapped my ass suddenly, and I sank farther down with a yelp.

"Stop trying to squirm away and ride my fucking face."

I could feel myself rising. I was going to come already, embarrassment be damned. There was nothing I could do about it. Except just before I crested over that wave of pleasure, Massimo moved his tongue and kissed the inside of my thigh.

"Hey!" I protested.

"I told you to ride my face and take what you want . . . you're not coming until you do that."

"What?" I demanded. "Why?"

"Because you need to stop hiding from your pleasure, your body . . . from taking what you want. Stop worrying what other people are thinking."

I sighed. Like it was so easy to change habits you'd had for a lifetime. Like it was so easy to go against my programming.

Another slap on my ass had me crying out. It didn't hurt half as bad as it should.

"No sighing at the teacher, my little stray."

I huffed and pushed myself up to my feet. I looked down at his face, taking in his smug grin.

"What? You're going to try and get away without coming? Can you stand it?"

Nope, but I was tired of being the only one who was an undignified mess. The image of him yesterday when he'd come on my panties, his face exquisitely tortured, returned to me. Hmm, that was right. I didn't need to even use my imagination to torture him right back. I held on to the wall and turned around so I was facing his feet, and then I sat back down, lowering my pussy to hover just over his face again.

"Decided to be a good girl after all?" he murmured.

I could feel his wicked smirk on my skin. He was enjoying my discomfort way too much.

Time to even the playing field. Shifting my ass backward, I leaned forward and rested a hand on his thigh. It flexed, hard as stone, even through his pants.

His cock was still harder than ever, and when I put a finger out to touch it, it leapt against his belly.

"What do you think you're doing, *micetta*?"

"Giving you a taste of your own medicine," I called back, then leaned down and licked up the side of his dick.

He went still at that first, hesitant touch. I angled his dick so it was easier to lick the head. He tasted musky and salty and not bad at all. Something deep inside me hungered for more of that taste as soon as I drew back.

I leaned back down and closed my lips around the tip of him, hollowing my cheeks and carefully pushing my mouth down around him, taking in as much as I could manage.

"Fuck," he muttered, his voice muffled beneath my pussy. "Are you trying to drive me insane?"

"Mm-hmm, keep me company," I murmured, popping off his dick, only to return to the same position.

I bobbed up and down, going on nothing but instinct. It wasn't polished. It wasn't smooth. I went too far down and choked when his rounded end pressed into the back of my throat, and was rewarded with Massimo's soft curse. Gradually, while I'd been concentrating on turning him on as much as he turned me on, I'd started to grind on his face. I'd forgotten my embarrassment; I'd forgotten everything but how good it felt.

He fucked my clit with his long, probing tongue as I licked his dick, sucking and tasting and enjoying the way his thighs twitched beneath my hands.

I started to rise again, and this time there was no stopping me. I closed my hand around the base of his dick and pumped the shaft, sucking on the head. My orgasm hit me like a freight train. I clenched my thighs around Massimo's head and moaned around his cock. I writhed on him, working my hips on his face to draw out my orgasm, making stars explode in the darkness all around me.

I still pulsed with pleasure all over when a tug on my hair pulled my head back and his dick from my mouth.

"Good girl, you came all over my fucking face, and it was the hottest thing I've ever seen or tasted. Now it's your turn, little stray. You said you were hungry . . . swallow me down, every single drop."

He guided my head back to his dick, and I sank down, enclosing him in my mouth. I returned my hand to pumping him, and he twitched under my fingers. He swore now, a litany of curses leaving his sinful lips, urging me on, praising me. It sounded like a prayer.

Then he gave a guttural cry, and his body tensed. His dick seemed to expand in my mouth, pulsing along my tongue, and then he was coming. My mouth filled with hot, salty liquid. It was new, foreign and strange. Globs of it fell from the sides of my mouth where my lips were stretched around him. He came and came, filling my mouth and making it run over.

"Swallow, angel. Fill that empty belly up with me."

23

MASSIMO

The next day, the police arrived a couple of hours after the anonymous call was placed, courtesy of my IT guy.

From the attic room, I watched them pull up outside the institute just before lunch. Dark clouds gathered, and the sun had barely broken the gloom all day.

Two cars drew up, and a couple of officers and detectives entered the building below. Calling in the police made things difficult for me, but there was no other way to deal with Benedict's disappearance.

Besides, it was time to leave Hallow Hall, and it couldn't be allowed to continue the way it was. It had to be shut down.

I sat on an old crate, my sniper rifle in hand, and rested the butt on the floor. In all my years in war-torn areas providing aid and emergency relief, I'd seen a lot of dark shit. A lot of things that would haunt my nightmares for a long time to come . . . but Hallow Hall might be the absolute worst.

The men who ruled this place weren't at war. They weren't scrambling to survive, or to protect, or even to conquer and take power.

They were merely indulging in their perversions and making money while doing it, while hiding behind a mantle of holiness to deceive their victims.

They were the worst people I'd ever encountered, and that was really saying something.

I watched the police walk around outside the institute studying the footprints at certain spots, looking at the fence and the security cameras installed high up on the walls. I knew they wouldn't find anything on them. Those were purely for show.

The snow started to come down harder, turning the air white. The surrounding trees were absolutely covered in it, their branches pushing against the power lines that ran along the back of the building.

I was just about to go and make sure the cops would find what I wanted them to find when the power went out.

The attic room plunged into darkness, and exclamations of shock and screams echoed around the building below.

The day seemed to get gloomier outside as Hallow Hall went dark.

It felt like a bad omen.

I found Katarina in the dining hall setting up candles. Tatiana, the little ragamuffin who was usually glued to Katarina's side, tripped along in her shadow. When she saw me, my angel drifted toward the window as nonchalantly as possible, crossing her arms and staring out at the storm. She wore the same faded, dingy white sweatpants and T-shirt she always did, and yet, in the glowing candlelight, she glowed like the sun. I understood now . . . that glow had nothing to do with her obvious beauty. It came from within. The only thing the darkness ever really loved was the light. We were evidence of that.

"Have they asked you anything yet?" I wondered, stopping beside Katarina to gaze out the window.

She shook her head.

"They've only just finished with Pavol and Dr. Blackwood. They're looking around in Benedict's office."

I nodded. That was all to be expected. Italian police weren't exactly known for their efficiency, a fact that I'd taken plenty of advantage of in the past. However, now, when I wanted them to discover something, they dragged their feet. Typical.

Tatiana tugged on my cassock. The little girl had gotten over her initial fright of me, and now nothing stopped her from speaking to me whenever we crossed paths.

"What do you call a bear with no teeth?" she asked solemnly. She was slowly working her way through her list of jokes.

"I don't know, what do you call a bear with no teeth?"

"A gummy bear," she said, and then giggled.

The sound was too sweet and pure for this place, and I couldn't help but smile.

"So, what's the plan?" Katarina murmured.

She lingered at my side, pretending to fiddle with a box of matches. She looked beautiful in candlelight. She looked beautiful in all lights, actually. I fought the urge to touch her.

"We wait. We play along . . . and see where the police are taking this."

"Won't Pavol tell them about you? You're not supposed to be here," she said quietly.

Was she worried about me? I didn't know how to respond to that. I wasn't sure if anyone had ever worried about me.

"Neither are they. Vargas was excommunicated from the church," I told her. I hadn't mentioned it before. I hadn't wanted to set her off worrying about her mother, seeing as she'd apparently been such a devoted follower of his.

Her eyes widened. She took a moment to process that information. I'd just heard from Giada this morning regarding Pavol's and Benedict's backgrounds, and they were no less shocking.

"Both Pavol and Benedict worked in medicine before losing their licenses and joining the Church. They barely made it a year before dropping out. They're cosplaying as holy men and using it as an excuse to do whatever they want. This place has no connection with the Church anymore."

She stared at me, as shocked as if I'd just told her that the world was flat. I suppose in her own way, I had. Her world as she'd known it for three years was never as she'd believed it to be.

"Sister Vera?"

"A former nun who left in disgrace."

Katarina shook her head, stunned.

"Soon, Pavol won't be a problem, and there will be no record I was ever here. But their investigation into what's been happening here will see it shut down." I was confident the police would at least do that much. Even if they were somehow on the payroll of Hallow Hall or Centrium Group, not everyone in the department could be, and I already had stories ready to leak in major national papers that would force scrutiny.

Hallow Hall was finished.

"I-I can't believe it," Katarina said numbly. "My mother has no idea. I mean, I don't think she does. She always held Vargas in high regard. Always at the front during sermons, always volunteering, always giving our last spare penny to the collection plate." She shook her head ruefully. "Now she'll have to see how wrong believing him was. It'll break her heart."

I held my tongue, the truth weighing on my conscience. *Fuck.* How was I supposed to tell her the truth right now? Since I'd found out about her mother, we'd been under constant threat. Katarina's meltdown in bed, the tears that had threatened to wash her away, weren't gone. They were lying in wait. Waiting for her to be free of this place and process all the terrible things that had happened to her here. To heap her mother's death on top of that was unthinkable. I wouldn't do it. Not now.

"Let's worry about the real world when we get out of here and not before, okay? One thing at a time, *micetta*."

She blew out a long breath and nodded. Fucking hell, she was strong. She'd just had her world tilted yet another time, and she was already adjusting.

She was an impressive woman . . . and all mine.

"Did you leave your . . . evidence?"

"I'm betting this whole place is crawling with evidence once they dig deeper, but I'm about to do that now. Nothing says 'investigate further' than finding a freezer with organs hidden in the fridge in the kitchen."

She wrinkled her nose, maybe wondering for a moment how I'd removed said organs. The answer to that would be badly . . . but no one was going to use Benedict's rotten old organs anyway. They were just the smoking gun to push the detectives into a full investigation here at Hallow Hall.

Tatiana wandered off to color, and Katarina remained by my side.

"I should go with her."

I nodded.

She continued to loiter. "We never talked about the money in the safe . . . I was supposed to figure out the combination and pay you what I could."

I raised an eyebrow at her teasingly. "Are you telling me you haven't already done that? I told you I don't work for free."

She flushed, her gaze dropping to the floor before rising back to my eyes. "I'll get the money somehow. I promised, and I'll keep that promise."

I fought a grin. She had no idea.

"I'm not interested in your money. You haven't worked that out yet?"

She chuckled awkwardly. "I know . . . all my firsts, too. But we've almost covered them all, haven't we? I mean . . . except for the—main event."

Her cheeks were pink as a rose petal. My chest ached at the sight. An ache that seemed to grow the longer I was around her. The only thing that soothed it was to hold her tight against me.

"But there are so many firsts to cover . . . an infinite number, really," I murmured. "First apartment . . . first trip abroad. First marriage and first honeymoon . . . first boy, and first girl. First retirement . . . first funeral."

My words had struck her dumb. She just stared at me. I lost the battle of not touching her and reached out to push one hanging lock of hair behind her ear.

"I have many firsts to take from you. A lifetime's worth."

She opened her mouth, probably about to protest, but I stepped away.

"I'll find you later. Be a good girl and keep your head down. Stay out of trouble . . . even though I know it's hard for you." With a wink, I turned away and headed out of the room.

I had detectives to make suspicious.

I returned to the attic room once I'd poked around and seen where the detectives were in their investigation. They were going through the papers in Benedict's office while Pavol and Dr. Blackwood watched silently from the hallway. Blackwood I still didn't have a good read on, but Pavol was sweating bullets. He mumbled to himself, pulling at his collar and generally looking like a guilty bastard. It seemed he'd also been partaking in the spiked wine from their private lounge.

I made sure not to be seen. I didn't want the detectives to come asking me anything. To fix the mess I'd gotten into with the unplanned killing of Benedict, I needed to get out of here clean . . . and take Katarina with me. I had a hunch that Pavol wouldn't say anything about me. He thought I was here to keep an eye on him on behalf of Centrium Group. He wouldn't want to rattle his sponsor's cage.

I'd had a few close calls in my years building my reputation as L'Ombra, but this was the closest. I was invested because of Katarina. I was worried because of Katarina. I was taking risks because of Katarina.

For the first time since I was a teenager, I had something to lose, and it was making me impulsive and uncontrolled.

The stairs to the room at the very top creaked ominously, and it was nearly pitch-black except for the candle I was holding to light the way. The window of the attic room showed the denseness of the falling snow.

I went to it and looked down as candles were lit in the chapel below, barely visible through the snowstorm.

I stood aside and watched the patients of Hallow Hall file into the small chapel on the snowy grounds. The detectives had just left. The snow was really coming down now, but Pavol hadn't canceled the vigil he'd decided to hold for Benedict. It was performative, of course. Pavol was paranoid about the cops and what they might find wrong with Hallow Hall. He was going out of his way to appear above suspicion.

As for me and Katarina, we would have to wait until tomorrow for the detectives to find the most vital evidence. I had done what I could to shut this place down. It would have to be enough. I pulled my phone from my pocket and dialed a number.

It rang a few times before a familiar voice sounded over the line.

"Lucciano residence." The words were followed by a long, hacking cough and throat clearing.

"Paolo, you sound like the Crypt Keeper."

"Well, isn't this place a crypt? No one ever comes here except me," Paolo, my housekeeper going on ten years, said with contempt.

"Well, don't get too excited, but I need you to get the house ready for a guest."

"Which ex-military friend is it this time? Are they going to sleep on the floor again, or should I make up a bed?"

"She's not ex-military," I told him, and silence came over the line. "She's not just a friend, either."

A low chuckle sounded. "*She*? Well, that's a different story. Should I make up the guest room or . . . will the lady be staying with you?"

"With me, from now on."

Paolo's voice was warm now. "Certainly, I will see to that immediately. Do you happen to know what her favorite flowers are? Wine, fabrics, books, foods?"

The rapid-fire questions made me chuckle.

"I don't know any of that, but I will in time. For now—snowdrops. She likes spring flowers."

"Ah, yes, snowdrops, a symbol of resilience and fresh beginnings, resurrection. A beautiful choice."

"Calm down and don't go over the top. You're not a cartoon

clock trying to make Beauty fall for the beast. I can handle that part."

He sniffed. "So you say. When can I expect you?"

"Tomorrow."

He squawked in protest and promptly hung up.

I pocketed my phone and made my way downstairs toward the chapel for the vigil.

I joined the end of the snaking line of patients forced out in the snow and followed them into the drafty chapel.

Instead of sitting at the back, I took the creaky stairs upward to the gallery. It was dark up there, and the air was close. Incense and the oily scent of the lamps and candles permeated the air. I walked to the edge of the barrier and stared down. Below me, patients from Hallow Hall continued to mill about and find seats. One drew my eye immediately. With her long blond hair strewn around her shoulders like golden satin and her curious eyes, my gaze found Katarina right away.

Ah, there she is. My angel.

She glanced around. Searching for me. As soon as her gaze hit mine, her shoulders relaxed a little and a faint smile touched her lips.

No one looked at me the way she did. Like I was her savior. Like I was a man who might one day be worthy of a real life, a family, and all the things I'd long ago given up hoping for. And suddenly, I couldn't be without her for one more second. Tomorrow, I'd take her from this place and bring her home. My home would be her home. And she would be mine. A home at last. It was more than a man like me could dream of.

I lifted a hand and crooked my finger at her. She dropped my gaze. Would my little angel obey the call of her devil?

She turned and started to walk upstream to the people flooding into the chapel. Anticipation roared in my veins as I waited for her to appear at the top of the creaking stairs. A quick scan reassured me that no one in charge had noticed her slipping past.

That meant that for the duration of the mass, she was all mine.

She walked up the stairs, her white sweatshirt and pale hair glowing in the candlelight.

I was sitting in the second pew from the front, invisible from below.

Music played downstairs, a shitty organ recording, while the chatter died down among Pavol's congregation. The man wasn't even a real priest, so how he thought he could lead a mass was beyond me.

Katarina walked unerringly across the rough floorboards toward me. She was a woman who looked better in the graying, old institute uniform than other women did in head-to-toe couture. Her goodness glowed, and she was smiling at me. My heart beat fast. My palms dampened. I was a nervous schoolboy watching the most beautiful girl in town approach, but this time, she'd chosen me.

Me, the worthless sinner. Me, the original stray.

"What are you doing up here?" she asked, sinking down into the pew next to me.

I threaded my fingers between hers. This was a hand that deserved the finest jewelry money could buy. When we got out of here, I'd spoil my angel rotten.

"Waiting for you," I told her, and pressed a kiss to the back of her hand. "Waiting to be alone together."

I parted my lips and grazed my teeth against her skin. A gentle bite. She jumped, and then her cheeks flushed, a wave of pretty, innocent pink washing up her neck. Since I'd become a connoisseur of her body, I recognized it as the same pale dusty rose of her nipples. I wanted to paint my bedroom in that shade and see it every day.

"What? Father Lucciano, don't tell me you're interested to hear what a disgraced former psychiatrist has to say about God?" Katarina teased. With intense interest, she watched my lips brush her hand.

I shrugged. "What can I say? I guess I'm going to hell, but I'm not interested in lessons on morals from a man like Pavol . . . I'm here for something more."

She raised an eyebrow. "Such as?"

"You," I murmured. This woman had taken over my thoughts effortlessly, and I was a slave at her command.

She smiled, a small, secret thing, and then wet her lips.

"What for?" she wondered.

I dropped her hand and patted my lap.

"Come sit here and I'll show you."

A grin twisted her lips, and she stood just to move over and sink down on my lap. I cradled her back to my chest and hugged her closely. It reminded me of the morning after we'd signed our deal with a bloody kiss, when Blackwood had given her an MDMA-laced sedative that had made her desperate to be touched.

My cock stiffened at just the memory of that first, desperate touch of hers. I'd been determined not to participate in her frenzied reach for relief, and yet had come in my goddamn pants like a teenager.

She gasped as I flexed my cock on her ass. Her weight on me was sweet torture.

She evidently felt the same, because she moved tentatively on me. I wrapped one arm around her waist and pressed my face into the nape of her neck, using the other hand to collect the heavy fall of her hair into a rope and tug her head to the side. My mouth found the delicate skin under her ear, and I traced it with my lips, and then tongue. She squirmed, rubbing my cock with her cunt, hidden from me by the many layers between us. This was going too far. I was too hungry for her. One wrong decision and my mask of control would shatter, and I'd take her against the wall beside us and not care who knew it.

"Stop now, unless you want to be fucked in this church during mass," I said.

She paused before deliberately gyrating again. I hissed through my teeth.

"I'm not joking, angel."

"Well, neither am I," Katarina said, and looked over her shoulder at me. Her eyes were hooded, her lips pink and rosy with arousal. "I'm so tired of being scared and worried. I want to feel something good. I want to feel you."

I closed my eyes for a moment, her words sinking through my worthless body and embedding in my soul.

"Angel . . . you—you'll be the death of me, and I'll go smiling," I whispered, and slid the hand I had on her waist under the elastic of her sweatpants.

Her panties were damp. My girl was wet and desperate for me.

I inched my fingers under that cotton and finally found her cunt, hot and wet and mine.

Ghosting my fingers leisurely down her slit, I watched her close her eyes and gasp softly. I nipped her earlobe with my teeth.

"Don't be a naughty girl in church. Pay attention," I teased, and sank a finger inside her.

She was still tight, but there was something about that slick grip that told me she'd accommodate me. Because she wanted it to be me. She wanted me inside her.

The thought nearly shredded my last vestige of self-control.

"Lose the bottom half," I told her in a rough whisper. I unbuttoned my cassock, jerking down the fly of my pants and pulling my drooling cock free.

She stood between my legs and jerked down her pants and panties. I cupped her beautiful ass, pulling the cheeks apart to see her pretty holes.

"I can't wait for you one more day, *micetta*. I've been waiting for you my entire life, and I'm finished. You've ruined me," I murmured.

I tugged her back to my lap, this time facing me. I cupped her face and kissed her. She settled herself on me, her bare pussy pressing against my red, angry cock. Nothing between us, finally.

She slid up and down me, coating me with her juices, until I was slick and ready. I dipped my hips and angled the head of my cock just inside her. I fucked her shallowly, just the tip entering her sacred cunt. My hand strayed to her clit, and I rubbed it in slow, deliberate circles.

She whimpered, a soft, vulnerable thing, and I twisted her head with my free hand to hold her mouth near mine.

"What do you want, Katarina?" I asked.

"I want more," she moaned on my lips. "I want all of it."

"Not here," I whispered. I had grand plans for fucking this girl for the first time. I needed my own bed and uninterrupted time . . . days of it. I needed a bath nearby to ease the aches, and fresh sheets to make her comfortable on again before I fucked her once more. I needed time to fit her cunt to me so carefully, she'd understand that it could never take in someone else. I had to make her as desperate for me as I was for her.

"Yes, here. I'm tired of everything but," she grumbled, attempting to sink farther onto me.

"Oh, you are, are you?" At her disgruntled tone, a chuckle rose in my chest.

"Yes, I am. I want more, and you're going to give it to me," she announced against my lips.

I could feel her smile stretching over mine.

"Hmm," I said, the desire to do just that burning through me.

The effort of holding back was nearly painful. The lower half of my cock throbbed and burned, desperate to be buried inside the object of my obsession. My addiction. My fascination. My affection. She was all of them at once.

"You think I'll just give you what you want? We have no protection, angel." It had been so long since I'd fucked someone I didn't even carry condoms, and I certainly didn't bring any on a job. That part of my life had fallen away, not that I'd been overly interested in it to begin with. Still, as the throes of youth faded, my drive for vengeance, and to find a good way to die, had overtaken everything else inside my head. Even my body had been subject to that strict control.

"I don't care. I haven't had a period in years," she said.

That stilled me. "You haven't? That's something we'll have to see to, *micetta*," I said, breathing on her forehead, concern tugging at me. "When we get out of here, I'm going to take good care of you, angel. You just have to let me."

She pushed down on me once more, taking advantage of my stillness to make me sink farther inside.

She moaned, half pain, half pleasure; she passed the halfway point, and gravity sank her down the rest of the way, then she was fully seated on my cock.

I felt her barrier break. This first she'd given me, she'd given without fear. It was a mighty gesture. A fearsome thing. I wasn't sure I'd ever met a braver woman than Katarina Dmitrova, a girl who could still smile and joke and laugh and love after all she'd been through. A woman who saw right through the act I put on for others to the tarnished soul I really was, and still take me inside herself.

"Fuck," I muttered, and pulled her closer to my chest. Her cunt squeezed my cock like it was trying to snap it right off. It was painful, honestly, and she had to feel the same.

"Does it hurt?" I asked.

She nodded. She had her hands curled in fists on her lap, and her body tensed, absorbing the pain.

"It hurts me to hurt you," I admitted, a whispered confession. "But I don't mind it."

"Because?"

"Important things . . . hurt. Life-changing things *hurt*. So hurt . . . and hurt me back, so we'll always remember it. This, and us, together here. The beginning of it all." My words traced against her temple.

She shook in my arms, held together through sheer determination and desire.

I circled her clit again, and slowly, oh so slowly, the tension melted from her. Her cunt stopped trying to strangle me, and new wetness flooded down my shaft. I lifted her an inch and then let her fall.

Her breath stuttered, and she grimaced.

"I know I'm big, but I know you can take me. No one else could fit me like you do. We were designed to fit," I said to her, lifting her and lowering, lifting and lowering, all while rubbing her clit.

She started to move on her own, her inner muscles cramping less now and sucking me in instead.

"That's it. That's perfect. Fuck, you are perfect, inside and out," I said on her lips and kissed her.

Below, Pavol droned on in his fake mass, reading words he had no right to. It could have felt wrong. Craven, even, to be joined like this with Katarina in a holy place . . . but it didn't.

It felt sacred. It felt like a benediction. She was my salvation and all I needed.

Slowly, she grew more confident, rising and falling and fucking me with abandon. The sound of flesh slapping filled the air, and I could only hope they couldn't hear it below, because I wasn't stopping. No fucking way. Not when I was this close to heaven.

I thrust up into her as she rode me hard, moving instinctively on me, bucking her hips and finding her rhythm. When I pulled away from the kiss, she let out a moan that I was sure was going to send someone up here to investigate. Then I'd have to stop to carve their eyes out right there, before the cross, for daring to look at my angel when she came undone. I slid my hand over her mouth, silencing her moans, and she licked at the pads of my fingers, working me faster and faster. She'd never done this before, and yet, nature had taken over. Her body urging her to take what it needed, driving her to come, pushing her onward. It was the greatest thing I'd ever experienced. Transcendent.

Her eyes bulged as she got close, and worry flashed across her brow.

"It's okay, Kat. You're going to come, and I'm going to be right here, holding you when you do. Nothing can hurt you. No one can take you. I'm here, and I won't let you go," I whispered to her.

Her eyes fluttered shut, and I felt her lips mouth my name against my hand. Then she tightened all around me. Her pussy squeezed tight, sealing me inside her, and she went rigid in my arms.

I couldn't hold back one more second. Cum surged, hot as lava and fast as lightning from my balls and into her. I came endlessly, locked in a moment of perfect peace. The feeling of her all around me, my arms filled with her, the smell of her skin in my nose, the peace and quiet of the church, the drone of the faraway mass . . . Even the wooden pew beneath me was comfortable.

A perfect moment, frozen in time, ours forever.

When she was peaceful, her body slack and sated, I carefully pulled off my dog tags, on a long chain and never missing from my neck, and reached for the small necklace she always wore. It was a tiny crucifix on a chain. I took the cross off and slid it onto the chain holding my dog tags. There. Both of us together on the chain. The symbol of my commitment to this woman. For years, abroad in foreign lands, I hadn't cared if I lived or died. Only the dog tags would be left to identify my body. Wherever they fell, that's where my body would take its last breath and finally leave this world. Now, though, they were no longer mine to hold. They were hers . . . as was my life. Now, she held it in the palm of her hand.

I passed the chain over her head and tucked it into her sweater.

"What's this?"

"Let's call it a promise." I smoothed her hair back.

Below, the patients of Hallow Hall shuffled to their feet and started to sing.

"Are your garments spotless? Are they white as snow?

Are you washed in the blood of the Lamb?"

"Tonight, rest and recover, save your strength," I said to Kat when she drew back with a contented sigh.

"And tomorrow?"

"Tomorrow, we finish what we started." I tucked her hair tenderly behind her ear. "Then we get the fuck out of here and never look back."

24

KATARINA

If Hallow Hall was spooky at the best of times, with harsh fluorescents, TVs blasting from rec rooms, and radios blaring at nurses' stations, it was downright eerie in the tomb-like dark.

Candles were dotted along the corridors, but not enough to illuminate the gloom, since there was little to no light coming in through the windows. The snow swirled angrily. Would this sudden snowstorm kill all those brave snowdrops pushing through the frozen ground? Would it kill the bud on the tree outside?

I stared out at the white filling the air like cotton wool, strangely transfixed by it. It was beautiful and dangerous. The most alluring combination.

Without my meaning for it to, my mind shifted to Massimo.

His words from before were pinned in place in my mind, never far out of sight. Our agreement was just that, a deal I'd struck with a devil. It wasn't something real.

Right?

"But there are so many firsts to cover . . . an infinite number, really. First apartment . . . first trip abroad. First marriage and first honeymoon . . . first boy, and first girl. First retirement . . . first funeral."

My pulse thudded hard at the thought of him. I'd started to look for him in every room. I felt safe knowing he was nearby. Tendrils of feelings had started to stretch out between us, invisible but strong. I'd thought those creeping feelings had only been going in one direction, from me to him.

What if I was wrong? What if he felt it, too?

"Good night!" Tatiana called to me as she walked down the hall with one of the nurses, holding her hand.

I nodded to the nurse. She was one of the good ones. One of the ones who was clueless about the darker side of Hallow Hall. She mostly cared for the very elderly, the patients whom Benedict and Pavol didn't mess with. Hallow Hall's function as a nursing home was its only positive contribution to the world, and I was pretty sure it was only used as a cover for its real purpose.

"Good night, I'll see you in the morning," I called back to her.

She nodded. "Maybe we'll get to go outside and make a snow bunny!"

"A snow bunny? Why not a snowman?"

"A man is too big," Tatiana said wisely, and waved one more time before skipping off.

She nearly ran right into Dr. Blackwood, who was coming the other way. He approached and stood at the window beside me.

"Some storm, isn't it? The heavens are angry."

I slid him a sideways look. "So, you believe in all that? I never pegged you for the religious type."

"I suppose I believe as much as you, or any other bystander. In a lofty, esoteric way."

I considered those words and shook my head. "My faith isn't lofty or esoteric. I believe in God. I believe in a wrathful, vengeful God. I believe in hell for sinners. I believe they burn. Do you?"

I turned to look at him.

He chuckled and shook his head. "No. I don't believe I do, at the end of the day. I don't believe in any of it, when you put it like that."

"Then why work here?"

Blackwood raised an eyebrow at me. "To help people."

I stared at him for a long time. "I can't tell if you're being sarcastic or not."

He sighed and tilted his head to the side. "I don't want to upset you, Katarina, but the way you're acting is very close to how you do when you're off your medication. Are you sure Father Lucciano has been diligent in making sure you take it?"

I simply nodded.

"I noticed he was conspicuously absent when the police were here," Blackwood continued.

"Why would he get involved with Hallow Hall business? He's barely been here a minute," I said as casually as I could.

"And yet, two men in charge have either died or disappeared in that time."

I shrugged. I felt like Blackwood could see right through me.

He shifted and checked his watch. "It doesn't matter. I'm here to come and get you. Father Pavol wants to talk to you."

Fear immediately streaked through me. Go and see Pavol now? There was nothing I wanted less. Did he suspect me? Did he know what we'd done last night?

An orderly appeared beside Blackwood.

"Come on now, Katarina, don't be difficult."

I bit my tongue as the orderly took my arm in a firm grip. Running away wasn't going to help matters. I had nowhere to go. Massimo was around here somewhere. Just the thought comforted me. After three years alone in this place, having an ally felt better than I ever could have imagined.

"Okay, sure. Let's go."

• • •

Pavol was in his treatment room. As soon as I stepped in, the claustrophobic air suffocated me. Candles burned on every surface. Pavol sat at his desk, drinking from a wineglass and tapping at the surface of his phone.

"Why is nothing fucking working?" he snapped as Blackwood stepped in.

The orderly stayed by my side, his gaze blank and uninterested in the scene before him.

Whatever Hallow Hall was becoming, it was clear that the veneer of professionalism was fading day by day.

Pavol looked at me and narrowed his eyes. "Weren't you the last person to see Benedict? What do you know?"

I put a hand to my chest, feigning shock. "Father Benedict? I have no idea. Has something happened to him?"

Pavol glared at me and stood. He rounded the desk, slurping down more of the wine, and stopped just in front of me.

"You know, Katarina, you are one of the longest-residing patients in this place. All these years and all these treatments, and it seems you still lie like a sinner . . . and look like a siren, ready to steal the soul of the good men who try to help you."

He reached out and touched my hair. When I flinched, he grabbed a fist of it and yanked my head forward. The sudden attack had my pulse hammering. I hadn't expected it. I'd gotten so used to the usual routine of abuse from Pavol that I had stopped thinking of him as someone capable of strength.

That had clearly been a mistake.

"You, bitch, have been a thorn in my side and a fucking cocktease for years. 'Katarina's off limits'—it's all I've heard for years and years." He sneered at me. "Like you're so special."

"Why am I off limits?" I burst out, desperate to finally know. It was a question that had haunted me for so long, I couldn't stand not knowing the answer.

"You really don't know? You're such a dumb bitch." He yanked my head farther down, and it was now nearly between my legs. "Blackwood," he snapped. "Hurry up. Let's see if Benedict really made any progress or not."

Before I could open my mouth to scream or try to move . . . I felt it.

A sharp prick in the back of my neck and then a piercing feeling.

I finally got the scream out, but my head was pushed down too far for it to be a loud one. Blackwood injected something into my neck, and Pavol held my head there until it started to swim. He let go when my body slumped, tension leaving my muscles.

A veil of fog descended over my mind, heavy and thick, coating things and leaving me numb.

I couldn't think. I couldn't focus on anything. Pieces of me were falling through my fingers and I couldn't hold on to them.

They fell, and so did I.

PART II

PURGATORIO

And I shall sing about that second realm
Where human spirits purge themselves from stain,
Becoming worthy to ascend to Heaven.

—Dante, *The Divine Comedy*

25

KATARINA

I woke suddenly, or at least my consciousness did. My thoughts were scattered, and I had the feeling like I'd just restarted my brain. My neck ached and my head throbbed. The floor beneath me spun sickeningly as I blinked. When I was able to focus on the room, two male voices were arguing.

Slowly, I straightened up and glanced around. *Where am I?* I felt like I'd just woken from a long sleep, but I wasn't in bed. I didn't know where I was.

Rise and shine! Finally you join me.

I jumped. The voice spoke quietly, but the sound carried from wherever she was sitting. I glanced around looking for the person who had spoken.

I was in an office, and there were shelves with medical texts along one wall, and a leather sofa. In the corner was a privacy screen. I stared at that the longest. It was familiar, somehow. Candles burned all around. Outside the window, the sky looked black and white. There was no woman. Whoever had spoken must have left. Confusion pressed down on me, making me feel small.

A man in a black priest's robe stood before me, his face flushed. He stared over my shoulder at someone else.

"Katarina, how are you feeling?" a deep voice asked from behind me.

I swung around to see whoever had spoken. A man in a white lab coat. I peered between him and the man dressed like a priest, perplexed. What the hell had I been doing when I'd fallen asleep? Was I sick?

No. They are.

I spun around again. It was the woman's voice. But no one stood there. Unease crept through me, and my palms began to sweat. My chest felt like I couldn't draw a full breath.

"Katarina," the priest urged me to answer.

"Okay." What else could I say? Okay, but I think I might be hearing a voice inside my head? Okay, but I lost my mind somewhere and don't know where to find it?

"That's good," the man in the white lab coat said, moving in front of me and shining a small light into my eyes like a doctor.

Ah, that made sense. He was a doctor.

"Do you remember why you're here?" he asked.

I opened my mouth and froze. The answer was just there, not far from my lips, but it was held back somehow. I couldn't quite reach it. I shook my head slowly.

The man in the priest's robes smiled. A nameplate sat on the desk behind him.

Father Pavol. *Pavol.* I waited for some feeling of recognition at the name, but it didn't come. Fear skittered through me. My head felt painfully empty.

"That's fast-acting. Excellent. I need to send word to the director that we've at least achieved one thing with all this shit going on."

"I don't think the director will be very impressed in the end, seeing as you've somehow managed to let the cops in here on your watch," the other man said sharply, a name embroidered on his lapel.

Dr. Blackwood.

Pavol sneered at him. "What do you know about everything I've been handling here? It's not your place to worry about the director or the business. You're just here to keep the patients alive until we want them otherwise."

Get out of here. Now, the woman's voice whispered in my ear, and this time I didn't wait to see where it was coming from. I trusted her somehow.

Blackwood shook his head and reached into his pocket.

"You still think that, don't you? You still don't know who works for the director and who works for you."

Pavol paled. "Lucciano works for the director, that's why he was sent here."

Blackwood pulled his hand from his pocket, something black and shiny in his grip. A gun. I froze at the sight. The doctor had moved around the far side of the room, his eyes locked on Father Pavol.

He shook his head and sighed.

"It was never Lucciano. He's here for training. It was never the guy before him, either. It was always me. And the director is fucking sick of your flagrant mismanagement. I'm afraid he's going to have to let you go."

I watched through my dreamlike confusion as Blackwood raised the gun toward Pavol and, before the priest could step away, shot him in the chest.

The sound was suppressed by a silencer, but I still jumped. Pavol reared back from the impact, careening into the table behind him and knocking over the multitude of candles. His numerous bottles of spirits also fell, some smashing on the floor. The fallen candles made contact with the spilled liquid, and with a loud whoosh Pavol went up in flames.

I jumped up, backing away as the burning man flailed around the room. The curtains went up next.

"Jesus, what an idiot, he can't even die gracefully," Blackwood muttered, and took my arm in a steellike grip. He guided me from the room as thick smoke clogged the air. The windows shattered behind us, oxygen feeding the blaze. A scream rent the air, and it took a long moment to understand that it was coming from me.

Blackwood went for a fire extinguisher on the wall and tried to go back in, but he soon gave up. I edged away from him up the hall, watching him tuck the gun away somewhere under his coat.

"Fuck," he swore, watching the growing blaze. He turned to me. "Get out of here, and wait outside for me."

"Why?" I asked. Who was he to me? Why would I wait for him?

"Because I told you to. I'm your doctor, Katarina, I want what's best for you. So do what I say."

"You're my doctor? You just killed someone," I said, the words jumbled and thick in my mouth.

He nodded. "To save your life. That man wanted to hurt you. He's hurt a lot of people. He'd have hurt more in the future. I did the world a favor."

"You should have called the police. You can't just kill someone," I cried, hysteria making my voice thin and sharp. Smoke flowed out of the burning room, and I coughed.

Go on. Unless you want to burn to a crisp.

I started at the voice. There was a long line of mirrors on the wall, and I could see myself clearly in them. I was alone. There was no woman whispering in my ear. She sounded like me, but confident and all-knowing.

She was inside my head. The certainty hit me like a gut punch.

I was hearing a voice inside my head that made more sense than anything that was happening outside it.

Was I crazy?

"Kat. I know this is all scary, but you don't need to overthink anything. Just trust me."

Blackwood put his hands on my shoulders, and I shuddered. His touch felt wrong.

"I've taken special care of you here, you just can't remember that right now. I've cared for you on behalf of your mother, Elena, and your fiancé, Ivan."

Fiancé? The name Ivan meant nothing to me, but Elena? That name clicked somewhere inside me, soothing my fear and pain for a moment. A comfort that could never be denied.

Elena. Mom.

"You know my mom?" I asked, gripping on to his white coat.

He nodded. "She wants me to bring you to her. We need to go."

Go to my mom? She was the only thing in my head that I recognized. In the empty, echoing hallways of my mind, there was only her.

"Okay, take me to her," I agreed. My thoughts were getting foggy again. I glanced at the room beside us where a huge fire raged. I shied back from it.

"There's a fire!" I exclaimed softly. I had no idea how it had started, but it was spreading. It was dangerous.

Blackwood considered me carefully and nodded. "Yes, we need to get out of here. You go raise the alarm and wait for me outside. I'll be there soon, and I'll take you to your mother."

I left Blackwood in the hallway, which was getting increasingly hot and smoky, and ran up the corridor toward the double doors at the end.

As soon as I pushed through, a fire alarm screamed overhead. Some of the doors along the hallway opened, and other people looked out, dressed in white sweats and looking just as confused as I was.

"Fire! There's a fire!" I shouted to anyone who would listen.

People gathered in the huge foyer and then poured out the doors into the storm. As soon as I stepped out, the chill in the air stole my breath, and I couldn't see anything except for the orange blaze of the building. Snow fell thick and fast. It was freezing.

Above me, windows blew out, and a whooshing sound filled the air.

"Fuck—the oxygen in the operating room!" someone yelled, and then a boom sounded and the ground seemed to shake.

I fell to my knees in the gathered snow and covered my head with my hands. People screamed and cried all around me. I was too close to the blaze. I could feel it raging at my back.

I sensed the whole place was going to go up.

Cold soaked through my sweats as I stumbled up and slogged through the thick snow, putting more distance between the fire and me, watching more and more people leave the building.

A man appeared, coughing and covering his face with his sleeve. He made his way toward me through the crowd wearing a white lab coat with the name Blackwood embroidered on the lapel. Did I know him?

"Stay here, I'm getting my car. We need to leave."

"Where are we going?" I asked, but he'd already moved away.

I glanced back at the door, where a man was just leaving, and something sharp clenched in my heart. The snow seemed to stop falling for a heartbeat. Even the fire faded for a second.

He was tall and broad, brooding in a way that was magnetic. Stubble wreathed the lower half of his face, and his dark eyes were piercing, even across the distance between us. He was huge. Imposing. Scary. His dark priest's robes smoked as he left the blaze. With a background of fire and smoke curling off his shoulders, he mirrored a devil who'd come to claim souls for hell.

And he was staring right at me.

I stumbled back, falling against the freezing stone of the chapel wall behind me. My foot slipped on a metal bowl hidden under the snow, and I nearly fell.

The man walked toward me.

You know him, the voice of insanity said inside my mind.

She was right. Didn't I know his name? It was on the tip of my tongue, but the damn brain fog made it hard to remember. He was familiar in a way that made my heart pound.

Lucifer. The light-bringer.

He walked right up to me, the crowd parting before him.

"Are you all right?" he asked, his deep voice sending shivers over me. His sooty hands closed on my face, cupping my cheeks and tilting my head back for his inspection. His gaze ran over my features, checking for injuries.

I just stared at him.

"What happened? Do you know?" he asked.

I shook my head slowly.

He turned to the crowd. Muttering to himself.

"It looks like everyone—wait, where's your little shadow?"

"Who?"

"Tatiana. Have you seen her?"

Tatiana. Chubby fingers curled around crayons and knock-knock jokes. I didn't get a visual of her, just an impression.

"I-I don't know," I admitted.

Lucifer narrowed his eyes at me and then tilted my face to see it better. He ran the backs of his fingers down my cheek. It was a surprisingly gentle touch for such a terrifying-looking man.

"Stay here. Don't move. I'll find you."

Then he faced the institute. Looking left and right to search the crowd, he spied a nurse. She ran toward him, gesturing wildly at the building, tears streaming down her face.

The demon nodded, clenched his tight jaw, and put his head down. He glanced back at me for a long moment.

I found my feet taking a step toward him before I could register even moving.

He shook his head once, forbidding me closer. Then he turned back toward the blaze and walked unerringly into the burning building.

See . . . I told you he was a demon.

I couldn't breathe properly. My throat was tight and my lungs cramped. Something crawled up my throat as I watched the man stride back inside.

Fear?

A car horn sounded behind me, and I whirled around. Dr. Blackwood, sitting in the driver's seat of a small black car. He pushed open the passenger-side door.

"Get in. I'll take you into town."

"What about the patients—the fire?"

"Emergency services are already on their way. The patients will travel into town as well."

I hesitated. I was freezing cold, my limbs shivering in the snow, and there was nothing I wanted more than to get in a nice warm car, but . . .

It felt wrong. Leaving when everyone was standing outside felt wrong.

Leaving before that man had emerged from the fire felt wrong.

"Katarina, your mother is waiting for you. Get in."

My mother.

I was moving toward the door before I could stop myself. I slid into the warm interior, and thoughts of my mom filled my head. Yes, I'd go home and see my mom. Comfort at the very thought filled my chest. Despite the fog in my head, she was clear.

Blackwood reversed the car, and that nagging feeling that I shouldn't be leaving like this reappeared. If only I could think more clearly.

A chain around my neck threatened to strangle me, caught in my sweater. I tugged at it. It was long, with a pendant hanging far down my chest, caught between my breasts.

I pulled it carefully free from my tangled sweater.

Blackwood sat forward, staring intently at the dangerous roads. Fire engines streamed past us on the way to the institute, disappearing in the rearview mirror.

It wasn't a pendant, I realized, when I uncovered the whole necklace.

Smooth flat disks, rectangular and printed with a name . . .

Dog tags.

I lifted them to the light and tried to make out the tiny letters.

Lucciano, Massimo.

Lucciano?

Blackwood swore. He steered the car through snowy streets. Torino was beautiful under its thick, white layer of snow. Arcades bracketed the road, with their elegant marble colonnades marching down the street, protecting the sidewalks from snow. We passed the twin baroque churches of Piazza San Carlo, and I glimpsed the spire of Mole Antonelliana piercing the skyline in the distance. I knew this city. I used to live here. It was clear, while everything else was murky.

We halted at a red traffic light. On the right was a train station lit up brightly in the darkness. Inside, people milled around.

It all seemed normal. A world that I had nearly left behind forever.

The dog tags felt heavy between my fingers.

Get out of here now, while you can. Go!

The voice inside my head was insistent. Maybe it made me crazy, but I listened. The man beside me was tense and fidgeting. Did I know him? Suddenly I couldn't even remember getting into the car. Then I saw the back of his hand. A fine spray of red decorated his knuckles. There was no cut to explain it. I knew at that moment that the blood wasn't his.

I yanked the door handle and unclipped my seat belt at the same time. Instinct drove me onward. I couldn't explain it, and I couldn't ignore it, either. I just needed to get away.

Blackwood shouted after me, but I left the car door hanging open and ran for the pavement. The light changed, and car drivers honked at Blackwood.

I didn't dare look back. Something inside me urged me to run away from that car and that man, and I didn't have time to question it.

I hit the sidewalk and slid on the ice and snow, going down on one knee hard. But I didn't have time to stop. I scraped my palms on the ground pushing myself up and staggering the last few steps into the train station.

Heat and humidity hit me as soon as I got inside. Some people gawped at me and then looked away. I must have seemed strange in my all-white sweatsuit and sneakers, bloody knee and hands, a frantic glimmer in my eyes. My face felt chalked with ash and soot from the fire.

I put my head down and moved to the wall, walking quickly along it. Should I hide out in the ladies' room? Wouldn't that be the first place Blackwood would look for me?

What if I was overreacting and the man was just trying to take me to my mother's house? Despite how much I tried to believe that, I just couldn't.

There was a small kiosk at the end of the waiting hall with stands of magazines and newspapers outside. I dove between the rails and paused. I had to get a grip. I didn't even know if Blackwood was following me.

I lingered there, pretending to choose a magazine, peering over the top of the rail whenever I dared. My heart sank as Blackwood entered the station.

I scuttled farther back, my breath rasping painfully. I couldn't seem to catch it.

He glanced this way and that, and then started in my direction. He was going to find me here.

Suddenly, someone touched my arm and I nearly screamed. I spun around to find a young woman, maybe my age, maybe younger, standing beside me. She had draped a heavy, fashionable puffer coat around my shoulders. The thing nearly hid my entire institute uniform.

"Here," she said quickly, and pulled a woolen beanie hat with a pom-pom onto my head. Then she stepped between me and the rest of the station and tugged me over to a display of gardening magazines.

"What are you doing?" I murmured, confused and mistrustful.

"Just looking at magazines with my friend," she said back quietly.

"I-I don't know you?" I asked, more of a question than a statement.

"Not yet." The girl gave me a half smile and then glanced forward. "Keep your head down, he's coming."

I stared at the magazines, my eyes swimming. This sudden act of kindness from a stranger was all it took to make me tear up, apparently.

I swiped at my eyes, tension beating through me. I waited to see if Blackwood would find me despite my makeshift disguise.

After a few minutes, the girl beside me relaxed.

"He's gone out the emergency exit at the back. He must think you came in and went right back out to confuse him."

I stepped away from her and stared around. She was right. Blackwood was gone.

"Thank you so much for your help. I don't even know what to say—"

"You don't have to say anything. You see someone in trouble, you help, right?" The girl studied me with concern. "Do you have somewhere to go right now?"

I shook my head. I could go to my mother's, but it was bound to be the next place Blackwood would look for me. He'd been on his way there, or at least had been pretending to be. My mind was so cloudy, it felt dangerous to wander around while I didn't remember what the hell was going on.

"I think I need to find this person." I lifted the dog tags from my sweater.

The girl eyed the name thoughtfully. "Lucciano, Massimo." She dropped the tags. "You don't know who he is, but you wear these?"

"I know, it doesn't make any sense, does it? I can't make much sense of anything lately, to be honest."

She stared at me, clearly puzzled, but not afraid.

"Lucy," a sharp voice said beside us, and I nearly dove to the floor.

"It's fine, Nina. I've got it under control," the girl who had helped me said quickly.

A woman stood beside us, alert and professional. Something about her screamed security. She wore all black and had her deep-red hair in a severe bun. Her gray eyes were watchful and full of assessment. She took me in from head to toe, a frown creasing her brow at the odd sight I made.

The girl, Lucy, turned back to me. "Well, I'd invite you home with me, but I'm only here on a work trip. I've got a hotel room for a few nights, though, and you're welcome to hide out there."

"Lucy, no!" the woman in black protested, clearly alarmed.

"Yes, Nina," Lucy argued back. She had an air of confidence that was at odds with her age. Maybe she was rich? Or maybe she was just used to having her say.

"You see a woman who needs help, you help," Lucy repeated her words from earlier.

"My job is to keep you safe, no one else," Nina argued back softly.

Her job was to keep her safe? Was she a bodyguard? Why would this girl need a bodyguard?

"Yeah, and she's with me. Enough arguing about this in public, you're drawing more attention than anything else. I'm done talking about this," Lucy said abruptly, then turned her attention to me. "Do you want to go to the police?"

I shook my head. Not until my head cleared. I had no answers for their questions.

"I don't think I can make myself understood right now. I'll go tomorrow, when I'm calmer. But why are you helping me?" I blurted out.

Lucy shrugged. "People have helped me when I needed it before. People have even helped me when I didn't deserve it. You never know what someone is going through . . . I've learned that the hard way. I'm Lucy, by the way."

I'd learned that there were two types of people when it came to helping others. The ones who walked away, afraid to be dragged into someone else's issues, and the ones who ran toward the trouble to help. To find the latter felt like a miracle.

"Katarina," I said, and stuck my hand out to shake hers. I waited for a bad feeling or a tingle of intuition that I shouldn't trust this kind stranger, but it didn't come.

She seemed genuine. And I had no alternatives. I'd have to trust her for now, at least.

"Katarina. Can I call you Kat?"

I nodded.

"Let's get out of here," she said decisively.

I nodded. "Let's."

26

KATARINA

Lucy was a student in her final year at a prestigious culinary school in Florence. We went back to her hotel by taxi and soon were locked safely inside. She was in Torino for a few days to take an exam.

"I can't believe this snow," Lucy said, gazing out the window. "We never get this down South."

She'd just ordered a whole lot of food from room service, and we were waiting for it to be delivered. Nina, her bodyguard, was outside the door. I wasn't sure how to ask her why she needed one.

She'd very patiently reminded me of her name, the bodyguard's, and why she was in the city three times already. My short-term memory didn't seem capable of holding more than half an hour of time. It was horrifying. I'd never been more confused.

"I have someone I could ask about your missing soldier," she said, coming to sit on the sofa. This wasn't just a hotel room, it was a suite. Lucy wasn't a poor student, that was clear.

"Who?" I stared at her, confused.

Until she nodded toward the dog tags around my neck hanging out of the cozy white knit sweater dress she'd let me borrow.

"Oh, him." I picked up the metal disks and stared at the name etched into the surface.

"Who could you ask?" I wondered.

"Someone who's like a sister-in-law to me. She's actually pretty impressive with tech. I bet she could find him."

"I don't even remember getting these, that's the problem, or when or where I got them."

I held the dog tags in my palm. They felt oddly precious to me.

"Are they from a family member? Or a boyfriend? As far as I know, they're sentimental things to part with."

I shrugged. Under the dog tags was a small crucifix, the only thing I recognized.

"This is mine." I held up the cross. "But the rest, I don't know."

"Is this memory loss thing new, or . . . what do you remember?"

I took a deep breath and thought about it. "I've been in the hospital, I think. I don't know where. I've been staying there for a long time, I think. My mom is waiting for me to get out. There was a fire . . . I don't know what happened."

"If you've been staying in the hospital, how come you ended up running into the *stazione centrale* in the middle of a snowstorm?"

I shrugged. "I don't remember."

"What's your whole name? You want my friend to look you up, too?"

That I knew. Just like I knew my mother, I knew my name. The rest of my life remained shrouded in fog.

"It's Katarina Dmitrova."

A knock sounded at the door, signaling room service had arrived.

Lucy stood and crossed to the door, peering out quickly before she opened it wider.

The waiter wheeled the food in and then left. Smells of pasta with tomatoes and basil hit the air, and I groaned.

"Come on, let's eat, and tell me more about what you remember," Lucy offered, sitting at one side of the table.

My stomach growled loudly, and I joined her.

"That'd be a short conversation," I said with a sigh, and sank into a chair beside her.

The hotel suite had a real-life dining room area. There were three bedrooms and two bathrooms in the place. It felt like an apartment. The quiet luxury felt entirely foreign to me.

The food tasted better than anything I could remember having eaten before. The texture of the pasta and simple, strong flavor of garlic and basil was so good it brought tears to my eyes.

"Are you okay?" Lucy asked, quietly watching me as I struggled through my fifth mental breakdown of the day.

I shrugged. "Honestly, I'm not entirely sure."

She nodded. "What are you going to do after this?"

I swallowed a lump in my throat. "I need to go and see my mom, but I can't yet. I need to lie low until my head clears."

She didn't ask why my head would be so confused, which was good, because I had no idea how to explain it. My thoughts were slippery, falling through my fingers like water. I couldn't seem to keep things straight, and everything felt like it was held back, just out of reach. It was frustrating, and at the same time, I knew I'd felt like this before.

"Well, I'm here for a few more days. Stay as long as you need to."

I studied her. She was small, with red-brown hair and big hazel eyes. Despite her coloring, she didn't seem to be Italian, not to mention her American accent.

"Why are you helping me?" I asked. "Are you some kind of saint, or are you—do you want something from me?" It came out rude as hell, but I had a deep-down certainty that no one helped me without wanting something from me. I knew in my gut that I'd learned that the hard way.

She set down her fork and took a moment to think of her reply.

"If you see someone who needs help, you help. My sister taught me that. She's the best person I've ever met."

I smiled at Lucy. There was such honesty in her words, I didn't doubt their sincerity. A soft smile touched her lips as she spoke, and I envied her that beautiful sisterly bond.

I was all alone except for my mom. I missed her so much at that moment I could hardly breathe. All I'd ever wanted was a family to fall back on. A place to belong, to be protected, to be whole. I let out a held breath, urging the damn tears back that seemed to hover, never far from falling.

"So, stay here, let Nina protect both of us for a bit. We'll work out what to do. Maybe after a good meal and a good sleep, your head will be clearer."

I nodded and reached out to grab Lucy's hand when she went to stand.

"Thank you," I murmured. "Seriously, thank you. I think you might be saving my life."

It was a dream. I knew that it was a dream. It had to be.

In it, I ran down a white hallway, and everything burned around me.

I reached a door at the end and nudged it open. It stuck on something. I shoved harder. The obstacle gave way, and the door swung in. This room wasn't white. It was red. Bloodred. Blood dripped off every surface, pooling on the floor. There wasn't a single inch of white left. Blood as far as the eye could see.

"Kat!" A kid's voice broke through my horror.

I spun around to find her. *Tatiana.*

A person strode down the hallway, fire trailing in his wake, licking up around his ankles, touching his priest's robes.

His eyes stared into my soul.

Massimo.

I woke with a cry, a hand touching my shoulder.

"Wake up! You're having a nightmare!" Lucy's worried voice broke through my swimming thoughts.

Right. Lucy, the girl from the train station. The hotel. Dr. Blackwood.

Massimo.

The fog in my head had cleared. I'd left it behind in the night, finally escaping it.

I pushed out of bed. Lucy hovered beside me.

"What did you dream about?"

"I—they weren't dreams. I remembered," I got out. Panic clutched my chest in an unbreakable grip. The night before filled my mind. Going to Pavol's office. Being injected. The fire. Being outside and confused. Massimo in the snow, looking for Tatiana. Massimo going back into the burning building. They'd given me something again, and it had made me confused, but it had worn off. How long had it lasted? A day?

"You need to breathe. You're hyperventilating. Calm down and tell me everything."

I nodded, taking the glass of cool water she passed me and sinking into a chair.

"It's a long story," I warned her.

She shrugged. "I've got time. Tell me."

So I did.

After, Lucy sat for a moment, stunned by the convoluted tale, before twisting for her phone.

"I need to find Massimo. I don't know what happened after he went back into the building. He could have been hurt. He could have . . ."

No, he couldn't be dead. It wasn't possible. I refused to even consider it.

"Okay, right. We need to find him. And as for the doctor you ran away from, he sounds just as dangerous as the other men who were in charge. He needs to be caught."

"Yeah, but how? Without Massimo, I can't even dream of being a match for Blackwood."

"We need to talk to my brother-in-law."

"Who's your brother-in-law?"

"He's someone who can . . . protect people and deal with problems," she said somewhat evasively. "He's the reason I have Nina outside."

"He must be someone important. A politician?"

She shook her head. "Not exactly. He doesn't have a conventional job. Anyway, we need to talk to him, or at least the woman I told you about earlier. My IT guy."

"Okay. Let's speak to her . . . maybe she can find Massimo."

Lucy nodded and dialed on her phone, putting it on speaker and setting it on the table between us.

It rang and rang. Just when I thought no one was going to answer, a voice came over the line.

"You're lucky I barely sleep, kid," a woman said.

A deep, rumbling male voice spoke in the background.

"I'm sorry, it's an emergency," Lucy said quickly.

I could hear when the woman on the other side of the call snapped to attention.

"What's going on?" she asked with intention.

Lucy took a deep breath. "This is going to sound crazy, but I met this girl last night. She was running away from someone—someone dangerous. She was staying at this place in Torino, a hospital of some kind."

"Hallow Hall," I leaned forward and said toward the phone. "It's a Church-run, kind of, home for unwed mothers and the elderly, some psychiatric care."

Silence reigned for a long moment before the woman on the other end spoke.

"You're shitting me."

"What?" Lucy raised an eyebrow at me.

"Kid, you have a very special talent, like an eerie ability, to walk right into the shit, every single time. Trouble finds you, Lucy. It's a gift, or in my case, since I'm forced to care if you live or die, a curse." The sounds of rustling covers filtered through, and the phone speaker being jostled about.

"What are you talking about?" Lucy called.

A man, his voice tinged with an Irish accent, spoke instead of the woman. "She's off to get her laptop fired up. How are you keeping, kid?"

Lucy smiled toward the phone. She obviously liked this guy. "I'm good. I just want to help Katarina, and I don't know how."

"Well, if my wife can do anything brilliantly, it's tell other people what to do. She'll sort it out, don't you worry your wee heads about it. Katarina, was it? I'm Bran."

"Hi." I waved my fingers toward the phone before realizing how dumb that was.

"Hi. And my better half, the one who's scurrying around bare-arsed right now getting her computer all fired up is Giada."

I smiled. I couldn't help it. There was something incredibly comforting about these people's dynamics, their confidence. They were clearly family in some way or another. The jealousy hit me hard for a moment.

"Right, I'm here," Giada said. "Nice to meet you, Kat. I can call you Kat, right?"

"Sure," I said, having the feeling that any disagreement would be ignored.

"Where's Massimo?" Giada asked, brisk. "Sorry, Father Lucciano."

I stared at the phone. "What?" I slowly asked.

Lucy's face reflected my shock. We hadn't mentioned Massimo on the phone yet.

Giada sighed, sounding impatient. "I know, wow, surprise, I already know some of what's going on! Worlds colliding and all that. Let's marvel at the wonders of fate later . . . Where is Massimo?"

"I don't know," I managed. "There was a fire at the institute—"

The sound of tapping came over the phone. "So I see. A big one. That place is trashed. Good."

"Massimo went back inside to look for a little girl who lived there," I told Giada. "That was the last time I saw him."

"Mass went on a rescue mission?" Giada chuckled. "You can take the boy out of the Col Moschin, but he's still a damn bleeding-heart hero under all that psychosis."

She tapped away a little longer.

"What are you doing?" Lucy asked.

"Checking hospital records for anyone who died last night." Giada's voice was dispassionate, while I felt like the bottom just fell out of my world.

"Nothing for his name, and they should be able to ID his body from his dog tags."

"He doesn't have them." I pulled them from my borrowed dress. "I have them."

There was a low whistle in the background from Bran. "Oh, he *likes* her, likes her."

Giada ignored her husband. "Okay, well, there don't seem to have been any admissions for severe burns, so . . . he's probably okay and out there looking for you right now."

Thank God.

I dropped my head into my hands and stared at the carpet. My heart raced. I couldn't take it. The dog tags swung against my dress, gleaming dully.

Lucy rubbed my back. "What should we do?"

"I can't find Massimo if he doesn't want to be found. The man's a ghost. L'Ombra," Giada said.

L'Ombra? *The Shadow.*

"The best thing you can do is wait until he finds you, which he will. In fact, if he gave you the dog tags, he probably already knows where you are."

"What do you mean?" I wondered.

"It doesn't matter. I'll try and get in touch with him, but the man changes phones like socks."

"She also needs to get to her mother," Lucy said. "That's where she needs to get to in the city, but she's scared that the men searching for her will be waiting."

Giada was quiet for a long moment and then swore under her breath. "Wait for Massimo. Don't go anywhere until he makes contact. Mass will sort it all. Lucy, don't miss your exam. Katarina, stay in the hotel, and I'll send another bodyguard to help out. Worst-case scenario, if Mass doesn't get in touch soon, I'll send you a passport, and you come here to New York. We'll take it from there."

"New York? I can't go to America without my mom," I told her quickly.

She paused. "Right. If Massimo finds you, you won't need to. He'll take over, okay? Just wait until he comes for you."

I nodded. She and Lucy exchanged a few short goodbyes and hung up.

"She's . . . a character," I said lamely.

Lucy laughed. "She's a stone-cold bitch, and I love her."

"She sounds great. I can't understand how she already knows about Massimo and Hallow Hall, though," I mused.

Lucy shrugged. "If Giada knows someone, it means she's probably helped them with something at some point. She said Massimo was in the Col Moschin, the Italian Special Forces. Maybe she knows him through her older brother, Elio. Elio was a colonel or something, I think. He's my brother-in-law's best friend."

I nodded. "I see. And do they all work in this . . . unconventional business you mentioned?"

Lucy's eyes slid from mine, and a stab of nerves went through me. Was she lying to me?

She nodded. "Yes, they're all involved. My sister, too. All of us, I guess. It's a family business." She trailed off and then glanced at the clock. It was morning already. The sun was far from being seen, but the snow had stopped. "I need to get to the assessment kitchen early to prep. I wouldn't go if it wasn't an exam."

"Don't be silly! Don't miss your day to sit around here and do nothing but hide out with me. I'll be fine. Your help is already so, so much."

She nodded. “Nina won’t let me leave on my own, but Giada said she’d get someone down here to watch the door.”

I nodded reassuringly. “Like I said, it’s already so much to have a place to hide. Thank you.”

“Stop thanking me every two seconds!” Lucy smiled and stood, stretching this way and that.

I felt bad that she was going to be so tired for her exam, but there was a determined energy about her that told me she was going to be just fine.

“Now, I need to look human and get out of here. You need to go back to bed and sleep more,” Lucy said, stern.

I laughed at her tone. “Yes, Mom.”

27

MASSIMO

"Sir, you can't just leave, you've been hurt," the nurse said for the tenth time as she hovered at my side.

I fought the urge to bite her head off and relaxed back onto the bed. *Fucking hell.*

"How long will it take?" I asked instead.

"Not long. The doctor has been really busy seeing to those injured in the fire."

"And the little girl I came in with?" I asked.

They'd split up me and Tatiana when the ambulance had arrived at the hospital. A fucking beam had fallen on me just as I'd reached the door of the burning building last night and knocked me out for hours. An entire night. Hours I couldn't afford to lose.

"She's being treated for smoke inhalation. She's doing just fine." The nurse gave me an encouraging smile and reached for the iodine-soaked gauze she was using to clean my burns.

They were superficial at best. Some on my hands and arms. The very minimum you could expect if you went into a building where burning beams fell from the sky.

I'd found Tatiana hiding in a cupboard in the kitchen.

I'd come damn near to not finding her at all. A thought that didn't bear thinking about. She'd run out of her room and hidden before the nurses went to check on her.

She'd already been unconscious from the smoke in the air when I'd found her. Those burning moments, carrying her out of the building, shoving and pushing the fallen beams away from us, had taken me back in time to my years in the military. Then the ceiling had fallen, and it had been lights out. There was another patient from the institute in the bed next to me, and he'd told me that Katarina had gotten into a car. Blackwood's car.

My blood burned at the thought of her being with him. Where the hell had he taken her? I didn't have my personal effects. The damn nurses had taken all of them from me when I'd come into the hospital with Tatiana, and they'd insisted on treating the burns on my hands and arms.

Now I sat in a paper gown without my phone or the ability to call Giada or check my tracking app.

Thank fuck I'd given Katarina the dog tags. The tracker inside was linked to an app on my phone. I could sign into the program from somewhere else, but the fastest thing would be to get my own phone back. I had exactly one thing in my possession that I was sentimental about, and that was those tags, hence the tracker. I could only be grateful I had a way to find Katarina quickly, once I got out of here.

The nurse finally finished cleaning the burns. I watched men in cop uniforms passing up and down the hallway. The detectives were back, the ones who'd left just before the fire, and a hell of a lot more officers. I supposed that the case was turning into something a lot more involved. A disappearance, a suicide, and now a fire.

Suspicious. I needed to get out of here before they decided to question me, too. I had to find Katarina.

What felt like an hour later saw the nurse sticking fresh bandages over my wounds and stepping back.

"Are we done? I need my stuff back—my clothes and my phone."

She nodded, and her eyes darted to the curtain guiltily.

"Don't worry, Mr. Lucciano, or should I say Father? I have them here," a male voice said from the gap in the curtain.

I held the nurse's eye for a long moment. She'd been stalling me. *Perfect.*

Standing in that gap was the same detective who had been at Hallow Hall before, holding my priest's robes and phone.

"I would love to have a chat, too, while we're here," he said with a smile.

Fuck me.

"So, tell me again why you were at Hallow Hall? Since you aren't actually affiliated with the Church?" Detective Margoni was a persistent fucker, I'd give him that.

I shrugged. "Hallow Hall Institute has no affiliation with the Church either, just a lot of old men who liked to cosplay as priests. I was following their dress code."

Margoni frowned at me, and my fraying patience snapped.

"Listen, Detective, I appreciate your zeal, it's very impressive, but you need to look where the real problems are, like why has a place like this been running for as long as it has right here in Torino? Why hasn't it been investigated before?"

"It's registered as a private hospital," Margoni pointed out.

"A private hospital that doesn't appear to make any money and people barely pay any fees to attend? Yeah, that sounds aboveboard."

Margoni sighed. "Do you know how stretched thin we are in the city? If there are no complaints about a place, then why would we go and poke into it?"

"Don't ask me to explain your ineptitude. Now, if you're finished asking me to do your job for you, I need to get going."

Margoni shook his head. "I don't think so."

"Are you charging me with something?"

"For years there was nothing going on at Hallow Hall, and then you arrive, and the men in charge are either missing or dead."

"As far as I'm aware, one tragically took his own life, maybe because of the fucked-up shit they'd been doing up there, and that spooked the other two. They ran away, scared of answering for their crimes." I slipped my hands behind my head and stretched my back. The interrogation room at the small station that Margoni had brought me to wasn't the most comfortable place.

"That's a bit too convenient for me," Margoni said.

"Sure, now you hate convenience, but turning the other way for decades was fine," I muttered, and tutted at him. "Shame on you, Detective."

He narrowed his eyes at me. "Whether you have anything to do with the death and disappearances and fire or not, you were still there pretending to be a man of the cloth to fool the patients. We don't take that lightly here."

"So charge me with something," I dared him. I needed to get the fuck out of here, and the sooner they let me out of this room or moved me somewhere, the sooner I could escape.

"I don't have to charge you with anything until you've been held for twenty-four hours." He pushed back from the chair and stood. "So I'll see you at the end of that time. Let me know if you want to talk."

"Margoni! What about a phone call?" I shouted after him as he walked out. Anger and frustration welled up inside me. I had to leave and find Katarina, now. Every minute that passed was another that she was with Blackwood. Why had she gone with him? What had he done to make her?

Dark fury like I'd never known filled me as I sat and simmered in it. I'd find my little stray and kill everyone who had touched her. I'd kill everyone who had ever scared her or made her cry. I'd kill everyone who had looked at her wrong. I'd kill every single person involved in Hallow Hall Institute. They were already dead.

The thought that they might have already hurt her played on the edge of my mind, but I couldn't face it right now. Compartmentalizing was how I'd survived as long as I had. Everything went into a box, only to be thought about when it was relevant. It was how I'd coped with all the things I'd seen and done. One box for what I'd found in a school in a war-torn land. Another for a fellow soldier dying in my arms, his legs blown off by a land mine, clutching a picture of his pregnant wife. Another for the last moments of all the marks I'd killed on contracts. Another for the terrible fear brewing inside me at the thought that I'd already failed to protect the one person I cared about.

Nope. That went into a box with the lid jammed on top. That particular worry would only waste my time when I had none to spare.

First, I'd find Katarina and make her safe and protected forever . . .

Then, they'd all pay.

Every single one.

28

KATARINA

Lucy left with Nina at her heels. I wandered around the fancy hotel suite, tried watching TV, and finally just sat at the window and stared out over the city.

It hadn't changed much in the time I'd been away, yet at the same time, it looked completely different.

I'd missed so much. Three years. Three years of life lost to Hallow Hall. It felt like a nightmare I couldn't wake up from. I'd spent three years half asleep, dreaming, confused; and when I was lucid, following orders, toeing the lines of monsters. I was bereft. I was angry. I was all the things I could feel, all at once.

I still found it hard to process that Vargas, Benedict, and Pavol were all dead. It seemed impossible. They'd grown so large and invincible in my mind, the knowledge that they'd actually died, and right in front of me, no less, was still processing.

Maybe one day I'd wake up and believe it. For now, it was too much to hope for. In a few short weeks, Massimo had come into my life and completely changed it.

Massimo. My heart raced at the thought of him. He was out there in the city somewhere. Searching for me? I hoped so.

What if he wasn't? What if he felt his job was done here? What if he was hurt? He'd gone into the fire for Tatiana. He was angry. He was brave . . . He wasn't as irredeemable as he thought he was. Just the thought that he might be lying somewhere unidentified in a hospital . . .

I couldn't even stand to consider that idea. He had to come for me . . . he had to. We weren't finished with our deal. At least, I hadn't delivered my part yet. Giving him my first everythings. He'd wanted so much more than I'd thought.

I could only hope he'd track me down. Everything between us felt unfinished. Meeting him had felt like a beginning, not an end.

All morning, my mind turned to him in a never-ending loop. I wondered where he was and what he was doing. Was he injured? Did he find Tatiana? Was she okay?

It was around lunchtime when the doorbell rang.

I jumped to my feet, hope hammering in my chest. Could it be him?

I rushed to the door and put my eye to the peephole.

Dr. Blackwood stood in the hallway outside the door.

I stumbled back, suddenly feeling sick. Oh my God, he'd found me? Why? Why wouldn't he just leave me alone?

I stared at the door as I tried to get my breathing under control. I had to calm the fuck down. I was inside and he was outside. The door was locked. He couldn't get to me if I didn't let him in. Unfortunately, the new security that Lucy's sister-in-law had organized hadn't shown yet. I was alone.

Still, it was okay. He couldn't get in, I kept telling myself.

Then, a man with a trolley appeared at the end of the hallway.

Blackwood turned to speak to him, gesturing toward the door. He flashed some kind of lanyard that was around his neck. Was he claiming to be checking on a patient? The kid with the room service trolley seemed conflicted. He glanced up and down the corridor. Blackwood impatiently looked at his watch like he was in a hurry to check on someone.

I backed away from the door. He was going to get in, one way or another. I just knew it.

I couldn't stay here.

I ran through the hotel suite, shoving my sneakers on and pulling a heavy cream winter coat out of the closet. I'd just have to owe Lucy this one.

There was a terrace outside that attached to the one beside it. It didn't seem very security savvy, and Lucy's bodyguard hadn't been happy about it, but maybe the hotel figured that the people who stayed in such luxury, high-end suites wouldn't be sneaking around and stealing from each other's rooms.

Anyway, right now, I was grateful for it.

I stepped out onto the terrace. It had stopped snowing, but it was still very cold. My feet slid a little on the ice coating the flagstones. I shut the French doors and headed to the metal barrier between the two suites.

The room next door seemed to be unoccupied. There wasn't anything out on the terrace that would indicate another guest was staying there. I had to risk it.

I climbed up on the partition, my hands freezing on the icy metal. Slowly, I lifted my leg over the side, swaying scarily when I was halfway over, but I gripped harder and kept going. I couldn't look away from the wall toward the city. We were ten stories up. It was the kind of height that would make my head spin, and I was dizzy enough as it was.

Slowly, I lowered myself on the other side of the barrier and nearly collapsed in a heap on the balcony. I had to keep moving.

I scrambled across the terrace, slipping and sliding, reaching the glass doors. With a quick prayer, I closed my eyes and pushed it.

It slid open. Relief hit me. I'd fully been expecting it to be locked from inside. That was the kind of luck I usually had, but today, it had worked out.

I slipped inside. The room was quiet, empty, and clearly unoccupied. I locked the door to the balcony and paced the living room, trying to think through my problem.

I could stay here, but Blackwood would work out I might have gone to a neighboring room. Hell, my footprints were pretty obvious at the back. I should have taken some time to go back and forth and make it confusing. Then again, there was nowhere else to go once I was out here, so he'd still find me. I couldn't stay here, I realized slowly. The desire to stay in the warm comfort and safety of the hotel was overwhelming, but I couldn't give in.

I had to leave, and I had to do it right now, before Blackwood got access to this room, too.

I crossed the room toward the main entrance and listened to the hallway outside. It was silent. Next, I peered out the peephole. Not a single soul passed by. If I was going to go, I had to go now. Slowly, I eased the door open. It felt like every single clunk of the electronic lock opening was a shotgun blast.

The hallway was silent. Blackwood and the room service guy had probably entered Lucy's suite. I had to go.

I started down the hall, jogging close to the wall. When I got to the bank of elevators, I second-guessed my decision to take one. I went for the stairs instead. I padded silently down the stairs, ears straining for any kind of noise that would alert me that I wasn't alone.

I made it all the way to the bottom and out into the foyer safely.

Maybe I could do this. I really could. I was more and more confident with every passing minute that I didn't get caught.

Outside on the street, I raised the hood of the heavy winter coat. I should wait somewhere nearby to watch for Lucy coming back, I decided. She had security with her, and her IT guy seemed like she could help with a lot. I shouldn't just disappear on them.

I headed to an alley to the right of the hotel. I didn't have any money, so I couldn't wait in any of the nearby cafés.

In the alley, steam poured out of a vent in the wall, immediately fogging the cold air. A generator hummed, and it was less cold than being in the direct freezing wind blowing overhead. I leaned on the wall and shivered, folding into a crouch.

Outside, the street was bustling, considering the cold day. The people of Torino getting on with their work, taking kids to school, walking their dogs. Everyone too busy to notice a girl huddled against the wall.

Then I saw him.

Blackwood.

He'd left the hotel and stood in front of it, trying to hail a taxi.

He had his phone clamped to his ear, but I couldn't hear what he was saying from this far away. He waited impatiently for the taxi, checking this way and that, a pissed-off expression on his face.

Where are you, Lucifer? I thought. *Aren't you coming for me?*

"Don't worry," said a man speaking on his phone, walking in my direction up the alley, "I've found her."

It took a second for the words to register. The man didn't pass me by. He stopped right in front of me. Massimo?

I stared at the black dress shoes on the sidewalk before me and then brought my gaze slowly upward. The man was wearing a heavy overcoat, and in the years since I'd last seen him, he'd only gotten meaner looking.

My eyes met his, and I knew I was screwed.

I hadn't seen Ivan Markovic in three years, and yet I knew him immediately.

Just like I knew my freedom was over.

"I've found my wayward fiancée at last." His voice was full of mocking.

I sprang upward, but Ivan had been expecting it.

I felt the all-too-familiar sting in my neck before I even saw his hand move.

No. I didn't want to get lost in my head again. Please, no. No!

"Come with me, Kat. It's time to finally finish what we started." Ivan grabbed me as I swayed, lifting me effortlessly.

The last thing I saw was Blackwood standing by a waiting cab, the interior a yawning black pit.

It swallowed me whole.

When your mind is not your own, you become an unreliable narrator. You learn to mistrust yourself. At worst, you feel betrayed by your own mind; at best, you become apathetic to the events around you. You have no control. You have no focus. You have no organization of thought. You are just a person reacting to things without context, existing in the heat of the moment without a past or a future.

You stop caring about any of them anyway. They stop being real.

I was in a taxi on my way somewhere. Men were talking loudly in the smoky interior of the cab. I put my hands over my ears. I didn't want to hear.

"Sergei is pissed, so the sooner we pull this off the better. Where'd you find the priest?" the man beside me asked. He had a lanyard around his neck that said he was a doctor.

Where was I going with a doctor?

The other man twisted from the front seat. He was familiar. He made me think of my mother somehow.

"Where are we going?" I managed to ask, though it felt like my tongue was too big for my mouth.

"Home, don't you remember?" The man in the front laughed.

I stared down at my clothes.

"I don't want to go," I found myself muttering.

"I don't give a fuck." The guy in the front was still watching me. "Don't you get it yet, Kat? Nothing you want has ever mattered."

Satisfied with those cutting words, he turned back around, tapping on the dashboard merrily.

"Step on it. It's fucking freezing out here," he said to the taxi driver.

The doctor was sitting beside me in the back. I turned to study his face. It was almost familiar.

"I don't know that man," I told him quietly.

He shrugged. "You don't know anybody."

"That's not true. I know . . ." My mind came up blank. "I know my mother."

I latched on to the thought of her. Her smell, the way her hair felt tickling my nose as I hugged her.

The doctor ignored me.

I turned to the window, putting my hand to the door. I tried the handle as discreetly as I could.

"It's locked. You think I'm falling for that twice?" The doctor sounded tired.

"Do we know each other?" I wondered.

He let out a short, frustrated breath. "Fucking hell," he muttered. "What a mess we've all made of your head, Katarina. I'm starting to wonder how much will be left, when all is said and done."

"Hopefully not a lot," the guy in the front called back. "She'll be a much more pleasant wife without all those irritating opinions of hers."

I opened my mouth to protest, but what was the point? They were laughing at me. They were cruel . . . and I was stuck with them.

Alone.

You're not alone. You have me. The voice inside my head was startling. I jumped. She sounded just like me. *Great.* I was hearing voices. I'd gone insane.

I stared out at the white city rushing past until the view blurred with tears.

We pulled up outside an apartment building a little while later. I had no clear concept of time. It was stretching and bunching like unruly fabric.

I was hauled out of the cab into the snowy night and then forced up cold stone stairs and into a small, shabby apartment. Inside was stuffy, the product of too-hot radiators and no air. It was old-fashioned, like it had last been decorated twenty years before, and the surfaces of tables and counters were cluttered with bottles and plates.

"Shit, Ivan, would it kill you to keep the place clean?" the doctor demanded, following us into the apartment.

"You clean it if it bothers you so much, Mr. Uptight, OCD,

Can't Take a Little Mess Lying Around. When I have a wife, I'll have all the cleaners I want, and I won't have to live in this shit-hole anymore." The man, Ivan, pushed me down a short hall and into a dark room.

A small double bed stood in the middle of it covered with a hand-crocheted quilt, and a host of religious icons decorated the walls.

"You can go ahead and get ready for bed. I'll be there soon." He gave me a smirk that turned my blood cold and then left me alone.

A scraping sound came from the door. A lock turning on the other side.

I sank onto the bed, feeling sick.

Outside in the hall, they argued.

"What the fuck are you talking about? You can't sleep with her before you're married and you get approval, or you're a dead man!"

"What he doesn't know won't hurt him."

"It wasn't what we agreed on, Ivan."

Ivan let out a frustrated sigh. "You are such a fucking stick-in-the-mud, and you always have been."

The sound of their voices moved away down the hall, and I glanced around the room. There was a window, but when I went to check it out, I saw a slender latticework in the shape of bars across it. There was no way out except the door. The locked door.

I sank down to the floor and took in the idols on the wall. I recognized most of them. The Madonna, and Saint Nicholas of Myra. Sitting directly over where I sat slumped was the most recognizable. An angel with gleaming wings and a golden sword. Archangel Michael. Defender against evil. I groped for the cross I always wore at my neck. A habit that apparently predated my confusion. My hands met cool metal disks. There was something else on my necklace, but I couldn't quite see what in the darkness. The only light fell through the window and onto the wall, illuminating the icons. I gripped the awkwardly shaped jumble on the chain and stared at the picture of Michael.

Please, please. Someone, somewhere . . . help me.

29

KATARINA

The night felt never-ending. The only blip in my solitude was the doctor visiting me again and injecting me while I struggled to wake up from my half-slumber. After that shot, I fell into a deep, drugged sleep.

I woke up with the man who told me his name was Ivan leaning over me, shaking me hard enough to rattle my teeth. Where was I? Why was I here in this unfamiliar house?

"Move it. We're late."

He yanked me up by the arm so hard something tore in my shoulder, making me cry out. Ivan ignored my sound of pain. I struggled to my feet as he pulled a moth-eaten white lace dress from the huge, dark-wood wardrobe at one end of the room.

"Wear this."

I looked distrustfully at the dress.

"Now!" he shouted roughly, sending my nerves on high alert. He pounded a fist against the door on his way out. "Put it on now. If not, I'll put it on for you and I won't be gentle."

As soon as he left, I grabbed the dress. I didn't know exactly why I was sure, but I believed his threat. Tears dripped down my cheeks as I took off my clothes and tugged the old dress over my head. It smelled like mothballs. The lace was scratchy and the sleeves restrictive. I saw myself in the mirror and glanced away. I resembled a sacrificial virgin in the old-fashioned dress, and having met the man who was waiting for me, it wouldn't be much of a stretch to think I could be.

The door banged open, and the same man appeared. Someone lurked behind him in the hallway in a white lab coat. A doctor? He had a syringe in his hand, and I instinctively backed up, but he advanced too quickly.

The needle burned like a wasp sting as it went into my thrashing arm.

"You're ready? Let's go." Ivan turned away, expecting me to follow.

I did, slowly. "Where are we going?" I asked.

We left the small apartment and stepped out onto a dingy, cold landing.

"Church."

I was shivering by the time I got out of the car beside a small church, tucked away down a quiet street. Ivan manhandled me out of the back seat and crouched beside the driver-side window.

"Go and get it over with." The doctor sat at the wheel.

"You don't want to come and see? Three fucking years I've been waiting for this. It had better be worth it."

The doctor nodded at me. "It'll be worth it. Trust me. I'll see you later."

"Come on, lazybones, let's go to a wedding," Ivan said.

Now the odd, Gothic-looking lacy dress made sense. Though wearing a white lace dress to another woman's wedding felt tacky.

Ivan smirked at me, and there was nothing tender or caring about the expression. He seemed full of sadistic energy. I wondered what it must feel like to be so energetic. I could barely keep my head up. I wobbled after him, stopping once to retch. I felt so sick. Ivan barely gave me a second to recover, tugging me along and muttering about how disgusting I was.

Inside the church was quiet and still. I swayed on the spot, and a priest approached. There was no one else there. Were we the first to arrive?

"This is her?" The priest eyed me doubtfully.

Ivan nodded.

"Okay, well, let's get started." The priest sounded resigned. He kept glancing around nervously like he was doing something he shouldn't be.

He led us to a small dais and faced us.

"What's happening?" I asked Ivan.

He smirked. "We're finally getting married. I've waited fucking ages for this, so don't ruin it."

"Married?" Something inside me told me this was wrong. I had to fight. I had to stop it. But my muscles refused to move, and that crippling apathy washed over me.

What was the point? I could run, but where? I didn't know where I was or where to go. I had no numbers or even names of friends in my head.

I'd never been more alone.

He led me through the empty church, past the deserted pews to the altar, which was positioned under a gigantic wooden cross.

The priest turned to us and nodded meaningfully.

My apparent fiancé passed him a thick envelope of cash.

"Dearly beloved, we are here today to join Ivan Markovic and, um . . ."

The priest looked at me, and I stared blankly at him.

"Katarina Dmitrova," Ivan supplied.

". . . Katarina Dmitrova together in holy matrimony."

I felt sick. I could barely stand up. I was hot and cold, like I had a fever coming on. I clutched at Ivan's arm to stay standing. Something burned against my chest, and I dug around for it in the neckline of the lacy dress.

I pulled it free as the priest went through his lines.

It was a chain. The kind someone in the military might wear. It had a name on it. I peered closely at it, Ivan and the priest not even noticing that I wasn't listening. I'd seen it before. I was sure. It felt familiar.

"Then, in the power vested in me by—"

Boom. Boom. Boom.

Something hard knocked on the heavy old wood door of the chapel, the sound echoing throughout the room.

Boom. Boom. Boom.

The sound seemed to shake the entire place. It felt for a moment like it was coming from underneath the stone floor. Like someone was knocking from the very underworld itself.

Then, someone cleared their throat.

"I think you've missed a section, Father." The voice was deep and rich, arrogant, and something else—furious. Yes, there was fury in the tone.

It weakened my knees.

The priest stared into the darkness beyond the nave. "Who dares to interrupt a wedding?"

Footsteps sounded. Someone walked across the stone floor somewhere, but there were too many shadowy corners to see where he was coming from. The acoustics of the church made the voice echo around.

"You missed the section where you ask if anyone objects to this marriage."

"Who the fuck is there?" Ivan demanded, and drew something from behind his jacket.

A gun.

The sight of it was like a punch to the gut. I tried to step back, but he kept me close.

"Go ahead and do the ceremony properly, Father. We'll all wait," the voice continued.

Ivan peered into the murkiness and took a step in that direction, apparently going to investigate who was speaking.

Then there was a strange sound, like a zipper being drawn quickly closed, and a chunk of stone flew out of the pillar beside Ivan's head, gouged out by a bullet.

I stared.

The priest cried out, covering his head and calling for God.

"I said . . . do the ceremony properly, Father, I won't ask again," the voice continued.

"Does anyone here object to this union? If so, speak now or forever hold your peace." The priest's voice trembled.

"I'm so glad you asked." The man stepped out into the light, so much closer than he'd seemed.

He was dressed like a priest, but his clothes were burned and torn. He was tall and broad, so fucking broad, he looked like he could hold hell up with the strength of those shoulders. Bandages covered his hands but didn't seem to have impeded his aim.

He leaned against a pillar and met my gaze. His midnight eyes were ringed with full lashes. His lower face was bearded, and for a second I could feel the scrape of that beard against my chin, but then the memory was gone. He had a gun at his side, fitted with a silencer.

"I object and I will not hold my peace."

Ivan pointed his gun at the newcomer. I could feel his hand shaking beside my face. The demon of a man laughed like it was a joke. Ivan seemed to think better of it and brought his gun to my head, pressing it into my temple.

"Stay back, or she dies."

The man sighed and used the tip of his weapon to scratch his temple. It was such a nonchalant move. He was a man used to dealing in death. None of this fazed him.

"How predictable," he drawled. Then he focused on me. "I would tell you how much it pisses me off when people threaten to break my things . . . but you're not going to live long enough to make it worth the energy. You're already food for the worms."

"Because?" Ivan demanded. "We've never even met!"

"So? I've killed a lot of people I've never even met . . . You're actually quite special, because today I'll kill you for entirely personal reasons."

Ivan gripped me closer. "What personal reasons?"

The man pointed the gun at the priest, who was trying to creep away.

He whistled. "Oi, Father, I can't let you go now that I know you're willing to wed an unwilling, drugged-up woman to whoever comes along and pays you off. I'm sorry. I'll see you down there later, okay?"

"Down where?" the priest mumbled.

"Hell. Wait for me." Then the shot sounded. A muffled *pop*.

The priest fell to the floor before the sound had even finished.

Ivan roared with fear and outrage. "Man, what's your fucking problem?"

"You are. You and men like you. The ones who think women and children in our world are just chess pieces to maneuver where you need them. You're my fucking problem. Add to that the fact that you've touched that which is mine, and I'm afraid your fate is decided."

"What's yours?" Ivan demanded. "Her?" He shook me and then pushed me a few steps away.

I stumbled into the altar.

The newcomer chuckled. "Yes, her. My little stray. My woman, soon-to-be wife, and future mother of my kids. It's not your desire to marry her that sealed your fate. It's that you even glanced her way. That you thought yourself worthy of touching her—oh, and that you tried to take one of my firsts." He stared at me. "I'll be her first husband, and her last."

Ivan went to protest, to back up, his gun waving wildly, and a shot sounded. Only seconds later another shot zipped from somewhere, and Ivan fell. The smell of something burning and the coppery scent of blood filled the air. Around me, the bodies lay, both dead as fucking doornails, matching bullets between the eyes. Executed with perfect ease.

I was frozen with terror as the newcomer walked toward me. He wrapped an arm around me just before I fell over, and he hauled me to his chest.

"I'm sorry I'm late, *micetta*," he murmured, his gaze moving across my face.

It had blood on it; I could feel it. A delicate spray.

"Are you going to kill me?" I heard myself ask through numb lips.

"Kill you?" he repeated, a frown furrowing between his eyebrows.

He ran his attention over my face, checking for wounds, perhaps, or deciding how he would end me. Something that looked like worry worked across those marble, statue-worthy features, and he slowly shook his head.

"No, angel, I'm not going to kill you. I'm going to marry you, and keep you . . . till death do us part."

I stared at the man who seemed more devil than human and lost the battle.

Darkness swooped over me like a veil, and I fell gratefully into that sweet oblivion.

30

MASSIMO

After Katarina passed out, I lifted her carefully into my arms, pocketed my gun, and made my way from the church. I called in some favors to have the place cleaned. The fucking detective had taken so long to process my paperwork and let me go, that by the time I'd charged my phone enough to check the tracking app, Katarina had already been on her way to the church.

Even a few minutes later, and that motherfucker would have married her. What the fuck was going on? I'd grabbed his wallet before carrying my unconscious bride from the church, and now, in a cab, I went through it. He was her so-called fiancé. He had been mentioned in her admission paperwork, though I hadn't thought of his name again until today.

So, he was Ivan Markovic. Well, it *had* been him. Now, he was just a body on the floor, soon to be chopped up and disappeared by professionals. I took a picture of his ID and sent it to Giada to look him up properly.

Then I turned to feast my eyes on Katarina. She slept sweetly against me. Fuck, I'd missed her. Even in the short time we'd been apart, I'd really fucking missed her.

She didn't remember me. Someone had drugged her again. I'd suspected it when I'd seen her outside Hallow Hall during the fire. There'd been a far-off look in her eyes that hadn't been right. One thing about Katarina was how sharp she was. She didn't just see everything, she saw beyond what others wanted to show. She saw inside.

The woman in the church wearing a bloodstained wedding dress hadn't seen anything. She hadn't been herself, and it hurt somewhere in my chest to think she was confused again. Alone, locked inside her own mind, when I'd told her she wasn't alone anymore. Whoever had drugged her was trying to make a liar out of me. I wouldn't stand for it.

As soon as we got home, it would be time to figure out why Blackwood and the holy trinity of fuckwits at Hallow Hall had kept her locked up for so long without killing her, or, given their MO, knocking her up and selling off pieces of her after she'd delivered. Nothing about Katarina Dmitrova's story made sense.

We took a cab across town. I held her in my arms. The fucking bullet that the fucker in the church had gotten lucky with had landed somewhere in my thigh. A non-vital place, clearly, since I wasn't losing much blood, so I ignored it. It had started to snow again. The stately streets of Torino shone with orange lamplight against the murky sky and falling snow. We stopped at a bustling ER, and I sent a message to an old Army buddy.

Half an hour later, I was carrying her into an exam room, and Filippa, one of my squad mates a lifetime ago, closed the door and eyed me.

"You don't call or write, and then text me from the parking lot that you need help with some woman who's injured? Mass, you know there are rules in a hospital, right?"

"And they don't apply to this patient," I snapped at her, my patience with the bullshit of the last few days growing dangerously thin. "She gets what she needs, when she needs it, or I'll go out to your waiting room and kill anyone who would be before her in your triage system, understand?"

Filippa sighed. "All too well. Why do you think I smuggled you in here? Put her on the bed."

I carefully lowered Katarina to the paper-covered bed in the corner, sliding my hand into hers to keep some form of contact between us during her exam.

Filippa eyed that touch curiously but wisely didn't comment while she took Katarina's vitals.

"She's out of it on something. Something strong. A sedative?"

"She was standing up and walking around earlier," I supplied in case it helped.

"Maybe she has a bit of resistance to it, but it got to her in the end. What else does she take, any regular medications?"

"She was taking carbidopa and levodopa for a while."

Filippa frowned. "Does she have a Parkinson's diagnosis?"

I shook my head.

Filippa tutted. "Then why in the hell would she be taking that combination? It can literally cause psychosis in patients who don't require it. Confusion and memory issues, lost time, nightmares, paranoia, voices in your head, you name it, it can—"

"Voices in your head?" I interrupted.

Filippa nodded. "It can cause a psychotic break that some never recover from. Trigger psychosis-like symptoms; it's a massive risk. Why was she taking it? Who would even prescribe that?"

"I don't know, okay? I don't know why, but I'm going to find out. She was off it for a while, and she seemed fine," I said. *Except for the voices.*

Filippa went to a drawer and pulled out a syringe and a tourniquet.

"I'll take a full panel and get her blood tested for everything I can think of. It's a starting point. Other than that, I'm going to give her a drip of fluids and saline. She's dehydrated and might not have eaten in a few days."

My gut clenched at the words. That fucker in the church had starved my angel. He had kept water and food from her, imprisoned her somewhere, when she'd already suffered that exact fate for three fucking years. Black anger billowed from my heart, the same cold, black hue as the smoke that had risen from the top of Hallow Hall as it burned, taking all the evidence of Pavol's, Vargas's, and Benedict's crimes with it.

"What can I do?" I asked hoarsely.

Filippa eyed me cautiously. I stood over them, fists clenched hard enough to draw blood.

"Go and calm down somewhere. Get a cup of coffee or some ice water. Try the matcha tea from the cafeteria. We'll be here awhile," Filippa snapped.

I turned away, my frustration not allowing me to make a civil comeback. I took two steps when she lashed out.

"Stop right there! You come to a goddamn hospital with that much bleeding . . . from what? A stab wound? And don't think to get yourself patched up?"

I stared down at my thigh. *Oh, right.*

"It isn't a stab wound," I told her coolly. "It's a gunshot."

My blood had been pooling around my boot, apparently, while I was standing over Katarina.

"Mass." Filippa seemed to be at the end of her tether with me. She stopped right in front of me and gave me the once-over. "What are you doing? Getting shot? Running around the city with unconscious women? I'm not even going to ask about the robes or the fire damage . . . Are you still doing all of this? Do you still not care if you live or die?"

Her voice broke on the last word. She was emotional like that; she always had been. A bleeding heart wrapped in a cool and analytical doctor's body.

"I do care. I'm here because I care about something finally," I said quietly.

Filippa sighed. "Revenge?"

I shook my head. "Her. That woman there. I care about her—enough to . . ." I was unsure where I was going with that sentence. It was a fundamental shift, soul deep. For so long, I'd lived with emptiness inside, knowing the end was only ever one bad call away. Most of the time, I welcomed the knowledge that life was fleeting and fickle and at any moment it could all be over.

Until now.

I care about her enough to live.

"Who is she?" Filippa asked, curious.

"She's my responsibility," I heard myself say. "Mine to protect. Mine to save. Mine to heal. Mine."

Filippa raised an eyebrow at Katarina's sleeping face. "She must be someone special to have broken through your bullshit and made you see sense."

"Which is?"

"Life is for the living. Now, I'm going to check that bullet hole, so I can sleep tonight knowing I did everything I could to actually give you a chance to live a real life for once . . . with the woman you love."

Love?

Filippa pushed me into the chair beside Katarina's bed and bustled around, setting up supplies for cleaning the gunshot wound. I studied my sleeping angel's face.

Love. So, that's what this terrible, precious thing was in my chest, the hope and fear all rolled into one. Love.

"Right, no bitching, or it'll take longer," Filippa said, wheeling over a tray and her chair. She tapped the bed beside Katarina's hand. "Foot up here."

I followed her commands. She pushed my robes out of the way.

"Okay, in the interest of passing the time, I want to know. Why the fuck are you dressed like the priest from hell?"

By the time I left Filippa's hospital, it was late afternoon. The snow had stopped again, but there were only a few souls braving the white streets. It was freezing. I'd borrowed blankets from the hospital to wrap around Katarina, but she couldn't stay outside for long. She needed a warm bed, hot food, and a fire burning in the hearth.

But first, I needed something. Something simple. Archaic. Something selfish.

But then, I didn't know any other way to be.

Our destination glowed orange on the white wall of buildings, all caked with snow. The lights burned through the small windows of the church, inviting passersby who were cold to come inside.

Inside, I quickly made my way down the aisle, the heavy scent of incense filling my senses. It was quiet within, with only a few people drifting around the hallways. I knocked on the closed door of the chapel before a familiar voice rang out.

"Come."

I pushed the door open and turned sideways to carry Katarina in without banging her head. The tiny chapel was dimly lit. Vittorio, dressed in very plain robes, straightened from his prayer position as I entered.

He was only slightly older than me, but there was a calm peace about him that I'd never achieve.

"Massi?" he said, looking over me and my armful of woman. "Please tell me she isn't unconscious."

"She's had a long day. They drugged her. Be mad at them, not me, Father."

I carried her down the short aisle to the altar.

Vittorio watched me with a pained expression.

"You left that out when you asked me to marry you both." He shook his head. "I cannot marry her while she's unconscious. She needs to wake up to agree."

"She agrees, she told me to tell you before she passed out." I sighed and tossed Vittorio a tired grin before my attempt at humor faded away. "Honestly, she's drugged, she won't agree to anything until it wears off. She won't know me . . . but we can't waste time. She needs to marry me so I can keep her safe."

"And you need to marry her why?" Vittorio asked.

"To keep her. I need to marry her just to keep her. Vittorio, she's mine, and I'm hers. I knew it the moment I met her. End of story. Don't make me hold a gun to your head."

Vittorio blinked at me, surprised by my vehemence. Yes, I was well aware of how much of a hypocrite I was, having just shot two men an hour ago for attempting to do what I was about to, marry my little stray without her consent . . . but I'd already condemned my soul to burn . . . what was one more sin?

He studied Katarina's sleeping face, and his gaze drifted down to my dog tags around her neck, tangled in her hair and only just visible.

"Very well, I'll do it, but if you're lying, you take the sin on your own soul, not mine."

"Deal. Let's get started."

I shifted Katarina in my arms, cradling her close. Vittorio went to stand behind the altar.

He started to speak in a low rush of Latin, crossing himself vigorously and gesturing toward me. Like I could be cleansed of the sins of my life. I'd long ago given up any idea of being saved. I didn't need salvation, or want it. I gazed down at Katarina.

I just needed her.

"What's happening?" Katarina murmured, her eyes blinking open groggily.

Vittorio glanced at me, but I nodded at him to continue.

She was waking up but not all the way. She hovered somewhere between sleep and wakefulness, the drugs tugging her downward.

I tightened my arms around her. "You're dreaming. This is all a dream."

Her eyes fixed on mine for only a moment before they slid shut again.

"Keep going, Vittorio. I can still shoot you in the head," I warned my friend.

He huffed but continued.

"Do you take this man?" Vittorio tossed to Katarina, but she'd gone under again.

"She does, and I take her. Get to the end, Father," I prompted him.

He shook his head, crossing himself again, and nodded.

"By the power vested in me by God, I pronounce you man and wife. You may kiss the bride, if you can," Vittorio said.

I looked down at my sleeping angel. My little stray, scrappy and determined and so full of stubborn, relentless hope, she shone.

I leaned forward, raising her face toward mine, and pressed a kiss to her forehead.

It was chaste. Respectful . . . the only concession I could give considering I'd just married her without her knowledge. I was the devil she'd always accused me of being, and I couldn't bring myself to care. Not now that I had her in my arms and our names together on a registry. I'd do it again, to keep her.

31

MASSIMO

Paolo was waiting at the door when I carried Katarina into the townhouse I kept in Torino's old town. The hallway was as dark and atmospheric as if I'd stepped through a portal into the seventeenth century.

Frescoes painted the walls, angels and demons battling for the fate of the world. The heavy marble banisters gleamed in the light from the antique sconces on the walls. This place had been a few days away from being torn down when I'd bought it. It was a relic, a gorgeous, fading one, and I'd decided to restore it instead of watching it crumble.

Now it was dark, and Gothic. Beautiful in a way that spoke to my damaged soul. Could my angel live here in the dark with me? Only time would tell.

There were four spacious levels, and my rooms were on the very top. The view of the city from the balcony was stunning. I carried Katarina up the stairs to the fourth floor, with Paolo trailing behind us.

"Is there anything the lady would like to make her more comfortable?" he asked, hurrying behind us.

"I will attend to her," I told him quickly. The thought of my old housekeeper providing anything at all for Katarina riled me in a way I couldn't explain. It went beyond mere possessiveness.

I reached the top floor and carried her through the expansive dressing rooms and opulent bathroom into the huge bedroom. An enormous four-poster bed with ornately carved posts dominated the room, which was hung with dark-red velvet curtains. A large mirror leaned against one wall, its glass shadowed with time but still catching the light in patches. Now I saw myself holding Katarina, a dark specter with an innocent maiden. Her awful white dress was bloodstained here and there, adding to the effect that I was a devil come to carry my stolen bride off to hell.

I advanced into the room, turning away from the mirror. I didn't need the reminder of what I was right now.

I set her down on the bed. The mural on the wall depicted a fair-haired maiden in a meadow with a shadowy robed figure on a black horse approaching. The meadow where the maiden sat was warm and bright, but the approach of the rider held a spreading darkness, and the painting behind him was altogether different.

It was only early evening, but suddenly I was exhausted. Since the fire, I'd done nothing but worry about this woman. Now that she was here, safe, in my grip, all the fight went out of me. It was a strange feeling, and one I'd never experienced before.

If I'd been more naive, I might have thought it was contentment, but I knew that didn't belong to a man like me.

I stripped off the dreaded priest's robe finally, and threw it in the corner, then moved to Katarina's clothes. The bloodstained wedding dress was a macabre sight. I didn't want another man's blood touching her skin. I didn't want another man's anything touching what was mine.

I cut the dress, turning it into simple strips that could easily be peeled off her. Her underwear was the same threadbare, grayish cotton kind she'd worn at Hallow Hall. I left it on her. When she woke, if she didn't know me, she'd be scared, and this woman had had enough of being scared to last a lifetime.

There'd be time to dress her in the finest silks and laces. Time to give her all the things her hard life had denied her.

First, I had to wait until she came back to me.

I tucked her under the heavy comforter and slid in next to her. I pulled her into my arms, breathed in the smell of her, and finally, slept.

The sound of metal rattling woke me. It was a quiet rattle. Careful. I opened my eyes before I moved so I could take my little stray in and see what she was doing before she realized she'd woken me.

Morning light streamed in the windows. I'd slept right through. It was unheard of.

Katarina stood at the door, carefully turning the knob this way and that, trying to get it to open.

"It's locked," I called to her, my voice rough with sleep.

She jumped. She'd wrapped a blanket from the couch around herself, and she nearly dropped it.

I shoved the bedding back and sat up, leaning against the ornately carved headboard.

"I had the housekeeper lock us in."

Her gaze darted around the room as she looked for an escape. "Why?"

"To keep you safe," I supplied, and pushed myself out of bed.

I was naked except for underwear, and she froze as her gaze ran up and down my body. She lingered on the bandage on my thigh. It had turned pink with weeping blood overnight.

"Who are you?" she murmured.

"Who do you think I am?" I sauntered across the polished parapet toward her, giving her plenty of time to get used to the sight of me. It didn't seem to be working. A pulse hammered in her throat, and her eyes widened as I got close.

She raised a hand in front of her. "Stop right there! I don't know."

Of course it had been obvious that she hadn't recovered her recent memories, but the confirmation was disappointing.

"Did we . . ." She wet her lips, and pink touched her cheeks. "Did something happen between us last night?"

I nodded slowly. "Something happened, but not what you think."

My cryptic answer did nothing to calm her down.

"What was it?"

We got married. Well, that wasn't technically true, I admitted, just to myself. I married her. I decided in that split second that telling her while she was confused and disoriented was a terrible idea.

"We'll talk about it later. First, I need to know how you are." I put a hand to her forehead before she could step back.

"What are you doing?" She seemed scandalized that I'd touched her.

"Checking you for a fever. Your cheeks are terribly pink, little stray, unless that's in response to something else . . ." I let my focus run over her, drinking her in.

She glanced down at my body, my insinuation clear.

Her eyes latched on to my cock, thick and hard in my briefs, and bounced back to my face, her cheeks only getting redder. Yes, I was hard as hell at the sight of Katarina in my home, her smell in my bed, knowing we were married. I was a simple man, at the end of the day . . . and having her here was affecting me more than I'd expected it would.

"I don't have a fever, I'm just . . . confused," she admitted, and looked away.

I nodded. "That's to be expected. You were drugged. It was something strong, but feel better knowing that you've been checked by a doctor and all is well. We'll know more about the drug later."

"Who would drug me?" she asked, and then narrowed her eyes. "Was it you?"

The suspicious and stone-cold bravery of that question while she stood alone and defenseless, locked inside a room with me, made me chuckle. She was there, my angel of vengeance with the steely spine and shining wings, just under the surface. No matter what those monsters at Hallow Hall had done to her, they'd never broken her.

She was unbreakable.

"Why would I bother drugging you, *micetta?* When I already have you here, under my command?" I lost the fight not to touch her, settling for brushing a lock of her hair back. It gleamed like liquid gold in the sunlight.

She raised her chin at me, refusing to be cowed. "To keep me quiet?"

I grinned at her. "But I like it so very much when you scream my name."

Her eyes widened. She turned away from me, trying to put space between us, to keep her cool. She stared up at the painting that filled an entire wall.

"It's Hades and Persephone. Their first meeting. It was in bad shape when I bought this place, but I decided to have it fixed instead of painting over it. A love story for the ages."

"It's horrible," she said flatly, and then glared at me. "He stole her."

"He loved her."

"He brought famine on the world for the sin of taking her."

I just shrugged. "That was her mother. Anyway, why would Hades care what happened to the world, as long as he had her?"

She shook her head. "If you find Hades relatable . . . you are beyond saving."

"I don't need salvation, angel. I have you."

"Angel?" she repeated, her head tipping to the side. She tested the word, as if she remembered being called it before.

For an endless moment, heat and memories collided. I could see her start to remember me, the drug finally wearing off, when a knock at the door broke that precious moment to shards.

"Mass, do you want breakfast?"

"*Cazzo*, Paolo, you have the most fucking annoying timing! Come in," I called out to him irritably.

Katarina fled to the bed and hid most of herself behind a velvet curtain.

The door opened, and Paolo came in, looking curiously for a sign of the woman I'd unexpectedly brought home. I didn't bring women here, to my home. I didn't bring women anywhere, really, as a rule. Relationships, even one-night stands, were a distraction, and one I hadn't allowed myself in years.

Paolo beamed as soon as he saw her.

"Miss Dmitrova." He held a silver tray with a tea set worthy of the Queen of England rattling on it.

Mrs. Lucciano. I ignored the possessive, dark growl inside me.

"Would you care for tea? I didn't know how you took it, with cream, or milk, sugar, lemon . . . the options are endless," he prattled on.

I was about to send him away when Katarina advanced toward him a little, her shoulders less tense. So, old Paolo was making her feel more relaxed? Then he could stay.

"Paolo, see to Katarina, whatever she wants or needs. I'm going out. I'll be back shortly." I nodded meaningfully to my housekeeper.

While I might be giving the appearance of ease, Paolo was under strict instructions not to let Katarina out of the room and to keep her locked in. I couldn't have her getting away before she remembered herself, and me.

I took one last glimpse at my stolen bride. The angel I planned to keep in the dark beside me. Even seeing her standing there in the glorious morning light, the painting of Persephone right behind her, I couldn't bring myself to regret it.

I left my new bride in peace, and she watched me go.

32

KATARINA

Paolo, the kind old man with the creased face and perfect tea, refilled my cup for the tenth time.

"But I just don't understand why I'm here," I told him earnestly.

He simply nodded, full of understanding.

"I should get home. My mother's house is near Cavoretto, if you know that area."

He shook his head. "I'm not overly familiar."

"Still, she'll be worried about me," I said. The words sounded like they must be true, even if I had holes in my memory the size of chasms.

"Massimo will take good care of you, Katarina. I promise you this," Paolo said.

I slumped down in the chair beside the fire, disappointed by his dismissive tone.

The old man wasn't going to help me, then, and I wasn't the sort of person to try and break an elderly man's hip, fighting to get away. Besides, there was something about Paolo that warned me he'd be a better fighter than I assumed. He might be old, but he was solid and spry. There was real strength in his gnarled grip. While I was just me. As weak as always.

I sipped the tea and treasured the way the warm amber liquid slipped down my throat, soothing me from the inside out.

The day had turned gray outside, but inside this house, the warm, intimate atmosphere was only heightened by the darkness. I enjoyed the fire warming my side. The seat was velvet and overstuffed. I could close my eyes and sleep for a week, but I couldn't afford to . . .

Because I didn't know where I was or how I came to be here. Rationally, I should be more upset about that than I was, but there was part of me that was just resigned.

Confusion was something I felt instinctively used to, as sad as that was.

Also, there was something about this place that felt familiar. Not the house, or Paolo, or the view from the window, it was something else. The smell? That would be a weird thing to be used to. The man whom I woke up beside?

Yes. Him. There was something familiar about him. A thread I couldn't stop pulling at to unravel the knots in my memory. He felt like the key to all of it. And while he was intimidating, terrifying, really, I wasn't afraid of him.

I wandered around the room, taking in the rich, antique furnishings.

"Massimo had this entire place restored, brought it back from the dead. He stopped it all from being forgotten. Sometimes people ask to rent out the place, or to film TV shows here!" Paolo chuckled.

"I take it he never lets them?"

"Massimo is a private man. The most private I've ever met. You won't catch him opening his home up to just anyone. In fact, you are the first woman he's ever brought here."

"Did he just move in?" I mused.

"No."

Oh, okay. That knowledge made me feel odd inside, and I ignored it soundly.

I walked to a long sideboard and picked up one of the photos there. It was a group of men in military uniforms. They wore heavy helmets and sunglasses, but even then, I recognized Massimo. He was the tallest and broadest. While the rest were smiling for the camera, he was just straight-faced.

I set the frame down and glanced over the others. There was a picture of him at some kind of ceremony wearing a suit and collecting a medal.

Paolo appeared beside me. "For bravery. He was the only man, during a bombing at a school, to run back inside while the bombs were still falling."

Suddenly, in my mind's eye, I saw him. Dressed in black, startling against a white backdrop, staring back at me for a moment before running into a burning building.

I set the photo down.

"He doesn't like to remember the past too much, or his accomplishments, I guess, but I do. Since I'm the only person here most of the time, he humors me and lets me put up the frames."

Next on the shelf was the medal, propped open in its box. The writing below the medal read:

Medaglia d'Oro al Valor Militare

Next to a name:

Massimo Lucciano

I stared at those words before my hand rose to my neck. I pulled the long chain out of the top of the cashmere sweater Paolo had given me and inspected the dog tags.

There it was. *Massimo Lucciano*. I'd noticed the necklace just a little while ago when I'd gotten dressed.

"Ah, his dog tags. I'm not surprised to see you wearing them," Paolo said. "If he values you enough to bring you home, then he certainly values you enough to give you those. Now, are you hungry?"

I found myself nodding before I could help it.

Paolo beamed again.

"*Brava*. I'll prepare lunch."

After lunch, which I ate with wild abandon, Paolo left me alone, and I found myself drifting off. I was stuffed full. The dining room of the townhouse was just as dark and Gothic as the rest of the place, but in here, deep-emerald velvet chairs and huge, jewel-hued threaded tapestries covered the walls. The gigantic dining table gleamed under the wintry light flooding in through the long windows. A whole wall was framed with Juliet balconies, and I could have stayed and gazed out at the white city streets of Torino all day as the snow fell. It was the most majestic city view I'd ever seen, despite having lived in this very city for many years. My neighborhood was nearer the bottom of the hills, much closer to Hallow Hall. It had taken three buses to get into the city center, while I'm sure Paolo could amble along the gracious sidewalks to the markets and shops in a few minutes. It was a level of wealth and luxury that I'd never experienced. Massimo Lucciano might not actually be from the underworld, but he was certainly from a different tax bracket.

"How was your lunch?" Paolo asked as he brought me an espresso.

I just stared at it for a long moment before reaching out to take it.

"I could make you something else," he started, seeming doubtful about breaking the unofficial Italian rule of only drinking espresso after eating lunch.

"No, this is perfect. I just think that maybe I haven't had one for a long time." I lifted the tiny cup to my face and breathed in deeply.

A hit of caramel and toasted nuts, then bittersweet dark cocoa from the deep roast.

I took a sip and closed my eyes, enjoying every second of the smoky sweetness.

A soft chuckle pulled me from my reverie.

"I don't think I've ever seen someone enjoy a simple coffee so much," Paolo remarked. "Most people forget to enjoy the little things. They become commonplace and worthless."

"Not worthless," I mused. "Forgotten. People forget all sorts of things. I didn't always lose my mind over coffee. Like I said, I think it's been a while."

Paolo crossed himself dramatically. "A life without coffee? *Che peccato!* How is it possible?"

A soft meow saved me from having to explain why I had no idea when the last time was that I drank coffee. I glanced down, and my heart melted. A black cat was winding around my ankles.

"Nox, don't bother your new mistress," Paolo reprimanded the magnificent black beast.

I crouched beside him.

"He's not! I love cats," I enthused. Nox. The Latin name for night, and this boy personified night . . . just like his owner, Massimo. Dark and dangerous looking, so graceful and aloof it bordered on cruel, inhuman beauty. But then Nox butted my hand forcefully, demanding attention and head scratches.

"Don't say that around Massi. He already brings home any bedraggled strays he finds outside. You'd think we were running the world's most expensive cat shelter." Paolo's sniff made his distaste known.

Massi. Paolo's approval for his boss was clear. The stern and terrifyingly intimidating man from this morning who'd assured me that he was actually saving me, not harming me, by keeping me here filled my head.

My heart melted a bit more, and a twinge of discomfort moved within it. Massimo collected strays. Was I just another stray to him? A damsel who needed saving? What did he want in return for his help? Was I another charity case to him? Wasn't I a charity case in general? I didn't even remember the last few days, or months. I could hardly afford to indulge in hurt pride right now. Anxiety clamped its steely hand around my throat.

Nox was a sweetheart, rubbing around me and purring loudly. I stroked his sleek coat and tried to put my worries out of my head.

"Pax is jealous. She's shier, but she's my favorite," Paolo said.

I followed his gaze to the stunning cat sitting on top of the sideboard situated across from the dramatic windows. She was white as the moon, with deep golden eyes. It was clear she was a girl. There was something delicate and feminine about her mannerisms as she straightened up and assessed me.

Gravy, I hope he's okay. The image of a little moth-eared cat filled my mind.

The name and image came to me suddenly. The thought was so natural and effortless, I knew he was real. I stood, my heart suddenly racing. Was I remembering things? I remembered Gravy, the stray. But where had I met him?

"If you're finished, I need to run out to the supermarket before it closes for dinner. I suggest a nap, after everything you've been through."

I let Paolo lead me upstairs.

"You wouldn't happen to know what that was and feel like filling me in, do you?"

Paolo patted my hand, tucked into the nook of his elbow.

"I don't think that's a good idea. It'll come when you're ready to know."

We got to the room I'd woken up in. The one that took up the entire top floor. Lavish didn't begin to cover it. The tub in the bathroom looked like one that ancient Roman emperors used to bathe in. It only added to the mystery of the man who had taken it upon himself to care for me here, in this otherworldly house.

I went into the room and let Paolo fuss over me, because honestly, he seemed happier that way. He tucked me into bed and put a white noise machine on that was discreetly hidden somewhere on the marble bedside table.

"You rest, and then Massi will be home later, and you can ask him your questions."

I nodded, tired suddenly beyond belief.

Paolo lowered the heavy velvet drapes around the bed, so the light was dimmed, and then the sound of the door shutting softly let me know that I was alone.

The bed was beyond soft. Dreamy, honestly. I started to drift away almost immediately, before a creeping feeling of anxiety came over me.

Lying there, I felt suddenly like a prisoner. It wasn't rational. It made no sense. Regardless, I sat up and opened the curtains of the four-poster bed. The room was serene and cozy. It wasn't a prison.

I thought about going back to sleep but knew that I wouldn't be able to before I proved to myself that I was free to leave here whenever I wanted.

I got up and padded to the door, my feet sinking into the plush rug.

I reached the door and turned the handle.

It didn't budge.

I tried it again, twisting it this way and that. It didn't move a single inch. I was locked in. Just like a prisoner. And just like that . . . I lost it.

Panic clawed up my throat and made it hard to breathe. My skin felt like it was going to crawl off. It was an involuntary reaction. A trauma response buried deep. I didn't remember why it set me off so violently, but my body clearly did.

I banged on the door. "Let me out!"

Silence met my cry.

I banged harder. "Paolo! Let me out of here. Open the door!"

Silence, and then a throat cleared.

"I'm sorry, Katarina, but you're not to roam free in case you leave and get lost."

"That's not your decision to make, or your boss's. It's my decision to make. I get to choose!" I banged on the wood, my hand starting to hurt.

"I'm afraid I can't." His tone wasn't that of someone who would change their mind. He'd locked me in on his master's orders, and there was no escape. I was powerless. Voiceless. Controlled. Imprisoned.

"If you don't, I'm going to make him regret this!" I warned Paolo.

"So be it." His final response.

That motherfucker. I turned around and headed for a lamp right beside the door and kicked it over before I could overthink it. It fell with a hard crash and shattering of glass.

There were no sounds from beyond the door. I headed for the

sideboard and the decanter and crystal glasses there, picking one up. I threw one against the wall and then another. A scream left me, unbidden and unstoppable.

I lost track of how long my anger and fear raged. Frustration filled me, so thick it choked me, fogging my thoughts. When I finally exhausted that fury, the room was a mess. Regret spread inside me. All the beautiful things in this painstakingly restored room hadn't deserved to be smashed up. But then, I didn't deserve to be locked up and have none of my questions answered. This shit was just things, and I was a person, not a possession.

After the anger passed, the tears came.

Endless tears. Rivers of salt. I made my way back to the bed and pressed my face into the pillow, crying and crying until it felt like my lungs might give out.

Somewhere in that torrent of feelings, I wore myself out. Sleep came on the heels of my exhaustion, and I thought no more.

33

MASSIMO

After I went by Filippa's hospital to talk about Katarina's results, I answered Giada's call.

"Finally, you pick up. Didn't you see that you have a hundred missed calls from me?"

"Yes I did, but I had somewhere to be before I called you back. I had to find someone I'd lost in the mess that was the end of Hallow Hall. Someone important." Not to mention that Paolo had been calling me nonstop to report on Katarina's movements, including the fact that she'd decided to smash up the bedroom. I hurried back at that news.

Giada was quiet for a moment, and then I could hear the smile in her voice. "I told her you'd find her. I was so right."

"You told her what? You've spoken to her?" I asked, confused. I came to a stop in the street.

"Mm-hmm, yes, I have. She called me . . . well, someone close to me called for her."

"Tell me everything," I demanded.

Once her story was over, I stood at the side of the road watching cars pass, turning the road to gray slush. It was cold, but I couldn't feel it. The inevitability of fate felt like it was closing in on all sides.

Katarina had run into Renato De Sanctis's sister-in-law? It was almost enough to make a believer out of me.

"I told her you'd find her, and you did."

"She knew me? I mean, she was looking for me? When was this?"

"Bright and early yesterday morning. Why? Is she not looking for you anymore?"

"No. She's not. She doesn't know me. They've done something to her." I fought to keep my anger calm. They were dead. They got what they deserved.

"Shit, really? What are you going to do with her?" Giada asked.

"I married her."

"What?" Giada's voice exploded over the line. "Why? You married her, as in it's already done? You just told me that she doesn't know you . . ."

"She was asleep for the ceremony. I'll tell her all about it when she's feeling back to herself."

"Why wouldn't you just wait?" Giada said, exasperated.

"Because she's mine, and it's time everyone knew it. We won't be parted again," I told her resolutely.

She was quiet for a long moment and then whistled softly. "So, you're like in love with her . . . or obsessed . . ."

"Both. She won't be taken from me again."

"Okay, okay, I'm not trying to take her anywhere, jeez. Lucy is panicking about where she went."

"Tell her that everything is fine," I commanded.

Giada chuckled. "Sure it is, she's just married to some asshole she doesn't know. Absolutely fine."

I cast my eyes toward the sky, thinking of my angel in my room right now, worn out from breaking things, safe and sound in my house.

"She knows me. She knows me like no one ever has. Soon, she'll remember that."

"You hope," Giada added.

"I know."

She sighed. "Take it from someone who had a few memory problems a little while back. There's nothing scarier than some big, terrifying guy telling you he's your husband when you don't recognize him. Take it easy with her. Make sure she's better before you tell her."

"I will. Don't worry. Her well-being is my topmost priority. Also, I need you to find someone's address for me. A doctor from Hallow Hall. He goes by Blackwood and seems to be the real deal as far as I can tell."

"First name?"

"You need one? I thought you were the best at this," I reminded her.

She scoffed. "I am the best, and that cheek is going to cost you extra."

"Bill me, just find his address."

"Okay, okay, I'll call you later."

Giada hung up, and I climbed into my car at the curb. Blackwood had driven Katarina away from Hallow Hall before I could leave and find her again. He'd obviously helped to keep her drugged. The kind of shit they were giving her wasn't over-the-counter stuff. There had to be a real doctor in the mix somewhere.

So Blackwood needed a little visit. I had questions, and revenge to exact. My angel's story didn't quite add up, and I needed answers. I'd present his severed head to Katarina as a wedding present if she seemed so inclined.

Good idea, I congratulated myself, and turned the car toward home.

I came into the kitchen of the townhouse just as Paolo set a tray with coffee and cakes on the island.

"I'll take this upstairs," I said, picking up the tray.

"Are you sure she wants to see you?" Paolo hurried after me. "I made some headway earlier, if you want to leave it to me."

He bumped into my back when I stopped abruptly.

"As touching as your concern is, I can handle my wife. Don't worry."

"Your wife?" he nearly squeaked. "She never mentioned . . ."

"She doesn't know yet."

I had the pleasure of striking Paolo speechless as I headed upstairs.

I climbed the endless stairs slowly, tugged upward by the pull of Katarina. I'd be able to find her in the dark, with my eyes closed . . . something inside drew me toward her whatever chance it got. A little red line of fate connected us both.

I reached the door and set the tray on the console table across the hall before taking my key from my pocket and fitting it into the lock.

I turned it quietly, hoping I wouldn't wake her if she'd been sleeping.

"Rise and shine, *micetta*. Paolo made snacks."

The curtains were closed, keeping out the late-afternoon sunlight, the room shrouded in gloom. I peered through the darkness toward the bed. The covers were rumpled and tossed around . . . but the bed was empty.

I stepped farther into the room to find her, then I felt it.

A sharp sensation at my neck. Something piercing pressed against my throat.

"So, you're awake," I drawled.

She was silent, refusing to even give me her voice.

"Hungry yet? I brought you something to eat."

"Your man locked me up in here," she said just behind me.

Something that had been clenched tight the entire time we were apart relaxed at the sound of her voice.

I nodded. "For your own safety. I can't take the risk that you leave here and run away before you remember everything."

"He locked me up in here—alone." Her voice was low, and she was clearly hurt.

Her words sank through me. *Fuck.* I'd ordered for her to be locked up, just like the men in Hallow Hall had. Last night, I'd known it would hurt her to be locked up alone, and that's why I'd stayed by her side. Today, I'd been distracted with wanting answers, and Paolo had carried out my wishes a little too enthusiastically.

I turned, and the sharp object pressed harder into my skin, but the pain didn't register.

"I'm sorry, I didn't mean for that to happen," I told her slowly.

"You locked me up, Mass. Took away my choices. Controlled me."

Mass?

I twisted my head to see her, needing to look into her eyes to see if what I hoped was true really was.

She stared up at me, her eyes accusing. The glare was hard to meet, and yet, at the same time, precious. Because she knew me. She really knew me.

"I didn't know what to do—I'm sorry," I admitted.

She sighed, her shoulders falling from their position up around her ears. Her hand dropped to her side, and the shard fell to the floor with a small smash.

Her face twisted slightly, her lips drawing together, and her eyes filled with tears.

"I got lost again," she whispered, so quietly I almost couldn't make her words out. "I got so lost in the dark again—alone."

"You're not lost anymore. You'll never be lost again, and you're not alone anymore. From now on, it's you and me. I'll never leave you alone in the dark again."

A tear ran down her cheek, and then a sob that she was trying to fight slipped out. The sound was like an accusation, and I knew in that moment that I'd never let this woman cry again. She'd cried a lifetime's worth, and she was finished with that. I'd make sure of it.

"I thought you'd gotten hurt in the fire. I thought you might have died," she confessed, tears running freely down her cheeks now.

She started forward, and I opened my arms to catch her.

She hugged me around the middle, throwing herself into my arms, and I let her momentum spin us around, clutching her tightly to me.

Breathe. Now I could breathe again for the first time in days.

I pressed my face into her hair and inhaled deeply, filling my lungs with her. She was here. She knew me. Not alone, not anymore.

"I was so confused . . . I couldn't remember you, but I knew I'd forgotten something important," she muttered against my chest. She raised her head and looked at me. "It was you. The feeling that I'd forgotten something vitally important . . . It was you."

The space where my heart used to be burned. Fuck, it hurt. Finding a kindred soul after a lifetime of loneliness wasn't a small feat. For a man like me, it was a miracle. I was unlovable, and yet . . . she loved me.

I couldn't put any of that into words. All I could do was show her how much I'd missed her.

I leaned in and kissed her, and she kissed me back. Her hunger stole my heart even more. Soon there'd be nothing left of me, and only her inside me.

I pulled her more firmly into my arms and turned us around, kicking the door shut and heading for the bed. I carried her to the edge and then sank down on it, holding her carefully so she wouldn't fall.

I settled my weight just off her, so she wouldn't be crushed, and then deepened the kiss. My tongue sliding along hers, my hand cupping her jaw, then circling her neck. Thrusting against her soft, pliable body, needing more. Always more. I needed all of it. Every single inch of her.

My hands moved to her clothes. An old sweater of mine, and her panties. In seconds, they were on the floor. My own clothes followed. Her eyes widened as I lowered my naked body over hers. Her hard nipples pushed into my chest, and I could feel her heat between her legs, so fucking close it was all I could do not to sink inside her that very second.

"What are you doing?" she asked.

"Taking another of my firsts," I continued, sliding my hand down from her neck, between her breasts, and over her hips, and stroking her cunt. "First time I fuck you in my bed . . . *our* bed."

She shivered, biting her lip and trying not to cry out. My cock poked at the soft skin of her inner thighs as I ground myself on her. Her knee rose, and I guided it around my hips. I angled my aching cock just right and nudged inside.

It was like hitting a damn wall. She was so tight.

"Fuck," I let out in a rush.

"I don't think that's going to fit this time," she murmured, and then laughed.

She fucking laughed, while my cock poked at her tight little entrance and my body was desperate to be joined with hers.

My heart skipped a fucking beat. That was what she did to me.

My chest loosened with a chuckle, and I shifted to my side, slipping a hand down her body to her cunt.

"Hmm, it isn't, is it? My fault for skipping to the main course when I haven't even had my appetizer yet." I traced my fingers down her slit and moved suddenly, shifting to kneel before her. I pressed her knees to the bed, pinning her open.

She watched me with heated eyes. I leaned in and licked her. Her cunt was even sweeter than I remembered. I licked her from clit to ass and back again. I inched a finger inside and added another. She thrust her hips into my invasion. Needing more, I nosed through the wet curls covering her mound and burrowed through her slick folds to her clit. I licked and sucked circles around that precious little bundle of nerves, and her wetness coated my hands. I added a third finger, and her breath hitched.

She was getting there. I tongue-fucked her while she writhed beneath me, and when she came, her cunt spasming around my fingers, clenching tightly, I leaned up, moved across her, and pushed inside.

I kissed her deeply, holding her face in my hands like the priceless thing it was, and sank in deep, to the hilt.

She cried out on my lips. I'd only been inside her once before, which wasn't nearly enough to make it easier for her to take me.

"I'm sorry, angel. I'm sorry," I murmured, letting her adjust to my size.

I was sunk deep, and her muscles clenched like crazy around

me. Maybe I was pushing her too quickly after everything that had happened. She wasn't relaxed like she'd been that first time in the chapel.

Her nails were deep in my back, and when her eyes met mine, they were blazing.

"I'm sorry to hurt you—"

"Don't stop," she interrupted me to whisper.

When I didn't move, surprised by her words, she spoke again.

"I said don't stop," she demanded.

I pulled out a few inches then sank back in, and pleasure shot down my spine. Holy fuck. I wouldn't last long inside my angel. She had not only destroyed my sanity, but she'd also dismantled my self-control.

She shook under me, and I gathered her close, my heart against hers.

"I got so lost," she murmured. "I missed you. When I thought you were hurt, my heart broke, and I didn't think there was enough of it left to do that anymore."

I shook my head, emotions crowding in and filling it. Tender and sweet things I'd never felt before. Precious feelings I had given up on experiencing in my miserable life.

"I will find you every single time you feel lost. I will never let you go. How they ever thought they could tame you, I have no idea. You are so much stronger and braver than they could ever conceive."

My hips were pounding her now, and I was close. I needed to come, to mark this woman and fill her up. We weren't using protection, and there was only a slim chance that she was on birth control. What if she got pregnant? *Good.* Then it would be harder for her to ever leave. That damn devil in my head was satisfied. It would be harder for her to stop loving me if she was tied to me by a child . . . or three. I wanted her pregnant with my child, wearing my ring, in my bed, on my lap, at my table, all around me, all the time. A fresh start to have a real family, and they would be loved. I'd die before they ever doubted that.

She had changed me, from the inside out. I wasn't the same because of her. I never would be again. A light in the darkness.

"You shine," I whispered on her skin, and changed my angle to hit her clit with my pelvic bone.

She cried out, stiffening, her nails biting deeper, but I didn't stop.

I didn't slow even a moment and showed no mercy, because she'd shown me none. She'd stormed my heart and claimed it before I'd even realized I still had one.

When she came again, her whole body jerked. She got impossibly tight, so tight I couldn't even thrust anymore. Instead, her cunt squeezed along my cock and milked my fucking orgasm right out of me, drawing it ruthlessly from my balls.

I couldn't have stopped it if I'd tried.

34

KATARINA

I trailed my fingers over the rich brocade of a tapestry hanging on the wall of the library. An actual tapestry.

Maybe Massimo was the lord of the underworld after all; his home would certainly suit that role. It was impressive, and so beautiful, it was hard to believe it was real. Art and antiques filled the space. Dark wood and soft furnishings of velvet and satin. The windows faced the most stunning view of Torino. A grand piano stood in the library, and a harp. A freaking harp. Everything looked like it had been brought directly here from a secondhand sale at a royal's estate.

This was how kings lived.

The kitchen kept the theme, gothically dark but spacious and airy. A display of pomegranates sat on the huge marble island, calling to mind the Hades and Persephone painting upstairs.

Very funny.

Massimo had left a few minutes ago to get breakfast after sweeping up the remains of my smashing session.

He'd sent his housekeeper away yesterday so he didn't have to hear me screaming all night. It was just him and me, here in this house that felt like it had slipped through the cracks between worlds. A place separate from time. A bubble of safety from the storms raging outside.

It was quiet in the library. He had a library. I loved this house. *And this man.* I sat on the rug before the hearth. There was a fire already burning in the grate. Nox and Pax wound their way around me. Nox confident and curious, getting right onto my lap. Pax held back, coming slightly closer each time. I petted Nox until Pax seemed to feel safe enough to edge closer. She allowed me to stroke her after smelling my fingers for a good minute. A little later, I was bracketed by the two cats, as different as night and day. They snuggled into my sides, and I let my fingers wander through their fur and watched the flames dance in the fireplace. I hoped that Gravy had found someone else to feed him. I wondered if I went up there to call for him, he'd come to me. I could ask Massimo if he could become a member of the household. Sure, he wasn't regal like Pax and Nox, but he was a bundle of love, and I'd love nothing more than to hold him again.

Once the cats got bored of my petting, they wandered off, intertwining their tails as they went . . . the night and the moon, diametrically opposed and yet perfectly paired. I went to browse the books in the library.

I wandered past the stacks, enjoying the feeling of the cloth-bound spines under my fingers.

All the classics were covered here. Boccaccio's *Decameron,* Dante Alighieri's *Divine Comedy,* and *Il Canzoniere* by Petrarch.

I pulled a copy of *The Divine Comedy* from the shelves and went to sit in the chair before the fire.

Nel mezzo del cammin di nostra vita
mi ritrovai per una selva oscura,
ché la diritta via era smarrita.

The first lines called to me. I felt their meaning deep in my soul.

Midway upon the journey of our life
I found myself within a dark wood,
for the straight way had been lost.

The straight way for me had been lost three years ago, when I'd come home to Ivan Markovic and Father Vargas with my mother in her small, humble sitting room. A part of me had been angry at her for a long time for what I'd seen as a betrayal. But over time, that pain had ebbed. She had feared for my mortal soul. She'd trusted the wrong people. She was the only family I had left. Still, she had helped bring me to that wood where Dante had begun his journey through purgatory, hell, and beyond. Would I ever reach the end?

I was so engrossed in the book, I didn't notice the presence leaning over the chair from behind me until he spoke.

"Before me nothing but eternal things were made,
And I endure eternally.
Abandon all hope, ye who enter here."

Massimo translated easily. He switched effortlessly between English and Italian with a skill I envied. I glanced up at him. I couldn't get used to the sight of him in civilian clothes.

I shivered. "That has to be the creepiest part of this whole poem."

"Maybe so, but for you, it's also the most prophetic."

I frowned up at him askance, and a contented grin played around his lips.

"For I will keep you eternally, and you shall never leave me. Don't bother hoping for it," he murmured.

His hands went to my hair, and he stroked through the strands.

"So, you're my stalker now?" I attempted to lighten the mood, but honestly, what had happened yesterday was pure madness. The church and rushed ceremony were a blur of memory. I'd woken up thinking I'd imagined it.

"Hmm, maybe I am." He pulled my hand upward and pressed a kiss to my ring finger. At some point during the night, a huge ruby surrounded by diamonds had appeared on it. My hand felt heavier thanks to its opulence.

I stared at the jewel twinkling in the light.

"Why did you give this to me?" I wondered. It wasn't a small ring. It was a statement. I just didn't know what it was a statement of.

"Why? You don't like it?"

"It looks like an engagement ring," I mused.

He nodded. "Shall we just make it official then?"

"Make what official?"

"Getting married."

I stared at him for a second and then laughed. "Very funny. I'm not adding another responsibility to the load I've laid on your shoulders. You've already had to do a hell of a lot of crap for me. I'm not adding marriage to the list."

He was quiet for a long while, but it wasn't a peaceful silence. Finally, he took my hand and rubbed his fingers over the ring he'd put on it.

"It belonged to a noblewoman of the Savoy family. She used to live right here, in this very house," Massimo told me. "Paolo swears her ghost haunts these halls."

"Did she have a happy life?" I asked.

"She killed off four husbands who failed to please her and died with her children all around her, pampered, spoiled, and powerful, so, I think so."

"Powerful," I muttered, turning the ring this way and that. "I wonder what that feels like."

Massimo watched me. "You already know more than you think. Locked up in Hallow Hall with your mind intact, your wit razor-sharp, and your goodness unspoiled? That's power, whether you realize it or not."

I shook my head, sure that I wasn't worthy of that kind of praise. I'd only just survived in that place. That was hardly powerful.

"They didn't break you," he urged. "Don't you see how strong you are?"

I shook my head. "I don't feel strong."

He just shrugged. "Yet, that doesn't mean you aren't. How are you feeling?"

Now it was my turn to shrug. "Okay, I guess, though I kind of miss not having any memories. The last three years aren't something I'm eager to think about."

"And you don't have to. You have me now. I'll think about it, keep your tally and settle your scores."

"And Mira? I want to know what happened to her child. I want to make sure it never happens to someone else at Hallow Hall."

"That shithole is no longer. It wasn't a small fire. It's gone. They won't be rebuilding. I don't want to upset you, angel, but I found out some information from my doctor friend about the medications you've been on."

"What is it?" I felt worried for a second that he was going to sugarcoat it, conceal things to protect me, when all I wanted was the truth. It was my truth. It was my right to know it. Luckily, he didn't even try. By the time he finished telling me everything, I was shocked and furious. The rage threatened to blacken my vision.

"So, you're telling me that Ivan was giving me these drugs from our very first date?"

Massimo nodded. This was news indeed. I didn't know what to make of it. It meant that I'd been Ivan's target from the very first second we met.

"He was slipping you something that could cause side effects like voices . . . which you developed. You then went to your doctor about it, and that gave them a reasonable excuse to put you in Hallow Hall."

"I still don't understand why they wanted me there to begin with." I had so many unanswered questions, and it was driving me crazy. Maybe my mom could shed some light on it, though I already knew she had really believed that Hallow Hall would be good for my soul.

Massimo sighed. "I know. We'll find out together, and now that the drugs have stopped . . . you shouldn't hear the voices as much, if at all."

I took in that information. It had never been anything other than a side effect of a medication I should never have been taking. It was hard to get my head around.

"So, it wasn't angels after all? Are you disappointed?" I asked Massimo.

He chuckled and shook his head. "Science is one thing. I have my own opinions on you, my little angel of vengeance."

"Didn't you hear? I was never talking to angels, I was just tripping on the wrong meds," I pressed.

He shook his head. "You can't make me believe anything. You

saw me when I first walked in, without any prior warning of the kind of person I was. You saw me, and I saw you, angel. I know what you are, just like you know what I am."

"But you're not a devil or a demon. You're a man who takes in stray cats and ran back into a burning building for a little girl. You're the man who restored this beautiful house instead of letting them tear it down. You care about things . . . you just don't let anyone know it."

"I care about you, and I don't care who knows it. I'll shout it from the rooftops so everyone knows," Massimo murmured. His voice was deep, seductive, and sitting in the firelight, his face painted with hollows and shadows, making him look like a work of art, he was impossible to resist.

"If I didn't know better, I'd think you were trying to get in my pants, Father Lucciano," I teased him.

He pushed me back until I fell onto my elbows. We'd been sitting on the rug before the fire, and suddenly the location seemed too intimate. I wondered what the rug would feel like on my naked skin.

"Just trying? I better step up my game if I want to keep you satisfied, little stray. You're awfully demanding," he said, his dark eyes dancing.

"Are you complaining?" I wondered.

He prowled across me and laughed, and the dark intention in his voice sent goosebumps down my spine. This man was sin personified and, God help me, I was crazy about him.

"The day I answer yes to that, I've been body-snatched. Call the cops," he said, giving me a wicked smile as he lowered his head to kiss me.

He was just about there when the doorbell rang. It echoed through the house.

"Shit, Paolo's not here," Massimo murmured. "Fuck it, ignore it."

A banging followed, loud and authoritative.

"Police, open up!" The shout reached us on the fourth floor.

Massimo frowned. "You know I was kidding about calling the cops."

I scrambled up. "What do they want?" Suddenly, all the illegal shit that Massimo had done felt like a huge flashing sign above our heads.

"I'll go and see. Stay here, just like this, don't move," he instructed, clearly not bothered at all about the cops visiting.

He left the room, and I rushed to follow. I listened from the stairs but couldn't hear much.

"We're taking you in for questioning regarding the potential arson at Hallow Hall," a loud voice announced.

I froze on the bottom step and watched the sight before me. Massimo in handcuffs. It was wrong on every level.

The detective who had been at Hallow Hall the day of the fire stared at me.

"Unless you have a warrant for her arrest, look the fuck away," Massimo growled at him, looking mad enough to almost break the handcuffs apart with sheer, brute strength.

"We are only interested in you," the detective said, and nodded to the officer holding Massimo's arm.

He found my eyes with a hard stare. "Wait for me here. I'll be back as soon as I can."

Then, he was gone.

I'd fallen asleep at the TV when Paolo appeared to announce a visitor. I was immediately wary, considering everything that had happened, but when I followed him to the sitting room and saw

Lucy, my fear melted. I hugged her hard, and she hugged me right back.

"Thank God, you're okay," she murmured. "I was so worried when you were gone."

"How did you find me?"

"Giada found Massimo's address. I figured I'd check here." She glanced up at her bodyguard. "We're just going to talk. Go take a break."

Nina considered her for a long moment and then stalked a little distance off.

Lucy let out a long-suffering sigh. "Apparently I find trouble too easily, so I need to be babysat."

"At least she's watching out for you," I argued. "It's not safe . . . anywhere, it seems like, these days."

"Yeah, well, especially when you're a girl," Lucy added.

We exchanged pained smiles.

"So." Lucy pushed her hair back and sat up straighter. "Tell me what happened after you left the hotel."

I caught her up on what I remembered, shivering at the memory of Ivan. I'd hoped to never see that monster again. At least he was gone now. Gone. I hadn't wrapped my head around it. Lucy listened to my rambling and my anxiety about Massimo.

"Okay, that's a lot. You've been through hell, basically, in the last day." She tapped her lip and seemed to ponder something. Then she straightened up and nodded. "Well, I have a few hours before I need to make my train. What are we doing to turn this day around?"

I shrugged. "I don't know. Massimo doesn't want me to leave the house. I can't believe the police were here. What if they charge him with something?" I chewed my lip.

"What about your mom, though? We could go and see her,"

Lucy suggested. "You said that the other guys are dead . . . so as long as we're careful, why not?"

Excitement and nerves flared in my gut. Go and see my mom?

"If you want to, that is," Lucy added.

I nodded. "Yes, I want to. I want to very much."

Nina had a rented car, and we drove to my old address.

"What if she moved?" I worried, gazing out the window.

"And what if she didn't? Let's go and see!" Lucy pushed open the door.

I got out after her. Nina walked in front of us toward the block of apartments.

Tension and anticipation beating through me, I pressed the buzzer on the door and then waited.

Moments passed.

"I guess she's not home?" Lucy suggested.

Suddenly, the intercom crackled to life.

"*Buongiorno?*"

"Hello, I'm looking for someone who used to rent this flat, or maybe she still does . . . Elena Dmitrova?" I said quickly.

"I'm sorry, I don't know about any previous tenants. We've lived here two years."

Two years! All this time in Hallow Hall, I'd been imagining my mother here, in this apartment, and she hadn't been.

"We could check the church? You said she went there often," Lucy suggested after I thanked the person on the intercom and they hung up.

It was finally a sunny day; the world gleamed white and pure and clean where the sunlight fell on the snow. I didn't want to go home and obsess about Massimo in police custody.

I turned in the direction of the church. "Let's go and see."

The church was quiet as we entered and glanced around. My heart fell when I saw that she wasn't inside. Sure, she might be at work, but we'd passed the tiny seamstress shop where she'd been employed, and it had been closed. She might have changed jobs, though. It *had* been three years.

A nun walked down the aisle, and Lucy bustled over to her.

They spoke quietly as I stared up at the stained-glass window that I'd looked at every Sunday for years, when I was younger. The world had felt like a safer place then, before I'd known a place like Hallow Hall even existed. Now that I knew about the evil of the people who worked there, I couldn't forget it. I was forever marked by that wickedness.

The sister walked away, and Lucy and her bodyguard talked softly. Lucy seemed upset.

I wandered toward them. "What's wrong?"

Nina moved away, turning to face the door, giving us privacy.

Lucy seemed pale, her dark eyes bright. She watched me steadily, making me nervous.

"Seriously, what's going on?"

"I asked that nun about your mother, since you said she used to come every day."

I nodded. "Did she know something? Was she already here today?"

Lucy was quiet for a long, long moment, and when she spoke, her voice was soft. "She wasn't here today. She hasn't been here in a long time. The sister remembers her, though, she spoke very highly of her."

"She changed churches? I guess after Vargas was excommunicated, maybe," I rambled.

Lucy just watched me.

"What? You're making me nervous."

Her hands reached out and touched mine, threading our fingers together. "There's no easy way to tell you this, so I'm just going to do it. I don't want to lie to you. The sister remembered your mother, and she remembers what happened to her . . ."

"What happened to her?" I repeated, my heartbeat slowing down. "What happened?"

Lucy blinked, a tear appearing on her lashes, and I knew.

In my heart, in that second, everything changed.

"No," I whispered softly, shaking my head like that could change reality. "No, it can't be."

Lucy took a deep breath. "She said she's laid to rest here in the churchyard."

I couldn't stop shaking my head. "I don't believe it. It's a lie—show me."

It took half an hour to find her headstone. The snow had been falling for days since the terrible storm the night of the fire, and no one had cleared the headstones in the old graveyard. My mother's final resting place was right before the wall met the woods behind the church. The world was still as I cleaned snow off the entire thing and confirmed it for myself.

Here lies Elena Dmitrova. A mother.

My attention caught on the date of her passing. I couldn't stop staring at it. Two years ago? For two years, I'd been held hostage in Hallow Hall, believing it to be the only thing I could do to keep my mom safe. It had all been a lie. Not only had I been there two years longer than I'd needed to, but I'd missed being with her in the end. Lucy had already called Giada to ask her to look into how it had happened. Cancer. She'd always hated going to the doctor and had avoided it at all costs. When she'd finally gone, it had been inoperable.

I sat on the ground beside the grave for hours. My feet and legs were frozen through, but none of it mattered. The only person in the world who had cared about me was gone.

"We should get you home," Lucy said. She'd given me time alone with the grave for a while before returning to urge me to go and get warmed up.

I couldn't stop staring at the name of my mother, written in stone.

"It's too cold out here, Kat. You'll get ill."

"What does it matter? What does any of it matter anymore?" I mused. I couldn't seem to cry. It was like the tears were frozen inside me and they wouldn't thaw enough to fall. Maybe I'd feel better if they did, but right now, they burned inside my chest.

"Because she wouldn't want you to get sick. Right or wrong, everything she did was what she thought was best for you, misguided or not."

"And now I'll never see her again. Now I have no one." My words lashed at my heart. There was no emotion there. It had all been burned away.

"Don't say that—"

"It's true. You don't understand. You have your sister with you through everything. You can't imagine what it feels like to know . . . you are alone."

Lucy touched my back, and I fought a flinch. She didn't deserve my anger. She didn't do anything wrong. It was me.

"You have Massimo, don't you?"

Massimo. The cold inside my chest warmed as I thought of

him. A safe harbor in the storm. God, I hoped the police would be done with him and let him go. I couldn't stand being apart for too long.

My gaze dropped to the ground. Half frozen and thawed, the shape was hard to make out, but when I picked it up, I knew.

A bouquet of snowdrops. My heart froze inside my chest, the sense of betrayal cutting through me like a knife.

Everyone in my life had tried to control me, manipulate me. Every single person had taken my choices away from me.

I'd thought my own personal demon was different, but those snowdrops didn't lie.

He'd been here. He knew . . . and he'd never told me.

"He's just like the rest of them," I muttered to the wind. "I can't trust him."

I sensed Lucy's concern; it was suffocating. I rose slowly, my knees screaming at me.

An electronic ringing filled the air, and Lucy answered her phone, watching me warily the entire time.

"Is that Giada?" I asked her.

She nodded and passed me the phone. "Do you want to talk to her?"

I put the phone to my ear.

"Katarina? Are you okay?"

"Did he know? He knew, right? You both did."

Giada was quiet for a long moment and then sighed. "Would you have told you, considering the state you were in? He was trying to protect you. You've remembered him, so you *know* he cares about you. More than cares. He loves you, in his own twisted way."

"Love?" The word was strangled.

"Yes, love. No matter what else you think, he would never have married you if he didn't love you. He's no saint, as you know all too well."

A shocked exhale left me, the ring on my finger suddenly a lead weight.

"Married?" I echoed. The ice from the gravestone had crept into my heart, and now it was encased.

Giada must have heard my surprise and cussed a long stream of Italian down the phone. "Don't fucking tell me he didn't tell you yet."

"No. He didn't tell me. He decided to keep it from me, just like my mom's death. Thanks for all your help," I said stiffly.

"Katarina, you guys just need to talk everything out. Letting go of control doesn't come easily to Massimo."

I hung up abruptly and handed the phone back to Lucy. She had a hand clamped over her mouth, having clearly understood what had happened from the one-sided conversation.

"He married you—when?" she said, breathless.

I shrugged. "Last night? When I was . . . unconscious, I guess."

Lucy watched me with a look that was awfully like heartbreak.

"I'm sorry to get you into all of this. It's not your problem. You must think you stumbled onto the set of a soap opera," I muttered, then bit my lip when Lucy stepped forward and embraced me hard.

Her hug was unexpected but so, so welcome.

She held me tightly. Her hand soothed circles on my back. I would have cried then, if there had been even an inch of warmth left in my chest. But I couldn't. Everything was cold. And I felt finished.

"I'll leave here, you're right, it's too damn cold." I drew back from Lucy's arms.

Her relief was palpable. She nodded quickly.

"It's a shock. Give it time to sink in. All of this has been so hard, and terrible, and it will take time to process," she babbled.

We walked toward the exit of the church grounds. My feet crunched over hard ice and sank into unplowed snow. At the gates, I turned and glanced back at the path toward my mother's grave. I didn't want to leave. I wished I could just go back there, curl up, and lie on her grave, and finally fucking rest, with the one person who had been my family. Yes, she might have believed others over me in the end, but she was still the only person I'd ever had.

I nodded at Lucy, but I knew in my heart that I couldn't recover from this. Ice had formed around my heart, jagged and spiky. I could barely breathe it hurt so much.

Somehow, pathetically, it was Massimo's betrayal that hurt the most. I'd thought I was someone real to him, not just another puppet dancing on invisible strings. I'd been wrong.

"Is there anything else you need?" Lucy asked as Nina drove us back into the city.

"Do you have any money?" I asked bluntly. I didn't have a penny to my name. I'd have to ask Massimo for it. I'd rather die.

She reached for her wallet. I was past feeling embarrassed or ashamed of my situation. I was homeless, penniless, an orphan . . . the list went on. There was no room for pride in situations like mine.

"Thanks. I'll pay you back one day," I promised her.

She shook her head. "Please don't. I just want to help."

She looked so beautiful, sitting there worrying about me. I touched her hand.

"Thank you for everything you've done for me. Seriously. I don't know what happened with you in the past, but you saved me. Thank you."

She shook her head slowly. "Why does everything you're saying sound like a goodbye? What do you need the money for?"

I squeezed her hand and turned away to stare out the window. "I can't stay in this city anymore. I-I don't understand why they won't leave me alone, but I'm not safe."

"Massimo would keep you safe," Lucy offered quietly.

A smile that tasted bittersweet touched my lips. "Safe, and controlled, and imprisoned. Different cage, same life. I just want to be free," I said.

"But you care about him."

I nodded. "Yes, and that's what hurts the most. I just want to make my own choices for once. It shouldn't be a luxury, but it's become one to me."

Lucy sighed slowly. "I get it. More than you realize. If you want to leave the city, come with me. Nina and I are going back to Florence this afternoon on the train. Come with us."

"I couldn't impose. You've already helped me so much."

"I have a far-too-big apartment, and the city is beautiful, and it's far away from here. And as for helping selflessly . . . honestly, it's been nice . . . having a friend." Lucy jerked her head toward Nina, sitting in front of us. "Most people are scared off by Nina, and me . . . sometimes."

"You?" I laughed. "What could be scary about you?"

"I can be more impulsive than I look. Apparently, according to my sister's husband, I can be a handful."

She appeared so innocent while saying it, I couldn't help but laugh.

"I can't imagine it, honestly."

"Well, stick around long enough, and you'll see," Lucy said, and sighed again. "I manage to get myself into more than my fair share of trouble."

"Well, you do approach random bedraggled strangers running for their lives in train stations instead of turning the other way like everyone else."

Lucy's face lit up with an impish smile. "I don't want to pressure you. The train is at five P.M. Just know that you're welcome to come with me. The choice is yours."

The choice was mine, for the first time in my life.

The ice wrapping around my heart hardened as a blizzard stormed inside me.

35

KATARINA

Warmth hit me as soon as I walked into Massimo's townhouse. Paolo greeted me at the door.

"We will have to get you a key," he said with a soft smile.

I shook my head at him. "Not necessary."

He followed me up the stairs. "Are you hungry or thirsty or anything?"

"No, thank you. I'm fine."

But I wasn't fine. Not at all.

I went to the top floor, into Massimo's room, and shut the door behind me. The room smelled like him. A sob threatened to break through the cold in my chest, but it didn't quite manage it.

Checking the clock, I saw I had some time until I met Lucy. I sank onto the edge of the bed, then flopped back and inhaled that scent for the last time. Massimo. My Lucifer, my savior. The man who'd taken me out of the dark . . . and wanted to control me just the same.

I held on to the dog tags at my neck like a rosary until a knock at the door sent me upright. Alarm filled me at the thought that he might have returned. I didn't think I could leave him if he was here. I wasn't sure he'd even let me.

"Katarina? You have a phone call."

I followed Paolo downstairs to the antique-looking landline phone and put the receiver to my ear.

"*Micetta,* are you okay?"

Massimo's voice washed over me, bringing comfort and disappointment at the same time.

"I'm okay," I got out.

"You left the house? Paolo told me you went out."

"With Lucy and her bodyguard."

"I know, that's the only reason I didn't break the fuck out of here and come find you," he said, sighing roughly.

"How come you can call me?"

"I get a phone call."

"I think that's supposed to be for legal counsel."

"Fuck legal counsel, I didn't start the fire. I'm not afraid of the police. So, where did you go?"

I swallowed a shard of ice in my throat.

"I went to see my mother."

Silence met that confession. My hand was curled into a fist so tight my fingers ached.

Then another sigh.

"Katarina—"

"I just want to know one thing: Who put you in charge of making my decisions for me? Who gave you the right?"

"Angel—"

"Don't call me that! I'm not an angel. I'm not a saint, and I won't forgive you for this."

"Yes you will, because once you take a second to think about it, you'll understand why I did it. I didn't want to hurt you. From the moment we met, I didn't want to hurt you. I will never hurt you," he said in a rough growl.

"And marrying me when I was drugged and out of my mind? How do you justify that?"

More silence, and then his deep rumble.

"To protect you."

"Bullshit. What protection does your name give me? You just gave me another jailer to answer to, when I was free for the first time in three years."

"You wanted a family and a place to belong, someone to belong to. Someone who would care if you were hurt, who would slay your demons for you. Someone who would never turn their back on you."

I swallowed the angry retort that sprang to my lips at how he'd taken all the soul-destroying, personal things I'd told him and used them as an excuse to do whatever he wanted.

I tried to harden my heart to him, but it felt impossible. He was the only thing left that kept it beating.

I forced coolness into my tone. "But I never asked you to be any of those things."

"You asked me to kill for you," he snapped back. "You agreed to be mine."

"I agreed to fuck you, which I have. You made sure to do that as soon as you could. You chose to take that first from me while hiding the truth from me. You put lies between us and ruined it. You ruined everything," I said. The cold in my chest was now twinned with anger. Disappointment so thick I could hardly breathe.

"I ruined nothing. I saved you, and I will save you time and time again, as long as you need, wherever or whenever you need me."

"You'll save me? Except from you."

Silence fell. When he spoke, his voice was as deep as mantle.

"You knew who I was when you reached out and touched me, when you believed in me, when you shone your fucking goodness on me. You already knew who I was, and you didn't complain when it suited you."

Those words hurt to hear, because they were true, weren't they?

"I wanted to choose my family. I wanted control over my own life, and if you don't understand that and why I need it, you don't understand me."

Massimo chuckled darkly, but there was nothing amused in the sound. "And if you think I'm going to let you go in a fit of temper, you don't understand *me*. I made a mistake. I should have told you . . . I'll pay for it, with you by my side. I'll make it up to you, with you by my side."

"No you won't. I don't want to see you."

"You don't have a choice, we're married," he reminded me.

I let out a scoff. "And you think you aren't taking away my freedom or choices? Just listen to yourself."

He was quiet, a fuming, loaded silence.

"You're angry. You have the right to be. I'll be home soon, and we'll talk about it in person."

"No. I don't want to see you, and this isn't my home. I don't have one anymore. I am completely alone . . . and maybe that's what I need."

"Katarina—"

"If you really care about me, beyond wanting to possess me for some fucked-up reason, you'll give me the space I need. I'm going with Lucy. Her security will watch out for me."

"Going where with a De Sanctis?"

"Away. I'll call you when I'm ready."

"Wherever you go, I'll find you, little stray. Like it or not, you're my wife."

"I don't like it."

"You'll come around," he ground out.

"No I won't . . . unless you show me you're worth not giving up on. I need time; you'll give it to me, or our story is at an end. I need to know my choices *matter* to you. I need to see that you're not like them. I won't swap one prison for another. I'll die first."

Then I hung up and cried. The ice in my chest shattered and broke into a thousand shards. My initial freezing paralysis had burned out and melted at hearing his voice. Spitting my venom at him had cleared my heart of anger, and now there was only disappointment and sadness. Sadness for what had happened. Sadness for my sorry life. Sadness for my mother. *My mother.* Just the thought of her lying in the cold, hard ground for two years, without anyone to visit her grave, twisted my heart into pieces.

I cried and cried until my soul felt wrung out and exhausted.

I checked the time when my eyes cleared enough to see. I had to go.

I got to my feet, my knees weak. I swayed against the bed, unconsciously gulping long breaths of the air that smelled like Massimo.

"Wherever you go, I'll find you, little stray."

Right, he was the master at that, but I had a hunch that he had help. I untangled the chain around my neck carefully, pulled it free from my hair, and placed it on the covers. The dog tags had become a symbol of safety to me. Something to grip on to when the world felt too much. When I was alone and lost in the dark. The small crucifix twinkled, nestled beside the tags. Me and him, together on one chain. I should take the shining little cross off and take it with me. I should, but I didn't. I couldn't bear to remove it. I left it there.

I pressed a kiss to my fingertips and then stroked my fingers over his name.

Then I turned around and left.

I had told Lucy I'd meet her on the street outside the townhouse. I waited, watching for the familiar sleek black car that Nina drove her around in.

The traffic was busy, winding slowly up the road. Ice slicked the pavement in places where the snow had started to melt.

Florence.

Could I really go there and leave Massimo behind? Would he really let me? I had to know the answer to that. It mattered more than anything.

After a while, a black car pulled up, and I made my way toward it. It stopped and turned its blinkers on, blocking the road.

I reached the rear passenger-side door and opened it—and then stopped.

It wasn't Lucy in the back seat.

Not at all.

Sergei, director of Centrium Group, sat against the plush cream leather.

I just stared at him, making no move to get into the car. What the hell was he doing here?

"Katarina, I'm so relieved to find you safe and well," he called out.

He made a move to get out, and I backed up, ready to run. I glanced around. I didn't see anyone else about to close in.

"Why are you here?" I asked numbly.

"I was looking for you. I've had a lot of people searching for you."

"Why?" I demanded.

He sighed and peered at me. "Do you really not know?"

Tension bunched in my muscles, telling me to run, or at least cover my ears. A terrifying foreboding filled me, and suddenly I didn't want to hear what he was about to say.

"I know this is a lot to take and it's out of the blue," he started, then stopped when a small voice spoke.

"Kat?" A little body wriggled forward, and I could finally make her out.

Tatiana.

I took a step forward, ready to try and grab her out of the car or die trying.

"Easy, Katarina, relax. I'm here to explain everything to you, and don't worry about Tatiana." He turned to the girl beside him. "She's my daughter."

Shock froze me to the spot. His daughter. Everything I'd ever heard about Tatiana's strange treatment in Hallow Hall fell into place. The fact that she was the only kid her age suddenly made sense.

Then, Sergei stared at me.

"And so are you."

I reeled back, slipping on a patch of ice and falling on my side. Sergei got out of the car and came to my side faster than I'd have thought possible for a man his age.

He helped me to my feet and cupped my face, ignoring my flinch and immediate attempt to wrench away.

"She's your half-sister. I know it's all a lot to take in, but I didn't want to lie to you anymore. I'm your father, and I want both my girls safe under my roof."

I looked between him and Tatiana, my mind reeling. I had no evidence that what he was saying was true. He might just be making it all up, but I didn't think so. Something inside my heart knew he was telling the truth.

"Come home with us. I'll explain everything," Sergei said, leading me to the car.

"Kat! Sit beside me," Tatiana begged from inside.

No matter whether he was lying or if he had an ulterior motive, it didn't matter.

I wouldn't let him take Tatiana anywhere alone.

I got into the car.

36

MASSIMO

I burst through the doors of the townhouse downtown and startled Paolo into dropping his watering can.

He cursed and crossed himself as I ran up the sweeping staircase.

"Mass! Wait!" he called after me.

I didn't stop. I couldn't. I tore up another flight, and another, and finally reached the top. As soon as I stepped onto the landing, I knew.

She'd already gone.

I couldn't feel her there at all. There was just the echoing emptiness I had lived with my entire life, until I'd walked into Hallow Hall and met her.

I stalked along the corridor, clenching and unclenching my fists. It had taken a fucking age at the police station, and once my lawyer had shown up, it had been clear they had nothing on me. It had simply wasted my time and forced me to be absent when Katarina had found out the worst news she'd ever gotten. Her mother was dead, and I'd kept it from her. Oh, and I'd married her without her knowledge . . . couldn't forget that particular fuck-up.

I checked around the room. She wasn't here, but the air still smelled like her. I closed my eyes for a second and breathed her in.

The longing in my chest was a physical weight.

Opening my eyes, I took my phone from my pocket and opened the tracking app I'd paired with the discreet device on my dog tags.

The little blue dot glowed right where I stood. I approached the bed and saw them.

The chain of my tags caught the firelight when I picked it up. I turned it in my hand. Her crucifix hung beside the tags. She'd even left that behind in her haste to get away from me.

I gripped the chain hard in my palm. Regret froze me in place. She was gone. She was gone and she would never come back, because I'd lied to her, kept things from her. I'd treated her just like the other men in her life who had done nothing but manipulate her.

In her eyes, I was the same.

"Mass," Paolo said, wheezing, finally making it to the top of the stairs behind me.

He shuffled into the room as I whirled on him. I grabbed him by his lapels. He was so light, one hard push sent him into the wall. I slammed my hand against the doorframe just beside his head.

"Why did you let her leave? How could you just let her walk out, without the fucking tracker, no less?"

Paolo was composed in the face of my aggression. He stared me right in the eye.

"Do you think that restricting her freedom would have furthered your cause with her? Do you think she would love you back if you became everything she hated?"

I let out a bitter chuckle. "I've always been everything she hated. If you'd have kept her here, I could have—"

"What? Tricked her? Found a convenient lie? Fooled her again? That's not love, and that's no way to start married life." Paolo raised his chin, defiant.

"No way to start married life? How are we starting married life when she's just left me and you watched her go?" I demanded.

The old fucker shrugged. "If you want to be her husband, *really* her husband, no games . . . You need to let her come back to you. You need to let her choose you."

I slammed my fist into the doorjamb again, wanting to smash it into Paolo's face and only just resisting.

"Get out of here before I forget myself," I rasped at him.

He pulled himself to his full, diminutive height, more dignified than I'd ever manage.

"Forget yourself away. You don't scare me, Massimo. I know you. You're not angry at me. You're angry at yourself."

I curled my hands into fists and tried to stop imagining wrapping my hands around Paolo's throat and squeezing until his unwanted insights stopped.

"Thanks for the dime-store therapy. Get the fuck out of my sight." I stepped back.

He took his time leaving.

Quiet surged into the room in his wake.

Her light was gone from my life.

And I was alone in the dark again.

Just like always.

"Have you gotten the information?" I said in lieu of a greeting when Giada called.

She sighed. "I'm doing well, thanks. How about you?"

"Giada. I need Blackwood's address. He's the fucker who got away, and I need to right that wrong."

"I know, I know. You're back to vengeance being the only thing you have. Wonderful."

"I don't want a lecture," I started.

"Well, maybe you need one! I can't believe you didn't tell her about her mother."

"When should I have done that?" I stopped my wild pace in the library. I'd been walking back and forth in the same spot for an hour, waiting for Blackwood's address. "Maybe when we were trying to escape a fire, or when she was in solitary, or maybe when I was busy killing the men who had hurt her, trying to keep her safe?"

Giada was quiet for a moment. I stood in front of the fire and let the heat scorch through my pant leg and blaze along my calf. The pain was good; it kept me from losing control completely.

"I'm not saying it was easy . . . but the right thing is seldom easy. It was never going to be an easy thing to tell her, and you—"

"Were a coward. I'm aware. I don't need you to tell me." I sank down into the leather chair beside the fire.

"It's not cowardly to be afraid of losing the person you care about—"

"The *only* person I care about. She's the only person I've ever cared about in twenty years. Afraid doesn't cover it."

Silence fell between us again.

"So, you could have messaged me the address, but you wanted to call to tell me I told you so?" I massaged the bridge of my nose. I had a pounding headache. I'd had it since that phone call when I was at the police station. The hurt in Katarina's voice had dug tiny daggers through my skull, right into my brain.

I'd have fucking nightmares about that phone call; it would haunt me.

"No. Believe it or not, I wanted to make sure you're okay."

"I'm fine," I bit out.

"Yeah, you sound great. What are you going to do?"

"Kill Blackwood."

"I mean after that?"

Darkness filled my chest, possessiveness sinking its teeth into my heart at the thought of a future without Katarina. The sheer strength of it stole my voice from me.

"You know that following her to Florence and watching her until she decides to give you another chance won't go down well, right?"

Giada's words had me shaking my head.

"And neither will instigating encounters where she's forced to rely on you."

Is she a fucking mind reader?

"Please. Even in your imagination, you're so PG," I snapped. "How about sneaking into her bed at night when she's asleep and fucking her and filling her up nightly until she's pregnant, and then swoop in and take care of her when she finally needs me again?"

Giada drew in a short breath. I'd finally shocked her.

"Or even more obvious: Take her and keep her somewhere quiet and isolated until she's so desperate to talk to someone that she talks to me. Until she's so desperate to breathe fresh air and feel the sun on her skin, she takes my hand."

My words were low, a bleak and broken confession of a damaged mind.

"You wouldn't do either of those," Giada uttered after a moment. "You wouldn't."

I swallowed the hot knot of fear and anger in my throat, though it returned immediately. It never left me lately.

"You don't know me, Giada O'Connor, not really. You have no idea what I would do for the woman I love."

"For, or to? You're not a monster, Massimo, not unless you let yourself be."

"Some of us have never had a choice in what we are. It's written in our bones. I hadn't expected naivety from Elio's sister. Interesting."

"It's not naivety. It's hope that you'll be a better man than you think you can be. I have to have hope to keep helping you," she trailed off.

"Yeah, well, I've never had any kind of hope, until her. She is my hope, and if I let her leave me, I might as well lie down on the street and die."

"Then die," Giada said suddenly. "Kill the monster. Become the man she needs. Be good enough for her. That's your only hope."

I bit down so hard I tasted blood.

"Send me Blackwood's address," I commanded.

My phone chimed a second later with the details, and Giada hung up.

37

MASSIMO

Dr. Blackwood lived in an old apartment near the center of town. Sure, it wasn't the best neighborhood, but it was the kind of place where people could go unnoticed. I was sure that the good doctor had a whole lot that he'd like to go unnoticed.

He had a top-of-the-line lock on his ancient door, but I'd never met a lock I couldn't get around. I had a set of picks in my pocket just for the occasion, as well as something to jam a home alarm.

Once I was inside, I listened carefully for sounds of habitation. There was nothing. It looked like Blackwood still had places to be during the day. I didn't like the thought that the psychopath was still out there in the city, treating innocent people.

He was a monster, just like the unholy trinity and just like me, and tonight, he'd answer for his sins.

His house was cluttered inside, the kind of place passed down through the generations, and in Blackwood's case, he didn't seem to have cleared out any of his elders' belongings.

With its wood paneling and brown carpet, the seventies were jealous of his avocado bathroom suite. I went room to room until I found his bedroom.

A king-size bed took up nearly the entire space. The bedding was in disarray, a pet peeve of mine. Maybe it was my years in the military, but a man who couldn't make his own bed in the morning didn't have any kind of discipline.

I wandered around the room. Though it was cluttered, there were few personal effects there. An old ID badge with Blackwood's face on it from a hospital downtown. Old train ticket stubs from years ago tucked into the corner of a mirror.

I sat on the creaky rocking chair in the corner of the dim room and waited.

I didn't have to wait long in the end. The sound of the lock turning echoed down the hallway only an hour later, and Blackwood entered the dark apartment.

The rustle as he walked told me he carried grocery bags to the kitchen. He sighed when he set them down. The apartment was so small, every sound carried.

Then he tossed his keys onto a hard surface, and his footsteps started my way.

He came in but didn't bother turning on a light. Instead, he shrugged off his blazer and loosened his tie in the moonlight. He hadn't seen me. He didn't seem to be on his guard at all. It was stupid and naive and certainly made my life easier.

I reached out to the table beside the rocking chair and clicked the lamp on.

Blackwood froze in the process of taking off his shirt. He was looking at the floor and didn't even raise his gaze to me when he spoke.

"So it's my turn," he said quietly.

Ah, so it wasn't naivety that had made him unaware of danger. It was resignation. How boring.

"Yes, it is finally your turn."

He dropped the ends of his shirt and faced me.

"You got a weapon on you?" I asked. "Going to try and take me off guard?"

Blackwood laughed; it was a strangled sound. "Would a weapon work against L'Ombra?"

I sat forward, the gun in my hand pressing against my knee, pointing at Blackwood.

"Ah, so we're dispensing with the formalities? How did you find out who I am?"

Blackwood shrugged. "I wasn't sure until now. You fit the description, and Vargas—he was sure someone had put a hit out on him. That's why his security was crazy, and he only let his guard down at the institute. He felt safe there."

"Yes, he did, didn't he? There in the place where so many young women should have felt safe . . . but weren't. He fell for his own PR, I guess. On your knees."

I jerked the gun down, showing Blackwood where I wanted him.

He sank slowly to the carpet and brought his hands up behind his head.

"You don't have to do that." I chuckled darkly. "This isn't a holdup. There's no way you're leaving here alive. If you tried anything, you'd be dead before you could realize what had happened."

Blackwood was quiet, letting his arms sag back to his sides.

"I have some questions that you will answer, if you want to die in the next hour. I am capable of making your death last all night, all week, all month. You understand?"

Blackwood nodded and blinked nervously.

"Why was Ivan Markovic so determined to marry Katarina? Even after all this time?" That fucking question had been weighing on me. It was all part of Katarina's mysterious story and why she had been relatively untouched in Hallow Hall compared to others.

"Ivan Markovic. He's my—he was my friend from school," Blackwood said, his voice heavy. "Father Vargas's nephew."

I sat back and let that sink in. "So, why marry Kat? Was he obsessed with her?" That was something I could easily understand.

Blackwood shook his head. "He didn't even like her. He was ambitious, though, him and Vargas, and when they learned about Katarina and her mother, they planned how they were going to use them."

"Use them for what?"

"To get rich and inherit everything." Blackwood looked up at me. "Katarina wasn't an ordinary patient of Hallow Hall."

"I noticed. Why wasn't she?"

"She was special. Off limits. She was only supposed to be there temporarily, until Ivan could scare her into marrying him. But then she saw what happened to her friend, Mira . . . That was three years ago. Vargas convinced the director that Katarina was safer in Hallow Hall. That her soul would be saved from the vices of the modern world, and her body would remain pure and untouched. The director is quite paranoid about the state of the world . . . especially for his family. Once Katarina's mother died, it wasn't even in question. Katarina would only leave when the director was ready to have her married and looked after by a husband. She could never live alone and be exposed to sin."

Blackwood laughed bitterly.

I went over the words that Blackwood had just thrown at me and seized on one particular phrase.

"For his family," I repeated.

"Katarina is the director's illegitimate daughter. Her and Tatiana."

I stared at him. I'd been expecting something along those lines. There was no other explanation for her treatment there, though Pavol and Benedict had hardly left her untouched. I supposed that they thought her medication regimen was enough to keep her confused and not remembering.

"The director," I repeated. "Sergei Stoyanov."

Blackwood nodded resignedly.

"How did you come to work there?" I asked, leaning in to look at Blackwood's face.

"Pavol recruited me. I interned with him when he was still practicing, before the trouble and accusations got his medical license revoked. I found out about the director and Katarina when I was working there. Ivan went out of his way to meet her after that. He thought she was his ticket to big money. He fancied himself boss of the Stoyanov family after Sergei died."

I nodded. "Okay, fine." I flipped the safety off the gun.

"Wait! Don't you want to know more?" Blackwood glanced around frantically, searching for a way to extend his pathetic life.

"Not really."

"The Stoyanov family doesn't just run Hallow Hall," Blackwood shot out.

I paused and lowered the gun a fraction. "Explain."

"They run a lot of these places. You might think Hallow Hall was just a one-off, a single abomination made possible because of Father Vargas and his influence in the community . . . but it didn't even start in Italy. It started in Bulgaria, and Sergei imported it. There are a lot of Hallow Halls in small forgotten places, all over. Italy, France, Croatia, Spain. It's been going on for twenty years in some cases," Blackwood said.

I took a deep breath, and my chest rattled. I felt the presence of my heart at that moment, an organ I had long believed dead. Now it hurt. It hurt at the thought of other Hallow Halls and other pregnant women disappearing.

A tight band of tension wrapped around my throat and pressed in.

"Where else?" I ground out. "In the South?"

Blackwood nodded quickly. He was excited that I'd taken an interest in his information, hastily tossed out to buy himself time.

"Yes, I've been collecting some of the patients' records and drug therapies—"

"Why did you stay there so long?" I interrupted, getting to my feet and standing over him. "You're a doctor. You're supposed to do no harm," I reminded him.

Blackwood glanced left and right, looking for a way to escape the simple question, and then shrugged. "Harm was going to come to those women whether I helped or not."

The pain inside my chest intensified. It was an excuse I was familiar with. The way I justified my own profession. I had more in common with Blackwood than I liked to think, and that was fucking depressing.

"Besides, the drugs I was developing there, with free rein, they'd change victims' lives," Blackwood continued.

"In what way?"

"The power to forget the things you didn't want to remember, to erase it. To be turned on by a pill slipped into a drink; instead of fighting it, she'd want it. The victim would become powerful—"

The shot was sudden, a flash in the darkness.

He slumped back against the bloody carpet, against the fragments of his sick and twisted brain.

I straightened up. I was breathing heavily, I noticed in a detached sort of way.

I was angry. I felt sick. I needed to know more. A swirling sense of foreboding had filled my head, and it wouldn't go away.

I left the bedroom with its stink of gore and copper and walked through the apartment until I found Blackwood's office. It was stuffed to the brim with boxes. His small desk in one corner had a box open beside it, as well as a laptop. He seemed to have been going through the boxes and categorizing the information. Searching for insight from old patient records. I stared at the boxes. They were the large, A4 size that you get in offices. There had to be fifty of them that I could see, and even more behind them.

I flicked the light on. I'd killed Blackwood with a silencer on. No one would be calling the police. I had time. I holstered my gun and reached for the first box, pulling it down from the top of the stack and opening it.

I had to know.

Dawn shined through the blinds of Blackwood's office when I reached the last few boxes. My eyes stung, and I felt numb. Numb to the horror of seeing name after name of patients the Stoyanov family had used and abused in institutes just like Hallow Hall. Some were experimented on; those were the older patients, the ones whose relatives were paying for their care. They ran unregulated clinical trials of illegal substances and sold the information—including the formula for making the drug—to the highest bidder. Then, there were the teenage girls. The ones who'd been pregnant when they'd arrived and gave birth to babies who were promptly sold on the black market. If the mother could recover and be confused enough not to understand what had happened, she stayed at the institute until someone could knock her up again, and the cycle repeated until she died or was killed, and then her organs were harvested.

I'd seen some awful things in my life. Bombs dropped on civilian hospitals, whole families dead at their kitchen tables, bodies riddled with bullets. I'd seen evil in its purest form, and I'd been naive enough to think that nothing could shock me anymore.

I'd been wrong.

My head felt black as pitch as I turned to close a box and accidentally knocked one of the last ones off the desk. The contents spilled out across the floor. I felt infected by darkness from reading the records. Tainted in my soul . . . and I was a man who had known from a young age that I was hell-bound. Shakespeare had been right.

Hell is empty, and all the devils are here.

I could practically feel the presence of Old Nick watching me as I read.

I had to get out of here.

I bent down and scooped the files back into the box. My fingers were clumsy, still clad in the thin latex gloves I used when carrying out a hit.

The papers in this box were older than the others, some even handwritten.

If I let the police have them, would they do something about it? Would they investigate, or would it be hushed up? I had little faith in the justice system. And families like the Stoyanovs would have connections. There was no way they'd managed to operate for so long without greasing the right palms. No, I couldn't trust the police with this. No way.

I needed to get these boxes to my IT guy. Giada would find the right people to process all the information, names, and locations. We could work out what to do with it then. Going to the media and whipping up a shitstorm was one option. That way the police would be under intense scrutiny and could hardly just brush it off.

Something had to be done for all the names in these boxes. Because behind every name was a person. I might be a monster, too, but there were lines that shouldn't be crossed, and this treasure trove of abominations wasn't something I could ignore.

I picked up a paper lying near my foot and looked at it closer. It had a woman's name and age, her address, even. The address was what caught my eye. It was far away from here, down South. Close to Naples.

I scanned over the paper, and the logo of the hospital in the top corner caught my eye.

A dove flying through a laurel wreath.

I stilled. There. There it was. The thing I'd been searching for. The thing I'd needed to see in real life and not just dusty memories.

My breath stopped, and even my heart ceased to beat as I took in the familiar logo. It was one I'd stared at on and off for years, researched, employed others to research. I'd hunted for information about this logo and always come up empty. When I'd left my uncle's house in a fury all those years ago, I'd grabbed the notebook of my mother's words but left the letter from the hospital behind.

I'd started to think it didn't exist. My memory was flawed. I'd been a young, angry teen and I was misremembering the name, the color, the style.

But no. I didn't make a mistake. It was right here, just as I remembered it.

Ospedale di Santa Maria, Napoli

The hospital that had sent me my mother's final effects after she'd passed in childbirth. The hospital Fabio had told me had buried my mother in an unmarked grave . . . the one he couldn't remember the name of. And Blackwood had the patient records.

I didn't know how long I stood there. Lifetimes passed maybe, in the blink of an eye, or maybe it was simply hours in real time. I died a hundred times in that silence.

When my phone rang, my body felt stiff and unused. I answered on autopilot. Giada's voice filled my ear.

"Good morning, Massimo." Her voice was soft, hesitant. It was very unlike her.

"What's wrong?" I asked immediately.

She sighed. "Lucy called. Katarina never met up with her. She didn't show. I figured she must still be in Turin somewhere. I didn't think she had a place to go, or money—I was worried, so I checked out the footage from Lucy's hotel. Kat left the townhouse all right, in time to meet Lucy and go to the train, but she got into a car just outside. I traced the license plate, and it's registered to—"

"Sergei Stoyanov, director of Centrium Group, boss of the Stoyanov family," I finished for her.

Giada was stunned into silence for a second and then sighed. "You want his address?"

"Of course I do."

There was the sound of keys clacking and then a deep voice spoke. Her husband.

"Right. I'm to tell you that busting into a Mafia compound to rescue the girl alone isn't smart. Also, Elio is still in Italy, not too far from where you are. I'm telling him what's going on, and you're going to wait for him to come and help."

"Negative. I'm not waiting. I'm not leaving Katarina with that man for a second longer than I have to."

"Massimo! If you die, then no one will save her," Giada reminded me.

Fuck, why did she always know the most annoying but true things to say at all times?

"I need a favor," I said, changing the subject. "I have important documents that need to be picked up from Blackwood's, and a cleanup crew would be appreciated."

"Got it. What documents?"

"Patient records. They've done this before, all over Europe. They're doing it now, all over . . . Giada . . . I found some letters with the dove and laurel wreath."

Giada was silent. She had been looking for that logo for months, trying to help me find my mother's last resting place.

"You mean . . . ?"

"I mean they did it to my mother. She was a patient." I could barely say the words. I'd read too often tonight about how they treated the pregnant patients. Was my mother in an unmarked grave, her body hacked to pieces, her organs harvested?

My head was swimming. The past and present were colliding, and I was losing it.

"Massimo," Giada's voice cut through the noise in my head. "I'll send people for the documents and the cleanup. Don't worry, I've got it. You go home and rest until Elio gets in touch. Then, and only then, you go and get your girl. Hold it together. She needs you."

She needs you.

Yes, she needed me. Katarina. My angel. The image of her filled my head, and my foggy vision cleared. New strength filled my bones and straightened my spine.

She needed me.

Nothing else mattered.

38

KATARINA

Sergei Stoyanov lived in a castle, or that's what it felt like, anyway. I hadn't seen much of it, considering that as soon as we'd gotten here, I'd been shown to my room, Tatiana to another, and been locked inside. I prowled the confines of my cage, frustration building in my chest.

Why had I taken the dog tags off? Why had making Massimo understand how deeply I resented being controlled been the most important thing, at a time when danger lurked around every corner?

I sank down on the bed. Because I was stupid. It was clear at this point. I'd lived quietly in Hallow Hall for years, as obedient as an abused dog, scared that they'd hurt my mother, when she'd been dead nearly the entire time. I'd let the injustice of what had happened to Mira continue for so long, when I should have been brave enough to die to bring it to light. I'd pushed Massimo away, and over the phone, no less.

I got back up to walk the perimeter of the room. It was richly decorated but had none of the antique, artistic charm of Massimo's townhouse. I looked out the window for the hundredth time. Bars slanted across it, and past them, I could see the bare branches of trees. We were outside the city. Somewhere quiet and elevated. Torino's city lights twinkled in the distance. A road ribboned below, but no vehicles had passed in hours.

I walked around the room again. When the knock sounded on the door, I jumped. The walls were thick, and sound didn't reach me easily.

The door opened, and a security guard in a black suit and shirt stood there.

"The director is waiting to see you," he said stiffly.

I nodded, not about to argue about leaving this room. I followed him, my thoughts jagged and anxious, little shards inside my head. Sergei was my father. And Tatiana's. It explained a lot, but it was still shocking. I couldn't wrap my head around it. My mother had told me that my father had died in Bulgaria, and it was part of the reason why we'd moved to Italy. Had she known that Sergei was alive and well and living in the same city as us? Yes, of course, she had to have known. Why had she kept it from me?

We went down a grand sweeping staircase and entered a luxurious living room.

A woman reclined against a sofa, dressed as if she was about to go to a gala dinner. Sergei stood, stiff-backed, in front of the fireplace. He turned.

"Ah, Katarina, you're here." He smiled at me.

I stopped just inside the door like a puppet whose strings had been cut, unsure what to do next.

"Come in, come in. Would you like a refreshment?" He glanced meaningfully at the woman on the couch, but she was engrossed in her phone and ignoring him. She looked to be about my age, maybe one or two years older.

"This is Rada, my fiancée," Sergei said. "Rada, my daughter Katarina."

Rada waved her fingers at me passively, though she didn't lift her eyes from the phone.

"Sit," Sergei said.

I walked into the room and sat on the edge of the brocade sofa. He watched me expectantly.

"Where is Tatiana?" I asked. "I haven't seen her since we got here."

"She's well and being cared for. It seems I was remiss in thinking Hallow Hall could provide a good education for a girl her age. She is quite behind, but it's not a problem now. She will have the finest tutors this city has to offer."

"Where is her mother?" I heard myself ask before I could question the wisdom of it.

Sergei took a moment to answer. "She is Italian and lives in Palermo. She wasn't well enough to take care of a child, so Tatiana was put into my care."

"And you sent her to Hallow Hall? That's your idea of care?" A jagged laugh left me.

Sergei frowned at me. "Why not? Hallow Hall is the ideal place to keep a young girl and woman untouched by the foulness of society. She could grow up there with her immortal soul intact and her purity untainted. As my daughters, your safety was of the utmost concern to all who worked in Hallow Hall."

"Her purity? She's six."

Sergei shrugged. "And yet, there are men who would seek to soil her body with their own sick desires."

"Your business partners, perhaps?" I shot out.

Silence fell around the room.

Sergei frowned at me. "What are you implying, Katarina?"

I swallowed a knot of fear and anger. "Nothing. Just wondering how old Rada is?"

Sergei scoffed and shook his head. "That's none of your concern. I'm starting to get worried that you lost your sense of decorum during your stay at Hallow Hall. I trusted Vargas to provide for your spiritual and emotional education, but . . . I'm wondering if he was lacking."

"He certainly didn't lack the evil to cut babies out of pregnant teens and harvest their organs," I spit, standing. Suddenly, I couldn't take being in the same room as this man.

"What are you talking about?" Sergei demanded.

"Are you honestly going to try and tell me you don't know what went on at Hallow Hall? You don't know what they were doing to their patients?"

Sergei shook his head, concern clouding his face.

"What's she talking about?" Rada said, sounding worried.

"I don't know, sweetness. I don't know."

He moved closer and reached out a hand to touch me, but I pulled back.

"Katarina, if you felt there was something wrong at the institute, why didn't you say something?"

I opened my mouth to protest. To explain why I couldn't sound the alarm on the whole operation, but all my words sounded like excuses.

"It's not that simple. They were all in on it, and I have no way to know that you weren't, too," I said, and wrapped my arms around my middle. "I want to see Tatiana."

Sergei nodded. "Of course, right away." He gestured to one of his men in the corner, then reached out and touched my arm. "Please, daughter, believe that I mean you no harm. I've only ever tried to protect you from the world. When your mother passed,

God rest her soul, I knew you needed to stay in Hallow Hall longer, to be safe."

I just stared at him.

He sighed. "You don't believe me? Your mother was the one who wanted you admitted in the first place. She'd heard rumors of loose behavior, and she was worried."

"How easy it is to blame the dead," I murmured. I knew well enough the sins my mother had committed against me. I didn't need this guy trying to control our story.

Sergei nodded again. "I know, she isn't here to defend herself, sadly, but she was just worried. She wanted you to get better from the voices you were hearing in your head."

I shook my head, not trusting myself to speak. The past was a tangled forest, dark and dense and easy to get lost in. I couldn't sort through those twisted branches. I didn't know which way to cut. I had no place to start from.

"I don't hear anyone in my head," I ground out. Fucking Ivan had been drugging me. The voices had never been real. I didn't feel like sharing that particular violation with Sergei night now.

"Then it worked. Your mother would be so happy to know that." Sergei reached out to pat my hand.

I drew it back out of reach.

"Kat?" A small voice tugged at me from the right.

Tatiana stood in the doorway. I pushed away the fear and anger crowding my throat and coloring my words and reached for her.

"Tatiana, come here," I called to her.

She was a blur, she flew to me so fast. She threw her arms around my middle and stole my breath.

"You stayed!" Tatiana exclaimed joyfully.

"Of course I stayed. *You're* here," I said to her quickly, giving her a hug.

"There was a fire!" she exclaimed.

I guided her onto the sofa next to me. "I heard! Was it scary?"

She nodded. "It was really scary. I ran away first. I smelled it. I looked for you in your room, but you weren't there."

"You looked for me? The first thing you do in a fire is get outside. Adults can take care of themselves."

Tatiana nodded. "I hid, but Massi says I didn't choose the best place."

"Massi?" I repeated, a dull ache blooming in my chest. God, I missed him. I'd do anything to see his face right now.

"Massimo. He came for me, you know? When it was scary and hot everywhere. I don't remember well. I was coughing so much. He carried me. I woke up in the ambulance, and guess what?"

"What?" I was aware of Sergei's gaze on my face but didn't want to turn and be reminded of where I was. I smoothed Tatiana's hair back. It was clean and shiny for once, though I didn't like the idea that someone here at this house had bathed her.

"Massi was still there. I opened my eyes, and he said . . . 'Knock, knock.'"

My smile was unforced for the first time all day. "Hmm, and what did he say?"

She giggled. "He said, 'I'm Colin.' I said, 'I'm Colin who?' And he said . . . 'I'm Colin an ambulance.'" She fell about in careless giggles.

I hugged her close.

The sounds of a game emanating from Rada's phone caught her attention. She got up and hesitantly approached the young woman.

"Are you playing a game?"

Rada barely glanced up from the screen.

"Mm-hmm."

"Can I play?"

"No."

Tatiana stepped away, disappointed. I was just about to say something when Rada spoke again.

"You can watch me, though."

Tatiana climbed up onto the sofa beside her, and Sergei passed me a glass with ice and a pale-amber liquid.

"Here. It's a mocktail, give it a try."

I held it with no intention of drinking.

"Now, that's an interesting story Tatiana has . . . a man who saved her. A man I had no idea was working at Hallow Hall. A man whose story doesn't add up."

I met Sergei's gaze unflinchingly. "What man?"

"Massimo, she said his name was."

I shrugged. "Oh, right."

"Did you know him well?"

"Hardly at all."

Sergei nodded and then pursed his lips. "Well, he's an interesting man. Very interesting. A useful kind of man."

"I wouldn't know."

Sergei looked at my drink. "Not thirsty?"

I didn't respond.

He sighed. "Very well. Let's get you turned in for the night. Rada and I have a dinner to get to. The chef in the kitchen will prepare you whatever you need. Eat together," he said, looking between me and Tatiana. "It warms my heart to see my daughters getting along so well."

When I failed to respond, he gave a resigned dip of his chin.

"I know you are angry at me. I understand. I relied on Vargas and the safety of Hallow Hall for too long. You should have come to live with me long before now, but honestly, it wasn't safe. Men like me have enemies aplenty."

"Aren't you just the director of a business?"

He smirked slightly. "I'm a powerful man, daughter, and plenty of people would like to see a powerful man fall. I'm sure you've heard that proverb?"

I shook my head. He took Rada's arm and started toward the doors.

"I've heard another, though, about power."

He stopped on the threshold as Rada huffed about the delay.

"'The bigger they are, the harder they fall.'"

He studied me for a moment and then turned away.

39

MASSIMO

I went back to my house to gear up and wait for the address from Giada.

Paolo fluttered around me as I strode down to the basement and punched the code into the keypad.

"I don't understand what's happening," he said, worried.

"What's happening is that Katarina never made it to Florence," I called to him, moving along the rows of weapons I kept down there. My stock was extensive. I had a private arsenal under the city and a weapon for every occasion.

Now I was dressed in black combat gear, the type with plenty of straps and hooks to fit ammo, knives, and guns into for easy access.

"You look like you're going to war," Paolo said miserably.

"Maybe I am."

The phone rang somewhere in the distance, but I didn't really register it until Paolo appeared and called to me.

"It's Father Vittorio."

I strode into the hallway and took the phone from him. "What?"

"What? I wanted to see how my friend was recovering. Is that a crime?"

"I'm fine."

"You sound it."

"I am."

Vittorio sighed. "Paolo told me what's going on."

I shot a dark glare at my housekeeper, and he sidled farther down the hallway.

"It's not your problem."

Vittorio chuckled. "You see, it kind of is, because you're my friend. You can't go alone."

"And yet, I'm going to. I'm not afraid to die, Vittorio, you know that."

"But you aren't afraid of failing and leaving her there?"

That question cut through the hot, urgent storm in my head.

"You need backup. Someone on your wing."

"I won't ask you to kill anyone, Vittorio. You've left that life behind."

"Yes I have, but I can watch your six."

I argued a little longer fruitlessly, then hung up. The only way to stop Vittorio when he'd made his mind up about something was to try and leave before he got there. But I had no control over that, seeing as Giada seemed determined to make sure her brother could arrive before she sent me the address. I had no idea what I'd done in my sorry life that made these people work hard to protect me, but they had to be fools.

I went upstairs and forced some food down. Bread and cheese, olives and tomatoes. I needed energy to fight. I couldn't afford to be weak.

While my hands moved mechanically, bringing food to my mouth, reaching for water, my mind kept returning to Blackwood's crowded office.

I couldn't stop seeing it. The hospital logo at the top of the paper. I couldn't stop Giada's voice from speaking again and again in my head.

Katarina never met her outside the hotel.

For the first time in a long, long time, I had something to fight for. It didn't matter if she was mad at me. It didn't matter if I'd fucked up beyond forgiveness. I'd told my angel that she wasn't alone anymore. I meant to keep that promise. No matter the cost.

The message came from Giada a few hours later. I'd nearly worn a hole in the parapet waiting for it.

Giada: *14, Corso Giuseppe Gabetti, Borgo Po.*

Elio is en route.

Me: *You seriously made me wait this long just to give your brother a chance to get closer?*

Giada: *Yeah, I seriously did, because I knew you weren't going to wait*

Me: *Waiting means giving that man longer alone with Katarina*

Giada: *I'm sure she can handle herself. She survived just fine before you came along. Girl's a fighter.*

I blew out a breath of frustration.

Me: *You should know, in the interest of our future work relationship, that trying to control me isn't going to work.*

Giada: *Isn't that what your wife said to you? Or you just don't like it when the shoe is on the other foot?*

I growled with frustration, her little dig getting under my skin. Goddamn it, she was right, after all.

Paolo hovered near the door when I headed that way.

"What should I do?" he fretted.

"I will send Katarina here. She'll either be with me or she won't," I stated flatly. "If she's alone, tend to her and call Filippa to check her over. Make her feel safe here. Later, once she's ready, get a lawyer to go over my estate with her. She's my wife and she'll be a very wealthy widow."

"Massimo!" Paolo exclaimed as I made for the door.

"And don't worry, I haven't forgotten about you either. I've left you the place on the coast. You've always wanted to retire to Amalfi, haven't you? The beach house you love. It's yours."

Paolo stopped dead in the hall and shook his head. I took him in for the first time in a long time.

"Why are you acting like you won't come back?" he asked.

"Because I'm a realist and I like to be prepared." I patted the old man on the shoulder. "I know my odds. It's not some guy who's taken my wife hostage. It's the head of the Stoyanov family, who lives in a castle-like compound. They're going to be armed and they're not afraid to kill. That's okay. It means we can play on the same level. Getting Katarina out and safe is my only priority."

"You should make it a priority to come home with her."

I didn't have an answer for that. My life had always been the expendable component. Not caring if I died had made me a lethal weapon, and caring about that now would only make me weak when I couldn't afford to be.

"Take care of her, I'm trusting you," I told Paolo instead, and stepped out the door.

It was dark outside, light flurries of snow whirling around the light from the lampposts. As I went for my car, a sharp whistle cut through the sleepy silence of the residential street.

I turned and saw them. Two figures in black walking toward me.

"Look who I ran into." Vittorio smiled and elbowed Elio in the side lightly.

Our former commander eyed me up and down. I'd only just seen him a couple of months ago, when I'd gotten mixed up in his business. I didn't know what to make of the fact that he'd come here for me. Vittorio, either.

"We just need Filippa here, and it's a reunion," Elio murmured, and stared up at the townhouse behind me. "This your place?"

I nodded. "I'd give you the tour, but we have places to be."

"Later then," Elio agreed, and then caught my eye. "After."

It sat unspoken between us that there might not be an after. The idea of that had never bothered me before, but now something festered in the pit of my stomach. A thrill of nerves I never usually felt. A fear of losing something before I'd ever really gotten the chance to have it.

"I can't take you, Vittorio. I can't make you break your vows—"

"I've already broken them. Who do you think sent you to Hallow Hall in the first place?" Vittorio's voice was pained and heavy.

I stared at him in shock. "You took out the hit on Vargas?"

Vittorio nodded. "Once I suspected what was going on with him, I had to find a way to end it. I needed someone good, someone who would make sure that whole place was shut down as soon as he got to know the real deal. I needed you. There aren't many killers for hire with a conscience."

A raw laugh left me. "What about your worries about my immortal soul?"

Vittorio hung his head. "Forgive me. I needed—"

"A monster? A condemned man?" I asked.

He shook his head, guilt written across his face.

I patted his shoulder. "It's okay. I understand. I wouldn't change it, not a single moment . . . because you brought me to her. Thank you. I'll owe you for the rest of my life."

Vittorio blinked, his eyes teary, then he cleared his throat. "Okay, well then, good. No more arguing about me tagging along, okay?"

"Enough chitchat. Let's gear up. I don't think a rosary or holy water is going to cut it," Elio announced. "You got a gun for the good father, Lucciano?"

It was a bizarre thing to see these two men, whom I'd once risked life and death with, standing there on this quiet, ordinary street. Suddenly, I was glad not to be alone. Glad to be someone valued by these two men, men better than I'd ever be. It was humbling. It made me feel things I had no experience with.

I grinned at him. "Do I ever. Come inside."

40

KATARINA

I ate dinner with Tatiana and then was forced to go back to my room while a staff member took her away. I was in my room for two minutes before I tried to open the door, only to find it locked.

My brain felt overwhelmed with all the information that had been dumped in it today, with finding out about Sergei, and Tatiana.

I didn't know how to process it all. I kept raising my hand to my neck, searching for my necklace that wasn't there. I missed it.

I flopped down on my bed and stared at the ceiling. Above all, I missed him. Massimo. My devil. I'd been rash and impulsive, and grieving, sure . . . but I'd made a mistake.

Thoughts of my mother pressed in now that I was alone. I was still processing her death, but oddly, it didn't hurt as much as it had earlier. The years of separation had numbed my feelings about her. The resentment and bitterness, wrapped up with love, had grown twisted in my mind. I'd loved her but I'd also hated her for allowing them to put me in Hallow Hall. I'd missed her, but

I'd resented the fact that she had listened to my depressed request to stop visiting me.

And now she was gone, and we'd never be able to fix things. It would always be left unfinished. But then, wasn't life often like that? Messy and complicated and not at all like you wished it would be? Wasn't love like that? My love for Massimo was no different. Messy and complicated . . . but none of that made it any less real.

A tear fell, followed by another one, and another. That frozen feeling in my chest loosened more and more with every passing moment. The shock had worn off, and there was only sadness left.

I let myself cry there, in the house of the man who called me his daughter. Just when I'd lost my last relative, two new ones had appeared. It was disorienting. I'd wanted a family for so long, and this was how that simple prayer was answered?

A scraping sound from the door sent me to my feet. Was Sergei back already? The lock turned, and the door swung open.

I stared and stared. It wasn't Sergei. It wasn't his fiancée, Rada, or anyone I expected to see.

"Shut your mouth, Katarina, or you'll catch flies in there," Sister Vera said, stepping into the room and shutting the door behind her.

I backed away, putting the bed between us.

"What are you doing here?"

"Surprised to see me?" Sister Vera asked, a smile playing around her lips.

"Just disappointed. I thought that maybe you'd died in the fire. I was planning your memorial and everything."

"Hmm, I'm sure you'd have said lovely things to remember me by," Vera snapped, as easily riled as always. She smoothed her expression and stared me up and down. "I see you haven't changed into the clothes that the director filled your wardrobe with. I told him it was a waste, but he is determined to spoil his eldest daughter."

"Sister—"

"It's just Vera now, no need to keep up the pretense. I haven't worked for the Church for a long time."

If Vera was dropping her mask of piety, it didn't seem like anything good was about to happen.

"I see. So, why are you here?"

"Well, now that Hallow Hall is no longer—until it's rebuilt—Sergei needed a hand with Tatiana. She can't be allowed to run free around here, and Rada wouldn't know how to properly discipline a child if her life depended on it."

Her dislike of Rada was clear in her tone. Dislike and something else . . . envy.

"I can look after Tatiana. I'm here now."

Vera chuckled. "Very funny. To think that you could look after anyone. You're crazy, Katarina, don't forget."

"I'm not crazy."

"Don't forget that I know you. I've been there with you for three years. I know you."

"No you don't. I'm not the girl in Hallow Hall who you can drug up and abuse anymore." Heat and anger rose in my chest and spilled out in my words.

"Are you sure about that?" Vera gestured around her. "This looks like being locked up to me."

Tension filled me, a heavy weight that didn't seem to move from my chest. I knew what I needed to ask but felt my courage failing me. But I needed to know, for Tatiana's sake as well as my own.

"Sergei told me he doesn't know about all the things that go on at Hallow Hall. Like what happened to Mira." I watched Vera carefully. "Is that true?"

Vera sighed and sat on the edge of my bed. I had to fight my instincts not to push her off. She eyed me up and down again, her expression scathing.

"What does your angel inside your head tell you?" she mocked.

Right. Of course Sergei was involved. He was profiting off it all. I'd long expected that the company paying the bills for Hallow Hall had been the one running the trafficking operation. Not to mention the conversation I'd overheard in the hallway between Benedict and Sergei, before Benedict had met his untimely demise thanks to Massimo.

"It tells me . . . that Sergei and everyone associated with Hallow Hall are sinners. And they need to pay," I said evenly, turning to grip the sideboard sitting just under the window. I needed that hard surface to hold me up. To give me strength for what needed to be done.

"Sinners? People like you aren't qualified to call me a sinner," Vera sneered, and got to her feet. "Anyway, I've wasted enough time here with you. I have Tatiana to mold in my image. I don't believe in sparing the rod when rearing a child. I'll finally get to teach that little brat how to act."

"No, I don't think that you will."

I sensed Vera moving closer in an attempt to hear me. She'd come here for a purpose, and she wanted to gloat and get my reaction. After all our time together in Hallow Hall, it was personal to her.

"I don't think you'll be around to teach her a single thing," I murmured, and then swung around.

The Bible in my hand was a hardback and thick. I put everything into that spin. All the fear and disappointment and regret of three years of imprisonment. I slammed the book into the side of Vera's face, and she spun around with the impact.

She went down hard, and I was already standing over her. I grabbed her by the hair as she flailed around on the floor and hefted the book again, beating her face with the spine, again and again, until blood dripped onto the carpet. Her nose smashed in, and then her eye.

She let out a gurgling noise. I dropped her bloody head and staggered back, panting. I could barely breathe. The sudden burst of exertion and the anger, thick and suffocating, made my heart pound and my head feel light.

She rolled away from me on the floor, curling in to protect herself. But there was no protection from the karma she had earned.

I drew my foot back and kicked her in her middle once, and then twice. All the times she'd maliciously dragged me to my BS therapy sessions to be abused and exploited. All the times she'd locked me in solitary. All the times she'd smiled when a patient begged her for help, before sending them away. All the times she'd sniped at Tatiana just for being a sweet little girl and punished her for no reason at all.

"The angel in my head doesn't exist, Sister, there was only ever me." I sighed and crouched near her head.

Her face was a bloody mask. I was shocked and intrigued at the same time. After years of inaction, years of torment and feeling powerless, I felt free.

"You reap what you sow. You are going to understand that tonight . . . and so is Sergei."

She gaped blearily at me. "You didn't come here to let your father take care of you?"

I laughed. It was funny, really. I shook my head.

"That man isn't anyone to me. I don't know him . . . But I know what he's done. I came here for Tatiana, and thanks to you, I'll be going to get her now." I fished the set of keys out of Vera's pocket and dangled them in the air before her. "Thank you for your help, Sister." I straightened up and stepped back. A quick check in the mirror showed me I was a little bloodied, but nothing too drastic. I made for the door, unlocking it and listening carefully before opening it.

The hallway was empty. I seemed to be in one of the turrets, since there was a perilous, winding staircase to my room that didn't go anywhere else. Sergei gets his daughter home and locks her in the tower. That seemed on-brand for him.

I reached the top of the stairs and peered down. It was quiet below, and I couldn't see anyone moving.

I'd just taken the first step when a rough grunt hit my ears. I twisted in time to see Vera barreling toward me.

"You don't get to win!" she roared at me, or tried to, through a mouthful of crushed teeth.

I didn't stop to think, I just acted. She went for my middle, and I spun around, throwing myself against the wall. She brushed past me, her momentum carrying her toward the steep stairs. Only one of her hands reached out and snagged my sweater, threatening to pull me with her.

We both came to a stop. I was pressed to the wall, bracing both our weights. She hung by that handful of fabric.

Her eyes met mine, and I saw her fear, and she must have seen my resolve, because her lip trembled and she shook her head slightly.

"Enjoy hell," I whispered, slowly prying her hand from my dress.

As soon as it was free, she started to fall.

She didn't have a good enough position on the stairs to stop herself. The shove I gave to her middle didn't help, either. One second she was staring at me, her face a crimson mess of exposed bone and twisted cartilage, and the next, she was gone.

She fell hard, building speed as she went. The stairs were dangerous, relics of a time before health and safety regulations. She landed halfway down with a hard crack, her neck's broken angle clear to see, even from where I stood.

There wasn't even a flicker of regret in me for taking a second life. I couldn't muster even a moment of it. All I felt was relief. I'd spent so long living among monsters, I'd become one too. I couldn't find even one part of myself that cared.

Now it was time to get my sister and get the fuck out of here.

The house was quiet as I walked down the plush-appointed corridors. Art decorated the walls, and console tables were bedecked with lavish flower displays. The scent of flowers hung in the air, more like a pall than a pleasant fragrance. It smelled like a funeral home.

Tatiana's room was on the opposite side of the estate from mine. The only close call came when I had to sneak to the lower level, cross the bottom floor, and go up the stairs. Two guys with buzz cuts and black suits stood around talking, but neither of them glanced my way. I supposed Sergei didn't consider his daughters much of a flight risk.

I made it to Tatiana's door without any trouble and unlocked it with the key from Vera's key ring.

When I pushed open the door, silence greeted me.

"Tatiana? It's me, Kat," I said to her.

Silence, and then a rustling sound.

"Kat?" her familiar voice called.

Then she popped up behind the bed.

"Kat!" She jumped up and ran over to me. "I'm so glad it's you!"

"Who else would it be?" I grabbed her and hugged her tightly.

"I thought she came back. Sister Vera," Tatiana said, her voice muffled against my chest.

She leaned away to look up at me, and I gasped. She had a split lip, and her eyes were red. She had been crying.

"Did she hit you?"

Tatiana nodded, and more tears fell. I hugged her again and smoothed her hair back.

"It's okay. Don't cry and don't worry. She'll never hit you again. I promise."

"I don't want to stay here anymore," she said.

"Neither do I," I murmured. Leaning down, I looked her in the eye. "Shall we go?"

Tatiana nodded. "But where will we go?"

Home. The image of Massimo's Gothic but oddly warm townhouse filled my head.

I shrugged. "I don't know yet, but anywhere is better than here, right?"

She nodded again, and I took her hand, leading her over to the wardrobe in the corner.

"Put warm clothes on. You'll need them outside."

I spied out the window while she got dressed. I could see the sweeping gardens of the property with a guard post manned by security at the very bottom of the driveway. We couldn't get out that way. We needed to go out the back.

"Come on, let's go," I whispered to Tatiana, and took her hand.

We started down the stairs. It was just as quiet as before; however, when we got close to the lower floor, one of the patrolling security guards had decided to do his job and paced back and forth.

I motioned for Tatiana to be quiet, lifted a heavy vase from one of the console tables, and positioned myself above him on the upper floor. I had an uninterrupted view of the top of his head as he walked in and out of sight. I took a few seconds to study his speed and movements, then I let go of the vase. It fell and hit him right on the top of his head, and he crumpled to the floor. Thank goodness the thick rug beneath him muffled the sound of the vase breaking into a dozen pieces.

I grabbed Tatiana's hand again, and we crept down the last few steps. The man had fallen on his side, and his jacket had flapped open. I stared at the shiny black handle of the gun in a holster on his waist. Before I could question it, I reached for it.

It was heavier than I'd imagined it would be. I gripped it and looked it over. The safety seemed to be on, but other than that, I had no idea if it was even loaded. Still, I felt safer with it in my hand.

I nodded toward a hallway branching off the foyer toward the back of the house. I hoped there would be a way outside from there. We went past a kitchen where the low sound of voices talking sent us running past. At the end of the hall, past the kitchen door and around a bend, was a set of French doors.

My heart pounded so hard I could barely hear anything apart from that drumming tattoo in my ears. Tatiana's hand was small and sweaty in my grip, but she held on to me tightly, and I her.

We reached the doors, and I muttered a quick prayer, turning the handle.

It didn't move.

It was locked.

Disappointment crashed into me just as I remembered Vera's key ring. I pulled it out and sorted through the keys I hadn't tried yet.

Attempting the one that looked the closest in size to the lock, I let out a tiny cry of relief when it turned.

The night air, freezing cold, washed over my face. We stepped out onto the frozen gravel outside the back door.

"What now?" Tatiana asked, shivering a little.

"Now we find the street." I gave her a smile that I hoped came off as playful and adventurous instead of terrified. I had no doubt that if Sergei found us sneaking out, the illusion of our being valued guests would soon disappear.

We started out across the lawn. The moon hung bright and low overhead, and I wasn't sure if it was a good or a bad thing. It illuminated the yard, but then it also made us more exposed.

We were halfway across when headlights swung past the house, approaching from the other side. Sergei and Rada returning from dinner?

I tugged Tatiana after me. We neared the tree line that surrounded the edge of the yard and the high fence. I made out a dark shape crouched low in the bushes. He seemed to be facing the front of the house, and we were able to get close without attracting attention.

The man didn't even turn until I pressed the gun into the middle of his back.

"I don't want to kill you—"

"Thank God for that," the man interrupted, and crossed himself.

I stared at him, sure I hadn't seen him correctly in the moonlight.

"We are leaving, and you're not going to try and stop us," I resumed my threat.

The man nodded. "I won't, I swear. In fact, I'll come with you."

"What? No you won't," I snapped, and backed up.

The man slowly straightened and held his hands out like he was indicating that he came in peace.

"I need a hand here. I'm out back, four o'clock," he said to no one, apparently.

"Who are you talking to?" I demanded.

"You'll see shortly. Someone who is very impatient to see you. But if you could do me a favor? Finding you was my job, after all. Don't tell Massi that you did my job for me, okay?"

"Massi? You're with Massimo?" I asked, things I couldn't name soaring in my heart.

"Wait, Father Lucciano is here?" Tatiana asked beside me.

"Yes, little one. Father Lucciano is here," a deep voice said, and then strong arms surrounded me from behind.

41

MASSIMO

EARLIER . . .

"What are you thinking?" Elio squatted beside me and Vittorio after checking the perimeter of the compound.

"I go in the front, Vittorio the back—he's to look for Katarina—and you be my eyes in the sky."

Elio nodded. He had his sniper rifle slung over his shoulder and an earpiece with his sister, Giada, on the other end. Between them, they could do a lot of damage.

"It would be less risky to sneak in, get Katarina, and sneak out."

"But far less fucking satisfying," I said with a growl. "Sergei Stoyanov isn't just the man who's taken my wife, he's the man who created the fine institution that killed my mother. He dies. Tonight."

Elio studied me for a long moment and then nodded.

"Go and get your vengeance, brother. You've waited long enough."

"Got it, Commander," I muttered, and saluted Elio before moving off, nearly missing his grin.

My former commander used to have quite the reputation for never smiling and basically being a serious stick-in-the-mud.

That had changed slowly when he'd met his childhood sweetheart again. Not quite a storybook romance, but I'd never seen him so happy. And God, I wanted what he had. I wanted it so much, I could barely breathe. In a few short weeks, my life had turned upside down and reformed around a new purpose.

Her. My angel.

"Sergei isn't home yet," Vittorio whispered in my ear. He was busy making his way around the back of the house.

"We could get the girl and get out of here before he even got home," Elio pointed out. "Take Stoyanov on another day."

I tutted softly, closing in on the front door, coming from an angle to check out how many men I was dealing with before they could see me.

"Where's the fun in that?" I mused, and chuckled when I counted the security presence. "Sergei left three guys on the door of the house where his precious daughters are inside. What a fucking moron."

"To be fair, three hardened Bulgarian Mafia men is probably more than enough to deter most guys," Vittorio whispered, sounding out of breath.

"What the fuck are you doing?" Elio demanded in a low voice.

Vittorio breathed heavily in our ears.

"There was a gate to climb over," Vittorio wheezed.

"Jesus, you need to work on your fitness. You sound like you're about to keel over."

"There isn't much time for going to the gym when you're a priest."

"Make time," Elio argued back with the same uncompromising discipline he'd always employed as our commander.

As I listened to them bicker, I closed in on the men at the front of the house. I ran along the back of a low wall that framed the front door and vaulted easily over it at the last moment, crashing into one of the men. They held semiautomatic weapons with laughable incompetence.

As soon as my boots crashed into the first guy, I was swinging for the next one. I lunged forward and cracked his head on the wall. The last guy turned slowly, and I pulled a knife from my vest and threw it.

Bullseye.

It hit him in the neck, and he pitched to the side. The first guy was attempting to get to his feet. I slipped the garrote out of my back pocket and came around behind him, sliding it over his head.

A short time later, I released his lifeless body to the ground. The second guy, the one who had been knocked out by the wall, stirred. I took my gun, fitted with a silencer, and stalked over to him. A shot to the temple, and he was gone.

A fine patina of blood sprayed over my chest and the mask over my face. It was a nifty piece of tech, giving me superior night vision, and it also used heat detection tech. I looked very similar to how I'd looked the last time I'd fought alongside both Vittorio and Elio, except instead of sand-colored camo, I was in unrelenting black, matching my soul.

I glanced up at the camera sitting above the door and wondered if Sergei was watching the footage in real time. My face was concealed, so the video being used against me wasn't an issue, and besides, I didn't think Sergei Stoyanov was the kind of man who could afford to call the cops. I tilted my head toward the camera, and just in case I did have an audience, waved.

Then I tried the handle. The door swung open. Sergei had really put too much stock in his three guards out front. I was just about to enter when my radio crackled to life in my ear.

"I need a hand here. I'm out back, four o'clock." Vittorio's voice, quick and low.

Without a moment's hesitation, I stepped back from the door and turned in the same direction he'd gone. I took off at a run along the side of the property, vaulting the fence and coming into the large, sweeping back garden.

"Someone's got him at gunpoint," Elio murmured in my ear. "I can take them out from here."

Elio, crouched in a perch somewhere with his sniper rifle, was absolutely unstoppable. The backup that no money could buy. His kind of skills and precision were priceless.

I caught sight of Vittorio in the distance, and the small figure before him, pointing a gun at his back. A smaller shadow stood just behind him.

"Scratch that," Elio said, a hint of warmth in his voice. "It's your girl. Seems like we've interrupted her saving herself."

My girl. Of course she was saving herself. She was a fucking force of nature.

I closed in on them, devouring the sight of Katarina, who was now slowly lowering the gun. Tatiana stood at her side. I pushed my mask up and approached them soundlessly from behind.

"Wait, Father Lucciano is here?" Tatiana asked in a small voice.

"Yes, little one. Father Lucciano is here," I growled, and reached for Katarina. I couldn't stand one more fucking second of space between us.

She jerked as I hugged her to me, breathing her in. I hadn't expected Vittorio to find Katarina so quickly. I hadn't even had the chance to kill nearly enough Stoyanovs yet, though I'd made a respectable dent in their numbers.

"I'm here. I'm here for my wife," I murmured.

She elbowed me in the side.

I let go, and she spun around and shoved at me.

"Your wife? What right did you have to do that, when I had no idea what was going on? Who are you to do that?" Katarina's voice rang out, her hands pushing at my chest. The anger was still there, apparently, now clouded with relief. I could see it in her beautiful face . . . her emotions written clear as day. Anger and most of all, relief, maybe even a hint of surprise.

"Your husband," I said calmly.

Her mouth dropped open in outrage. Her hand moved toward my face and met my skin with a slap.

"Who are you?" she demanded again, and a sheen of tears covered her dark-blue eyes.

Words didn't seem capable of conveying all the things I wanted to say to her.

So I kissed her. I'd always been a more action-over-words kind of guy.

She was shocked for a moment, but then she let me kiss her.

Fuck, it was like coming home after war. My body spoke to her. *Remember me, little stray. Remember this and us and everything we are going to be.*

Then she realized what she was doing, and her teeth closed on my lip. She bit hard. I had to give it to her, she could savage like the little stray I affectionately called her. Blood filled my mouth. Good girl. Us strays always needed to be able to defend ourselves.

She pulled back. Her pale skin was marked with my blood, dripping down her chin.

It was hot.

I wanted to wear her teeth marks. Her scratches were a badge of honor for a battle well fought and won. I wanted everyone to know.

"Who are you?" she whispered, this time more of a plea than a demand. Her eyes called to me, begging me to make the world make sense for her again.

I cupped her face, pressing my pinkie fingers into the soft, vulnerable underside of her neck, enjoying the feel of her pulse hammering against my skin.

"I'm the man who loves you. The one who will keep you safe, even from yourself, even when you don't want me to."

Then I kissed her again; I couldn't help myself. Her tears slid down her cheeks and between our lips. Salt and copper mixed as I slipped my tongue into her mouth, and she whimpered. When she swayed into me, her strength wasted, her fight out of juice, I moved back. She watched me carefully, her brilliant eyes ringed with wet, spiky lashes.

"I'm sorry. I'm sorry, little stray . . . I want to say I would do it differently, but honestly, I don't think I would. I don't think that there is anything I wouldn't do to keep you." I tucked her hair back behind her ears and cupped her face again. "I'd kill for you. I'd die for you. Everything else is just details."

She let out a long sigh. "You're an absolute maniac."

"Oh, he knows," Vittorio said, standing and watching us with a grin.

A small hand tugged at my pants, and I looked down. Tatiana smiled up at me.

"Knock, knock," she said.

"Who's there?"

"Carrie," she murmured.

I crouched before her. "Carrie who?"

"Carrie me home, I'm scared."

"Oh, sweetheart, it's going to be okay. You're safe now," Vittorio said comfortingly.

He was a man suited to comfort. I wasn't. I never had been, with my bloodstained hands and black soul. Yet, it was me who Tatiana pressed her little body against. I opened my arms, and she stepped into my embrace. Something fragile and too big to hold stirred in my chest. I caught Katarina's eye. She watched me carefully, her thoughts hidden from me. Fuck, I'd missed her. I never wanted to be apart from her again. I wanted a big house ringing with the sound of her laughter. I wanted to fill it with little baby girls who looked just like her to light up the world, and keep safe and cherish.

I straightened up slowly, and Tatiana went to Vittorio.

"Take them out to the townhouse. Wait for me and Elio there. We'll wait for Sergei to get home."

"No," Katarina's voice struck out.

"No?" I repeated, and turned to arch an eyebrow at her.

"I said no," she stated, and crossed her arms over her chest. "Not happening."

Before I could argue, she poked a finger into my chest. "If you're about to come up with some bullshit about keeping me safe and in the dark—I told you no. Sergei is my father. This is my business. I'm staying. You won't tell me what to do. You won't control me or make my decisions for me."

I stared at her, my need to keep her safe warring with my gut-deep knowledge that she needed this. She needed me to show her I could listen. I could understand her. Despite every tactical instinct I had in me screaming at me to refuse, I nodded.

"Very well. Vittorio, take Tatiana out of here. Elio, Katarina, and I will finish this."

"Oh, you've got it bad," Elio murmured in my ear with amusement. "I never thought I'd see the day."

"Shut it," I said to him, taking Katarina's hand in mine.

"While I hate to interrupt you getting put in your place, Sergei is home."

"Finally," I said, anticipation roaring through my veins.

Katarina glanced around, clearly wondering whom I was speaking to.

I grinned at her. "Today, I'm the one with the voices in my head. Let's go, little stray. Time to introduce me to Daddy Dearest."

42

KATARINA

We went in through the back door.

"Stay behind me, angel," Massimo instructed, stepping before me. In his black fatigues, bristling with weapons, he was a fearsome sight.

I nodded and stepped back, then followed as he advanced. He reached back and grabbed my hand, guiding it to the back of his bulletproof vest.

"Hold on tight so we don't lose each other. I can't take it a second time."

We advanced down the hallway, and Massimo's gun fired ahead of me. We passed the bodies of Sergei's men, fallen on either side.

The air smelled like fire and copper. The cooks scrambled out of the kitchen and ran for the back door, women for the most part. Massimo didn't look their way as we passed by them. We reached the foyer and crouched. Massimo pointed toward a table.

"You wait for me there," he instructed firmly, pulling a pin out of some kind of weapon.

He was in his element here. He wasn't afraid, and somehow,

neither was I. I felt like I was exactly where I was supposed to be, for the first time in my life, perhaps.

I nodded, and at his signal, ran for the table.

He tossed the object into the foyer, and smoke filled the space. Massimo slipped his mask on and walked in fearlessly. I couldn't see everything, but I made out enough of him moving around and taking down the men who had just walked in through the front door to know no one would survive this if Massimo didn't want them to. He was a one-man killing machine.

Silence fell, thick and heavy.

"Sergei? I think it's time we were introduced," Massimo called.

The silence had that particular quality of people trying to be quiet.

"I'm your daughter's new husband. I apologize for not asking your permission to marry her, it's just that I don't give a fuck about what you think," Massimo continued, goading in his tone.

There was a shuffling noise and then a flash in the smoke.

"You bastard! You think you can just marry my daughter?" Sergei roared, his voice rough with smoke.

Another flash. Sergei shooting at Massimo? No. No, that couldn't happen. He couldn't die.

"Where is my daughter? Tell me now, or you're a dead man." Sergei sounded so confident. Did he have a line of sight on Massimo?

"Stop!" I cried out and stood. "Don't hurt him."

"Katarina," Sergei snapped. "Come here."

Massimo was silent. Had he been hurt? I stumbled around until a hard hand closed on my arm. Sergei's face loomed out of the smoke.

"What have you done?" he all but spit in my face, then hauled me up the stairs.

I frantically searched the lower floor for Massimo, but it was still too shrouded in smoke to make out.

"And this is exactly why I needed you taken care of at Hallow Hall until you were old enough to marry. Ever since your mother came and told me that I had a daughter and she was eighteen, no less, it's been a fucking headache. Get up here."

He yanked me even harder, and I went down on one knee on the stairs. Fuck, that hurt. But I'd been hurt worse. I tugged back against him.

"Let me go, I don't want you to touch me," I hissed at him.

"I'm your father!" he roared.

"You're a fucking monster," I screamed back.

We'd reached the top floor, and now he pushed me through a doorway I hadn't seen before. It came out onto a platform on the roof. A helipad. I dragged clean air into my lungs and tried to keep up with his violent pace. Rada stumbled up the stairs behind us, tears falling down her face.

"Sergei! Wait for me!" She tripped and fell in her heels, but got up and followed.

He dragged me across the platform and then dumped me to the ground, taking his phone from his pocket. He still had a gun clutched in his hand.

"You think I don't know what you are?" I cried out. "You think you managed to pull the wool over my eyes? I know you're behind all the evil shit at Hallow Hall. I know you profit off the misery of all those poor women." I struggled to my feet. "You think I came here to be your daughter? To embrace you?"

I laughed, and Sergei stared at me.

"Why did you come here then?"

"I came here to kill you. I've been waiting three years. I'm done waiting. Tonight, the last monster behind that hellhole dies."

"Sergei! Why's she calling you a monster? What's happening?" Rada screamed. She was losing it and Sergei couldn't care less. In the distance, the choppy sound of helicopter blades beat the air. Sergei's escape route was opening up, and I couldn't let that happen.

He ignored his fiancée, stared at me hard. He shook his head. "You call me a monster? What about that man you married? What about yourself?"

"She's no monster, she's an angel of vengeance descended from above." Massimo called, stalking out from the door onto the roof. He had a gun trained on Sergei. "And as for me, yes, I am a monster, but I'm the man your daughter loves, and that makes me God's favorite monster. Thank you, *micetta,* for separating him from the fucking smoke below, I'll take it from here." There was blood on Massimo's ear and his mask was gone. Had one of those shots hit him in the ear? Panic threatened to engulf me.

Sergei waved his gun at Massimo. "Don't come any closer."

Sergei's movements were erratic and full of fear. Massimo's confidence was a stark contrast. He walked unerringly toward him, his gun never wavering.

"Let's both take the shot. I trust my aim more than yours, old man."

Sergei grabbed for me, but I scuttled back. He swore and grabbed Rada instead, dragging her up by the hair.

"Drop the gun or she's dead."

I staggered to my feet and put a hand out toward Massimo. The fear and betrayal on Rada's face broke my heart. How many lovers had Sergei used and discarded? Just like my mother . . .

Massimo didn't take the shot. He waited.

"Let the girl go, she isn't involved with any of this. Besides, you kill her and you'll follow seconds later. I don't miss." Massimo's words were a promise.

"Please, I was putting strays down since before you could walk!" Sergei shouted, and then cried out as a shot sounded. I screamed, scared that Massimo had decided to shoot through Rada after all, but Sergei's gun fell to the ground, and he clutched his hand to his chest, blood staining down his front. Rada fell to the ground, crying, and Sergei staggered back, turning and running now toward the helicopter that was coming in to land on the roof.

Massimo was a blur of movement sprinting toward Sergei, ignoring the terrifying blades chopping the air on the roof, which were getting lower and lower.

The helicopter touched down just as Massimo disappeared around the other side. Men in dark suits swarmed out. Had he seen them? What if they got behind him? Hurt him?

I couldn't let that happen. I took off around the other side of the helicopter, swiping Sergei's fallen gun from beside a hysterical Rada.

I saw them all at once. Sergei was posed on the step of the helicopter, new gun in hand. His men surrounded Massimo, one right behind him with a gun pressed to his back. His gun was on the ground.

I bit down my scream of fear, and the world seemed to grow very still.

"Sorry, I can't have you talking shit about strays. I've always been one, and now I'm in love with one." Massimo grinned at Sergei, seemingly unafraid of the threat all around him. Massimo's hand twitched at his side, a strange and purposeful movement, and suddenly the men around him were falling to the ground. I looked around wildly, wondering just whom Massimo had stashed around the property. I couldn't see anything, but those sniper shots had been professional work.

The man who was standing right behind Massimo, gun pressed into his skull, barely had time to realize what had happened before Massimo twisted, throwing the man's arm up and sending the gun flying into the air. It sailed away over the side of the building, and the man watched it go, before convulsing. Massimo sunk a knife into his throat, sudden and final. Massimo pushed him backward and he fell, then Massi turned back to Sergei.

A gunshot sounded and knocked me out my stupor. Sergei was the last man standing, but he still had a gun. His shot had gone wild, however, thank God. He pointed his weapon at Massimo again and I knew I had seconds to act. I ran forward, Sergei's gun in my hand, extended toward my father's back. I didn't trust my aim, but I didn't need to. He just had to know that he was cornered. I pressed the gun to the back of Sergei's head before he could take another shot, and he stilled. Massimo grinned at me and walked unerringly toward me, reaching my side in moments. Sergei remained frozen in fear at the end of my gun, his foot still poised on the step . . . and his freedom.

His voice rose over the noise of the chopper. "What do you both want? Money? You can have it. Power, to inherit the family? You can have all of it," Sergei bargained.

Massimo considered his words. "There is something I want from you. Sara Lucciano. Do you remember her?"

"What? Who? No, I don't."

"That's a shame. She died in one of your institutes twenty years ago. Died in childbirth . . . or so I was told."

"Who was she?" I asked Massimo, before realizing. "Your mother?"

Massimo nodded.

Oh my God. I couldn't look away for a moment. The mother Massimo had talked about. The one who'd heard voices, just like me. She'd been like Mira? My heart broke at that moment for her, and for Massimo, and for all the women and families ruined by Sergei and his cold-blooded moneymaking scheme. Profiting off the pure misery of others.

"Massimo?" I murmured.

His eyes were hard, lost in the past and fixed on Sergei.

"You won't kill me," Sergei called. He was trying to sound confident, but it wasn't quite working. "I'm the only parent she has left. If you care about her, you won't kill me. I'm her only chance at a family."

A muscle ticked in Massimo's jaw. I raised my free hand to cup it, trying to pull him back from the dark place he'd gone to.

"Mass?" I whispered.

He blinked and then looked down at me.

"It's true, this man created the place where my mother died. He's done what he did to Mira hundreds of times." I could tell that every single word cost him.

He sighed, his empty hands flexing at his sides.

"But it's your choice, my angel, if he lives or dies. You mean more to me than my vengeance."

His eyes burned into mine, and I saw that he meant it. He really would end his lifelong quest for vengeance and leave it unfinished if I asked him to.

It was my choice.

"Do you hear, Katarina? Call your pet killer off now," Sergei commanded. "Do not let him kill your only family."

"You're not my family," I said firmly. "Tatiana is my family." I stared up at Massimo. "My husband is my family."

Massimo's lips curved in the smallest ghost of a smile at those words.

"I don't need you, and the world certainly doesn't," I continued, and then nodded to Massimo.

He shifted his focus back to Sergei.

"Looks like you're dying alone, unloved and unremembered, Sergei." He went to take the gun from me, to take that final sin upon his own soul. Sergei must have felt the changeover, because he chose that moment to act.

He threw himself into the helicopter, and the thing lifted off the roof a millisecond later.

"No!" I screamed as the chopper rose. "He's getting away!" I couldn't bear the thought that he would survive this and go on living, despite everything he'd cost the world. Everything he'd cost me and Massimo.

Massimo lifted the gun and aimed at the helicopter. Shots sounded—from him, and from the sniper hidden somewhere on the property. The helicopter made it over the garden before the pilot was hit. The tail spun, as the gas tank was also pierced. Then it was falling from the sky. It didn't have a huge amount of altitude to make a massive crash, but there was enough height for it to hit the ground hard. Not only that, but the gas tank imploded at the moment of impact. A fireball roared up from the ground, scorching the earth and cleansing it from the presence of Sergei Stoyanov . . . forever.

He was gone and, just like that, the world was a better place.

43

MASSIMO

Katarina didn't complain about her cuts and bruises or the blood marring her clothes. She was silent on the way home, but her hand was curled in mine, so I took that as a win.

We got to the townhouse at the same time as Elio. He stared curiously at Katarina before we ducked inside. Paolo started to fuss over her immediately, whisking her away upstairs while Elio and Vittorio gathered in the kitchen.

"The little girl fell asleep after her bath. I don't think the poor thing has slept properly in days." Vittorio scrubbed a hand over his face.

Elio leaned against the kitchen counter, looking deadly and unruffled despite putting down nearly thirty men tonight.

"I've called the De Sanctis cleanup crew for the compound."

"Oh, and what's that going to cost me?" I asked, sitting at the table and feeling the weight of the world settle on my shoulders for a moment. God, I was exhausted. The adrenaline of the last few days pressed down on me like a two-ton boulder.

"A future favor," Elio said, and gave me a smirk. "In case you're interested in a different line of work, now that you're a married man, I was thinking that you join the team as a consultant. We work well together."

"I don't know if going from assassin to made man is an improvement or not." I sighed.

Elio shrugged. "Talk it over with the wife. Decide together."

"The wife. I don't know how long she'll be that, if she gets her way," I admitted. "She's not too happy with me about it."

Elio chuckled. "I know all about that, but I also know that the women we love are far, far too good for us, and far too forgiving." He made to walk past me. "Speaking of wives, I need to get back to mine. Come and visit us in Atlantic City."

"Is that an order?"

"It's a request. And as for the wife . . . give her a chance to choose you. It works wonders, I promise. That was advice, FYI." He winked at me in a very un-Elio move and headed out.

Yep, meeting the right woman had changed my stone-cold commander in an irrevocable way. I was jealous.

"So, what are you going to do with the little girl?" Vittorio asked.

"I don't know. We need to see about her mother," I said.

"I can make inquiries, or get your IT guy on it. If she has a mother, she might want to go back to her. If not, she has a home here. She's Katarina's family," I told him.

Vittorio grinned at me. "Yes she is, and so are you. Go and see your wife. I'll bet she needs you right now."

I found Katarina in the bathroom. Steam rose around her. She stood naked at the sink, staring at her reflection, bloodied and bruised. I wanted to kiss every dark mark on her delicate skin, but instead I gave her space. I closed the door behind me and caught her eyes in the mirror.

"*Micetta?*" I asked softly.

She stared at me for a stretched moment, and then a long line of tears escaped her eyes and ran down her cheeks.

"My mom died," she said simply. There it was, the grief she had tried to escape from but couldn't. The terrible, inescapable truth.

"I know. I'm sorry. I'm so, so sorry," I said to her.

Her face crumpled, and she fell apart. I was right there behind her, catching her as she fell.

She sank onto the soft rug of the bathroom floor, and I pulled her into my arms, cradling her close to my heart.

"I'm so sorry, my love. I'm sorry," I whispered into her hair while she cried and cried.

Later, an endless amount of time later, when the water had gone cold in the tub behind us and dawn stained the sky, she shifted against me, her tears all spent. The bathroom rug was surprisingly comfortable when she was in my arms.

"I'm sorry, too," she said, her voice rough. "About your mother. I can't believe that Sergei was the person you've been looking for all along. What kind of irony is that? That I would be his daughter . . . Your wife is the daughter of your long-lost enemy?"

"Not irony," I said. "*Destino*. Destiny brought me to you. The universe correcting the wrong of the existence of a man like Sergei and the awful things he did. Where there is darkness, there must be light. Balance. You and me meeting was just the universe getting the balance right again. I was always going to meet you, and I was fated to love you."

"You love me," she whispered, and glanced up at me. "I'm a mess. I'm crazy, haven't you heard?"

I smiled at her. "Didn't you hear? I'm crazy, too."

She nodded slowly. "Yeah, I did hear that somewhere," she murmured, and her gaze dropped to my lips.

I lost the battle not to kiss her.

I leaned forward and fitted my lips to hers.

PART III

PARADISO

But already my desire and my will

were turning like a wheel,

all at one speed,

moved by the Love that moves the sun

and the other stars.

—Dante, *The Divine Comedy*

44

KATARINA

I woke to the sound of laughter. It felt foreign for a moment as I lay there, perfectly relaxed, in a criminally soft bed. A deep tone and a light, girlish one.

Massimo and Tatiana.

I sat up, hearing Paolo chime in about whatever was making both of them laugh so much downstairs.

I stared at the ceiling, painted with a lavish night sky and stars that somehow seemed to twinkle.

I felt exhausted despite having just woken up, but oddly energized, too. I felt sad about my mother. Just the thought of her triggered a deep ache in my heart, one that I felt sure wasn't going to fade anytime soon. But I also felt at peace with it. The anger had passed. I felt so many things all at once, but most of all, I felt content to be where I was, exactly here. I was where I was supposed to be.

By the time I got downstairs, the chuckling had turned into full gales of laughter. They were in the kitchen and had been making pancakes, it seemed. There was flour on every surface, and batter splattered around. Massimo was manning the stove, flipping pancakes with a confidence that saw two pancakes out of five on the floor. Paolo was frantically trying to catch them with a plate and Tatiana was already eating, watching them and laughing.

It was chaos. It was perfect.

"Kat!" Tatiana saw me first, bolting out of her chair to get to my side. She hugged my legs. "You slept for a long time."

"I guess I was really, really tired." I smiled at her and ruffled her hair. I felt Massimo's gaze on my face, and weirdly, a frisson of nerves blossomed in my belly. Last night, I'd cried like my heart was breaking, and he'd simply held me. I didn't remember the rest, I'd just woken up in his bed. There was a sudden awkwardness between us, or at least, I felt like there was. We'd left things horribly before Sergei had picked me up. Awfully. I'd left his dog tags on the bed and walked out. I'd left him. And despite that . . . he'd come for me when I needed him the most. He didn't abandon me. He'd come in ready to burn the world down to reach me.

I searched my heart for the anger I'd felt when I'd found out about what he'd done. It was still there, but faded somehow. I felt lighter. Freer, somehow, of the heavy, dark emotions that had consumed me.

Tatiana tugged me toward the table. "We made you pancakes. I put the best ones on your plate."

There was a plate on the table piled high with crepes. I met Massimo's eyes as I sat down. He watched me steadily, his beautiful, dark eyes mysterious. I couldn't read the emotion in them, but they were full of it, whatever it was.

Heat crept to my cheeks at his study. Suddenly, I felt flustered and painfully aware of my bedraggled state. God, I was a mess. I'd only ever known this man when I was a mess. He, on the other hand, was perfect. I'd never thought I'd get used to him without his priest's robes, but the man wore everything well. Even now, dressed in dark, loose pants and a black T-shirt, he was hard to look away from.

Paolo staggered to the table. "What can I make you to drink, Mrs. Lucciano?"

Mrs. Lucciano.

I cut a glance at Massimo, who just chuckled.

"You just couldn't wait to call her that, could you?" he mused.

Paolo smiled. "Of course I couldn't, because that is who she is." He looked back at me. "Some of us around here were starting to worry that this man was going to die alone, that this house would never ring with the laughter of children—"

"Enough, Paolo. Don't forget, Katarina is going to Florence. Don't pressure her," Massimo called to his housekeeper, who stilled at the words.

I stopped, too, in the process of reaching for the honey.

"She is?" Paolo asked, echoing my own thoughts.

Massimo nodded. "She is, because that's what she wants to do, and my wife gets to do all the things she wants to do. All of her choices are hers."

I stared dumbly at the table, suddenly feeling tears gather against behind my eyes. His words split me down the middle. My heart swelled at the thought that he was letting me make my own choice and respecting it to the point of making sure it happened. That was the rational part of me. The other . . . felt like crying at the idea of being sent away. Go figure. What a mess I was.

"But when are you going? Am I going with you?" Tatiana asked.

I looked at Massimo, thoughts of my going to stay with Lucy pushed aside for the very real decisions that would have to be made about Tatiana.

"That's a good question," I told her, and took her hand on the table.

"Where do you want to go?" Massimo asked her carefully.

She thought it over for a moment and then shrugged. "I want to stay here with you."

"What about your mom?" I asked gently. Sergei had said she lived in Palermo. Was she looking for her daughter? Had Sergei simply taken her, or had something happened to her? We needed to check and see.

"I don't have one," Tatiana said with a certainty that broke my heart.

Massimo was watching me as my eyes stung. I blinked hard to clear the imminent tears. God, that hurt. The thought of little Tatiana alone in the world without a mom, hurt. It hurt for me, too, and for all the girls who'd lost their moms, and all the moms who'd lost their daughters. I thought of the baby that the unholy trinity had stolen from Mira . . . One day, they'd grow up to be a kid like Tatiana who'd never know their mother.

It broke my heart.

"Let's talk about it later, then. Don't worry, anyway," Massimo said in a low rumble. "From now on . . . this is your home. One that no one can take away."

Then he looked down at the table and grabbed a pancake, taking a bite of it plain.

"So, tell me, is this what we do next?"

"No!" Tatiana shrieked, distracted by the sacrilegious sight of someone eating crepes plain. "You have to put a topping on it!"

"I see," Massimo said with complete seriousness. "Paolo, bring the mushrooms, we need toppings."

"No!" Tatiana exclaimed, laughing merrily, and got up to chase Paolo away from the fridge.

Yes, it was chaos and it was perfect.

• • •

"You have a visitor," Paolo said later. Tatiana had fallen asleep in the library while I read to her, and I'd left her to her dreams. She had to be even more exhausted than I was.

I stood up, raising an eyebrow at him, wondering who it could be, when the door opened and Lucy walked in.

She crossed the room to me and hugged me tightly. The sudden movement stole my breath for a second. I was going to have to get used to hugs again. They felt so alien. I tentatively hugged her back.

"I'm so glad you're all right," she murmured, and pulled back to look me over. "No injuries?"

I shook my head. "Nope. None. Well, none that you can see." I smiled at her so she knew I was kidding. "Don't tell me you came all the way back from Florence to see me?"

Lucy sat down. "I only got halfway there before Giada told me what had happened. And I was just thinking that you'd decided to stay with Massimo, until she told me . . . I'm so sorry, it's awful."

"Don't be. I'm so tired of all of it. I just want to put it all behind me now," I admitted, realizing it was true as I said it.

"So what are you going to do? Stay here, or come to Florence?"

I shrugged, but Lucy sighed knowingly and gave me a warm smile.

"I knew it. I knew you'd forgive him. Promise me one thing . . . you'll at least come and visit."

I nodded, hearing the sound of Tatiana's voice in the hallway. She was awake.

"Have you told your husband that you've decided to forgive him and stay?" Lucy asked.

"There hasn't been a good time yet," I admitted. "And I'm not sure how."

Lucy considered my words. "Oh well, let him sweat it a little. It won't kill him," she teased with a wicked smile.

Lucy left a little while later, off to travel to Florence. Tatiana and Paolo were watching a movie in the sitting room while I sat in the kitchen nursing a cup of tea and wondering where Massimo had gone.

He'd been gone most of the day, and by the time he walked in, I was already missing him.

Our eyes met across the room. His cheeks were warm, having been out in the cold. It was snowing again. This winter felt like it might never pass. I couldn't imagine spring finally arriving, but it would. It always did. The silence felt still between us, like an untouched pond. I didn't know how to back down on my anger. I didn't know how to take back the things I'd said before. I wasn't sure where to start. Earlier he'd made it clear he still expected me to go to Florence. So . . . I should go . . . except I didn't want to anymore. I didn't want to be apart from him, or Tatiana or Turin. I finally felt at home, after so long.

"Have you eaten?" Massimo asked, breaking the silence.

I nodded. "We all ate a little while ago."

Massimo walked into the room, coming close to where I was sitting. He pulled out the chair opposite me and sat down, taking a small, rectangular-shaped package out of his pocket and placing it on the table.

"I meant what I said. I'm sorry about everything . . . all of it. About your mother, and the wedding . . . I should have given you the choice."

Emotion clutched my throat, making it hard to swallow. I didn't want to cry again today.

"I've never loved anyone like I love you, and . . . maybe it made me crazy." He grinned at me, making me smile back.

"I know what that's like."

"But I never want you to feel like you don't have free will. Like you're locked up . . . imprisoned. So go to Florence, and take your time. Leave me in the dark and make me pay for being a pushy asshole. Make me wait by the phone, and give me sleepless, lonely nights . . . I deserve it." His hand surrounded mine and squeezed. His dark eyes stayed on mine, unwavering. "But then, when you're done . . . come home. Come home, and I'll be waiting."

Those damn tears that had been threatening to overcome me all day started to spill when he pulled the necklace with the dog tags and crucifix from his pocket.

"One day, come home to me. I'll wait patiently and happily in purgatory until you do." He slipped the chain over my head, returning it to its rightful place. It felt right as it settled around my neck. Next, he pulled the ring from his pocket. The one he'd slipped on and never once told me was anything important.

He slipped it onto my ring finger. The ruby flashed in the kitchen lights, warm and beautiful.

He took my hand and kissed the ring. It felt like an unbreakable vow. A blood bond, like the one we'd sworn that dark night in Hallow Hall. The tension in my chest loosened, and all the heavy things I'd endured in the last three years felt lighter, suddenly, all at once. I was happy, I was loved, I was with family. Somehow, I had gotten everything I'd dreamed of, when I'd least expected it.

I should tell him that I'd decided to stay. I should say something, but the lightness in my chest urged me not to. Instead, I just nodded.

He looked disappointed in my lack of response but rallied when Tatiana came into the kitchen. He'd bought her bags full of toys and gadgets that she'd never had before, and she was going through them like it was Christmas.

I watched them play for a while until Paolo came through, and Massimo stood up.

"I have to go out," he announced, and my heart dropped.

"Why? You just got back."

He nodded, watching Tatiana and Paolo looking for snacks.

"I might be ready to let you go, angel, but I can't watch you leave. Even I don't hate myself enough for that." He met my eyes for one searing moment, and then turned away.

"Kat! Do you want to finish the movie with us?" Tatiana was there, climbing onto my lap. I watched Massimo go, taking in the defeated line of his broad shoulders and the tension filling his body. He was really suffering. It was real. He was letting me go, but it was costing him a lot.

"Kat! Are you listening?"

"Sure, of course I am." I focused on Tatiana, a wicked little plan forming in my mind.

45

MASSIMO

"If there was anyone I didn't expect to see here, it was you, old friend," Vittorio said, sinking into the pew next to me. His small chapel was a warm refuge from the storm outside. It had been snowing all day. Maybe the trains would all get canceled? A man could only dream.

"No need for holy water, I won't stay long," I reassured him.

He chuckled. "I think we both know you're safe from heavenly retribution. You're not half as terrible as you think you are."

"Tell that to my wife."

Vittorio sighed. "She's still upset? If you had listened to me, I could have saved you this headache."

"You really never miss a chance to say I told you so, do you?"

"I'm a priest, I preach—what more do you expect?"

I just shook my head and dropped it into my hands. I didn't want to go home and see my empty room. It would make it all too real. When I'd heard that Lucy and her bodyguard had come back, I knew it was for Katarina.

And I had to let her go . . . that much was obvious. If I wanted her forgiveness, I just had to do it, suffer without her, wait for her return. It was penance I wasn't sure I'd survive.

"Well, in that case, I'm going." I stood up. There was no point in delaying the inevitable. I had to get used to my new reality. I was tracking down Tatiana's mother. If she wasn't able or willing to meet her, then I had to adjust things for the little girl who'd be living with us. I had no idea how to explain to Tatiana that Katarina was going away . . . Maybe she wouldn't go because of her?

My heart leapt pathetically at the slightest sliver of hope that gave me . . . that maybe Katarina would stay, not because of me, but her sister.

"Yes, go on and get home. You've a family to look after now," Vittorio advised.

A family? When one of them wanted to escape me? I'd made a mess of my family before it had ever gotten started. It was just like me.

"I'll call you tomorrow," he called.

I waved over my shoulder. "Looking forward to it."

The townhouse was still when I entered, just as I'd feared it would be. Tatiana and Paolo were no doubt asleep at this late hour, and Katarina? She was probably halfway to Florence. I resisted checking the tracker on the dog tags. I'd at least wait until morning.

I made a mental note to check out houses in Florence, as well. If Katarina wanted to live in Florence, that was fine . . . there was no rule that I couldn't rent a place there, too, while she was there.

Fuck, I was doing it again . . . manipulating things. It came so naturally it was challenging to stop.

I climbed the stairs slowly to my room. I already knew it was going to smell like Katarina, and I was probably going to spend the entire night tortured and hard, wishing she was there. Fucking the mattress because it smelled like her would be a new low, but really, how long would that smell last? I had to take advantage of it while I had the chance.

I got to my bedroom and pushed open the door.

The covers were unmade, which I'd specifically asked Paolo for.

I stepped into the room and heard a creak coming from the stairs. I stilled, alertness flashing through me, pushing away my sadness and regret and filling me with adrenaline. Was there someone in my fucking house? A minion of Hallow Hall? A leftover man from the Stoyanov family? I turned silently and made my way back along the hall toward the stairs. The soft patter of someone trying very hard to be quiet met my ear.

I advanced down the stairs. There was a soft creak. I knew that sound like I knew every single sound in my house. It was the library door.

I reached it and pushed it open, waiting a moment to see if anyone showed themselves.

It was quiet inside, the fire banked but still warm. A single lamp was lit on a table next to a wingback leather chair, so the room was shadowy. Plenty of places to hide.

I stepped into the room and smelled it. As sweet as perfume, but priceless and unique.

The smell of an angel.

She moved quickly, but I was quicker, grabbing my assailant and spinning us both so her back met the wall. I made sure to cushion the blow with my forearm.

A flash of silver and a sharp prick to my neck. I was transported back to Hallow Hall and the way Katarina had begged me for her life . . . how the tables had turned.

Now I was the one begging her for my life, because without her, I was a dead man.

She looked up at me, alive and vital and so fucking real. She was here. She hadn't left.

She pressed the small knife to my throat, and I recognized it as one from my bedside.

"I'd ask what you're doing here, but I'm too fucking happy to see you," I admitted roughly.

She wet her lips, short-circuiting my brain.

"What do you mean, what am I doing here? This is my house, too, isn't it?" Her voice was throaty and low and undid me in ways I didn't know were possible.

I nodded. "This is your house. All my homes are your homes . . ."

She arched an eyebrow. "All your homes? Now you're just showing off."

I nodded and flexed my rigid cock against her belly. Fuck, it felt good just to press against her.

"All my homes, here and abroad, and cars, and investments . . . all yours," I murmured, rocking against her and ignoring the point of the knife.

"As long as we stay married, right?" she pointed out in a cool tone.

I shook my head. "In the event of a divorce, even if that's tomorrow. I thought you were going with Lucy?"

She swallowed hard and I watched her throat move with it. She was so fucking beautiful.

"I told you I wanted a choice . . . not that I wouldn't choose you," she said softly.

My heart was beating so hard I could barely think. My blood was racing and my cock straining, all to be closer to this woman. To consume her blinding light and keep it for myself.

My own personal salvation.

"So, are you telling me even with all the choices in the world . . . you choose me?" It sounded unbelievable, even to my ears.

But then she was smiling, a sunrise lighting up her face, and she nodded.

"Who else would I choose but my husband . . . the man I love . . . my own personal devil?" she murmured, letting the knife drop.

"Say that again," I demanded, hauling her into my arms.

"The man I love? Or my husband?"

"My husband. . . . Call me your husband again," I commanded.

She laughed. "You're my husband, you're not getting rid of me that easily. I'm here to stay, I'm afraid."

I pressed my face into the nook of her neck, lifting her against me.

"Thank fucking God," I murmured, pressing my pounding heart against hers. "Thank God," I repeated, the closest I'd ever come to a prayer. "The fact that you exist is almost enough to make me a believer."

"Really?" Katarina said softly, and leaned up on her toes to kiss me. "Show me then. I've missed you and I want you to show me."

"Fuck, you're killing me," I muttered, and carried her to the rug in front of the fire. "You destroyed me, dismantled every single cell and climbed inside. I'll never get you out," I said, more of a low chant than words that I was even conscious of.

She was only wearing a silky robe and pajama set. Now she wore pale ivory satin, fitting for an angel.

The material slipped down her body with a whoosh and pooled around her ankles. I was already kneeling before her and lifting one leg over my shoulder. She reached out for the mantelpiece, her eyes fixed on me as I leaned forward and pressed my face against her exposed cunt. I swiped my tongue up the length of her slit, dipping inside and then focusing on her clit.

She moved her hips, demanding my attention everywhere that made her shudder and twitch. I looked up at her as I fucked her with my tongue. She really was an angel, with her skin glowing in the firelight, her blond hair strewn in ribbons around her shoulders. Her blue eyes were unfocused, lost in pleasure, her hands in my hair.

I could die a happy man. She'd come back to me. She'd chosen me.

She was mine.

She came suddenly, a sweet little moan leaving her on a rush. Her cum ran down my chin and dripped onto my collarbones, and I was washed clean . . . a new man.

Her husband.

From now on, nothing else mattered.

I caught her when her shaking legs failed and pulled her into my arms.

"No passing out yet, I'm only just getting started," I murmured, and carried her to the wingback chair.

I settled onto the soft leather and cradled her on my lap, swinging her legs to bracket mine so she was straddling me.

I tugged my pants down just enough for my cock to spring free, desperate to be closer to her hot, wet heat.

She slid her hands under my T-shirt, almost shyly. She still had so much to learn about the power she had over me. How I was already her willing servant.

"You want me to take it off?" I teased her, flexing my hips so my cock brushed against her belly.

She nodded. "I like to feel your skin against mine."

"As you wish, *micetta*."

I tugged the T-shirt off and tossed it away, then stilled as Katarina's hand circled my aching cock.

"All this, just for me?" she teased me back, gently pumping my shaft.

"Everything's for you, today and every day to come," I gasped as she got braver and slid a finger across the head of my cock, teasing the slit at the top.

"Show me," she whispered, just like before. I knew what she wanted. I wanted the same thing. To be connected in all the ways we could. To be one.

I angled my cock straight up, and she rose on her knees and positioned herself over me. Then she was sinking down. Her cunt flexed and stretched around me, resisting letting me in before finally relenting. A thumb to her clit eased my way and made her moan. She'd already come and was so sensitive.

Finally, she was fully impaled on me. My balls pressed against her ass, and her tits pressed into my chest. I pulled her forward into a hug, remaining deep. I wrapped my arms around her. There was nowhere to go from here; we fit perfectly in the chair, joined as we were. I took a deep breath, feeling her heart against mine. I was exactly where I wanted to be . . . exactly where I wanted to live, really, from now on.

I don't know how long we sat like that, warmed by the fire, perfectly content. The only thing nagging at my attention was the desperate urge in my balls to come in this woman. To fill her up and maybe, just maybe, plant a seed. We could start our own little family, right here, tonight. Along with Tatiana, we could have a nursery full of kids to dote on and take care of.

I snaked a hand to her clit, less sensitive now and ready to come again. I rubbed slow circles against the swollen hood and gradually she started to move on me. Nudging up and down, slowly rolling her hips and experimenting with being in control.

I worked her clit faster, knowing that despite how much I was enjoying her slow exploration, I was only human, and I'd blow soon . . . but not before her.

She came first, always.

I rubbed at her clit, and she rose up and sank faster, working herself quicker and quicker, her thigh muscles clenched and tits bouncing gloriously.

I still needed to feed her up, clothe her in the finest materials, give her the best of everything. I couldn't fucking wait to do all of it. I wanted to spoil her like no one had ever been spoiled before.

Maybe one day soon, those beautiful tits would be full of milk. Fuck, just the thought of my angel feeding our child, taking care of a baby in such a natural, fundamental way moved something primitive in me. Something as old as time. I wanted to procreate with this woman. I wanted a family with her . . . people to protect and provide for.

Reasons to live.

She was moving erratically now, getting close to coming. She became frantic, moving fast, her pussy flooded with wetness. I felt her getting close to the edge and rubbed her clit harder to push her right over.

She clenched all around me, crying out. I kissed her hard and thrust up into her when she froze. Her cunt was so tight it was hard to move. She was milking me with those slick, pulsing muscles, and I couldn't help but follow.

I growled against her mouth as I came, a hand wrapped around the back of her neck, holding her face to mine, the other still working her clit.

I spilled inside her, sunk so deep she'd never get me out.

"That was amazing," Katarina murmured, snuggling into my chest and making no move to lift herself off me.

I was still hard, turned on by the very fact that I was still inside my wife.

"I missed home so much," she continued, and tilted her head to look up at me.

"So did I," I answered.

She smiled faintly. "You never left home . . . You were never Sergei's guest."

"Maybe not, but being here with you is the first time I've been home in a very, very long time," I confessed.

"Well, me too," she admitted. She looked so beautiful there, I suddenly wanted to see her in a white dress walking down the aisle toward me, everyone we knew looking on and understanding that she was mine.

"Do you want a real wedding? Something big, a fancy dress . . . whatever you want, you'll get it."

She shook her head. I was more disappointed than she was.

"No need for a wedding. I've never cared about all of that . . . but I have an idea for the honeymoon."

"You do? Somewhere exotic? You want to lie on a beach somewhere beautiful?"

She shook her head, a playful smile on her lips.

"Not even a little bit. But don't worry . . . you'll like it. It's right up your alley," she said mysteriously. I didn't care where we went or what we did. We could wait in line at the bank for two weeks if that's what she wanted to do; it wouldn't matter. We'd be together, and nothing else would matter.

I could have been lost in that moment forever, until . . . she shivered.

I stood up carefully, keeping her perfectly filled by my cock.

I started toward the stairs.

"Where are you taking me?" she squealed, and wriggled, making me groan. Cum worked down my thighs, released from Katarina's tight little cunt, still stretched by my cock.

"To bed, to warm you up, angel. Our night's only just beginning."

EPILOGUE

KATARINA

Spring was blossoming all around us in Naples as we parked the car as close as we could get to the site, and got out to walk. Fields of poppies and anemones lined the roads. We made our way through twisted olive trees, stepping over the cyclamens growing beneath. A haze had settled over the early-morning ground, as yet undisturbed by the crews of workers who were excavating the site.

Massimo was quiet, and I reached out a hand to lace my fingers through his.

We made our way through the trees that hid the charred remains of Ospedale di Santa Maria from where we'd parked.

Here, the extraction was well underway, with large sections of the ground already dug up. Tents had been erected to sort the uncovered remains.

I walked past a few of them until I felt Massimo's hand tug me to a stop.

"She's here, isn't she?" he murmured, looking across the wreckage of the hospital.

I nodded. "Yeah, I think she is."

He sighed, his hand tightening on the bunch of snowdrops we'd gone to five different florists to find.

"She's here," he said again, mostly to himself.

"And now she's not alone anymore. None of them are," I pointed out.

The excavation of Santa Maria had started quickly after the atrocities of Hallow Hall had come to light. Massimo had worked with a detective he'd met after the fire, who'd taken the case and run with it. Thanks to Giada and her sources, it had garnered a lot of attention.

The Church and twisted priests and exiled former doctors, organized crime and an isolated hospital just outside the city . . . it had all the ingredients that the public ate up. They wanted more information. They wanted justice, and the police had no choice but to give it to them.

I got to see firsthand how it was when you had tech skills, power, and money at your disposal to avoid suspicion. The deaths at Sergei's mansion were ruled as in-house Mafia fighting. With so many unidentified bodies to find on the grounds of Hallow Hall, the police couldn't really afford to care too much about Mafia men killing one another.

Next up, thanks to Massimo and his information from Blackwood's house, drip-fed to the police to direct the investigation, was the ruin formerly known as Ospedale di Santa Maria.

A river ran through the middle of Santa Maria's grounds. It was pretty, or it would be, if it weren't for the charred skeleton of the hospital.

Massimo stopped on the bank, transferring the snowdrops between his hands.

"She's here . . . all around me."

I pulled a snowdrop from the bunch and held it in the air.

"In that case, you don't need to wait to find her bones. We can honor her here. For Sara."

I dropped the flower into the rushing river and watched it get carried away downstream.

Massimo smiled at me and then followed my example, pulling one snowdrop, and then another, and letting them fall into the water.

His last goodbye. Closure, finally.

Later, we watched as the excavation started up.

"What do you think will happen to this place once everything is over with?" I wondered.

Massimo shrugged. "I don't know. Salt the earth and move on. It's a beautiful spot. It's a shame that the stain of such terrible things will remain here," he muttered.

"Hmm, it is a shame. I bet you could buy this land for a steal, once everything is said and done and all the investigations are concluded."

"And do what with it?" Massimo asked.

I thought about it. "Well, the weather is good here, dry and warm. It's close to the city. What about a cat rescue?" I suggested.

Massimo blinked at me. "A cat rescue?"

"Mm-hmm, for all the little strays."

"Finding Gravy and bringing him back to our home has really given you a false sense of confidence about how easy it is to look after animals," Massimo teased.

"Ha, not false confidence . . . just certainty that we could hire the right people to run it."

Massimo chuckled and shook his head. "I never know what the fuck you're going to say next."

I tossed my hair and grinned at him. "Don't you just love that about me?"

He was still smiling, and now he simply nodded. "Yes. That, and everything else."

Massimo disappeared as soon as we got back to the hotel, and I had a call from Giada.

"How was it?" she asked immediately. Despite her being half the world away, we talked every day. Even though Sergei had fallen, there were more locations with similar kinds of establishments to Hallow Hall that we didn't know about yet.

None of us would rest until we found them all.

"Grim, but there's hope there. Someday, it'll not be such a dark, depressing place."

"Good, though speaking of dark depressing places . . . I've got something for you."

She rattled off the address of a place in Palermo. I immediately thought of Tatiana's mother. Tatiana was right now happily in Turin, attending real school for the first time in her life, living in the townhouse with us and Paolo, and a kindly old nanny whom Massimo had brought in, a woman who seemed to think it was her job to spoil Tatiana rotten. I loved her already.

"You want me to forward the information to the cops?"

"Hmm, not yet, I think."

I turned to look at Massimo, who'd just appeared in the bedroom doorway of the beautiful suite we were staying in. Fuck the cops. They could clean up the sites and figure out who had died and trace their families, but I didn't trust them for more than that.

"Okay, shall I give it some time . . . say a few weeks? It would be sad if anything terrible happened to the folks in charge there."

"Yeah, it would be such a shame," I agreed, a wicked smile curving my lips as I looked at my husband.

I said goodbye to Giada and hung up.

Massimo approached me. I could hear the thundering sound of the bath running in the other room. The man loved to fuck in the tub.

"Who was that?"

"Our IT specialist. She has a location for us to visit . . . our second honeymoon stop point," I said with a grin.

"Hmm, why do I think this one never made it onto any top-ten destination lists for honeymoon ideas?"

"Let's just say it's specific to us," I murmured. I leaned up and threaded my arms around his neck. "Would you go to another Hallow Hall with me?"

"In a heartbeat," he answered immediately.

"Would you hurt someone for me?"

"Without question."

"Kill for me?" I added.

"Just tell me who, angel. You're my conscience. I kill on your command." He leaned down and grabbed my ass, hauling me closer.

"Good to know. So . . . you want to make a deal with me?" I teased.

"Hasn't anyone ever told you not to make deals with devils?" he said back, picking me up and carrying me toward the bathroom.

I nodded solemnly. "Yes . . . so I only make an exception for one. My own personal devil."

"Good," Massimo growled. "Don't go making me jealous. You're my wife. If someone needs killing, I'll do it. Now, let's seal this deal the old-fashioned way," he said, and put me down next to the bath. It was a huge soaker tub and was already steaming.

"With a kiss?" I asked with mock innocence.

Massimo laughed. "A kiss? Those babies aren't going to make themselves, *micetta*. Strip, wife. The water's waiting."

And so I did.

There was nothing I wouldn't do for my husband, the killer, the soldier, the sinner.

God's favorite monster.

ACKNOWLEDGMENTS

By book number 12, I thought this would have gotten easier. . . . Here we go!

I want to thank my team of editors, Lauren and Emmy, as well as the fab ladies from Dell. My alpha reader, Katarina, and brainstormers Kat and Sarah, thank you for putting up with my random messages at all hours. I'd like to thank Angela, my cover designer, and the amazing photography by Michelle Lancaster. Another big thank you to bestie Katherine, for all those walks and voice notes, and finally, my husband: my marketer, chef, chauffeur, accountant, personal trainer, and biggest fan.

PHOTO: JOANNA SILVESTRI

MILA KANE is a previously independent bestselling author. She is obsessed with cats, coffee, and antiheroes on just the right side of insane. She writes dark and dirty romance with the alpha-holes of your filthiest nightmares. She only writes *safe* stories . . . and no matter how dark and twisted the story might be, there will always be a happily-ever-after guarantee. Kane lives with her husband in Scotland.

milakane.com
Instagram: @milakanebooks
Facebook: @MilaKanewrites
TikTok: @milakanebooks

ABOUT THE TYPE

This book was set in Jenson, one of the earliest print typefaces. After hearing of the invention of printing in 1458, Charles VII of France sent coin engraver Nicolas Jenson (c. 1420–80) to study this new art. Not long afterward, Jenson started a new career in Venice in letter-founding and printing. In 1471, Jenson was the first to present the form and proportion of this roman font that bears his name.

More than five centuries later, Robert Slimbach, developing fonts for the Adobe Originals program, created Adobe Jenson based on Nicolas Jenson's Venetian Renaissance typeface. It is a dignified font with graceful and balanced strokes.